VICTORY'S VOICE

TRUTH FROM TAERNA BOOK TWO

VICTORY'S VOICE

ERIKA MATHEWS

Victory's Voice
Truth from Taerna Book Two
Copyright © 2021 by Erika Mathews
www.restinglife.com

Published by Resting Life
Cover design by Megan McCullough
www.meganmccullough.com

All rights reserved. No part of this publication may be reproduced, stored by a retrieval system, or transmitted in any form or by any means—electronic, mechanical, photocopying, recording, or otherwise—without prior written permission of the author. The only exception is brief quotations in written reviews.

All Scriptures are taken or paraphrased from the King James Version of the Holy Bible, Public Domain.

Quotation taken from *The Pilgrim's Progress: From this world to that which is to come.* John Bunyan. E. Marlborough, 1885. Public Domain.

ISBN: 9798708951915

CONTENTS

Chapter 1 1
Chapter 2 13
Chapter 3 23
Chapter 4 31
Chapter 5 47
Chapter 6 59
Chapter 7 75
Chapter 8 87
Chapter 9 103
Chapter 10 125
Chapter 11 135
Chapter 12 141
Chapter 13 153
Chapter 14 159
Chapter 15 177
Chapter 16 189
Chapter 17 203
Chapter 18 207
Chapter 19 217
Chapter 20 231
Chapter 21 235
Chapter 22 247
Chapter 23 257
Chapter 24 271
Chapter 25 279
Chapter 26 299
Chapter 27 311
Chapter 28 313
Chapter 29 327

PRONUNCIATION GUIDE

The Taernan language extensively uses the *ae* sound. Pronunciation is similar to the long *a* sound (*ay*), but with a distinct emphasis provided by the Taernan accent. The exception to this rule is the country name itself, which is pronounced *TAHR-na*.

Adon Olam (Ah-DAHN Oh-LAHM): the Master of the World, the Master of Eternity, the Master-Whose-Kingdom-Extends-Beyond-the-Horizon (Taernan name for God. In Hebrew, *adon* means Lord and *olam* means "to the horizon," often translated "eternity.")
Yeshua (Yeh-shoo-ah) or Mashiach (Mah-SHEE-ach): the Son of *Adon Olam* (Taernan and Hebrew names for Jesus and Messiah/Christ)

ELLISIA'S FAMILY

Ellisia Kostan (Ell-EE-see-ah KAW-stan): a seventeen-year-old with a passion for books and learning
Carita (Cah-REE-tah) Ellith: Ellisia's older sister, married to Kaelan
Kaelan Ellith (KAY-len ELL-ith): Ellisia's brother-in-law
Elanor Ellith: Kaelan and Carita's baby daughter

THE ELLITH FAMILY

Laelara (Lay-LARE-a) Ellith: Kaelan's twenty-one-year-old sister
Kelton (KEL-ton) Ellith: Kaelan's quiet eighteen-year-old brother
Kethin (KETH-in) Ellith: Kaelan's sixteen-year-old brother, who loves people and animals
Liliora (Lil-ee-ORE-a) Ellith: Kaelan's thirteen-year-old sister

THE ROHAEA FAMILY

Caeleb Rohaea (CAY-leb Ro-HAY-a): Ellisia's friend from Syorien, who is like her big brother
Mae: Caeleb's older sister, who is married and has triplets
Jaeson (JAY-son): Mae's husband
Daenia, Elkaena, and Naethan: Mae's baby triplets

THE DOEKH GROUP

Cormac (CORE-mac): financial manager
Don Rhaea (DON RAY-a): professor of literary philosophy who teaches at Amadel Academy
Jaefa and Jaeta (JAY-fa and JAY-ta): Researchers, authors, and scene creator brothers
Jolyn (Joh-LYNN): a student at Amadel Academy
Uncle K: quantum physicist specializing in sound waves, Jolyn's uncle
Maeve (MAYV): molecular scientist
Miss Loaw (LOW): marketer, book-seller
Pia (PEE-ah): professor of physics, teaches at Academy. Ryna's mother.
Ryna (RY-nah): a student at Amadel Academy
Zena (ZEE-na): housing caretaker and planner, wife of Don Rhaea

OTHER CHARACTERS

Aethelwyn (AY-thel-winn): a bubbly Academy student who goes by Wyn
Anthea (AN-thee-ah): an Academy student, known as Anni
Dresie (DRESS-ee): a neighbor girl who is close to Ellisia
Ellrick (ELL-rick): a wise elderly friend
Fraexo (FRAX-oh): a man Ellisia meets while traveling

Saera (SA-rah): an eight-year-old girl who helps Mae with the babies

PLACES

Amadel Academy (Ah-mah-DELL): a school of higher education near the palace in Syorien, also known as the Palace Academy

Frydael (FRY-dayl): the town that Ellisia lives near

Syorien (See-ORE-ee-en): the capital city of Taerna

Taerna (TAHR-na): the country Ellisia calls home

In the beginning was the **WORD,**
and the word was with God,
and the word was God.
The same was in the beginning with God.
All things were made by Him, and without Him
was not anything made that was made.
IN HIM WAS LIFE,
and that life was the light of men.
John 1:1-4

And they
OVERCAME HIM
by the blood of the Lamb, and by the
WORD of their testimony;
and they loved not their lives unto the death.
Revelation 12:11

NO WEAPON that is formed against thee
shall prosper; and **EVERY TONGUE**
that shall rise in judgment against thee
thou shalt condemn.
This is the heritage of the servants of the LORD,
and their righteousness is of me, saith the LORD.
Isaiah 54:17

1

A BLUR OF images paraded before her mental vision, sprung from the slightly-yellowed page open on her lap. Curled in her favorite main room corner chair, Ellisia let her imagination travel as rapidly as her eyes. Dukes and drama, intrigue and investigation, foiled plots and feisty populace—every word seized her fancy as her mind rapidly painted each scene in vivid pictures. Her only focus: what the next chapter might hold.

She stuck her thumb under the corner to begin the page turn. Wishing to reread a particularly mysterious sentence, she wavered between pages for a brief instant.

Rap, rap.

Ellisia started, raising her head to glance towards the front door. Judging by the insistent force of the knock, someone had been trying to gain her attention for some time. She sighed, stuck a crumpled bit of paper between the pages, closed the book, and went to the door. Evidently she wouldn't be finishing her story tonight.

Fumbling with the rusty metal, she lifted the latch.

"Reading again." The dark-haired girl on the step didn't even bother with a question mark. "Of course."

Ellisia sighed and grinned at the same time. "Of course," she echoed. "Come in, Dresie."

The neighbor girl stepped past Ellisia. "Carita's not home?"

"Not just now. And the baby's with her."

"Ah, how convenient for me. I hoped we could chat a bit." Dresie's dark eyes roved about the sitting room before landing on the book Ellisia had been reading. "I don't suppose you'd like to head outdoors any more than you usually would."

"Not really." Ellisia returned to her chair. "It's far too cold. I can't wait until this winter is over in a few weeks."

Dresie threw back her head, a merry gilded laugh emerging. "You never used to mind the cold, as I recall. Remember when we'd play outside for hours as young girls? With Dixaen? And remember how you'd outgarden both of us?" She paused as her eyes flitted across the bookshelf in the corner. "We used to write about such times in our story journal . . . you still have that, don't you?"

Ellisia murmured assent. "I can't tell you where it is though . . . I haven't looked at that for an eternity."

Dresie's fingers moved quickly across the titles. "It used to be back in this corner." She pulled out several volumes, then reached back for a thin, worn cover wrinkled behind them. "Here. Just see."

The lids fell open, and crooked letters sprawled faintly across the pages. Ellisia scanned them, suddenly transported by the few vivid words and the gaps filled in by her memories to that autumn afternoon.

NINE YEARS EARLIER

"Books? You'd better believe there are books, Ellisia. Why, whole rooms full of books—you can't even begin to imagine. Rooms bigger than your whole house. And shelves up to the ceiling."

Dreamy wonder shone in her eyes as she gazed at Caeleb's animated expression. A whole roomful of books at once! "Have you read them *all?*"

A laugh rang out. "No, I haven't. Even you couldn't possibly read all those books in one lifetime. One of my favorite BookHalls is in Amadel Academy—we call it the Palace Academy."

"What's that?"

"It's a school where students learn about anything they want to—and get a certificate in that particular field." Caeleb leaned back on his hands, his gaze trained on the sky for a moment before returning to Ellisia's rapt expression. "They do have a BookHall, though, and I enjoy going there because I can usually find a book more easily than at the Palace BookHall."

"The Palace BookHall." Ellisia's words were an awed whisper.

"You'd *love* the Palace BookHall." Caeleb plucked a blade of grass and tossed it at her. "You wouldn't know what to do with yourself. Or rather, you'd have more to read than you'd know what to do with. You'd never leave. Shelves floor to ceiling. Three stories, at least. All filled with books. And, guess what?" He leaned forward conspiratorially.

"What?" She forced the whisper out, hardly able to breathe. Three stories of books! What next?

"They're all lined up by color. Each topic is a different color. So when you walk in, it's a stunning rainbow array of blues, greens, reds, oranges, yellows, purples, browns—floor to ceiling, mind you. And you'd tire yourself out before you reached the other side of the room."

"Tire myself out . . ." The echo drifted into nothingness. "Caeleb, I'm visiting that BookHall someday."

"I'm sure you will, princess." Caeleb grinned before pushing to his feet. "Looks like Dresie and Dixaen are back. Want to play Captured Bases again?"

"Of course!" She leaped up.

Several rousing rounds later, sunlight stretched the shadows into comically tall versions of their noontime selves, and Caeleb had disappeared inside to talk grown-up business with Kaelan.

"We need to go back home now, Dixaen," Dresie's black braids flapped as she dashed around the yard scooping up the bases. "Grandfather said we must come when the sun touched the hilltops, and there it is now."

"Get the ball, too, Dresie," Ellisia returned. "Put it in the kitchen lean-to." Seizing a stick, she began erasing the lines they'd drawn in the dirt to mark the boundaries.

She'd reached the other edge of the yard when Dresie came flying back, panting heavily and braids flying. "I can't open the lean-to. It must be locked."

"Locked? No, it can't be. We just got the things out of it earlier. And Carita never locks it while we're still playing." Ellisia followed her friend to the lean-to and took a deep breath as she tried the handle.

It wouldn't budge.

"Can you go through the front door?" Ellisia asked.

Dresie disappeared, only to return a moment later. "That door's locked, too."

"What? No, it can't be." Ellisia breathed deeply once again as tightness welled up inside her. They couldn't be locked out of the house. Carita would never do that.

Yet testing the door confirmed Dresie's words, and Ellisia's heart sank yet further. Knocking loudly yielded no response, and Dixaen's strength added to the girls' efforts still failed to move the handle.

"What will we do?" Dresie's face drooped as she bit her lip. "You have to get in for the night."

Ellisia thought rapidly. There was no other way in. One of these doors had to open. Where was Carita? Why didn't she hear?

A passage Carita had often sung to her shot into her mind. "Behold, I stand at the door and knock . . ." And there was that other song from *Adon Olam*'s Word: "Knock, and it shall be opened unto you."

Adon Olam had said it. It must be true. Ellisia couldn't open the door, and Carita wasn't there, but *Adon Olam* was there always. Softly Ellisia sang the words, then louder and more boldly as she banged on the firmly-shut door. "Open!" she commanded the door. "*Adon Olam* says it shall be opened. So open and let us in!"

Her right hand reached for the handle as her left hand continued to pound—and the door slipped open. "Thank you," Ellisia said, stepping in.

Dresie brought the bases in and silently dropped them in the box where they belonged. "It opened," she whispered. "It *opened*. It was *locked*." She gazed around as if expecting to see Carita standing there somewhere.

"*Adon Olam* opened it for us," Ellisia said matter-of-factly. "Or He sent one of His angels to do it. I knew He would. He always does when I say it for Him. He knew we needed to get in."

Ellisia blinked at the words in the journal. Nine years ago, and she still remembered the relief when that door had opened. Carita had been busy upstairs and hadn't even heard their knocking. And that conversation with Caeleb ... she hadn't penned much of it in the journal, but every word had been seared into her heart. She'd dreamed regularly of Academy and the BookHall since that day.

"Remember when you told the door to open?" Dresie's voice cut into her musings. "It just did. I almost couldn't believe it." She flipped a page.

Ellisia shrugged. "I remember. I wasn't surprised. That wasn't the first time something like that happened."

"I know." A note of seriousness laced Dresie's tone. "I remember a few other occasions later. Ellisia, honestly, did it happen a lot?"

"Some. Not regularly, but I certainly noticed it. Just seemed like part of life to me."

"Do you remember when Grandfather was ill, and you told his disease to go away? I thought you were being too optimistic and unrealistic."

"And then you couldn't believe it when he recovered." Ellisia sank into the green chair and clasped her thin pale hands in her lap. "I expected that, too."

"Ellisia, there has to be more to this." The whisper was earnest. "You know my cousin just married a teacher from Doekh. Those Doekhans know so much more about things than we do here, and my cousin says some of them have studied the effect words have and why."

Ellisia's dark eyes caught Dresie's black ones. "Oh?

It's a matter of study there?"

"I hear so."

Her clasped hands tightened. "Then I'm going to learn. And find out."

"How?"

Ellisia shrugged. "I have no idea. But some way or another, I'll find someone who knows. You have no clue what it's like, Dresie. It's true—I sometimes say something, and, good or bad, later I see it happening. I've tried not to dwell on it too much, but now that you say it, I do believe you're right—it has to be more than mere coincidence. I guess I've thought it's like praying—you know how Carita prays. She prays; things happen. But if there's more to it, I'm finding out."

"Be careful, though." Dresie shut the journal and shoved it onto the shelf. "You don't know what you're dealing with. And I don't know how much I trust most of those people from Doekh. You know most of them don't follow *Adon Olam*."

Ellisia nodded. "I'll be careful."

Scarcely had Ellisia returned to her book after saying farewell to Dresie before a second knock sounded at the door. A sigh escaped her as she again rose to answer—no reading for her today. Was everyone in town out on social visits this afternoon? Her hand again sought the rusty latch.

Then she barreled forward, launching herself into the arms of the stocky twenty-seven-year-old man who stood outside. "Caeleb! It's so good to see you again!

What are you doing here? How's your grandfather? And your parents? What's the news? How long can you stay?"

"Ellisia." He returned the embrace with a broad grin. "Good to see you, too. You know, you've *still* grown since the last time I saw you."

"*Cae*-leb . . ." she scolded gently.

"Not really." His grin melted into a teasing chuckle. "But truly, it's good to be back. Syorien's social expectations do get tiring."

"I'm sure they do." She pulled back through the open door, shivering. "Won't you come in?"

Caeleb entered, swinging himself easily into the room and towards the chair that Ellisia had deserted. He picked up the green-bound novel. "Is it a good book this time?"

"One of the best I've read! Especially this year. Though I certainly haven't had many new books this year." She bit her lip as her eyes again ran across the pitifully small collection on the corner shelves.

"And why is that?"

She shrugged. "Not enough new books in town here, I guess. I've read them all. Either borrowed them from those who have them, or I own them myself." She plucked the book from Caeleb's hand and thumbed through it. "This one was one the storekeeper's wife picked up from a traveling merchant a month or two ago and saved for me until I could buy it. I'd love to be able to read a few more."

Caeleb eased onto the low divan and stretched his arms behind his neck. "Well, what would you say if I told you that I could give you a chance to do just that?"

The book clattered to the table as she whirled to survey him. "You can? You didn't bring more books, by chance?" She eyed the bag at his side with a slight frown—it hung as though stuffed with clothing and food, not books.

"Better than that." Reaching into his bag, he pulled out a piece of paper and handed it to Ellisia.

"What's this?" She unfolded it.

"A listing of all the certificates they're offering at Amadel Academy now. There's one that brought you to mind."

She scanned the list quickly, her heart racing. She knew that Amadel Academy—the "Palace Academy," as it was commonly called—was open only to select scholars, and not penniless ones like she was. And it was so far from her home here in Frydael . . .

A title jumped out at her. "World Literature?" she exclaimed. "There's such a thing?" Never once in all her seventeen years had she heard of someone who was certified in literature.

Caeleb leaned back, his hands again resting behind his head. "It's a new whim in Syorien. Don't know who decided to offer it or why, but there it is."

"Truly." Ellisia was whispering now. A trembling excitement seized her, and the hand still holding the list shook. Grayness swirled about the edges of her vision, but the words WORLD LITERATURE stood emboldened with crystal clarity before her eyes.

"I know how much you love books, and I know how much you want to continue your education. You've done an excellent job teaching yourself all these years, and I'd love to see that continue."

"But you know I can't . . ." Oh, how she wanted this.

"I know Carita can't afford to send you anywhere," Caeleb went on, plucking the list out of Ellisia's trembling fingers, "though I know she wants you to get all the learning you can. But I have a proposition." He grinned as he tucked the list back into his bag and folded his hands around his raised knee. "How would you like to come to Syorien with me and go to Academy?"

Ellisia's mind whirled. Academy had always been only a daydream. "With you? I couldn't just . . . How?"

"It's simple. You know I've been back in Syorien with my grandparents for a while. My parents are in the country currently. We've been living down the street from one of my sisters." He paused. "And now for the news you asked for."

"What news?"

"Family news, of course. What else would you want to know?" His eyes twinkled.

"About Academy." The words tumbled out before she could think. She clasped her hands tightly, trying to be patient. Could she truly attend Academy? What did Caeleb have in mind?

Caeleb grinned. "All in time. Family news first." His smile tantalized her. *What about Academy?* He continued, seemingly oblivious to her excitement. "My sister just had triplets. Healthy babies, all three of them. But she needs assistance, and for some reason she won't trust all the daytime care of them solely to me." He exhaled exaggeratingly, rubbing his palm across his bag, his nose wrinkled at Ellisia. "So—would you come to live with Mae, help her with the babies, and go to Academy?"

Ellisia's eyes widened. "I'd do anything to go to Academy. What does she want me to do?"

"Mostly just the ordinary housework, I think. She's been having a neighbor girl help her with the babies during the daytime, and she is adjusting to the care of them, but the other work could use a hand. I figure Carita's given you plenty of practice."

Ellisia wrinkled her nose. "Sure." She'd never

enjoyed housework as much as her sister had, but she'd accompanied Carita many times on missions of mercy to neighbors' homes in Frydael. She knew how to work, anyhow. "I'd do that. And—do you think I would be qualified to enter for the World Literature line? What does it involve? Can I get certified in that?"

"I'm sure you can do it easily if you set your mind to it," Caeleb encouraged her. "I'm not certain what it involves, but I assume it involves books in some form."

"Of course." Nervous excitement bubbled over into a chuckle.

"And yes, you can get certified in that field. It's a three-year program."

"When does it begin?"

"Beginning of spring. That's just two weeks away. Are you interested?" He grinned once more.

"Interested? Is that even a question?" Ellisia flew out of her seat and seized his hand, then released it and sat down again. "I'll go. If Carita will let me. When are you returning to Syorien?"

"I hoped to make a week's visit here . . ." When she didn't answer, he went on. "But they won't let me off that long. I'm leaving in five days. Can you be ready that quickly?"

"Can I? I could be ready tonight! I just have to pack my books . . ."

"There are plenty of books in Syorien, you know." Caeleb laughed.

She shook her head, an arch smile across her face. "You wouldn't understand. I certainly need to bring my favorites. There's something about a particular book you've read over and over. There's simply no other copy that will do."

"Can't argue with that one." Caeleb stood. "Now

where *is* Carita, anyway, that we've been left to ourselves so long?"

"She and the baby are over visiting Mrs. Jaelrven and her little flock. I suspect they'll be at it a long while yet."

"I suspect so." Caeleb agreed. "In the meantime, want to play a game of Trux?"

"Most certainly," Ellisia stated with alacrity. Skirts spinning, she headed for the cupboard and removed the game board and pieces. "If I can calm my mind that long. Are you sure I shouldn't start packing right now?"

"And leave my lonesome self to laze away on one of the sole four days of the only vacation I've had in months? Yes, Ellisia. Go pack. I'll manage." He pulled a despondent face, and wooden pieces slipped from Ellisia's hand as she doubled over in laughter.

"No, Caeleb. Trux it is. You are stuck with it now."

After an intense game—in which Ellisia came off winner amid much back-and-forth bantering—Caeleb excused himself. Laughing goodbyes were exchanged, then he touched his hat and moved out of the doorway, waving.

She waved back, unable to wipe the smile off her face.

She was going to Academy!

Five days later, Ellisia's bags lay packed and ready by the time a faint glimmer of pink touched the horizon. When Caeleb's silhouette appeared on the road, she bounded out the door before the wheels of the small wagon he sat atop had even stopped turning. He touched his hat, the reins dangling from his other hand. "Good morning, Ellisia!"

"Morning, Caeleb!" Ellisia felt her heart bubbling over. "What a glorious day, true?"

"Indeed." Caeleb's eyes sought the horizon for a long moment, and Ellisia's followed. Bands of purple and red streaked the sky, intertwining with the promise of daylight to come. Stillness hung over the hilly countryside, but foremost in Ellisia's mind danced the bright lights and whirlwind of excitement that was Syorien. Soon, very soon now, she'd be at the center of it all.

Carita stepped out the door, carrying one of Ellisia's bags. Caeleb swung off the wagon, took it from her, and loaded it in the back. "Oh, yes." Ellisia capered back towards the house, retrieved her last bag, and returned to the wagon.

"Goodbye, Ellisia." Carita's voice was sober, but encouragement seemed to shine from her eyes.

"Goodbye." Ellisia could hardly let herself stand still even long enough for a hug. Carita had received Caeleb's proposition for Ellisia seriously enough, but she'd been supportive and grateful to him for the opportunity, and she hadn't once offered an objection—though Ellisia could tell that the thought of parting with her only sister pained her. Carita had cared well for Ellisia ever since the two girls had been orphaned fifteen years ago. "I'll miss you. And that baby. Tell her goodbye for me, too."

"I will." Carita released Ellisia. "Remember, seek *Adon Olam* daily. He will continually guide you in every new experience."

Ellisia nodded, her eyes already back on Caeleb, who climbed into the wagon. She hopped up beside him, waving to her sister.

"I kept a book out of my trunk to read on the way," Ellisia informed Caeleb as the horse trotted into the quiet Frydael streets.

"Why am I not surprised?"

"You should be surprised that I didn't bring a whole bagful of books to read on the way," she retorted. "But I have to save some to read at Academy."

"Is that so?" Caeleb replied. "I told you there will be plenty more when you arrive."

"I hope so." She couldn't repress a little bounce, and the wooden seat creaked dreadfully. "You know there's nothing I'd rather do than read."

"And birds can fly."

She was in the highest of spirits, and he matched her mood. The morning and afternoon flew briskly, and by nightfall they'd reached a small two-room hut recently constructed for travelers on the road to Syorien. Settling in for the night went swiftly, and soon both slept deeply.

A tiny rustling noise aroused Ellisia. Suddenly wide

awake, she froze. What was that? Ought she to rouse Caeleb? But no, perhaps it was only a rodent in search of a midnight snack. Relaxing slightly, she soundlessly rose and crept to the window. Her muscles instinctively tightened as her eyes swept the trail and woods. A dark figure, outlined against the snow-streaked path, crept towards the cart.

Withdrawing at once, Ellisia dodged the chairs, stools, and bags between her and the door to Caeleb's room. Feeling for Caeleb's bed, she shook him, hissing in his ear. "Caeleb! A marauder!"

Caeleb was immediately on his feet and at the door, Ellisia at his heels. The figure had just reached the cart, but as the door opened, a head shot up, then a form fled into the woods. Caeleb called out, then followed a short distance, Ellisia clutching the doorpost.

Within moments, Caeleb returned, shaking his head. "He's gone."

"Did you see who it was?"

"He had a long dark beard and a bright orange cloak. Probably belongs to one of the wandering bands around here. I'm glad you heard him before he could do any damage."

"Are you sure he didn't do damage?"

"He wasn't carrying anything with him." Caeleb swung on his cloak. "But let's check it out."

An inspection of the cart revealed that all remained in order. Caeleb patted the horse, transferred a few items to the hut, and told Ellisia to go back to sleep.

Ellisia went to her room, but she stole back to the window where she could see the cart. Caeleb had pulled it closer to the house, but instead of coming back inside, he climbed into the cart. When after several minutes he did not emerge, Ellisia sighed and returned to bed. He *would* stay out there the rest of the night, wouldn't he? She wished that they had been able to identify the intruder. What if he returned? She rubbed her palms together jerkily. Carita would say that her thoughts were vengeful and not kind. *Adon Olam* would not be pleased. Yet still Ellisia yearned for some sort of retribution. Such people didn't deserve a place in this world.

She rolled over, shutting her eyes. Yet sleep eluded her. She tried one position after another to no avail. Her thoughts wandered over the events of the day—her early rising, the last-minute packing, the parting from Carita. Carita's final words rose to her mind.

Uff. Why now. She didn't want to think of Carita's reminder to seek *Adon Olam* now—not in conjunction with the marauder. Why couldn't she just fall asleep? Did *Adon Olam* care more about the marauder than her night's rest?

The longer she tossed and turned, the more convinced she became that He did. She tried cramming the pillow over her head; she tried counting as high as she could—anything to go to sleep. She didn't feel like praying or meditating on *Adon Olam*'s word. Someone else could be generous and merciful. It wasn't right for the man to go around preying on innocent people; someone needed to stop him.

At last, she pulled the pillow off her head with a defeated exhale. She wasn't gaining anything by lying here fighting her conscience. Though her mind and emotions still rebelled, she tried to focus her thoughts on *Adon Olam*.

"Love your enemies." The words sprang unbidden to her mind.

She pinched her eyes shut again. She wasn't about to wait for the rest of the passage that would surely follow.

"*Adon Olam,* thank You for what happened tonight. That man needs You, and I ask You to bring him to You. And—bless him for it." She bit her lip. "I bless Your name. So be it, even so."

She rolled over, her mind easier, and soon embraced the welcome unconsciousness of deep sleep.

The next morning dawned refreshingly warm. As the horse tossed his head under the bridle and the old boards groaned under Caeleb's shifting form, Ellisia climbed into the cart and pulled out her book. Perhaps it would serve as an effective distraction to block out the bright sunlight and the dripping sounds of last-melting snow.

Yet long before the sun stood overhead, Ellisia could only moan in defeat. The wagon's jerky motion gave her a headache and a stomachache. Both her eyes blurred and stung. Her back ached from the cart's jolting.

"How far to Syorien?" She didn't care that her tone was a complaint.

"It's a good two days' journey at this pace," Caeleb replied. "The roads have been much improved in the past few years. Have you ever been out this direction before?"

"Never." Ellisia sighed. One more reason to be discontent with life. She'd always wanted to see the world through more than the pages of her books, but never before had the opportunity presented itself. If only she would stop aching all over. Would the entire journey be this miserable? A slight grin threatened at the thought. Half of her books portrayed journeys idealistically, and the other half depicted them as excessively uncomfortable. The latter books were unquestionably more accurate.

At least she wasn't riding a horse. As shaky as the cart was, it was better than jolting about on horseback all day long. Not that she minded riding horses; she actually enjoyed it at times—much more than Carita ever had. It was just that she didn't fancy relying solely on a horse for an entire day's transportation.

An ear-piercing shriek from a distant tree snapped her to attention. She leaned forward. "What was that?"

"A panther." Caeleb's words were tense. He pulled the horse to a stop.

"A panther?" Alarm filled her voice. "Where?" Silly question, but she couldn't help herself.

"I don't know." He pulled out his long knife and reached for his bow.

She reached for her own knife, buried in a pile of blankets beneath her.

"Caeleb, do you know how to fight a panther?" Her tone trembled. Never had she seen a panther, but she'd heard so many stories . . .

"I have never done it, but I understand the theory."

"Will it chase us—or attack us?"

"Let's hope not." The words were grim.

"I've read about it, but I never expected to have to do it." She looked back down at her knife and the blanket pile, fingering the second bow beneath. "Oh!" A sudden thought struck her.

She snatched up a blanket. "If it pounces or comes within range, let's try to trap it in the blanket. Then it won't be able to see, and its claws won't be so dangerous through the blanket."

Caeleb's glance took in the size and weight of the blanket. "It might work . . ." he agreed. "It'll be a short-range fight anyway unless we can spot it soon enough for a bow—and it stays still that long." He grabbed a second blanket.

Again the scream rang out, much nearer this time, and Ellisia couldn't stop the stab of terror that pierced her heart. Tree branches to the north were shaking. Ellisia tensed, willing herself not to dive beneath the blanket pile, all her senses trained upwards.

A crashing in the underbrush startled her. Her gaze shot downwards as a man stumbled out of the bushes at a dead run, terror plastered on his face. He sped down the path towards the cart, the tree branches just above him bounding back in unison as the panther easily kept up.

Ellisia comprehended the situation at a glance. The panther was much too high for knife work. She yanked the rest of the blankets out of the way and whipped out her bow and an arrow, aiming it at the panther and ready to release.

A flash of color below slowed her motions.

The man wore an orange cloak and a long dark beard.

"Caeleb!" she hissed, glancing his direction.

He'd seen it already. "Fire, Ellisia," he commanded tersely.

Still she hesitated. In a second it would be too late—but this was a different situation entirely. The panther was chasing the marauder. It probably wouldn't bother them; it had prey already. And the man deserved it.

"Uff!" she groaned, and released the arrow. The panther lost its grip on the branches and tumbled to the ground, bouncing off foliage and underbrush on its way down.

Ellisia snatched up another arrow and sent it after the first the moment the panther hit the ground. It ceased squirming and lay still. The man, still running, glanced back and stumbled over an exposed tree root. He tumbled to the ground and lay still for a moment.

Then he opened his eyes, half turned, and gazed at the cart. Relief flooded his face, though terror lingered.

Ellisia froze. Now what? The man couldn't have

recognized them, but he clearly recognized the cart.

Caeleb leaped down from the cart and strode towards the panther. After ensuring that it was indeed dead, he returned to the man on the ground.

"Welcome, stranger," he greeted. "Can we be of assistance?"

The man turned his face away, perceptibly tensing.

"Are you injured?" Caeleb continued.

Still no answer.

Caeleb gently put an arm underneath the man and helped him rise to his feet. The man still did not speak, though he immediately assumed a defensive posture.

"Where are you headed? Can we give you a lift?"

The man shook his head. Caeleb led him slowly towards the cart, but he planted his feet and refused to come closer.

"It's all right," Caeleb assured him. "I know that you remember us, as we remember you, but *Adon Olam* has placed us in your path again and enabled us to save your life from the panther. We hold no ill will towards you."

"It's a wonder you don't," the man mumbled, shaking despite his evident efforts to remain rigid.

"*Adon Olam* holds no ill will against us for the many wrongs we have done him," Caeleb said gently. "We hold none against you. He did not allow you to harm us last evening, and He did not allow the panther to harm you today. Thank you, *Adon Olam*. My name is Caeleb," he added to the man.

Ellisia slowly slid off the cart and walked towards them. "I'm Ellisia." Her words did not match the kindness and enthusiasm of Caeleb's.

"Fraexo," the man volunteered.

"Where are you from?" Caeleb asked.

"I'm not from anywhere," he mumbled. "Used to be

from Syorien. Times are bad there. Have to fend for myself. Not even my friends . . ." His eyes darted here and there.

"Can we offer you assistance with anything?"

He shook his head. "Why did you stop? The panther wouldn't have chased you. You didn't have to involve yourself."

"Because *Adon Olam* is the master of our lives and not we ourselves," Ellisia spoke up. "I didn't want to shoot the panther. I was angry at you because of last night. I—I wished you harm. I didn't want to shoot. But *Adon Olam* did it in me. I couldn't just let the panther . . ." Her voice trailed off as well.

"Who is this *Adon Olam*?" Fraexo's eyes met hers for the first time.

"He is the Master-of-the-Universe. He is the Lord-Whose-Kingdom-Extends-Beyond-The-Horizon. He is the Everlasting One, the One who lives inside of me. He desires to live inside of us." A warmth sparked within her. The words poured from her. "His kingdom is forever. He created us, and when we allow Him to rule our lives instead of living on our own, He directs and guides us into His ways. Then we can ask whatever we wish and it will be done for us. He implants true life inside of our being. He causes our ways to prosper as we allow Him and His words to live in us! He can change you, give you a new heart, and make you new. His Son has died for you—you do not have to be trapped in this lifestyle any longer. He says that in Him, you are a new creature. You are His. From henceforth you will no longer serve yourself or please yourself. You will serve Him."

Her face was warm and her excitement was high. Suddenly she stopped speaking. The words had ceased to flow.

Fraexo stood as if stunned. Slowly he nodded. "It is so," he said, a light dawning on his face. "I believe it is so."

He slowly pulled free of Caeleb's grip and stumbled back down the path, away from Syorien.

Ellisia and Caeleb looked at each other. "Well, that was that," Caeleb said at last.

They both climbed into the cart and started down the road. Ellisia said nothing; she couldn't. She simply sat, her heart still and her emotions numb. Who was she? What had she said? It was as though someone else *was* living inside of her. While she knew that was true, she hadn't expected to feel it so literally.

At last, she reached for her book and turned pages automatically. She didn't lose herself in reading this time, however; she read slowly and precisely, her mind taking in each word. Instead of immersing her consciousness in the plot, she found herself processing the story neutrally and rationally, as though she were an outsider.

What was the matter with her?

She didn't say another word until they reached the outskirts of Syorien.

3

ACCORDING TO CAELEB, his sister's home stood near the outskirts of Syorien only a few blocks from the Palace Academy. While they approached the city, his descriptions played through Ellisia's head as she stretched her aching shoulders and gazed eagerly from side to side. Here and there, houses rose from muddy yards. Narrow alleys stretched out of sight, filthy and rundown. Potholes, mud, and dust puffs characterized the roads. Garbage collected in precarious heaps around each home. People sat on tiny porches with puffs of smoke emerging from their mouths, or with a worn or dirty book in hand.

Ellisia shivered. So far nothing came close to matching her vivid imaginations of Syorien's splendor. She desperately hoped that Caeleb's sister didn't live in this repulsive part of town. "Why is it so filthy?"

"Because no one cares to maintain it," Caeleb replied. "They are busy seeking their own pleasure. A few might keep things in order, but their efforts are negated by the majority who simply do not care."

Ellisia averted her eyes from a pothole filled with refuse and stared at the book in her lap. She'd already read it twice on this trip, but it wouldn't hurt to begin it again—far better than observing the squalor of her surroundings. She turned back to page one.

"You know, sometimes you can miss out on real life by burying yourself in books all the time," Caeleb mentioned.

Ellisia wrinkled her nose but didn't look. "If that"—she extended a discrete finger towards the filth around her—"is real life, I don't care if I do miss it."

"The observation and experience of real life will always prove more worthwhile than those of fictitious life," Caeleb told her, "and the grime, unappealing though it is, can broaden your experience and understanding. It can open your mind to the reality of what is happening in the world and what you can do to better the situation. It can keep you alert to your surroundings and give you insight into what the real issues of society are."

Ellisia sighed and closed her book, taking in her surroundings with critical eyes, solely from an academic standpoint. "All right, then, what can I learn from *this*? Let me see. Dirt is disgusting. Potholes should be filled in. Dirt roads do not hold up well over many years of regular use. When people do not care about their surroundings, the surroundings turn to chaos. And above all, people were not meant to live so closely together in large cities."

Caeleb laughed. "A decent start, but that's not exactly what I meant."

Ellisia frowned. "What then?"

"For instance, look at the people. Look at the faces. They are humans with souls just like you and me."

Only the jolting of the cart broke the silence as her eyes roamed over the faces. Most were listless and dull. She gazed into the face of a young woman who leaned on a tiny porch railing. Her hollow eyes stared deeply from her pale cheeks. Not one expression exuded energy or passion for living.

She shuddered. "The people appear even more awful than the houses and streets."

"I know," Caeleb agreed. "Isn't it horrible? And yet *Adon Olam* could completely change them if they would allow Him to."

"But they don't know Him." Ellisia felt something foreign bubbling in her heart—something both poignant and goading.

"I know." Sadness laced his tone.

Ellisia slammed her book down on the cart floor behind her. Grabbing the post at the side of the cart, she pulled herself to her feet, heedless of the cart's still-swaying motion. "Everyone!" she shouted. "Listen! *Adon Olam* is Master and Lord! Hear His words! Let Him enter into you, and He will change you! He will raise you up from your circumstances and give you true, abundant, real life!"

As the horse cantered past each home, she looked into the eyes of those outside. Some of the people came to their doors and stared at her. Some pointed with jeering face. Some pretended not to hear her. Some turned their heads to listen, and their eyes followed her as she passed.

Words poured forth from her. She had forgotten herself. She had forgotten the mud, squalor, and potholes; she thought only of the people—poverty-stricken, hopeless, and lifeless, without a purpose for living or a reason to awaken each day.

Caeleb said nothing, but continued driving the horse.

Silence overcame her as they traveled. Ellisia slumped back down on the seat, but the passing sights pierced her consciousness. They had passed most of the poorer district and now entered a street that was not nearly as populated. Although signs of poverty remained here and there, the alleys slowly gave way to middle-class farm-like plots. Garden patches and small barns adorned the open areas surrounding the houses. Some dwellings even boasted various livestock milling around in fenced squares and triangles.

At the end of the road, Caeleb turned the cart onto a narrow dirt path. Trees lined either side, their branches nearly devoid of growth but hinting at tiny buds to come.

The path ended at a low shed flanking a boarded house. "Here's Mae's house," Caeleb announced. "Welcome home, Ellisia."

Ellisia swung her head from side to side. "Thank you," she whispered, still dazed. For the next three years, this was home. A wave of homesickness for Carita and her family washed over her momentarily, but she pushed it away and scanned her surroundings.

The wooden house sat in the middle of a clearing in the trees. A garden and a smaller shed stood off to the side. An open grassy area stretched in front, and trees clustered beyond the house.

She stepped out of the cart and followed Caeleb to the house. He knocked.

The door flew open and a tall young woman greeted Caeleb enthusiastically. At once Caeleb was motioning towards Ellisia and Mae was speaking again. "Happy to have you here. You are eager to attend Academy?"

"Oh yes," Ellisia spoke up, enthusiasm surging back to her heart in a rush. "It's been a life dream of mine, but I never imagined that I would be this close to realizing its fruition."

More pleasantries followed as Caeleb and Ellisia stepped into the small house. Chairs graced the edges of the walls; a closed door adorned the back wall. A table and woodstove occupied the far-right corner; another door stood shut to Ellisia's right.

She took all this in quickly as she and Caeleb stood just inside the doorway. Mae brought them tumblers of water and invited them to make themselves comfortable, chatting companionably as they seated themselves.

"My little helper went home for the day already," she

told Ellisia, "but she'll be back tomorrow. She's eager to meet you. I'm sure you'll get along well. Her name's Saera. She will continue to assist me while you're away at Academy, but I look forward to your help during the mornings and evenings—before she arrives and after she leaves for the day. I tell you, it does take a lot out of one to care for three tiny babies. One doesn't have enough arms in which to hold them all when they all cry at once! And someone is always awake, someone is always hungry, someone needs clothing changed—it's a challenge."

Ellisia nodded as Mae chatted on. Mae, apparently, was as talkative as Ellisia herself. That was one thing to be grateful for. She didn't mind carrying on conversation with silent folks—the awkwardness bothered her little, and she could easily manage the conversation on her own—but conversing with other talkative people was always enjoyable. She studied Mae more closely: tall, brown-haired, with a plain face that still somehow reminded her of Caeleb. Her eyes spoke of weariness, but she had a pleasant air.

A man stepped through the back doorway, a baby in his grip. He swooped down next to Mae, who grasped his arm fondly. "Ellisia, meet my husband, Jaeson. Just finished outdoor tasks for today—it's so nice to have him close by so often. Jaeson, this is Ellisia."

"Good to meet you, sir." Ellisia's eyes met his without hesitation.

He returned the greeting. "I am grateful you are here. Your assistance will be most valuable to our family."

"I'm glad of that," she replied. All at once she felt oddly shy in his presence—something unusual with her. Perhaps it was the effect of his precise words and manner, coupled with his meticulously neat appearance. She felt nervous to make a mistake in front of him.

A small whimper from the back room sent Mae

heading for the closed door. She returned with a baby on each arm. "When one wakes up, usually they all wake up," she told Ellisia. "This is Daenia"—she motioned to the yellow blanket and the squirming body underneath—"and this is Elkaena." She nodded to the green blanket. "No one can tell them apart at first. But you'll learn quickly."

Caeleb and Ellisia both peered at the identical pink faces.

"They're cute," Ellisia commented. "But yes, I'll have a hard time telling them apart."

"Elkaena's blankets and accessories are green, Daenia's are yellow, and Naethan's are blue," Mae told her. "It helps to be able to tell them apart somehow for those who don't know them so well." She turned to the blue bundle Jaeson held. "This is Naethan. Our little son."

"He's as cute as his sisters." Ellisia touched his tiny fist. He grasped her finger tightly and yawned.

Mae nestled the girls into a wooden cradle and stirred a pot. "The food is ready to eat. It will just take a few moments to get it on the table."

Caeleb rose. "I'll bring in your things, Ellisia."

"You'll be sleeping upstairs." Mae glanced at Ellisia. "There's a bed all ready for you—Saera saw to that."

Several moments of bustling activity later, Jaeson and Caeleb seated themselves at the table. Ellisia dallied near the cradle, pretending to be fascinated with the babies, as Mae sat down, then she slid into the remaining chair. Her leg banged awkwardly against the table leg, and she drew it up underneath her, hoping no one had noticed.

Supper was a simple meal of stew and biscuits. For once, Ellisia felt no inclination to fill the meal with conversation.

Before the last of the biscuits disappeared, a knock sounded at the door, and then Caeleb was welcoming his grandparents inside amid many joyous greetings.

"We were on the way home from a prayer gathering," Caeleb's grandfather explained, "and we decided to stop in. We can bring you home if you're ready," he said to Caeleb.

Ellisia slipped into a corner chair and listened as Caeleb's grandparents filled him in on all that had happened in his absence. She wished she had a book, but she supposed it would be most impolite to read just now. Mentally she counted the days—five more until Academy began. How would she spend the intervening time? She supposed she would have work to do at Mae's home, and perhaps she could visit the Academy. Would Caeleb come for her and show her the way? Would it be safe to travel back and forth alone in this city? Would there be teachers at Academy who could unlock the secrets of the effects of her words for her? And when would she be able to visit that much-dreamed-of BookHall?

After several minutes of lively conversation, goodbyes were exchanged as Caeleb prepared to leave with his family. His grandmother stopped to take both Ellisia's hands in hers. "I'm glad you've come, dear." The smile was sympathetic. "I know you're here for a reason, and I pray *Adon Olam* shows you."

Ellisia could only nod, though she felt the weight of the words as the grandmother disappeared out the door.

As Caeleb followed his grandparents, Ellisia silently stepped out after him, wrapping her cloak around herself as she walked. "Thank you." Her words were quiet. "For bringing me here. For finding this opportunity. And all." She fell silent, her eyes on the dusty trail.

Caeleb took a step towards the cart. "You are very welcome."

Silence stretched between them. "Are you tired?" Caeleb asked.

"I don't know; why?" Ellisia tried to shrug off the question.

"You're so quiet. It's not like you."

She bristled. "Okay, I'm tired. Do you have to point it out?"

Even as the words left her mouth, exhaustion swept over her. She hadn't noticed it before. Frustration welled up inside. What was the matter with her?

"I'm sorry," Caeleb said quietly. "I'll come by sometime tomorrow or the next day to give you an Academy tour, if that works. Midday, while Saera is here, if that's all right with you."

She nodded, willing her tempestuous emotions back down.

"Have a good night, Ellisia."

Once upstairs with her belongings, Ellisia slipped off her shoes and sank onto the bed. It was larger than her bed at home. The window overlooked the remnants of a glowing sunset, and a small table and chair reflected the last evening light. A chest of drawers rested next to the bed, and the trunk Caeleb had hauled up for her waited nearby. Ellisia relaxed her toes against the braided rug. This would be an excellent place to study—if the babies were quiet long enough for studying in this house. Three babies! No wonder Mae needed help.

Yet if only she could start Academy tomorrow…

She was asleep almost before she pulled the blankets over herself.

4

ACADEMY. THE WORD blurred into her consciousness as she clutched the pillow and rolled over. She blinked, and suddenly energy surged. Perhaps Caeleb would take her to visit today! In last evening's fog of tiredness and emotion, she couldn't remember exactly what he'd said. She pulled the gray blanket back and hopped onto the frigid floor. Daylight illuminated the small window, and she tiptoed over to see what prospects it held.

Shadows shrank and vanished from the landscape around her. Although the sun was rising from the other direction, the grass below her shimmered, dripping and emerald, where early rays of sunlight frolicked and danced. Sunbeams sparkled on tree branches, lending a peaceful, familiar glow.

But buildings—gray-tinged mossy stone, crumbling brick, peeling log—also stretched over the expanse, marring the otherwise untouched beauty of the morning. Still an excited tingle swept through Ellisia as her eyes rested on one and yet another of the mottled constructions. What as-of-yet untapped potential might those homes and shops hold for her life! People with knowledge she'd never dreamt of . . . books with cultures she couldn't yet imagine . . . education on all her heart desired . . . an undiscovered world lay within those decrepit structures. And today, she was the explorer.

Her toes curled tightly, willing warmth despite the frigid floorboards. How should she spend the day? Perhaps she ought to settle into the room more thoroughly before Mae needed her for other work. It would be best to get acclimated as quickly as possible so that she could find what she needed when she needed it and would not be delayed when Mae wanted her, when the babies screamed all at once, or when it was time to go to school.

She twisted away from the window, but then turned back. Just because she was no longer at home with the daily reminder of Carita's form at the window early each morning didn't mean she wasn't perfectly aware of the importance of the long-engrained habit to facing the day, particularly the unknown of today. She'd keep to her old patterns here, even if Carita wouldn't know. Her fingers fiddled the windowsill's smooth oak. If only she could also mimic Carita's devotion, passion, and fervor.

"*Adon Olam.*" Her tongue moved, but the words weren't in her mouth. She was keenly aware of each phrase lodging itself firmly behind her temples before releasing above. "Be with me today. Guide me. Be with Carita and her family. Bless them. And be with Mae and the babies, and Jaeson. And Caeleb. Be with me and cause me to do well at Academy."

She stopped, the train of mental words fading out into the distant air. For the hundredth time, how *had* her sister found so much to say to *Adon Olam* at the window every morning? A sigh escaped as she pulled a book out of her trunk, aimlessly flipping and perusing before absently setting it on the table.

Academy. Enshrouded in a conscious daydream, she arranged the rest of her books, papers, and quills on the table and her clothing in the drawers before slipping down the stairs. From the intermittent cries below, the babies had evidently been awake for some time, so she had no fear of waking Mae.

A clock ticked loudly in the silence of the main room as she tiptoed over to the stove, examining its features. Behind her, a latch clicked open before Mae's hushed voice marred the stillness. "A good day to you."

"A good day to you as well." Ellisia's eyes flicked that direction as her fingers traced the stove handle's curves. Mae didn't appear any better rested than she had last night. "Is there something I should be doing right now?"

"I am so disorganized in the mornings, especially with all this." Mae's hand swept a vague circle towards the woodstove and table. "I think you can create your own routine here. Just make sure the basic housework is done, everybody's fed, things look presentable, and so forth. There may be different jobs to be done on different days, but the normal routine should be fairly simple for you to fall into."

"I see," Ellisia declared slowly, not seeing much of anything at all. She hadn't expected to be given a free hand in the housework. Most of the neighbors she'd helped when she'd gone with Carita had very distinct methods of operation. Having triplets must make a difference.

"Saera usually arrives an hour after breakfast," Mae continued, withdrawing a cup and a tight-fitting lid from a box. "You and she can work together after that point—she'll show you her routine—though once Academy begins, you won't be here at the same time much anymore."

"So—what do you usually eat for breakfast?" Ellisia asked.

"Anything you can find," she replied. The cup swiped against a blue and yellow cloth on a wall hook. "I'm not particular."

Ellisia glanced from side to side, a sinking feeling in her stomach that may or may not have been related to hunger. Was she expected to scrounge around, find Mae's food supplies, *and* come up with a meal on her own in someone else's home? Not only that, but cook breakfast for Mae and Jaeson as well? And would she have to do it while Mae herself was standing in the kitchen? This was certainly the definition of awkward.

Her feet dragged as she turned back to the stove and began to fiddle with the fire, pretending that it needed more kindling and yet failing to decrease her discomfort. Who was she to decide that someone else's fire needed more fuel? What if she did something totally contrary to Mae's notions? She was only a young girl after all—not by any means an experienced housekeeper. Carita had always handled the oversight of the housework.

Thankfully, Mae moved back to the bedroom without taking any further notice of Ellisia. Ellisia let out the breath she'd held, replaced the cover on the stove, and glanced around.

A small yet bulky box sat in the corner where Mae had been. Oaken-board shelves and cupboards lined one wall. Food must be in one of those places. She opened the cupboards first. Sweet potatoes, carrots, meal—sweet potato meal, judging by the color and odor—a partial loaf of bread, leaven, salt. Clearly Mae didn't have an abundant variety, but all the basics were there. Hopefully Jaeson wouldn't object to eating the same breakfast every day.

Uncertain, she stirred the sweet potato meal into a pot of water ready on the back of the stove. It seemed to stick to the pot, so she added more water from the kettle and kept stirring until her spoon felt as if she was dragging it through bread dough. Was she cooking it too long? If only she'd taken time away from her books to ask Carita to show her how to cook on the new woodstove that

Kaelan had surprised them with last spring—who'd have guessed that she would need more than basic fireplace cooking abilities? Ellisia frowned at the thick mess clustered on her spoon. Why did food matter as long as it was something to hold body and soul together long enough to finish the next book?

Frustrated, she pushed the pot to the edge of the stove, then quickly shoved it back before she could predictably tip the entire gooey mess onto the kitchen floor. Why had she never paid attention when Carita had made porridge for breakfast? This was getting ridiculous. She tried adding more water, but it didn't seem to help much. Tears stung her eyes, and her hands, already warm from working at the stove, grew moist. How could she serve this failure to Caeleb's sister?

Finding a clean spoon in the box on the floor, she dug it into the sticky mixture. Perhaps it wouldn't taste as bad as it looked.

It did. She wrinkled her nose and tossed the spoon onto the table. The porridge stuck on her tongue, coating the roof of her mouth. It felt impossible to swallow.

"I wish this breakfast were at the bottom of the Ressian Sea," she muttered, slamming the pot onto the table. She at least wasn't going to let it burn too.

Still, she was hungry. Another quick search of the cupboards revealed nothing she could cook to redeem herself—and Mae probably wouldn't want her wasting food anyway. Perhaps she could eat fruit?

Sighing, Ellisia turned back to the dish box on the floor. She found a few bowls and set them on the table, then added spoons. As the back-bedroom door creaked, she whirled to the stove, pretending to be stoking the fire once more.

Mae sat down at the table and used her right hand to fill two bowls from the pot, a green-clad baby on her other arm. Ellisia dared not sneak a second look. What else could she occupy her hands with? If only she could replenish the kettle—but where did Mae fill it?

At least Mae said nothing, only stuck spoons in the bowls and carried them back into the bedroom.

Ellisia breathed a sigh of relief when the door shut once more. But she had to eat. She shuffled to the table and filled the remaining bowl.

The last spoonful of the mush still clung stubbornly to her violently shaking spoon when the telltale *creak* sounded again. Ellisia froze. She didn't intend to stare, but her eyes involuntarily followed Mae as she walked to the cupboard, took out the small bowl of salt, and retraced her steps once more. Just outside the bedroom door, however, she pivoted. "Ellisia, would you like salt?"

"Yes please." Her ear-tips tingled. How had she forgotten the salt? Banging her head against the table seemed a fitting, if socially inappropriate, response at this juncture. Why had she agreed to keep house when she didn't know the first thing about managing a home? Wasn't there an easier way to go to Academy?

The salted porridge still wasn't very appetizing—and it was almost cold by now—but at least the salt improved the flavor somewhat. Slowly each spoonful disappeared.

She set the used dishes together on the table. Where did Mae wash them? In that green basin, certainly—but where did she fill it? Irritated, Ellisia spun, banging her ankle against the table leg. She was as out of place as a cow in the garden.

Without a second glance, she bolted upstairs. Stuffing a book into her pocket and throwing on her cloak, she dashed back down the stairs and out the front door.

Maybe it wasn't safe to roam the streets of Syorien. She didn't care. She'd go find the Academy or perhaps even the BookHall, Caeleb or no Caeleb. She wasn't spending another moment in that cramped kitchen—not just now.

She'd barely reached the end of the path to the road when she nearly bumped into a small girl. "Uff!" The girl let out a small shriek, bolting back a few steps.

"Sorry." Ellisia inhaled, truly contrite.

The girl's eyes sought Ellisia's dark ones. She couldn't have been more than eleven, her clear, pale face highlighting her alert, knowing eyes. Those eyes studied her face, her dress, her hair. They stopped on the hair.

"You're Ellisia, true?" the girl asked.

"That is my name. And you?"

"Saera," the girl replied. "I live just there"—she motioned behind her, across the street—"and I help her." She lifted a slim finger towards Mae's house.

"You're Saera," Ellisia repeated, as if to herself. The girl had the most open, innocent, yet understanding and knowing face she'd ever seen. Her brown hair was long, wavy, and pulled back from her face. A small cross hung at her throat, and her light blue dress was simple but becoming under the cream cloak. But it was those eyes that captivated Ellisia. Wide, all-seeing, knowing, tender, innocent, young, and bright—she'd never seen such eyes.

"Yes. I'm on my way to help Mrs. Mae this morning," Saera offered, almost timidly. "You will be helping her when I'm not there?"

"I believe so," Ellisia replied abstractedly, pulling her gaze out of Saera's eyes and onto the face. *Agree, even if you're entirely uncomfortable and unsure.* She grasped the advice that sprung unbidden to memory. "I've been trying to help her this morning."

"I'm sure you were a great help." Saera's words were halfway between a question and a declaration.

"I certainly don't know about that . . . Not by making breakfast . . ."

"Why?" Saera asked.

Ellisia met Saera's gaze squarely for a moment. "See for yourself." The girl was going to the house. She would see the unwashed dishes on the table, the remnants of the clay-like porridge still in the pot.

And the owner of that pair of innocent eyes will clean it up. The niggling voice in Ellisia's head irritated her. She ought to go back and ask Saera where to wash the dishes. But her heart thumped in resistance—either from pride or selfishness. Perhaps both.

Instead, with a nod to Saera, she continued out to the road. She turned right. Only when she reached the end of the street did she realize that she didn't even have a general idea of which direction Academy was in. She only knew that it was somewhere nearby—but Syorien was a giant city.

A glance over her shoulder revealed that Saera had already disappeared up the tree-lined path. There was nothing for it. She'd have to brave the city and its unknowns alone.

Or go back.

The thought was as unwelcome as it was unbidden. Not a chance.

And so she wandered for several hours, willfully putting Mae, Saera, and the housework out of her mind for the time. This was her opportunity. Mundane duties couldn't stop her.

Streets and houses, fountains and trash piles, shops and street children—all paraded past her striding figure, then blurred together in the distance behind her. Pleasure houses, music halls, entertainment centers, Locals, show halls, pharmaceutical dens, game fields, and trivia halls loomed and disappeared. She passed one medical center. But no Academy or BookHall appeared to her searching eyes.

The sun climbed to its peak. Ellisia paused at a dusty intersection, stretching her muscles and gazing from side to side with weary eyes. Was there really anything worth seeing in this city? If there was, she certainly hadn't discovered it yet. No doubt her very first turn had been miscalculated—this certainly wasn't the part of Syorien she'd hoped to explore. She glanced with disgust from the squawky reed-instrument player on one side of the road to the beady-eyed hawker of ratty-edged scrolls on the other, then stepped into the street to avoid treading upon a prone figure in the path, unconscious of anything going on around him. Was there truly an Academy in this horrid city? Perhaps the simplicity of Frydael was more valuable than she'd thought—if only she were walking upon its clean streets, among its friendly neighbors, and past its sparse pleasure-houses suffering from disuse.

"Books! Books! Good books!" A shrill voice across the street caught her attention.

Books! What were the chances that they would be something worth her interest? She obviously couldn't find Academy on her own. Ellisia crossed the road and stopped in front of a garishly-painted cart lined with books to match. She scanned the titles. Worthwhile or rubbish? Some of them looked promising.

"What kinds of books do you sell?" she asked, addressing the gray-cloaked woman towering behind the stand.

"All sorts, miss." The voice was monotone and betrayed no information.

"What is the quality of their content?"

"All very good, miss." The tone was the same.

Ellisia sighed. "Are there advisories connected with these books? Any of them?"

"No, miss."

"How much?"

The woman named her price. Ellisia pursed her lips and pulled out a book that appeared to be less jarring than the others. Was this a good read? Surely decent books must be available somewhere.

"Where can I buy the best books in town?" she asked.

"Here, as well as anywhere," the answer came back. "We are supplied by the best researchers, authors, and scene creators employed by Amadel Academy, endorsed by the palace."

The palace. Ellisia shivered. Nothing about that title recommended its products to her. But still the books loomed in front of her. Their fascinating lure tantalized her appetite. She hadn't had a new book to read for much too long. There would be one good one among them, would there not? She paged through the one in her hand.

Her eyes were drawn to the story, as if a magnet lay embedded within. She read the page—and the next and the next, unable to tear herself away. What the story was, she hardly could have told, except that she must read the end—she must know what happened.

After three pages, she jumped at a sudden sound across from her. The gray-shawled woman had cleared her throat. An odd expression darkened her face. How long had Ellisia been reading? Her face burned.

"Money, please," the seller demanded.

Ellisia closed the book. "I do not wish to buy."

"The time reading my book must be paid for." She held out her hand.

Ellisia hesitated.

"If you do not wish to accept these terms, you may simply buy the book," the woman added.

Ellisia glanced down at the book she held. She *did* wish to find out what happened—but a nagging feeling in the back of her mind warned her against this type of reading material. Yet she could hardly define the hesitation even to herself. Though it didn't seem to be an evil book, something about it made her uncomfortable. The thought of bringing it home for Caeleb and Mae to see made her heart flutter and her hands withdraw. "No, I will not pay for it," she said. "I do not want the book. I did not mean to read it. Only the spell of it enchanted me for a moment. May you be content with that? You ought to know what charm a book may have for a reader."

"That I do. Especially a book like that one." Her eyes gleamed—was it sympathy, greed, or excitement?

Ellisia pressed her lips together and stepped up to the stall, nothing daunted. "I did read a page or two of your book, but such previews are allowed before purchase. If you intended to charge passersby to open your books, ought you not to have advertised that on your sign?"

A nearly imperceptible softening appeared around the woman's eyes. "May I then interest you in a different work?" she asked, her tones more friendly. "If you do not wish to purchase a story such as this excellent one penned by the illustrious Jaeta, perhaps you may be interested in this textbook of philosophy containing the research of some of the best professors at Amadel Academy and in Doekh."

Doekh. Ellisia's mind flitted to Dresie's words. *Those Doekhans know so much more about things than we do here, and my cousin says some of them have studied the effect words have and why.*

Almost before she knew it, the textbook was in her hands, and her fingers trembled slightly as they turned the leaves, careful, however, to avoid losing herself in the pages this time. Though evidently a scholarly work, it appeared unlike any academy book Ellisia had ever seen before. Thoroughly fascinated, she still almost shrank from the unknown knowledge it might contain. Did a slight darkness seem to pervade its pages, or did she merely imagine it?

The text appeared to be mainly psychological analysis of the relationships between the mind and the physical world. Ellisia's eyes scanned the pages. She'd never read anything at this level before. The implications of mind and matter—the relation of self to the outside world, the techniques for manipulating the outside world using the mind—Ellisia had never heard such things.

"I will take this book." She raised her head to meet the dark-eyed gaze of the bookseller.

A smile bloomed across the bronzed skin. "That is wonderful. You are an Academy student?"

"Yes—that is, I will be, I—"

The bookseller nodded as Ellisia managed to hand over the coins for the book. "I see how it is. Let me know if you love this book, and I assure you I have plenty more. And here—" Ellisia found a slim volume slipped into her palm. "It's my little gift to you. No charge."

Ellisia nodded, not willing to converse further with the woman now that she had the book. A tingling spread through her fingertips as she stepped backwards and into the street, clasping her purchase. There was something in this volume—she knew it! Would it hold the secrets of the power of words? Would it be able to explain the odd circumstances she'd noticed throughout her life? Even just now, she'd spoken to the bookseller that she wouldn't be paying for the time she'd spent reading the storybook, and the seller, though evidently quite determined to receive payment, had inexplicably backed down.

Pivoting, she walked quickly back in the direction from which she'd come. She'd visit Academy some other day. Just now she had a book to read.

An hour later, she'd made no progress towards Mae's house.

Chiding echoed in her being. How had she been so

careless? This entire day was a mess. She knew better than to get lost in a strange city. She had thought that she had carefully marked the streets in her head so that she would be able to return, but apparently not. She couldn't make heads nor tails of the complicated city street system.

Walking wasn't getting her anywhere. Dropping on a bench between two slender saplings, she drew a deep breath and tried to focus as she reckoned her chances.

It was her first day in Syorien. She couldn't rely on wanderings to get her home.

She knew no one in the city but Caeleb and Mae's family. The chances they'd locate her, even if one of them knew to come looking, were almost nothing.

Mae's home was obscure enough; no landmarks or status distinguished it or its street from many others she'd passed. Asking a stranger for directions would get her nowhere. Caeleb's home *might* be known among followers of *Adon Olam* . . . but it would hardly be safe to wander about asking about *Adon Olam* here so near the Palace District.

Adon Olam. Her eyes idled upon the books on her lap, lost in thought. Was that a way home?

Things had happened after she'd spoken them before, but she'd never purposely spoken words to cause something to happen.

It was worth a try, wasn't it?

Ellisia drew a deep breath, gripping the thick volume with all ten rigid fingers. How was one to begin when speaking like this?

"My feet know the way home and will walk in it." The words were raspy and tremulous. She swallowed, and her eyes squeezed shut. Somehow it seemed easier to believe the words her mouth spoke that way.

"Thank you, *Adon Olam,* that You have led me home."

The words faded, and Ellisia wondered what would happen next. Slowly she got to her feet, and, trying not to overthink each step, set out down the road. If only she could walk with her eyes shut . . .

Streets again blurred together before her, but she kept on, low repetition of her words emerging every now and then. Her heart beat rapidly, but she resisted the urge to glance around her or become distracted.

"Ellisia!"

The call jerked her out of her daze. The road she was turning on—why, it was Mae's road, and Caeleb stood at the end of the Mae's pathway, calling her name.

Concern etched his features as he looked her up and down once she reached his side. "Are you all right? Where have you been?"

She shrugged. "I'm fine. And I was out for a walk."

Caeleb grasped her shoulder. "Mae and Saera both said they hadn't seen you since breakfast."

Ellisia nodded, still slightly dazed.

"I came for that tour, but I suppose you're hungry and worn out now." Caeleb's brow furrowed. "I intended to show you around the city so you could find your way about on your own."

"Thank you" was all Ellisia could manage. She swallowed, then tried again. "I do believe I shall need it."

"Where did you go?" Caeleb asked again. Then his gaze rested on the books in her hand. "Shopping already? Finding books in this town?" The barest grin smoothed the creases in his forehead. "I might have known."

"Yes, and this is a textbook that I hope will help in my studies," Ellisia spoke up. "But for now—yes, I'm ready for a meal and to get off my feet."

The kitchen seemed as cramped as ever, but Ellisia was thankful to sink into a chair and allow Saera to bring her a plate. What was on it, Ellisia couldn't have told, nor what comments Saera and Caeleb may have made as she silently ate. Once her plate was empty, she readily accepted Caeleb's suggestion of an hour's rest in her room before the Academy tour.

Refreshed and rested, Ellisia bounded down the stairs at the end of the hour to join Caeleb with a clear head and renewed enthusiasm. Within a half an hour, the wide marble steps to Amadel Academy stretched before her.

Ellisia threw her head back, her breath catching as her senses absorbed the stature of the building. Overlaid in pure white marble, the walls gleamed brightly in the afternoon sunlight. Huge pillars towered higher than three stories. Large windows and doors lined each level, and porches stretched out invitingly beyond each door.

Even her wildest dreams had never pictured such a magnificent building. When she expressed something of this to Caeleb, he merely grinned. "Wait until you see the palace," he told her, "and the other governing buildings. And the palace music halls and entertainment centers. This is one of many. Yes, it's stunning, but it's not unusual here in Syorien's palace district."

"Still . . ." Her breath caught, and words failed her. This building would be her daytime home for the next three years. This was where the keys and tools of education were contained. Here was where she'd unlock the mysteries of books and academics and learning and words and so much more. The reflected beams from the glistening marble shone upon her face, dazzling her eyes.

Surely this was a fitting shrine in which to begin her devotion.

Her awe only increased once she stood beyond the wide double doors. Almost in a daze, she stepped from one gorgeous room to the next. She passed desks and tables, chairs and quills, books and shelves, walls, closets, parchments, scrolls, and nooks. She gasped over enormous paintings, life-sized portraits, elaborate landscapes, and countless gems of abstract artwork. In the music halls, she ran her hand across harpins taller than a man, ornate viols, and many other instruments that she didn't recognize. Everywhere throughout the stately halls and classrooms she caught glimpses of things she'd only read about.

When at last they reached the Academy BookHall, however, all power of speech fled. Her breath hitched in her throat as she caught the doorway for support. Upward, for the full two stories, books rose in rows all around her. Spiraling stairways, with intricately carved designs in steel painted red, ascended at intervals. Matching pillars braced massive balconies and walkways that lined each wall of books. In front of her sat an immense white oak table and countless chairs, each carved in a pattern matching the stairways and rails.

Even in her wildest imaginations fueled by her most fantastical books, Ellisia's visions had never approached what it would be truly like to stand in such a room. Mechanically, as in a dream, her feet stepped forward underneath her as she tiptoed across the rug. Her hand stretched out in front of her, her fingertips hungry to graze the spines of the books before her.

She tipped her head back to scan the titles on the wall. They were not arranged by topic, nor by category, nor even sequentially. Rows of bright red books sat above rows of yellow books and orange books. The opposite wall held rows of blues and greens. Directly above her on the next balcony were books in every shade of brown.

She sighed, her fingers coming to rest on an orange-red book before her.

This was where she was meant to be.

5

THE REST OF the day swept by in a blur to Ellisia. She knew little else until supper was over and she was back in her own room at Mae's with the door shut and Caeleb's footsteps fading down the narrow stairway.

She pivoted on her chair, staring at the wall as visions of Academy played over and over through her head. She could see it now: she'd learn so much there; she'd read—oh how she'd read!—all the books she could find time for; she'd study, and perhaps she'd discover something about spoken words that would fit together the disjointed pieces of her own experience.

At last, she turned towards the table. Her new books beckoned temptingly, but she knew she wouldn't be able to keep her eyes open even for a chapter, and she wanted to give them the proper attention they deserved.

Sleep would be the next best thing. She could read in the morning.

Dawn streamed through the window when consciousness touched Ellisia's features. Immediately she was awake, rolling out of bed with a glance first at her books and then at the window.

No doubt it was past breakfast time already. Her stomach protested, and, once dressed, Ellisia hurried down the stairs, the aroma of sweet potato porridge tickling her senses.

Satisfaction flooded her as she noted the empty bowls and the pot still steaming on the table. Someone else had made breakfast today; she could get to her books all the sooner.

No one disturbed her as she hastily swallowed down the porridge before disappearing back to her room. Once she'd made herself comfortable, her hands grasped the thin volume that lay atop the thicker textbook. She might as well see what it contained.

It proved to be a story—a strange tale of dark powers and enchanted gifts. Though riveted by the plot, as always, she found her soul repulsed by the imagery: people speaking death and watching it occur before their eyes; freezing a friend by a mere touch; lightning that flashed from people's eyes to others' hearts; breathing out fire and ice; hearts that caught words, actions, and thoughts, twisted them, and shot them out or secretly planted them where they would harm others—all for the advancement of the wielder.

How could humankind do such things? Why were people so selfish? But as she read, the story tugged on her. One by one, each of the gift wielders attained his heart's desire. Some achieved fame; others grasped power; others secured long-desired positions. Some gained friends; others defeated longstanding enemies.

One specific wielder attained her desire of penning the most famous book in the world. Ellisia's imagination soared at the possibilities. Here was a dream so nearly aligned with hers. Even though Ellisia had never been a writer, she knew so intensely the emotions attached to books—the pull, the lure, the excitement, the beauty, the imagination that books inspired. The word pictures used by the wielder-author exploded vividly to life in Ellisia's mind, and the joyful relief of the author's success mirrored itself in Ellisia's own soul. *She* could identify with this!

At last, she pushed the book away from her. She really ought not to lose herself in its pages in such a manner.

Although the darkness of the story hung over her mind, a calm filled her. She was in control.

Her hand automatically reached for the textbook below, and the pages fell open on the table.

One must lose himself or herself, yet one must never forget about the psyche. The psyche is quintessential to the success of the endeavors of the mind. Voluntary reduction of the psyche will result in parallel reduction of the control of the mind. Magnification of the substance of the self, however, will trigger extensive advancements in the hypothalami . . .

Ellisia's mind stuttered, attempting to wrap her brain around the unfamiliar concepts. Fascinated, she continued. She'd never considered the relationship between mind and matter before, and she'd never read text of this caliber—but her intellect rose willingly to meet it as she flipped to the beginning and read on. Could it be possible that her mind had a true and scientific effect on the physical world around her? Obviously mind was stronger than matter; it seemed to make perfectly logical sense that the power of the mind could influence mere physical matter.

Several chapters lay on the left-hand side of the book lids when a small sound behind her startled her. The young girl with the piercing eyes stood at the top of the stairs, looking at her. Ellisia spun away from the table, closing the volume before her with a sudden inexplicable desire to conceal her studies from those in the house. What was this girl doing in her room?

"I apologize for intruding," the girl spoke softly. "Mrs. Mae told me that I'd find you up here most likely. She wants me to show you some things."

Ellisia nodded and stood quickly, reaching for one of her old books to slide over the new ones before following the girl down the stairs.

"I'm washing the clothing today," the girl spoke up.

Ellisia nodded as she placed her foot on the next step, wincing at its *creak*. Saera, she'd said her name was?

"Saera?" Ellisia drew the name out hesitantly.

"That's me," the girl replied. "I live down the way, and I've been helping Mae all winter already. Like I said, today is clothes washing. With all those babies, there are a lot of things to wash. It's fun to see who gets the biggest pile dirty every time. It's sometimes easy to tell because of the different colors, but you never know who gets their shared clothes dirty. So far, Dae is usually the worst. I thought it would be Naethan, because he's a boy, but it hasn't been yet. He has been quite neat compared to Daenia."

In the kitchen now, Saera opened a tiny, almost invisible door in the wall and began filling a tub from a spout concealed there. So that was Mae's water source! No wonder Ellisia hadn't been able to find it.

The full tub thudded onto the table next to a crate overflowing with baby clothing. Saera climbed on a chair and swished the garments one by one in the water, adding soap from a small dish next to her.

Ellisia still stood, staring at the child. She was so fast! How could such a small girl wash clothing so quickly?

One by one, each tiny garment slid into an empty tub on the floor. Once the crate was empty and the tub filled with clean clothing, Saera dumped the used water into the garden, then she wrung each garment and placed it back in the empty washtub.

"Now we hang them outside." Saera slid the tub to her hip and opened the back door.

A thick rope stretched just below shoulder level from a corner of the house to a tree. Saera expertly fastened each garment to the rope with handmade clips, then brought the empty tub back to the house and stacked it with its mate in the corner of the room.

"And so that's how we wash the clothes here," she

explained. "Not very difficult."

Ellisia still only stared, feeling clumsy as she watched Saera's quick movements. She was supposed to help the girl? But no, she would usually be at Academy while Saera washed the clothing. Perhaps this was to prepare Ellisia for a crisis where the babies had soiled all their clothing after Saera had gone home for the day.

For the rest of the day, Ellisia followed Saera around as she worked. Saera chatted about this and that—the work, the babies, her own family. Eventually finding both her hands and her tongue, Ellisia joined in with the chores and the chat, though Saera still performed most of the tasks herself and only faraway topics managed to pass Ellisia's lips.

When at last Saera said farewell and disappeared down the long path towards the road, Ellisia shut the door behind her with a small sigh. When was the last time she had been this tired simply from being at home? Her feet felt as though she'd walked a day's journey. Her shoulders ached. To top it off, cooking the evening meal had scarcely begun. At least today Saera had lingered a little longer than usual to give Ellisia a few cooking pointers and detailed instructions for supper preparation.

Stumbling back to the wood stove, Ellisia stirred the iron pot, her mind running through the list of ingredients Saera had said she would need to add. How had Saera had so much energy? She hadn't even looked the slightest bit exhausted from her labors, though Ellisia knew Saera had worked far harder than she herself had.

Supper, thankfully, escaped being a complete disaster. Mae and Jaeson at least didn't make any comments as the clay bowls landed upon the table. Once the dishes were done at last, Ellisia found her arms occupied with Naethan as Mae retreated to the bedroom to feed the sisters.

Ellisia let a slip of a grin escape at the small face. Wide awake, he batted his tiny fist at her. She grabbed it, and he held onto her finger, kicking and cooing happily.

With a deep breath, she relaxed her shoulders and then leaned back. Maybe she could get used to living here after all.

But she still couldn't wait for Academy to begin.

The intervening days alternately crept and flew until finally Ellisia found herself in the entrance hall of the Academy. She clasped to her chest the sack that held her books and pens, willing her beating heart to still as her gaze followed the pattern of the deep red carpet and the costly white chairs staggered across the room. She perched in one, her hand tracing the polished lines of the dark wood armrest.

Her gaze left the adornments of the room and landed upon the faces of the students: lounging or sitting stiffly, milling about, admiring the artwork, or grouped tightly, conversing in subdued voices. Face after face she scanned, searching. Oh joy that another here must share the passions of her heart! Back in Frydael, few had understood or sympathized with her passion for books and learning. Laelara had told her it was a waste of time—an impractical daydream. Uff. Impossibly practical Laelara had never had patience for reading or academics. No Syorien adventures for her—she still kept house for her younger siblings and served her father as he grew older. A small smile accompanied a mental shake of Ellisia's head. Why anyone would prefer housework to bookwork was far beyond her.

Kethin, too, never thought much of books, only his sole care seemed to be his animals—though he did seem to be unusually popular about town. Animals she could forgive him for; they could be quite likable, insofar as they related to the stories in the books she was reading. And

Liliora was more interested in people than in anything academic.

But Kelton! Ellisia's smile deepened slightly. Eighteen years old, he was someone Ellisia could understand, in spite of the fact that he spoke so infrequently. His brown eyes were always serious and seemed to hold secrets she could not fathom. He had much more patience with Ellisia's passions and interests than any of his siblings had. Thoughtful and kind, he enjoyed a good book on occasion. Not stories though—Ellisia had tried in vain to interest him in some of her favorites, and though he was always polite and usually read what she gave him, it was clear that some of her stories were simply not his type.

Perhaps he would like her new book on the mind.

A gnawing feeling crept up that he would either like it very much or completely reject it. But still, he might possibly understand what it meant to her. His perception was so quick. Ellisia wrinkled her nose. How had Kelton never attended Academy? But then, he'd never been one to wander far from home, clinging to his family with loyalty and devotion.

She snapped to attention as a hush fell across the now-crowded room. She followed the crowd's gaze and spotted a tall man outlined in one of the spacious doorways leading further into the building.

"We will come to order," the man cried.

Everyone immediately silenced.

"My name is Doen Haerra. I will be your Overseer here at Amadel Academy. We thank you for choosing the joyous and pleasure-filled halls of Amadel Academy and we wish you all success in your quest for personal fulfillment and self-actualization."

Ellisia straightened, leaning towards the man. Despite his formal terminology, surely she could learn from him!

He continued. "I will now call out each line of study along with the number of the room in which each one will begin. When your line of study is called, please make your way quietly to the specified door. Your instructors will be waiting to give you further direction." He cleared his throat, adjusted spectacles, and turned to a guidebook. "Door 1: Accountation. Door 2: Architecture. Door 3: Art, General. Door 4: Art, Taernan Historical. Door 5: Art, Modern . . ."

Sinking back into her chair, Ellisia tuned the voice out. At this rate, it would be a while before he reached World Literature. Her eyes roved the perimeter. Every door had opened, and from some of them came flashes of grey and scarlet instructor uniforms. Which door would be hers?

A thought struck her. This room only was big enough for perhaps thirty or forty doors, yet she was sure there were more than forty lines of study. Her gaze snagged on the corner, where a lofty staircase, almost hidden behind wall sections, rose to the second story.

More doors must be upstairs.

At last, Doen Haerra called, "Door 56: Literature, World!"

Ellisia rose and followed the rhythmic flow of other students to the corner and up the stairs. Doors and streaming students blurred past her until at last a sign marked 56 solidified in her vision.

A bearded man stood at the door. Ellisia nodded to him as she entered, unsure of the proper greeting.

Boots scraped and books thumped as students claimed plump chairs standing in circular formation around the room. Ellisia slid into one of them, holding her breath carefully until she was settled.

Once the stream of students slowed, the bearded instructor at the door propped it open and turned towards a larger chair at the back of the room.

Ellisia fastened her gaze on him as if magnetized. She'd read about schools like this, but still warm beads rose on her forehead as her heart quickened in anticipation. She was sure she was in for a day of new experiences.

"Good morning." The man's voice was a rumbly tenor, something like Ellisia imagined her grandfather's might have been. "Welcome to the study of world literature. My name is Don Rhaea, and I can assure you that you have made a fine choice in entering this field of study. Taernan, Doekhan, Arkalian, and Draconian literature spans the generations and has influenced the course of history. As we dive into the details of literary development and changes throughout the ages, my hope is that you will acquire a new appreciation for the written word and for those who have gone before in crafting it, perfecting the skill, and recording it for our edification, enjoyment, and posterity."

Ellisia drank in the words, her chin lifted. Here was someone who understood her passion for the written word. How much she would be able to learn from him!

The gold-wire hands of the ornate clock above the stair spun away the hours as Ellisia toured the rooms she would be using most as a student of World Literature, received several new study books and materials, and met some of her fellow students. About twenty other students, both male and female, were studying World Literature. During one of the study breaks, she introduced herself to a lingering group of girls—a fair-faced one with narrow blue eyes, a girl whose copper tresses cascaded freely like Ellisia's own, and a girl with long black hair that hung over her back like a cloak. Ellisia drew a breath of relief as Jolyn, the blonde girl, smoothly carried on the conversation, including Ellisia in the remarks on the classes and books, their day, and plans for later.

Throughout the day, little comments and mannerisms here and there quickly revealed to Ellisia that Don Rhaea's views did not align with her own on many accounts, but what did that matter in the overarching sunshine of his views on literature? Anyone who so sincerely declared that "literature is worth studying—more than that, that it is the most noble and enlightening field of study" was an applause-audience worth having, as the old show hall saying went. With such affirmation behind her, energy surged from her fingertips to the very depths of her heart; surely there wasn't anything she couldn't accomplish.

However, the day wasn't all books, words, and glamorous declarations of the value of literature. Ellisia also discovered that several other topics would be included in her course of study: accounting, bookwork, organization, cultural studies, and methods of entertainment, to name a few.

And so her feet shuffled slowly as she headed homeward to prepare supper that evening. The tinge of regret weighing on her heart wasn't for how the day had gone—she had known that literature wouldn't be the sole component of her studies—but it seemed such a waste. Why should she spend her time learning bookwork, culture, and pleasure when she could be using the time on books and words?

She wondered if literature studies had a physiological or psychological line. Perhaps she ought to switch lines. For a moment she contemplated the thought, her eyes fixed on a moss-mottled rooftop across the way, heedless that her shoe tips scuffed themselves on the small stones in her path.

Suddenly she jerked alert at a sharp pain in her toe. Her gaze sought the dust. A sharp piece of tin spun away from her foot. She sighed. Evidently her shoes weren't thick enough for such pressure any more than her mind was sharp enough to sort through the implications of changing Academy lines just now.

Back at Mae's, she prepared supper, ensured that both parents were supplied with bowls amid the chaotic racket of the triplets' evening routine, and tidied up the room after the meal. She brought in the clothes from the rope outside, folded them neatly into the tub, and placed the tub outside of Mae's room where Mae would be sure to find it.

Despite the monotonous tasks that mechanically passed through her hands, her mind swiftly liberated itself to faraway worlds and imaginations. The instant the chores were finished, her quick footsteps retreated up the stairs to the solitude of her room. Her new books, arranged neatly on the table with the older ones, received a moment of caressing admiration. How her heart warmed at the thought of new words, new books, new ideas—ideas that had not passed through the careful scrutiny that had filtered most of the books available in Frydael.

Only an instant she stood. The next moment, seated at the table with an open volume before her, Ellisia lost herself in the mysteries of mind-bending, word-power, and psychological connections. There could be no more fascinating way to spend an evening.

THE FIRST WEEK of Academy flew by in a blur of new studies, chats with students, thought-provoking statements by professors, breakfast, supper, chores at Mae's, and a glorious few hours of reading each night before bed. Yet by the second week, chore-time had somehow expanded, shrinking her reading time, entirely squeezing it off the schedule on one occasion.

When morning dawned, dishes rattled and porridge bubbled earlier than usual as Ellisia worked on a desperate attempt to fit a few extra chores into the morning routine and leave additional evening reading time. The Academy hours couldn't be condensed, but perhaps her work might be.

Once the double white doors swung shut behind her at the end of the afternoon, she took the marble steps two at a time, not caring how she might appear and wishing she didn't have to prepare the evening meal. Why did she seem to get so little time to focus on what mattered most to her? Surely with the extra work she'd done this morning, she could steal a few extra hours with her books tonight.

When she'd finally passed Jaeson in one of the fields and slipped in the house, a darkened quietness enveloped her. Saera must have already left for the day, and Mae was probably in the bedroom with the babies as usual.

Without a second thought for the chores that waited for her, she slipped up the stairs as quietly as she could. The last thing she needed just now was one of those babies screaming as though her wails could bring the entire city racing to her bed to fulfill every urge or want.

Ellisia flung her bag onto the bed and reached for her textbook.

Mind is the principal thing, therefore never subject the mind to the desires of the body. As the body—in each of its variegated and individual parts—is subjected to the will and authority of the mind, the whole person becomes one in harmony with the forces of the world and of the psyche . . .

A door slam from below roused her at last. The lump that had jumped to her heart rose to her throat as she nervously closed the textbook and shoved it under the others. How long had it been? Jaeson and Mae would be expecting the meal.

When she reached the foot of the stairway, she groaned inwardly. Used spoons and bowls littered the table. Water spread a trail from under the basin across the floor to the front door. Muddy boots lay where they'd been kicked off partway into the room, a black trail stretching behind them as though it was only after several steps in that the wearer had realized that he ought to remove them. A forgotten blanket lay crumpled near the bedroom door. The last sunbeams barely reached the windowsill, shrouding the room in evening shadows.

Ellisia had never seen Mae's house in such a state. Why hadn't Saera left it clean? Frustration welled, and she spun this way and that, trying to decide what had to be done immediately. Ellisia was late. Supper was late.

Everything was late. And she hadn't done any work this evening. As quickly as she could, she dragged the tub to the miniature door, filled it at the spout, and piled the dishes from the table into it. She tried to ignore the mud on the floor, but several times her shoes grazed the edge of one of the footprints, smearing it around the room as she bumbled about between the stove, the box, and the cupboard, attempting to locate something reasonably palatable for the meal.

After the fourth time—nearly spilling onto herself the cup of hot water she carried—she gave an impatient exclamation and headed for the ragbag. Late or not, she'd have to clean the floor first. She smothered the thoughts boiling in her heart and tried to work rapidly, but every move she made seemed only to smear the mud more horribly across the floor. Why did nothing she did seem to go right? She took a deep breath, refusing to let the sizzling emotions inside her heart control her mind. She must not give in. Mind, not body. Mind, not feelings. She breathed deeply a few times, then scrubbed the cloth over the floor in a more controlled manner.

At last the floor was clean, the dishes were clean, and the sweet potatoes on the stove were soft. Ellisia piled them in an earthenware bowl and covered them with a plate just as Jaeson exited the bedroom, shutting the door so softly behind him that Ellisia jumped when he stepped forward.

"Mae is not well today." His voice was low.

Ellisia shut her eyes, taking another deep breath. She would not react. Enough temper had already boiled within her that evening.

"I will bring her the meal." Jaeson uncovered the bowl that Ellisia had just set down.

Ellisia rescued one sweet potato for herself and nodded as Jaeson carried the bowl into the bedroom. Sinking into a chair, she sagged against the table. At least they shouldn't need anything else from her tonight.

She rebuked herself for the thought. She ought to be sorry that Mae was ill. Caring for three infants would be enough to tire anyone out.

But the regret didn't reach her heart, and Ellisia was keenly aware of that. Her book filled her thoughts. There had to be a way for the theories on the pages to transcend the parchments and become her own life's reality.

Late that evening, Ellisia finally closed the book again and leaned across the bed to blow out the lamp. She pinched her eyes shut. They felt gritty and sore, and the back of her head throbbed.

An hour later, she'd turned over on the bed countless times. A frustrated sigh escaped, and she squeezed her eyes shut against her piercing head. What was the matter with her? Grimacing, she half sat, then sank back down, too tired to do anything but sleep, yet too restless to fall asleep.

Her studies would be a task tomorrow.

Yet even in her tired fog, her mind spun around her book. She'd read it nearly three times already, yet still she wanted to keep reading. Were there other books like this? Was there a second volume somewhere?

She needed more time. Her hands reached out to the book in the dark, but even as she did, she knew that she wouldn't be able to hold her eyes open long enough to read even a single page.

Perhaps she could bring it along to Academy.

Ellisia awoke with a throbbing headache, her eyes still gritty. She stumbled through the morning meal and work, then set off for the Academy.

The cooler morning air refreshed her slightly, and she was alert by the time she reached Academy, her book tucked firmly under her arm. Pulling the door open, she crossed the entrance hall and climbed the stairs to the literature room. She still had a passage to analyze before studies began that morning, but she pulled out the volume she'd brought instead. Page after page fell away under her eager, heated eyes.

"You're reading Wulf?" a voice interrupted.

Ellisia started, nearly closing the book before catching herself. It was only Jolyn. She met the girl's pale eyes.

Jolyn tilted on her narrow-heeled boots, clasping her own books to her chest. "He's an interesting author with lofty ideas. I don't identify with everything he says, but it's a fascinating read for the growth of mental capacities and imaginations."

"You think so, too?" Ellisia drew in a breath, careful to let it out softly. "I have found him quite enlightening. Many of the ideas are concepts that have never before crossed my mind. I'd love to read more on the subject."

"Have you been to the BookHall yet?" Jolyn swiped her hair back from her face. "Several of his works are here as well as more on the same topic by other authors. I haven't read them all, but I've read a few. You should check them out."

"Where are they?" Ellisia asked. "I'm afraid I haven't gotten the system of the BookHall down yet."

"I'll show you." Jolyn glanced at a timepiece on a nearby shelf. "Do you have time now?"

"I do," Ellisia replied without hesitation, squelching the thought of the passage she needed to analyze. "I have nothing pressing—certainly nothing as important as this." Wasn't this the true reason she'd come to Academy?

Jolyn led Ellisia down the corridors to the BookHall.

"I've noticed that the books are arranged by color, but I have not been able to make sense of the classification system yet," Ellisia confided.

"It's quite ingenious," Jolyn replied. "The colors are also topical to some extent. For instance, we'll be looking in the pale orange section for the books you need." She motioned to the book that Ellisia carried, which, true to Jolyn's words, had a pale orange spine.

Ellisia glanced from the book in her hand to the towering shelves surrounding her. "What if someone writes a book on this topic in another color?"

Jolyn shook her head. "All books that are printed here in Syorien are colored according to the Thaerrian classification system. In that system, all psychology books are pale orange. It was partly the imagination of King Thaerre, but mostly the scheme of his chief librarian. Most of the BookHalls in Syorien are grouped according to his system now. It does make for a pleasing array of color."

"How many BookHalls are in Syorien?" Ellisia asked, her mind on Frydael's single dusty and decrepit BookHall, fallen into disuse many years before.

Jolyn shook her head and mounted the stairs to the second level. "I have no idea. Several, I'm sure. I only go here and to the Palace BookHall. More books than you've probably ever imagined in your life. More books than even I will ever need."

Ellisia craned her neck upwards as she followed her friend. "More than here, I gather?"

"Oh yes. Maybe twenty times this many."

Ellisia's eyes widened as they swept the towering shelves. "Truly." It was more of a statement than a question, a hoarse whisper of renewed awe.

"It's quite the collection—certainly a vast variety from which to choose." Jolyn paused, her hand resting on a support pillar next to the pale orange shelves.

Ellisia didn't reply—her imagination bounding as her mind again traveled the well-worn grooves of her own mental version of the Palace BookHall, now expanded by Jolyn's description and resplendent with all the glory Ellisia had ever invested in the image. Surely she could find time to visit soon ... she'd hoped Academy work would settle a bit and she could slip away ... but was it open to just anyone? And where was it located?

Jolyn turned from scanning the shelf. "If you want books by Wulf, you should go there. I think they have his whole collection there. That's where I've read most of the ones I've seen."

"Then what are we wasting time here for? Let's go!" Even the pale orange section seemed pointless now. If Jolyn was familiar with the Palace BookHall, it would be best for Ellisia to take advantage of the knowledge while she could.

Jolyn glanced at a timepiece. "Literature starting soon."

Ellisia's eyes traveled after Jolyn's. "Oh." She'd entirely forgotten class and her assignment. "After studies today, then?"

Jolyn nodded. "I can do that. I intended to get over there sometime this week anyway."

"Excellent! Meet you on the steps afterwards!" Ellisia's boots clattered down the stairs, echoing among the rows as she retreated to the literature room. She'd still get her assignment finished before class if she hurried.

The gold-wire hands of the great clock above the stair had never seemed to turn so slowly, but at last Ellisia escaped to the marble steps where Jolyn soon appeared at her side.

To Ellisia's delight, scarcely a quarter of an hour later she roamed the shelves in a wide building far exceeding even her wildest dreams. Compared to this, even the impressiveness of the Academy BookHall was puny! She hadn't known so many books existed in the world.

"I could live here," she gushed, her hands tracing over the titles on the first shelf inside the door. She tipped her head back. "So many books! This is—what—five stories high, perhaps?"

"Yes. Five stories. Books from top to bottom. But you can't eat and sleep books," Jolyn retorted, roaming past the many rows of red and pink titles.

"Shows what you know," Ellisia muttered without thinking, but the tones were faraway and almost dazed.

Then she shook herself. Why did books do this to her? Sometimes she couldn't even think straight. They seemed to take over her mind, pulling her towards themselves.

"Five stories," she whispered. "All books." She walked to the end of a row and let her gaze travel down the straight path. She could barely see the other end. Turning her head, she noticed that the path the other way wasn't any shorter.

"This building is massive."

"Yes. The kings don't do anything by halves."

"When was this built?" Ellisia asked.

"I have no idea. Before my time."

Ellisia walked to the wall. "I wish I knew."

"You could probably find out if you truly wanted to."

Ellisia grinned. "One of these books probably records the history of this place. In all this information," she waved her hands vaguely towards the ceiling, "they had to have run out of books and started writing down any random thing that happened in their lives."

Jolyn giggled. "Wouldn't surprise me. A collection like this? Half of it could be trash."

Ellisia stared, a hint of a frown crinkling her forehead.

"Not *trash*," she stated strongly. "*Not* trash. Even the worst written book has value. They are words. Words are power. Words are valuable. We need words. And if they are written, it means that those words were important to someone."

"But not to us necessarily." Jolyn turned a corner and disappeared down another of the rows that spanned the area.

"They could be just as important to us as to anyone though," Ellisia argued, following. "If the author thought it was vital to record, we can find their value too. We just have to see through the author's eyes."

"Maybe, maybe not." Jolyn's voice drifted back. "But as for me—I wouldn't want to read all of these even if I could read them in one second each."

"I would," Ellisia breathed, not caring whether her words reached the girl's ear.

"Here's Wulf," Jolyn called, stopping partway down one of the pale orange shelves. "See here . . . fifteen—no, seventeen books. The whole set."

Ellisia joined her. "Here's the one I have." Her fingers halted on a familiar title. "And here's the one he wrote next." She pulled out another volume. "They let you take these home?"

"Yes," Jolyn confirmed. "It's a strict system, though, so you don't want to lose them or be late in bringing them back—but you can take up to ten books at a time."

Ellisia cracked the book open, savoring the crispness and sharpness of the pages. Most of the books she was used to reading at home were on parchment or browned paper—not whitened paper like this. "Wulf must be a wealthy author."

"More like the kings wouldn't allow books for this Hall to be printed on anything of less quality. That's what they say at Academy, at least. I would be surprised if there are many wealthy authors around. Taernan authors, especially."

Ellisia paged through the book for several minutes in silence. "I'll take these three," she decided at last, pulling the next two books by the author into her lap along with the one she held. "I won't read them that fast anyway—I might have to bring them back before I'm done with them. But this way I won't lack for something to read."

Jolyn had chosen a title of her own, and Ellisia's steps pattered after Jolyn's to the front of the room where she noted in a blank record-volume which books she was taking and filled out the page with the required information.

Back on the road, Ellisia drew in a deep breath. "Thank you for showing me this place. I will certainly be back."

"You have to, if you don't want to get in trouble." Jolyn playfully shoved her. "You're addicted now. No turning back. Weekly visits for you." She winked. "But you are welcome. Glad to be of service." Her steps slowed as they reached the intersection. "Here's where I turn off. Academy's just down there, so you should be able to find your way home easily enough." Jolyn waved her bag down the street in the general direction of the school. "And I hope you continue enjoying Wulf as much as I have. See you tomorrow."

"You too," Ellisia responded, a grin working its way up to her face.

She turned the corner and paused to watch Jolyn disappear down the other corner. With a happy sigh, she bent her steps homeward. So much on her mind! Her steps rang lightly and joyously as she traversed the upkept streets of the Palace District.

As she turned up the path to Mae's house, she already heard the babies screaming—all three of them, in concert, their separate voices making distinct shrieks as she approached. She sighed. *Everything* seemed to go wrong at Mae's home.

For a moment, she considered not going indoors. She could stay outside and read in relative peace and quiet. But the trip to the BookHall had already made her late. She oughtn't to stay away another minute.

She reluctantly headed inside and hurried up the stairs to put her books away before plunging into the chaos in a wild attempt to create some sort of order out of the evening chores.

Despite the constant bedlam at Mae's, Ellisia easily devoured Wulf's books in three days. The moment studies were over on the third day, she traced her steps back to the Palace BookHall. She scarcely wanted to admit, even to herself, that she'd read the books so quickly simply to earn herself another trip to the BookHall. It exerted a strange yet thrilling pull upon her—something that she couldn't quite explain. As she'd told Jolyn, she would indeed be content to live there for the rest of her life.

Maybe she could. She only had to support herself in Syorien. Right now she boarded with Mae and helped with the chores in exchange for lodging and meals. Her gaze fixed on two squabbling crows. If she could earn her board elsewhere, she wouldn't need to do housework and daily chores for a living. She'd be able to go to Academy and spend time doing something she liked better.

Such as books.

The seed of desire stirred within her heart. She'd visited, as she'd always dreamed, but she knew now that one visit—or even a hundred—could never be enough. What would it take to get a job at a BookHall?

Her dreams dulled with a practical sigh. Few would give her such a job, she was sure. In Frydael and the surrounding area, women rarely held public jobs. Assisting husbands or fathers in their work, yes. Caring for children or doing housework, yes. Minor private jobs, yes. But any other job was difficult to attain unless one had someone to speak for her—and Ellisia certainly didn't have anyone here.

By the time her steps reached the bronzed pillars of the five-story building, she had made up her mind that she wouldn't give up so quickly. She would try her hardest to attain a position here in the BookHall.

Accordingly, once she had filled out the return paperwork for her books, she roamed the massive corridors and balconies, searching for someone—anyone—who might be employed at this place.

In a hidden nook towards the back of the long rows, a tall man with spectacles sat behind a table. Papers and parchments littered the surface before him, and his brow creased heavily as he rhythmically pointed a quill up and down a sheet in front of him.

Ellisia paused at what she hoped was a respectful distance and waited until he looked up.

"How may I help you, miss?"

"I have come to enquire about the functioning and system of the BookHall," she began. She didn't want to give away too much information all at once. "I am a student at Amadel Academy and I am looking for more information on how BookHalls are run—specifically this one." Her gaze escaped, following the upward rows of shelves and walls.

"We have a section that may provide you with all the information that you require," the man told her. "Pale blue. Second level, front side."

"Thank you; I will look into that." Ellisia took a step closer to him. "But I would also like information from you."

He pushed back his paper and stared inquiringly at her over his spectacles.

"You are employed here?" she asked.

"Part of the time."

"You do paperwork?" She took in the stacks surrounding him.

"Primarily."

"What other sorts of positions are available here in the Palace BookHall?"

"BookDusters." He threw down his quill. "Different ones who come in periodically to ensure that the books are in order and to clear away the dust that tends to settle upon them from time to time. Indeed, this is truly a massive task—one that employs more young men from the streets than many other places."

"I can imagine." Ellisia made a mental note of the fact. "What else?"

"The Scribe comes in from time to time to review the lists of books in stock and add to it as he deems necessary. Sub-scribes go over the lists of new books, approve them, and make the necessary preparations to import the books and categorize them. Then we also work with the PrintHall. You might want to visit there for information on what they do, but they are very closely associated with us. We also have a partnership with various researchers, authors, and professors around the city."

"Thank you," Ellisia's fingers itched to create more than simply a mental list of what he was saying. "Is that all?"

"Those are the primary employees of this BookHall—other than the usual staff that goes with any palace hall. There are other positions from time to time, but we usually fill those as they are available. We do have an employment manager, but he manages position fillings for most of the major halls in this district, so he's not strictly a BookHall man."

"Interesting," Ellisia replied. "And how does one attain a position here?"

"I'm here because my cousin recommended me to King Damien." His calloused fingers wrapped around the quill, and he glanced at his paper before meeting her eyes once more. "It varies. Love of books. Knowledge of books. Power of words. Sympathy to the ways of the kings. Any or all of these can help ensure that you're a good fit here. Also, it has to do with the need. If we don't have a need here and someone is hired, we might send them to another Hall instead."

"Is the pay good?" Ellisia's heart beat quickly. Surely she would be an excellent fit here. If only she knew more of that elusive "power of words" she'd heard mentioned more than once now.

"Of course." The quill moved up and down the page once before the rest of the answer came. "We're working for the palace. The rewards are always good."

"Thank you very much." Ellisia stepped back, again eying the shelves longingly. "Do you have special benefits from working here? Like reading these books? Or taking them home?"

His gaze darted towards the entrance once before he replied. "We're allowed to take as many books as we please and the loan time is twice that of a normal citizen."

Ellisia's eyes widened, and she swallowed. "Thank you much for your time. This has been very helpful. I will be returning often, I hope, and I expect to make good use of this marvelous facility."

"You are welcome." Already the quill moved on the

papers once more, the shoulders again hunched over the table.

Ellisia couldn't help the grin that spilled onto her face as she made her way back to the pale orange books. Picking up the next one in the series, she headed for the front of the room and filled out the appropriate paperwork. There. That would do. Paperwork for only one book took less time, and if she only took one book, then she would be able to return sooner. Coziness and belonging seeped from the very shelves and tables—she felt more at home here than anywhere in Syorien. She wondered if the kings provided accommodations for their workers, and if so, if there were any in this hall. She made a note to herself to try to find that out on one of her trips.

Yet . . . this whole dream was no doubt unachievable. They wouldn't hire her. She might be an excellent fit in her own eyes, but convincing anyone else of that seemed next to impossible. She had no references or experience. She liked to read, but she knew better than to suppose that would be cause for notice. Power of words—she had that, too, but what did it mean? If only her books were more practical and specific—philosophy was fascinating, but at some point, she needed practical instruction. Dresie's injunctions returned to mind. Perhaps she could ask around at Academy—one of the professors would surely be able to guide her if anyone could. Then, perhaps then, she could focus on that for a time—enough to truly set her apart and fit her for any palace hall position she might desire. Yes, it was only a tiny speck of hope on a distant star, but she had to try.

For now, she ought to be back at Mae's. The job she had now might not be her favorite, but it had brought her here.

7

NO ACADEMY TODAY. Ellisia's first waking thought carried both anticipation and dread. Would it be a boon that allowed her extra time with her books, or would it only mean dawn until dusk with Mae's housework? As she smoothed the blankets on her bed and ran a comb down the length of her auburn curls, a longing welled up within her to spend uninterrupted hours pondering the concepts of her philosophy books, making notes, analyzing words in her own life, and planning her strategy for approaching the professors on the subject when next week's studies began.

As the sweet potato porridge simmered on the woodstove, as Saera arrived and joined her in the chores, as windows were scrubbed, rugs straightened, and floors swept, Ellisia's daydreams swiveled freely between the Palace BookHall and the theories of words propounded by her books. Here was something worth spending her time on—something worth learning. Once the midday meal was cleared away, once Mae and the babies settled in for naps, and once Saera had returned home, Ellisia paced her own room, too restless to settle down to her books as usual, though she yearned to lose herself within the pages now that she had a few moments.

At last, she tiptoed back down the stairs, avoiding the

squeaky one, and unlatched the front door. Pacing might as well be done in the open air.

A wave of spring's warmth ruffled her hair as she stepped beyond the house. Peak spring was not yet upon Syorien, though it certainly wasn't far off. With the back of her hand, Ellisia smoothed the wayward tresses as her boots left dusty tracks on the road.

Street after street fell behind her as she neared the Palace District. Instead of turning left towards the Academy and the BookHall, however, her feet hesitated only an instant before pivoting right. She'd explore the Market District today.

The sounds of a crowded marketplace assaulted her ears before she'd even turned the corner: calling voices, squawking and squealing livestock, rumbling of carts on cobblestones, constant footsteps, murmurs of a hundred conversations. Ellisia paused, her arm against a stone storefront, contemplating the sight before stepping foot within. Hawkers of all sorts lined the busy thoroughfare. Stalls, stations, carts, awnings: the dizzying and vivid array presented a sight unlike anything seen in Frydael. Boldly painted letters labeled various people's merchandise. Forward and back a constant line of passersby surged and swerved, stopping now here, now there, yet seemingly always in motion.

Ellisia plunged into the performance. As she strolled carelessly, her head swiveled to view stands of fresh produce, stalls of jewelry, tables of household wares, and displays of games, tools, clothing, sweetmeats, and books.

Before she knew it, she'd paused in front of the brightly painted bookstall, her eyes roaming the titles that her fingers lightly traced.

She recognized these titles.

Her eyes jerked up to meet the dark ones of the bookseller. Sure enough, the seller was the same one she'd purchased her textbook from on her first day in the city. Recognition rose in the bookseller's eyes as well. "You're back," she stated. "Welcome. You enjoyed your selection, I trust?"

"I did." Ellisia's eyes fell back to the titles. No doubt these works were quite inferior to many she could find in the BookHall—but now that she'd seen the Academy BookHall and the Palace BookHall, she could tell that these books were different somehow. Quite possibly they didn't follow the Thaerrian classification system that Jolyn had mentioned; hadn't the bookseller said something about her books being written by people from Doekh?

"Oh, it's Ellisia."

The familiar voice snapped her head to attention.

"Jolyn?"

"Didn't expect to run into you here." Jolyn set down several sheets of paper, placed a weight over them, then skirted around the edges of the stall to Ellisia's side. "I might have known that where there's anything like a book collection, you'd be certain to find it."

"I suppose I could say the same of you?" Ellisia's hand dropped from the titles, and she scanned Jolyn questioningly. "You're—helping sell?"

"One could say that." Jolyn tossed her hair before stepping to the next stall to seize another stack of papers. "Or rather," she called over her shoulder, "I'm helping more with their production than their sales, though I've done a bit of that. Helping my people when I don't have studies, you know."

Ellisia nodded, glancing from Jolyn to the bookseller and back again. She bit her lip, hesitating.

But Jolyn spoke again. "Oh, but I ought to introduce you. Miss Loaw, this is my friend Ellisia from Academy. She's in my world literature line, though you may have guessed that. Ellisia, this is Miss Loaw, our marketer, promoter, and distributor."

Miss Loaw straightened her figure, her right index finger touching her forehead for a brief instant in acknowledgment. Ellisia nodded back, her eyes scanning the woman's medium-toned skin and dark curls—a stark contrast to Jolyn's fair features. Just how were these two related?

"Pleased to meet you." The words floated airily from Miss Loaw's lips. Ellisia felt the dark eyes scanning her closely, and she shifted yet stood her ground. "So you are interested in world literature. A worthy pursuit."

"So I believe," Ellisia returned, unbending a bit.

"Indeed. If only more of the young of Taerna would recognize the merits of texts spanning the course of history and of the world. But alas, it seems so many are interested only in the present-day's entertainments."

"A sad prospect for Taerna's future, I fear," another voice spoke up from the booth next door, and Ellisia's gaze swung towards a tall and ruddy man whose black hair hung nearly to his shoulders as he continued. "Our future generations may not have much in the way of literature from this age of Taerna's history at all. It is a task bequeathed to us to fill this void and preserve our modern knowledge not only for the future, but for all uneducated societies."

Ellisia nodded, then spoke up, undaunted by the new face. "And yet we must have readers of the works as well. Were all literary students to merely write books, no one would be left to pass on the love of reading. Books unread are books unvalued, and thus books wasted."

"Not wasted." The man scrubbed at his middle finger with a thumb before sliding a pair of spectacles onto his nose. "There is value in the act of transferring knowledge and images to the page. There is value in knowing that they are preserved and may be read a hundred generations from now, if never before. There is joy in the mere act of creation of such works, and you will find that a strong coalition of avid readers still do exist."

"And much to their satisfaction, we still have new books for them," Miss Loaw put in.

"Ellisia, these are two more of my people." Jolyn spoke up. "Jaefa, you ought to introduce yourself properly before launching into literary arguments. And Jaeta, meet Ellisia."

Another dark head, as like Jaefa's as possible, rose from its hunched posture on the other end of the stall. "Pleasure to meet you," a rumbly voice murmured before the eyes again dropped to the book at the stall.

"Jaefa's an author; Jaeta's a scene creator for him," Jolyn explained. "They're working on some new experiments at the moment that I'm sure you'd find fascinating. Exactly your type of thing. Wulf-style."

"Oh?" Ellisia arched an eyebrow. This could be worth hearing. "What sorts of experiments?"

"Our current quest could prove groundbreaking in world history," Jaefa began, but Jolyn interrupted with a laugh.

"Of course. Jaefa always has a groundbreaking project in his pocket. If it's not one thing, it's another."

"You said he's an author, though?" Ellisia glanced from Jolyn to Jaefa. "An experimenting author?" Her brow wrinkled. Certainly authors often experimented with different types of stories or different forms of writing, but that didn't seem to fit with anything Jaefa had said so far.

Jaefa shot a glance over his spectacles towards Jaeta before replying. Jaeta, his eyes no longer fastened on his book, stared towards Ellisia and Jaefa warily and yet with a spark of interest. Something passed between the two men, and Jaefa turned back to Ellisia.

"Currently we are experimenting with the transfer of spoken words and their impact on written words," Jaefa explained, his eyes working across Ellisia's face, gauging her reaction.

She nodded, her expression guarded, waiting for him to continue.

"If spoken words could be transferred directly to the written page—no medium required—the entire process of book production could be radically transformed."

A spark leaped to Ellisia's eyes. "The descriptions—the characters—everything would be so much more real."

A slow smile spread across Jaefa's face. "Exactly. The middle medium would nearly be eliminated. The author could practically speak directly to the reader. The possibilities of such a theory are endless."

"There is scientific basis for this, I assume?" Ellisia leaned across the stall, her mind flying back to her own small experiences with spoken words.

"There is," Jaefa replied. "It's been researched extensively in Central Doekh, as well as by various smaller groups across the world. As of yet we haven't achieved a breakthrough specifically with spoken to written, but it approaches ever nearer each day we experiment." Pulling his spectacles off once more, he surveyed her. "You're a literature student, true?"

Ellisia nodded.

"How would you like to assist me with my next research project? I can tell you have a keen mind both for the written word and for scientific analysis. An assistant would be most valuable for me just now, and I could promise that you'd learn the very best and latest of Central Doekh's research. Such research isn't even widely taught in academies here yet."

Ellisia's heart rate accelerated. "You'd—you'd teach me that?"

The black head nodded, the dark eyes still locked on Ellisia.

She swallowed, her gaze flitting from Jaefa to Jaeta—both staring—from Miss Loaw to Jolaena—both busy tending the stall—and finally back to Jaefa once more.

"What do you say?"

Her mind flew to Mae, to Caeleb, to Academy, to her books, to Dresie's words to her.

"I'll do it." Her voice shook slightly, and her tongue traced a path across her bottom lip before she tucked it back inside. Her hand reached out and gripped the nearest book. "What is it you'd want me to do? And when?"

"After Academy hours would be a fine starting point." Jaefa's grin showed before he turned serious again. "You can come to our headquarters with Jolyn once studies are finished, and I'll show you what's needed."

"Oh." Ellisia bit back the word. When would she have time for this? Mae would expect her back for evening chores. "Could I—could I perhaps come today? And then—perhaps after the evening meal? I do have commitments . . ." Her heart sank, wondering when she'd ever find time to read now, but she drew a deep breath. This would only be temporary, and these people could teach her more than she was likely to find in books—at least for the present.

Jaefa nodded shrewdly. "I will want more regular hours later, no doubt, but whatever you can manage for the present will do. And—" He consulted a timepiece that hung around his neck. "I can spare myself from the stall today. Research above all. Come."

Rising, he gathered his books, papers, quills, and bags. Ellisia glanced around, met Jolyn's eyes, then stepped after Jaefa.

A brisk walk brought her to a stately brick house. Climbing the steps after Jaefa, she rubbed her palm across the smooth rail and followed him through the entrance hall and into a sitting room. Her footsteps echoed softly on the bronze-toned paved floor as she stepped towards one of the maroon-curtained walls. Jaefa sank into one of the plush chairs and Ellisia tentatively perched on another.

"As you know by now, I am a writer." He dropped his bags and pulled out a gilded volume. "Besides experimenting with spoken-to-written, I pen books to sell to the people. I am always in need of scenes to pen. I gain inspiration from that around me, just as a painter gains inspiration from the scenery." He ran his fingers down the quill and back up again. "For my next book, you will be my inspiration."

Ellisia bit her lip, her mind racing. She knew well what kind of books would be bestsellers in Syorien, and she wasn't sure she wanted anything to do with *that* sort of book. "Isn't—isn't there something about the research aspect that I could assist with?" she spoke up. "I'm afraid I would make a poor sort of heroine. I am no good at an act."

"The experimentation and research will be naturally woven about the story creation process, of course." Jaefa reclined carelessly, flipping practiced fingers through the book in his lap. "Besides, if you are not good at the act, you soon will be. The act is quite an exciting experience, I do assure you. Ask Jaeta when he returns. You and he would work together. He will create the scenes; you and he together will act them; I will write them."

Ellisia eyes escaped. This wasn't the kind of "help" she wanted to give. "I will tell you, if you merely need an actress, you have the wrong girl." She leaned both elbows on the chair-arm, her eyes staring directly at him and earnest sincerity lacing her voice. "I have tried to act. I can do nothing."

Still Jaefa's eyes darted carelessly here and there as his

fingers drummed a page. "You only think so. I've seen girls like you before. I know you'll catch on immediately. This sort of thing isn't for just any actress; it must be specific. You're into books; you have the imagination; and you'll be part of my groundbreaking experiment. Again, I'll teach you the latest of Doekhan wordology."

Ellisia's mind worked rapidly, both tempted and repulsed. This wasn't the sort of "help" she'd intended to give, but at the same time, it would be foolish to shut the door on this learning opportunity. Back and forth—then she lifted her chin.

"I'll try it. For a few days. But if I'm not satisfied, I won't stay."

"Fair enough." Jaefa touched his forehead, then dropped his eyes to the book in his lap.

At first, acting simply encompassed the normal daily routine—eating breakfast, dishwashing, bedmaking, strolls along the avenue—but gradually Jaefa's methods began to encompass other activities. He wanted to not only conduct his experiments but also write something that would sell well, and that meant something exciting—and morally questionable.

Day after day, Ellisia returned, her appetite whetted by the tantalizing tidbits of wordology that Jaefa dropped. As he had predicted, acting for him wasn't as difficult as she'd anticipated. When her conscience questioned some of her actions, she subtly implemented her new-found acting skills to feign sickness, tiredness, hunger, dullness, headache, or an urgent task waiting for her at Mae's—anything to remove herself from the thick of her new occupation without alerting Jaefa to the real reason behind her indisposition. Time and again she noted with interest Jaefa's inexplicable unquestioning belief in her excuses—his agreeable nod, his willingness to send her home or stop the scene, the ease with which he found a substitute.

Even her chores at Mae's seemed more bearable under the triple fascination of unlocking the vast stores of Academy knowledge by day, watching Jaefa's wordology maneuvers each afternoon, and poring over Wulf at her bedroom table by night, sitting up far later into the evening than before and often emerging in the morning with eyes heavily rimmed with red.

One thing only caused a niggle of unease to creep over her heart. She'd begged off acting for the evening, pleading a headache, though her head was as clear and painless as it had ever been. "Certainly," Jaefa agreed at once. "If you're not up for this today, I'm willing to try something else tomorrow. Rest and be well."

"Thank you." Ellisia nodded towards him before squeezing her eyes shut slightly, as though the movement pained her. She forced herself to stand still for the count of twenty.

"No. Thank you," Jaefa replied. "I've done this without you for so long, but it truly is a pleasure to be able to concentrate on my methods when I have you handling the scene details with Jaeta."

A grunt came from Jaeta's corner. Ellisia swallowed. "I'll see you tomorrow then."

Her shoes scuffed against the stones as she exited. Once outside, she drew a long breath. Now she'd have extra reading time! Somehow time with her books seemed more profitable to her own experience with words than her time with Jaefa was. He was certainly an "experimenter" more than a "mentor." She stifled a wry grin.

    Yet by the time the door clicked shut behind her at Mae's, a throbbing threatened her temples. By the time dinner was cleared away, it had exploded into a full-force headache that threatened her vision and turned her stomach. And by the time she'd dragged herself upstairs and reached for Wulf, she could only groan and bury her head in the grey blanket.

    So much for a feigned headache.

A GREY RAIN-CURTAIN hung over the city as Ellisia trudged over the mud-splashed cobblestones to Academy. An ache still pulsed at the back of her neck, threatening to invade her temples. Worse, a throbbing in her soul warned her that it was her own fault. What had she brought upon herself? She'd gone from feeling perfectly healthy to suffering an incapacitating headache in an hour just after she'd lied to Jaefa about having one. What a long day this would be.

Her studies passed in a blur. Her instructor droned on, entrenched deeply in the historical mysticism that had inspired the ancient Taernan literary period. Though any element of literature fascinated Ellisia, she preferred other branches of literary studies. She tapped her quill silently against her bag, idly watching the two girls in front of her whispering about a new baby cousin.

A heartfelt sigh of relief escaped when studies ended early that afternoon. Gathering her book in trembling fingers, Ellisia slipped towards the Academy BookHall. Perhaps she could find a few moments of rest before Jaefa needed her.

Her favorite chair was occupied. Ellisia pulled up short, too late. The figure glanced up.

"Oh. Jolyn." Ellisia's standing form sagged against a

plush couch.

"How's work with Jaefa?" Jolyn waived formalities with a sweep of her hand.

"All right." Ellisia sank onto the couch, her hand massaging her forehead. If only this ache would cease for good.

"Learning anything much?"

"A bit." Ellisia pushed herself upright. "So far it only seems he shouts at the page a lot when he's experimenting, and sometimes something sticks. I'm not familiar with all his tools yet—very scientific-looking for an author."

Jolyn nodded. "His normal method. Jaeta sets up scenes and Jaefa works on their properties to bring them to the page. It seems fairly simple to me, but I'm not an author by any means."

"Simple—perhaps if it *worked,*" Ellisia muttered, her hands covering her burning cheeks. She stretched her neck.

"What's the matter?" Jolyn's hands fidgeted with a page corner. "You don't like the job?"

"I like parts of it. But I'm not an author either, and even less an actor."

The narrow blue eyes surveyed her carefully. "Might I accompany you this evening?"

A shoulder lifted in a non-committal shrug. "I don't care." She desperately hoped Jaefa wouldn't set up anything today that she couldn't in good conscience take part in.

"Let's go early," Jolyn spoke up abruptly.

"Why? I was hoping to read—or at least get a bit of quiet."

"The earlier we go, the sooner we're done." Jolyn stuffed her book into her bag and swung lightly to her feet. "Besides, I want to stop at the diner for a mouthful of something. Come on. Just this once."

Ellisia reluctantly pulled herself off the couch and followed Jolyn through the halls and down the marble steps. At the diner, Ellisia blocked out all commotion around her and focused on her plate. Though she hadn't thought she was hungry, the wrapped meat dumplings and turned vegetables proved appetizing, and her plate soon emptied.

Jolyn provided them both with pastries for the walk home, and Ellisia silently munched as their steps echoed on the bricks. At the house, Jolyn led her up the front stairs that Ellisia hadn't used since her first tour with Jaefa. "We're not using Jaefa's back door?" she murmured as they padded across the porch towards the entrance.

"Why should we?" Jolyn shrugged and let them in.

Back in Jaefa's studio, Ellisia went through the now-familiar motions Jaeta set for her. Arms crossed, Jolyn leaned against the back wall, commenting now and then, offering pointed observations, and occasionally stepping in to assist with a difficult scene.

"Ah, very good," Jaefa announced at last, throwing down a quill and some sort of tubular contraption he'd been working with. "Now if only I could get it down properly without all the scramble. Jaeta, go at Ellisia next."

"Uff." Ellisia collapsed suddenly onto the couch. "I didn't realize how much energy this takes." Her hand crept to her middle, and she drew a pained breath. "I positively must have refreshments before I can continue. I'm excessively hungry—feels like three seasons since lunchtime."

"Hungry, are you?" Jaefa grabbed his quill, scribbling furiously. "Doubt Zena has anything coordinated for a meal just yet, but you're free to check."

"By that time, the mood will be lost." Jaeta's voice broke in with a small frown.

"She's hungry. Can't let her starve." Jaefa didn't look up from his page. "Go, Ellisia. Thanks for the assistance. I'll see you tomorrow."

Still the quill scribbled on, and Ellisia backed out of the room.

Jolyn followed. Once the door was shut, she turned quizzically toward Ellisia. "I saw what you ate at the diner. It was more than me. You *can't* be that hungry yet."

Ellisia shrugged, unwilling to explain.

Jolyn's eyes scanned her carefully. "You wanted to get out of there."

"Wouldn't any sane, reasonable girl at that point?"

Jolyn tossed her head. "I'm sure you could just say so. Jaefa never asks *me* for such scenes."

"I'm not so sure," Ellisia said slowly. "And yes, I made up an excuse. Hunger probably wasn't the best one just now, but it's what came to mind."

"At least I'm not worried about your physical health this way," Jolyn returned. "I couldn't even *think* about eating anything yet."

They turned the corridor to the long hall.

"Oh, no." Ellisia groaned, her hand flying again to her middle.

"What now, you silly horse? You needn't keep up the acting; it's just you and I here."

"I . . . forgot. I *am* hungry now." Ellisia bit her lip, a thousand dark thoughts flooding her mind as the yawningly empty sensation swept her stomach.

"Don't be silly! You just ate."

"I know. But I can't help it. I need food."

"You *just* said you made up the whole thing as an excuse." Jolyn stopped walking and turned on Ellisia, a frown creasing the pale forehead.

"I—I did," Ellisia replied faintly, bracing against the wall. "But that was before. *Now* . . . oh, why can't I stop doing this to myself?"

"Fine. Let's go to the kitchens. Zena will have something." Jolyn spun and continued, Ellisia following more slowly. "But there's certainly something about this—you say you're hungry when you're not, and now you are, when you shouldn't be . . . Wait. Has this happened before?" Again she whirled on Ellisia, but a light had leaped to her eyes and her demeanor had softened.

Ellisia nodded. "Something very like."

"Ah. I see." Jolyn nodded. "Perfect sense, of course. So let's find something for you." She opened a door, and Ellisia followed her down another series of halls towards the annoying sound of pots clattering and the tantalizing scent of meat frying.

"You aren't in your element with Jaefa, are you?" Jolyn asked.

"Not exactly . . ." Ellisia replied reluctantly, clasping her middle. "He's particular about his scenes. I'm certain I won't suit him for long if I keep begging out of this, but I do want to stay while I can and learn his theories of words."

"What in Taerna are you doing working for *him*, then, if all you want is the theories of words?" Jolyn grasped the kitchen door handle, throwing a shrewd look at Ellisia over her shoulder. "There are better ways to learn. You're more along the lines of Wulf, yourself. This words-to-books theory that the J-brothers are working on is a different line entirely. Yes, they overlap, but wouldn't it be a better use of your time to tap directly into the line you're looking for?"

"What do you mean?" The words were nearly a gasp as the door opened and a wonderful variety of appetizing aromas hit her.

"Here. Sit down." Jolyn pulled out a chair. "Zena, do you have something ready for Ellisia here to eat? She's famished."

"Certainly." A tall figure at the head of the table motioned towards two purple-capped women rushing from stove to table to spout. "A plate, please."

In a twinkling, a plate appeared before Ellisia, and without a word, she devoured its contents.

When at last Ellisia pushed back the empty dish with a contented sigh, Jolyn was at her elbow. "Come. I'll show you what I mean. This could be the breakthrough we all need."

After the fourth room that Ellisia thought surely must be their destination but proved otherwise as Jolyn continued straight through the maze of halls, Ellisia pulled up short, her fingers stretching out to grasp the straight back of a chair in the brown corridor. "Jolyn, stop. Please, where are we going, and what do you have in mind?"

"Oh." Jolyn halted and pivoted impatiently. "And we were almost there."

"Where?" Ellisia repeated.

Jolyn dropped into one of the other chairs, sending a shrill creak across the corridor. "Words. They have power, you know."

Ellisia nodded breathlessly, her eyes searching Jolyn's.

"But you don't know how it works."

Again, she nodded. Her heart raced.

"And you want to."

Another nod.

"You're searching for someone who knows what's happening, who can put the pieces together for you. You're reading Wulf, finding bits of the philosophical side that match your experience. But you're not sure how it all comes together practically."

Ellisia's fingers stilled with the rest of her. She could only stare.

"It just so happens I know a bit about that."

"Truly?" Ellisia found her voice.

"There's a reason I'm here studying world literature. I've always been fascinated with words and what they can do. My bent is slightly different than yours, I think, but I've got an uncle. Maybe a crazy uncle to some, but his wisdom and research are esteemed throughout the four countries. He's got a hold of some research and science in words that I think would be exactly what you're looking for."

"Is he—here?" Ellisia gasped.

"It just so happens he is." A smile touched Jolyn's lips before disappearing again in the corridor's dimness. "So—do you want to meet him? Do you want to talk to him? I would have thought, with your mania for books, that the J-brothers and their work might be more your style, but it's evident that's not working out. But my uncle, now—he's pursuing an entirely different line of experiments. The power of words on physical things, not on the page."

"Yes!" The word slipped out. "I'll meet him. He's your uncle; you introducing me should be perfectly proper."

"I thought so." Jolyn resumed her walk, and Ellisia followed. If only this could be the turning point she was seeking.

Jolyn pushed open a door that scraped against the carpeted floor. Ellisia stepped into the room, throwing a quick circular glance as she did so. It appeared to be a library—or partly a library. Near the center of the room, a dark-haired man reclined with his feet on an ottoman and his hand hidden by a large book.

A book had to be a favorable sign.

But then again, it was the attitude one approached a book with that counted.

"Good day." He glanced up, taking in Jolyn before focusing his attention on Ellisia. "Please, have a seat."

"Uncle, this is Ellisia, from my literature line. She's been working with Jaefa but doesn't find herself suited to his line of experimentation. She's wanting to learn wordology; she's had some 'experiences' of her own and I think you'd find each other mutually useful."

"A pleasure." He dipped his head towards Ellisia but did not rise.

She slipped into a chair across from him, surveying his beard, cloak, and boots—for little else could be seen. Tall and dark-haired, the new stranger reminded her of a seaman. Yet something professional marked his bearing. Despite the fact that he was dark and Jolyn was light, it was evident that they were related. The shape of their faces and set of their eyes mirrored each other's. To a keen observer, Ellisia was sure, many additional similarities undoubtedly appeared.

"Always pleased to meet those with an interest in this exotic line," the man continued. "It is in my power to confer upon you a very great honor and open up secrets in your life that you do not yet know exist. 'Twould be to your own advantage and benefit."

She folded her arms, slightly skeptical of his language. "If I'm only here to take favors, tell me your secrets and be done." That ought to do it—straightforward and to the point.

A laugh rang out, and the brown eyes twinkled. "Of course it's not that simple, girl—Ellisia. Merely laying out what I can offer before we find out what *you* can." He wiped invisible dust-flakes from the small table beside him before positioning his book precisely on it. "What sort of word experiences have you had?"

Slowly she repeated the effect her words had had—from her childhood to the present—leaving out all details as well as her personal speculations on each occurrence.

He listened without interruption, his hand on his chin, leaning forward with interest. When she finished, he seemed lost in thought for a moment before speaking up. "Have you ever experimented with words? Played with them? Seen their effect?"

Her startled response must be visible on her face. "Only once."

"Only once?"

"Yes, when I used them to find my way home."

"Have you known much of wordology or words themselves?"

"Not much. I always loved them. I've read constantly since I was tiny."

"Ahh . . ." He spun his thumb around his forefinger.

"Why?" she asked. "What is it?"

He did not answer, only continued spinning.

At last, he looked up. "Come. I will show you."

Ellisia rose and followed him to a door in the back wall, carefully avoiding the piles of neatly stacked papers that lined the walls and furniture. A sensation of brightness struck her as she stepped into the adjoining room—white walls, tables, floors, chairs, machinery: all seemed to gleam as though played upon by high noon's sunlight, though the one window was securely shaded and twilight must be approaching by this time. Panels, instruments, tools—all sat neatly arranged on work surfaces lining the walls. To the right huddled a collection of objects that struck Ellisia as out of place: a toy lion, a set of fine china dishes, a surgeon's knife, and a gardener's rake caught Ellisia's attention from the tops of their baskets. To the left, a shelf of mixes, chemicals, and potions covered the wall, neatly labeled.

Jolyn's uncle approached a large table in the center of the room and bent over some sort of large instrument with white metal and glass protruding at odd angles. The contrast between his dark figure and the bright room was striking, and Ellisia found herself moving forward to stand at his side as he twisted a dial and flipped levers on a panel.

Her eyes dropped from his hands to a label mounted to the side of the machine. The thick black letters stood out sharply, and her heart fluttered in her chest.

"SOUND VISUALIZATION."

Curious, she leaned forward, examining the dials that Jolyn's uncle was adjusting. Reaching up, he pulled forward a rotating arm that held two round clear tumbler-shaped protrusions, pressed another button, and stooped to squint into the tumblers.

A voice from her left prompted a nervous start from Ellisia, but she quickly steadied herself while mentally repeating multiple chidings. It was only something from the sound-visualization instrument—of course a sound-viewing instrument would use *sound*. Her gaze traveled from the uncle's, fixed within the tumblers, to the table where the voice rumbled. He *did* appear to be viewing sound—what did he see? Impatiently she glanced back at the uncle, but his eyebrows scrunched together as he focused. Biting her lip, she steadied her hands against the table. She'd have to wait.

Instead, she focused on the voice. "... bringing the lion to rest inside the bowl, tail curled."

A low-pitched squeal emitted from the device, and the voice fell silent as the uncle pulled back, his eyes now trained towards the baskets on the right. Ellisia looked too. The toy lion now lay in the basket of dishes, curled up inside one of the finely engraved bowls.

From the bowl to the instrument to the uncle her gaze traveled, asking the question her lips couldn't form.

He pushed the tumbler arm towards her with a half-grin. "Your turn."

"But—what—"

"Just do as I did. I'll manage the controls this time. Just watch. You'll see. And listen."

Automatically Ellisia's hand reached for the tumblers, pulling them towards herself, her curls slipping over her shoulder as she lowered her eyes towards the instrument.

At first, only a blur met her gaze—a swirl of curved transparent tumbler walls reflecting upon themselves the whiteness of the table. She heard a lever slide, a button pressed, and light flooded her vision. Then the voice began again, and a hand moved to point the tumblers at the sound.

This voice was different: slower, female, more distinct. Then it ceased, and other sounds replaced it: hands striking together, something dropping to the floor.

Ellisia focused on the source. Tiny ripples—like the waves caused by dropping a stone into a pond—emerged from around the sound box. Another lever slid beyond her left ear, and the ripples slowed.

Fascinated, she watched closely. *Hands striking together*, her ears reported, and her eyes picked up tiny ripples traveling outwards. A book dropped, and this time the ripples were wider, sharper, and farther apart. A cloth snapped, flicked by a wrist; the ripples were narrower yet rounder. The voice spoke again, and Ellisia was fascinated by the nuances visible before her as each word and tone proceeded across the table. She drank in each new variation, and she would have been content to gaze the rest of the evening had not the uncle shut the sound and light off. Then she reluctantly pulled back.

"You see?" he told her. "That's what the latest

Doekhan research is capable of—that and much more."

"It is incredible—wonderful," Ellisia breathed. "I could watch for hours."

"And yet this is merely the crust of the bread. There's more—so much more, even specific to words."

"But how does it work?" Ellisia glanced from the instrument back to the keen dark eyes.

"Quantum physics, my dear young lady. 'Twould take half a lifetime to describe how it works, but suffice to say that the world as we see it isn't always the world as it is. There is an entire network of interrelated atoms, sound-ripples, and invisible forces at work in the natural world, causing the effects that we see demonstrated outwardly. I've shown you tonight a bit of the scientific side of my work, but rest assured that the philosophical side is even more vast and wondrous." He spun about, replacing items that had been moved during the demonstration. "You find interest in this field, then?"

"Oh yes!" Ellisia's heart swelled in contentment like a flask left too long in the sun. "Please, tell me more." Her grin stretched towards her eyes.

"All in good time." He whirled again, his cloak fluttering about his ankles. "But first, what *you* can help me with. You've experienced the effects of words upon objects firsthand. That's something most people don't have the skill or knowledge to harness. You might be entirely untrained, but you have a talent that could become both useful and powerful. You see, my aim here is to discover the limits and abilities of wordology, to spread its knowledge among the Taernan people—particularly among intelligent students such as you—and to work towards national reform via these means. Already we are well established in the community, but I'm in need of Taernan students with a sharp mind and natural skills in this field to propagate the developments I discover here in my workstation."

"And you think that's me." Ellisia's tone was calm and steady now.

"I know it is you." The words were smooth and confident. "Or it will be if you wish it. What you've told me of your own experiences leaves no room for doubt. Furthermore, your eagerness for discovery and knowledge in this field will render this work all the more pleasant for you as well as enable you to effectively carry it out."

"What exactly would you want from me?" Ellisia spoke up firmly. Words waited—she couldn't get lost in these grandiose promises without some sort of concrete understanding.

"Your voice." Jolyn's uncle lowered himself backwards onto a tall stool, his eyes locking with hers. "Not only do the people of your country need the academic knowledge we're discovering, but our own depth of learning will enable us to raise living standards as well as improve the economic and social framework of the country—starting right here in Syorien. Your voice, as a rising brilliant scholar of Taerna, can bring about our desired results."

"I don't understand." Ellisia's hand gripped the edge of the table before her. "Why can't you do that yourself? Or Jolyn—she's a scholar in the same line. What do I have that you do not?"

"You have a gift." The words didn't hesitate. "Your whole life experience has led you to this point. You love words. Words obey you. You love books; you love to learn. And you're a native Taernan attending the prestigious Palace Academy. All these qualities we lack to some extent. My time, for instance, is needed here in my research room. Someone must perfect the methods as they are spread to the people, and that's my place. Each of us plays a key part, and you, Ellisia—you are the missing piece we've been needing."

Ellisia sighed. The man's tones were light, but the words bordered too closely on manipulative flattery for her taste. Not for a moment did she believe she was the "only one" or the "key figure." But what did that matter? He'd teach her the power of words, and she only had to spread that message to others. She supposed he'd give her more specifics later on.

"I know there are many other students you could work with," she said at last, her gaze straying back to the fascinating instrument. "I'm not deceived into thinking you'd fail without me. But yes—I do believe what you're saying is quite workable. In exchange for the knowledge of word power and whatever training you can give me, I'm willing to attempt a partnership here." She swallowed, her gaze again swinging between him and the instrument. "A trial partnership. If all goes well, I foresee this being beneficial to both of us."

The uncle nodded, his expression unchanging. "Indeed. In that case, you may return the evening after next and I'll begin your training."

Ellisia nodded back at him. "I'll be here. When would you want something of me?"

"Soon enough. But it's to our mutual advantage that you receive training first. How training progresses will indicate the timing of our next move." He whirled back to his equipment.

Ellisia stepped backwards with a nod. She could always get what training she could from him and claim the partnership wasn't suitable later on if she decided she didn't want to work with him. He'd asked to start with her training; he could hardly object. "Agreed," she said, her eyes again locked on the instrument. Had she truly just seen sound?

VICTORY'S VOICE

This was almost too good to be true.

9

Morning light highlighted the page of Ellisia's latest book, open on the table before her bowed head. A leaf flipped, and "Introduction" stared up at her, printed in bold, blocky letters. Her mind worked overtime to comprehend the concepts denoted under the slightly daunting but thoroughly fascinating title *Psychoneuroimmunology*.

Ellisia couldn't pretend she'd ever heard that term before—she certainly couldn't spell it if she tried. But the concept became clear to her as she perused the pages: the effect of the mind on the nervous system and the immune system. The idea was intriguing: the processes of the mind could negatively or positively impact human health and wellbeing.

She paused and flipped back to the list of chapters in the front of the book. She always skipped this list, preferring to jump right into the meat of the book rather than to read what she would be reading before she read it. But this time, she was curious what angle a book with this premise would take.

The list read like a full three-year line in advanced medicine:
Psychology
Neuroscience
Immunology
Genetics

Physiology
Psychiatry
Behavioral medicine
Pharmacology
Rheumatology
Molecular biology
Endocrinology
Infectious diseases

She swallowed. These were just the major headings. The subheadings and chapter headings, in smaller print under each one, were equally long and incomprehensible. Evidently someone's knowledge of medical and psychological science far surpassed anything that she'd known existed in Taerna.

She turned the page and scanned the "Writerly Biography" section. The description caught her attention. The writer was not from Taerna at all but from Doekh. Her lips twitched upwards. She should have guessed, after all Jaefa, Jaeta, and Jolyn's uncle had shown her. Although Ellisia had studied a bit of the history and culture of the surrounding countries, Doekh was one that she'd read very little on. She knew from some of her more recent studies—driven, she'd hardly admit, by her newfound association with Jolyn and her group—that it was the most advanced country in the world, particularly in the academic field. In fact, many scholars from Taerna, Arkal, and even Draco traveled to Doekh to complete their education due to the vast amount of knowledge accumulated by that country.

Ellisia skimmed the author's description. It sounded like the author had been born in Taerna but had traveled to Doekh at a young age. He'd been raised in the Doekhan education system and had continued his studies to the end of the line, obtaining certifications in Far Education and teaching.

Interesting. She flipped back to the beginning of the book and leaned back, her eyes focusing on nothing in particular out the square window. She supposed her own chances of studying in Doekh were non-existent. Such extensive travels demanded more funds than she could possibly hope to acquire. At least she had access to some of the riches of their culture and knowledge, thanks to books—and to Jolyn's uncle.

She rubbed her hand across the paper. Its quality was exceptional, even for the Palace BookHall. The pages were thin yet durable. The print was fine yet clear. No blurs or smudges marred the thin strokes. Ellisia smiled as her imagination escaped yet again. To work as a bookbinder in Doekh would be a dream lifestyle. Some places in Taerna still produced volumes on parchment. Ellisia's nose wrinkled, remembering the few worn books she'd borrowed from neighbors in Frydael. She'd rarely seen a new bound paper book back home—and now she'd scarcely seen a parchment book since she'd been in Syorien. As the Palace BookKeeper had said, the kings allowed only the best in their Halls.

Ellisia dropped her eyes to the page she'd flipped to and scanned the first sentence, her mind racing to keep up with the philosophical and scientific concepts. How many in Taerna were familiar with such things—such complicated branches of health studies, scientific studies, and mind studies? She grinned. She accessed the knowledge of the elite. Words could indeed give her power.

She turned to section one, settling back comfortably in her chair. This would be good.

Her mind traveled far, far away as she absently stirred together the morning's porridge. After several chapters of the medical textbook, she'd switched back to Wulf and his philosophical discourses. The readings had both awakened and puzzled her brain. Jolyn's uncle and the medical book emphasized the practical side of wordology—the effects that it could have when put to use in the real world. Wulf, however, dwelt at length on the philosophical side of the matter, strongly implying that wordology was best left in the hands of the scholars and the minds of the brilliant, as physical application would undermine the power of the inner mind itself.

Ellisia reached for the sweet potato meal, sifting it through her fingers as she mentally weighed both sides. If only she knew which one would be more beneficial to pursue just now.

The porridge done and the fruit cut into pieces, Ellisia swallowed her share before heading back to her room to retrieve her books. She shut the front door behind her softly as her feet found their own way towards Academy—she hadn't seen anything of Mae today. Now that she thought of it, she had heard babies crying several times during the night. Perhaps everyone was catching up on missed rest this morning.

At Academy, her lecture room was unusually vacant. "Professor won't be here for another two hours," a boy with thick dark hair falling over his forehead informed her as she glanced around quizzically.

"Ah. Thank you." Ellisia rested her bag against a table for a moment, pondering. What would be the best use of two unexpected hours? Reading, of course—or something of the sort—but where and how?

She made her way to one of the many study alcoves in the BookHall. Slipping into the oversized chair, she nestled down into the lush red cushions. Her hand reached into her bag; her book nestled on her lap, but she made no move to open it. Instead, her eyes fixed on a shelf across the room, though she saw nothing of it. Again, her mind wandered . . . that never-ending, nagging question of reconciling what Jolyn's uncle had shown her with the theories in her books taunted her. Perhaps neither viewpoint was entirely correct—perhaps both Wulf and Jolyn's uncle were partly right. After all, the uncle had mentioned the importance of the philosophical side. Perhaps more time with him would answer her questions.

Yet as she recalled the intricate setup of his workspace, she could hardly deny the importance he placed on practical application.

Perhaps she could see what her Literature professor thought of the matter. Another viewpoint might clarify things.

As soon as the postponed lecture finished, she asked Don Rhaea for a bit of his time. When he acquiesced, stepping with her into a study alcove, she poured out her experiences—the fascination of words, the textbook, the new thoughts and feelings.

To her joy and immense relief, he seemed to understand. He nodded throughout her story, and a kind smile crinkled his face. "This is the realization of who you are," he told her. "You are maturing and discovering both your identity and the deeper levels of worldly workings. Keep learning, Ellisia. Never stop learning. The truth will come in time, as will the power and joy you seek."

"But what about practical application? Will it overpower the mind? I've seen a little of the practical side, but the mental side seems even more powerful."

"The answer to your question will certainly come with learning," Don Rhaea returned. "Don't discount one to pursue the other. Learn—learn all you can. Open your mind, and you will find it strengthened. This is a power you can grasp for yourself even now."

"So—keep reading Wulf, and keep—keep studying the practical side?" Ellisia's brow wrinkled. She hadn't mentioned Jolyn's uncle.

"Without question. Follow up all avenues. You might not gain equally from all sides, but what you learn will feed your understanding as a whole." Don Rhaea stroked his chin with a finger. "Not many care to invest this deeply in these topics. Those who do will find advantages in this world by so doing. I would tell you to keep it up."

The rest of the day floated by as if in a dream. Her instructor had affirmed her! She was right—Wulf was right, and the uncle was right, at least for now.

The moment the day's studies finished, she sailed out the great doors down the white steps, her head held high. A thrilling surge raced through her. She could do anything—*anything* to study wordology, anything she wished.

Training with Jolyn's uncle—he requested her to call him "Uncle K"—flew by. She stared into the sound visualization instrument until long after her eyes glazed over and Uncle K's words began to slur together in her brain. He'd pointed out—in what anyone else might term "excruciating detail," but Ellisia found it barely sufficient for her curiosity—the intricacies and nuances of each sound, the various patterns the ripples made for different spoken words, and the different levels of energy contained within each wave. She found each nuance seared irrevocably on her memory, imprinted with a degree of detail unparalleled in her academic experience, even considering the ardor with which she'd always approached her studies.

Her own voice etched itself on her mind the most strongly. She couldn't help but notice almost immediately that the ripples and patterns in the air when *she* spoke were somehow different from those that occurred when Uncle K or the instrument spoke. At first she thought it must be her imagination, but by the end of the evening she could pick out her own words from the swirling ripples every time. They were cleaner, clearer, stronger, more defined. They seemed to move more quickly and reach their destination with more force, though, strain her eyes as she might, Ellisia could not find that they actually arrived faster or had stronger results than Uncle K's words.

Still, before Uncle K could dismiss her for the evening, she couldn't help but reach her fingers slowly in front of her face as she spoke again, grasping at the empty air that was not so empty as she'd always thought. At first, it was only her own breath rushing through her fingers, but then she thought she caught a bit of vibration.

"That's it, girl." Uncle K's voice swept into hers. His vibrations tangled with her own, and now she was sure she could feel something. "You're ahead of yourself now. Human nerve receptors aren't sensitive enough to distinguish sound ripples, but I have begun working on an impulse amplification glove. It fits over my fingers, and the fingertips will be fitted with special receptors that will theoretically enable the wearer to feel the ripples. Still in development—but I see that you're sensing something already." He touched her fingertip lightly, then pulled back. "Close your eyes. Clasp your hands together, as if you're catching the words. Focus all your energies into the tips of your fingers . . ."

Ellisia obeyed, but Uncle K's words still felt like simple air. She scrunched her eyes tighter, her brow crunching in concentration. Almost unconsciously, her hands cupped around her own mouth, catching the words that slipped forth.

"The fruit of *Adon Olam*'s Breath is love . . . joy . . . peace . . ." Each word emerged distinct and slow. The cupped hands echoed and magnified each vibration, and her palms tingled slightly at each word. With her fingers pressing against her face, she felt the vibrations amplified through her cheek bones, each one more distinct than the last. If she just focused hard enough . . .

But when she opened her eyes, Uncle K's own eyes bored into her, the unreadable intensity behind them intimidating.

She licked her lips, all sensations immediately falling away.

Three beats of silence followed. Three more beats of her heart marked each.

His voice, when it came, vibrated low yet clear. "One

thing we must lay in the open before we proceed." His arms crossed briefly, then hung again. "This *Adon Olam*. Where are you on that?"

Ellisia's mind whirled. What was he getting at? What did he want her to say? "I—I don't know for sure. I—"

The man's gaze broke, his weight shifting and arms swinging lightly again. "Ah. Just as well. We can also help you with that, should you wish to learn."

"What if I don't need help?" A hidden challenge taunted in her words.

"Understandable." He turned to nod to Jolyn as the door opened and she entered with a fresh candle to replace the flickering one on the wall.

What was he trying to portray with that smooth tone? Was he for or against *Adon Olam?* Ellisia's eyes bored into him, scanning and rescanning the unreadable.

"I'm sure a smart gal like you can find your own way in such a matter. But we'll be here if you need us."

A thought flashed into her head. "Suppose I *do* need you." She spoke in subdued tones, casting her eyes downwards. "I know I have so very much to learn, and so few means of procuring that knowledge."

"On the contrary," he replied, "you are an honored student of a most fine Academy. You study under masters and instructors who are well equipped to teach you."

"And you've been reading some of the best books," Jolyn piped up. "Wulf, for instance," she added as an aside to her uncle.

"Ah, yes, Wulf." Uncle K nodded. "No, my girl, I believe you are well equipped. I would enjoy further discussion at some point, but for now—a pleasant night to you. Jolyn, I have an envelope for you in my room." On his feet, Uncle K rearranged a few items on the way out, his niece following with a muttered "Good night" to Ellisia.

Left in silence in the dimness of a single candle, Ellisia swiveled her head from side to side. The voices of Uncle

K and Jolyn faded and disappeared behind the click of a distant door, and Ellisia drew in a deep breath.

She'd been so close. She could almost feel the words she'd spoken, and Uncle K had interrupted her. Perhaps she'd get on better without him after all—except that she needed access to this lab.

Strange that he'd retired before she was out the door. Perhaps he trusted her. Perhaps the envelope he'd mentioned was important. Perhaps he was tired.

Perhaps the lab was monitored and he'd see anything she did without him anyway.

She glared from side to side at each instrument, each box, each object. Any of them could be spies, but nothing looked remotely suspicious.

She didn't care, anyway. She wouldn't harm anything. She just wanted to learn.

Cupping her hands around her mouth once more, she again spoke—any random sentences that came to mind. Her eyes closed, she focused on the vibrations, but the rush of air that came with the words intruded, obscuring the sensation.

Briefly she wondered what it would feel like in an airless environment.

But words *were* air, so she truly couldn't separate them, of course.

Still speaking softly, she wandered from side to side, examining each instrument closely, but touched nothing.

In the far corner, amidst a wide assortment of tools and parts, lay a crude, futuristic-looking metal glove, gangly sensors looming upwards from each fingertip. Ellisia, fascinated, let her eyes travel carefully up and down each facet of the instrument. A leather strap fastened the apparatus around the wrist, and smooth, plain metal fit across a palm, a single silver strip crossing the back of the hand at the knuckles. From this base, flexible rods of some purple-tinted material extended outwards, forming finger shapes, with a small cap designed to extend over each fingertip. On each cap were fitted a dazzling variety of parts, gadgets, and pieces Ellisia couldn't identify—no doubt intended to pick up sound waves. From the leather strap, a spiderweb of thin purple strings fell away, each one ending in a small round clip.

Slowly Ellisia stretched out her hand towards it. Her mind easily fit together the pieces of how it was intended to work. Surely Uncle K wouldn't mind if she tried it . . . he'd praised her quickness and admired her initiative when she'd attempted to feel the word vibrations earlier.

The glove was a little too large for her hand, but the flexible pieces adjusted easily to cling to her palm and fingers, and she pulled the leather strap tightly around her wrist. With her left hand, she adjusted the strings, running them up her arm to—to what? Somewhere in the vicinity of the mind, most likely—but where?

She fiddled here and there, at last fastening the clips to the hair near her temples, near her ears, and at the base of her neck. Close enough. If she could feel something without a glove, anything she learned now would simply be a bonus.

There! It was on. She flexed her fingers, the metal cold yet oddly comfortable.

Again, her voice echoed softly in the quiet chamber. She stretched out her hand, reaching with the tips of her fingers, forcing them forward to the edge of the instrument.

"I know how this works." The words floated out of her mouth, as though someone else were speaking. "My fingers know what to do. I can feel the words."

Her other hand slipped forward on the table, discerning the pieces and tools and bits of metal, sliding forward to grasp a smooth pot. The cork slid off at the touch of a finger; her other hand slipped out of the glove and into the cool slipperiness within the pot. Her fingertips coated and tingling, the glove went back on. She pivoted to the sound visualization machine, again directing her voice through it. Her eyes closed.

The speaking began. Words poured forth, vibrating and reverberating in the quiet room, incredibly loud to her pounding head.

The gloved hand reached for them.

Words.

Afterwards, she could never remember the next few hours clearly.

She knew only that she was at the table, seemingly elbow-deep in words, their vibrations, the sound waves lightly rippling through the air before her. The nerve sensitivity of her fingers must have been enhanced, for every breath felt like a gale, each word distinct in its pattern. Light words, heavy words, fluttery words, graceful words—words. She'd been all across the table with them; she'd arranged them over the ledge. She'd been with them on the floor. Their fascination had lured her in. At last, she fell asleep where she sat, exhausted by the words, yet still drinking them in even in her sleep, vibrations and patterns dancing before her eyes in her silent dreams.

When she awoke, heaviness dragged at her before her eyes opened. A dull throb pounded in her head. She straightened her neck; how had she fallen asleep in such an uncomfortable position? She stretched out her arms and immediately felt the glove still attached to her hand.

She squinted, breathed out, and spoke, willing the words without any heed as to what they were or what the subject might be. She raised herself to the sound visualization table, squinting to see, to feel. The words were there. They didn't look mysterious or enchanting. They didn't sparkle or glow. They were simply words—mere air, bare ripples, minute vibrations, so subtle—but still words.

Words.

And she'd seen them. Felt them. Heard them. No, experienced them.

Back in the comfortable familiarity of her room, the single inch of candle on the desk flickering at regular intervals, the warmth from the fire downstairs radiating up to spread across her toes, all the house below soundly asleep—Ellisia sank down on the bed, shut her eyes, and let her imagination run wild. Words—words flying out of her mouth. Flying to the end of the Taernan borders, to the end of the world. Words shaping their path before her eyes. Words doing whatever she wished, pushing all before them to her whim. She saw men, women, and children running out of their homes to stare at the unstoppable flow of her words. She saw herself exalted on a mountaintop, the wind whipping through her hair and words pouring out of her mouth faster than she could stop them. She saw them tumbling and swirling, waving and lilting, glittering and glowing, in an exquisite dance with the air as they passed through, leaving their subtle mark on whatever they touched. Carefree words, beautiful words, grateful words, healing words, helping words, breathtaking words—words of passion, of grace, and of calm.

Then the scene changed. Words still flowed from her, but the atmosphere had darkened. No longer did they seem to glow—they were turning murky and almost unreadable, pulsing in jerky waves through the air before her. What was she saying? What was she thinking? Glee rose in her heart, and the words kept coming. Twisting and writhing, swirling, turning, and tumbling, driving all on before them. A veritable thunderstorm cascaded from her mouth. The ground under her trembled in a low quake, echoing the pattern of vibrations in the air. Muffled shrieks came from the houses to which the people had fled. A dark wall of words came rushing upon the town, engulfing it in darkness . . .

Ellisia snapped to attention, sitting up suddenly. Where had that come from? She lay back down, carefully focusing her imagination. Surely she could regain control and dream on.

Now the words tumbled again, like a light breeze. The air before her once more held a faint glow, as if illuminated by the words she spoke, her voice lower. People reemerged from their homes and laughed to see the words coming. Some of those from poorer homes began shouting about newfound riches and prosperity. Others began to sing and dance in the joy of restored lives granted to them. One man came racing out of the servants' quarters behind the palace, shouting about freedom and life and light. Ellisia, from the mountaintop, grinned. The words kept coming. She started shaping them, arranging them, playing with them, making them beautiful before her eyes. Books began pouring from the sky down to the people's homes. Some ran out and began reading immediately. Others took them inside, already buried in study, then never again emerged. Still others shrieked in terror and ran indoors to hide from the torrent of books bombarding their homes. Ellisia merely chuckled. She was seeing her dream before her eyes. She continued manipulating the words, using her entire body now, the power of an exalted soul squeezing through her heart and up her throat and out of her lips. Now it wasn't books raining down but knowledge—pure, unadulterated knowledge. Many drank it in greedily, but somehow each one seemed to be inebriated with knowledge, no longer behaving rationally. Others shrank from the flood. Many picked up pieces of it and began using it for their own gain. And as Ellisia continued perfecting her skill, many others came to her—though they could not approach her as she stood on the mountaintop. Still, they tried their best to get as close as they could, throwing themselves on their faces before her and bringing her every sort of gift and bounty and blessing imaginable. She grinned and sent another torrent of words to gather up the gifts and bring them to herself. They spun themselves into a beautiful mansion on the mountainside and created a sort of elevated throne underneath her from which she continued to pour words down the mountain.

After a time, she began to wonder what had happened to the people who had brought the gifts. She craned her neck to see over the mountainside to where they had been, but she could see nothing but a great pool of words.

Still the words kept coming, dancing and writhing and twisting. Soon she lost all sight of all else, forgot to wonder about the rest of the world, and simply reveled in words. Words spun around her. Words engulfed her. The entire world was nothing but glowing, blossoming, enchanting words.

Her head sank down and she knew no more for a time.

When she finally began to stir, light crept in the western window from the reflection of a red sunrise.

Every muscle in her upper body ached. She stretched backwards, trying to relieve the pressure, but her head began to throb. Why had she slept in her clothes? And why hadn't she gotten into bed properly?

She stretched until she was flat on the bed, then she closed her eyes. Coherent thought fled. Gradually it returned to her. The people. The words. The mountaintop. One memory stood out more clearly than any others—a glowing, a shining. A feeling of perfect joy and contentment. A feeling of right, of delight in who she was, of harmony and power and beauty and gifts. Oh, she would give anything to feel that again. What had caused it? Was it the talking? Her reading? Eventually she concluded that it must have been the beauty of the words themselves. As she closed her eyes, the memories of the dream enveloped her mind—she could remember the soft inner glow, the comfort of it all.

It was a dream. But all dreams had a basis in reality. And in this one, she'd just tasted a draught of her life's purpose.

Yes, words were her life. From henceforth she would devote herself to their study and application.

The crimson light from the window had risen into blindingly bright whiteness by the time Ellisia reluctantly rose and opened her eyes. Straightening her hair and clothes halfheartedly, she reached again for her philosophy book. She'd master it.

Ellisia didn't know how much later it was when a small tapping on the wall just down the stairs attracted her attention. She jumped, her eyes jerking away from her book. Saera?

"Who is there?" she called.

"Caeleb," the familiar voice replied.

She half-rose. "Yes?"

"Do you have a moment?"

She glanced toward her book once more. "Yes."

Another moment and Caeleb's form appeared at the top of the stairs. "Ellisia, how are you?"

"Fine." She didn't want to waste time on trivialities. She had better things to do. Without meaning to, she glanced back at the book she still held open.

His eyes followed hers. Her face burned under his inquisitive gaze, and she fastened her eyes to the floor, then yanked them up to his face.

He was staring at the spine of the book, seemingly unable to pull his eyes away. Then he raised them to hers. "A new book?"

"The one ... yes ... I mean ..." She took a deep breath, her brow crinkling. All this study and experimentation, and she still couldn't find the words when a human spoke to her.

He crossed the room in two strides and reached out his hand. Wordlessly she allowed him to take the book.

Caeleb's gaze still rested on the title. He deliberately opened it and leafed through a few pages.

Ellisia folded her lips together. In a burst, clarity returned to her mind. *Nothing*—and no one, not even her old, trusted friend Caeleb—would extract information from her that would jeopardize her new studies. She could match anything Caeleb said or did or asked. She lifted her chin and gazed expectantly at him.

"Is this what Academy is teaching now?" he asked, his voice so low and gentle that it startled her. "Is this what the literature line is? I had no idea."

Ellisia shrugged, waiting.

"I know Academy isn't given to promoting the ways of *Adon Olam*, but this—this!" He folded the lids of the volume carefully together and set it on her table, backing his hands away as if he didn't even dare touch it.

Another shrug. "You're right. *Adon Olam*'s name is basically not mentioned at Academy." She paused, glancing critically at his face. "I knew that already."

"So did I—but this. Ellisia, you know I want the best for you. That means your studies, your education, *and* your faith."

"Thanks. I knew that already too."

"You know that what you put in your mind will determine who you are and how you behave."

"So I've gathered."

"I know you have a critical mind, and I know you're quick to figure things out. That's why I thought Academy would be a good opportunity for you. A strong-minded woman like you—you can go through Academy and emerge with your faith stronger. Not to mention Carita praying for you every day."

"Yes. But I fail to see the point of this conversation."

Caeleb swallowed, taking a step back from the table. His eyes shut for an instant, then opened. "I'll try to speak straightforwardly to you this time. What I fear is that something smaller or more subtle will harm you, Ellisia. Large temptations and dangers you'll talk your way out of easily enough on your own, but it's the little things that you truly must guard against. Please, for the love of *Adon Olam*, for the love of your family, of your friends, of sanity, of rightness, of all you hold dear—I request as your friend that you to cease from reading these pages."

Ellisia steeled herself. She uncrossed her arms and flipped her hair over her shoulder. "As you said, I am aware. I am discerning and critical in what I read. I don't agree with everything, believe it as you choose or not. I came here to Syorien and Academy for the books, and I maintain that I can read what I choose. These books have not harmed me so far. On the contrary, I've learned much from them. They've broadened and exercised my mind. And, Caeleb . . . it's a textbook. It's science."

"Oh Ellisia." Caeleb sank down onto the bed. "Elli, don't you know? Can't you see? You, who have read so many books—both better and worse, good and bad—can't you see what *this* book is? Can't you see what it's doing? Books are not neutral carriers of academics, of entertainment, of passing time. They—their words, their concepts, their ideas, their philosophies and worldviews—possess power over your mind and heart. They change who you are. What you read is what you become. And Elli, I know you—this is not what you want to become."

"How do you know?" she challenged, defensive now. "Maybe it *is* what I want to become. Besides, the way you're talking now, I think you'd enjoy this book. Those are the kind of things it's saying."

Caeleb shook his head. "I've seen enough even on the few pages I glanced at. This book," he pointed, "is contrary to the Word of *Adon Olam*." His words were quiet, yet they rang with authority.

"Caeleb . . ." Ellisia shook her head. "That's just the introduction. Read the book itself—in context. It's not like that at all. On the contrary, it seems to match *Adon Olam*'s words quite nicely." She patted the cover. "Maybe there's more to me—and more in me—than even you ever imagined. I have a lot to learn, but you can't close my eyes to learning when it's finally starting to take me somewhere in life. There may be something in me that even I don't know yet."

"If there is, you can trust that *Adon Olam* will show it to you in His time and in His way." Caeleb's eyes sought hers again, and he reached for the book, holding it tightly against himself. "You cannot do it through your own study and your own efforts. You cannot use the ways of the enemy—and the ways of Taernan culture—to bring out that which He has placed in you."

He paused. Her eyes fastened on the floor, then rose and caught on the candleholder on the wall, the candle gone—burnt out during her imaginations last night. The memory swept over her, tingling in her elbows as she saw and felt it over again. Yes. *Adon Olam* had given her words, created her mind, and blessed her with the ability to learn and to speak. He'd given her the opportunity to understand the heaven-sent power that so many in this world had never recognized. The mind could achieve what the mind set out to achieve. Learning to use those abilities and gifts *was* seeking Him.

She met Caeleb's eyes once more, but he was speaking again.

"You have a gift, Elli—a special gift. *Adon Olam* has put wonderful abilities and skills in you, and He desires you to learn to develop and use them for His purposes. You—and me, and everyone else, but today, *you*—have a choice: will you do so in His way or in your own?"

"You can't tell me what to do or what my life choices

are. You can't narrow it down like that," Ellisia retorted. "How do you know that those two options are mutually exclusive? And how do you know that *Adon Olam* isn't using that book for good in my life?"

"The King of Light never works by the methods of darkness." Caeleb's words were soft.

"Are you going to give me my book back?" Ellisia challenged.

He sighed and relinquished it to her. "This is your choice and your life, Ellisia. I can't make it for you. I can only pray that you choose wisely."

He stood up, his eyes on her. She placed the book back on the table with a smile.

"But I didn't come to talk to you about this. I wanted to see how you are planning to spend your off days."

Ellisia relaxed as the atmosphere in the room lightened considerably. She shrugged. "Reading. Hobbies of my own. And always, always the cooking and cleaning. Babies don't have off days."

"Don't I know it." Caeleb chuckled.

Ellisia swatted at him. "Oh, stop. You don't know it. You never had a houseful of them, you youngest child, you."

"Oh? And I suppose *you,* you-other-youngest-child-you, are the expert now." Caeleb's eyebrow raised, and he swung himself up off her bed.

"I said stop!" She clattered down the stairs, taking care to shut the door quietly so as not to wake up any sleeping babies.

To no avail—he opened it almost before she'd let go, and he swooped ahead of her into the kitchen. "Where are you going?" he asked.

"Breakfast," she answered shortly. "Since I'm not to get any more reading time this morning, I ought to do my work. Late enough as it is." She flung open the food box, irritated at her own hunger as it flashed suddenly upon her.

"Ah, no. No breakfast for you." A hand shot over her shoulder, the box clapped shut, and Ellisia found herself spun around.

"Caeleb!" she scolded, whirling back to the food. She was in no mood for his games. She reached for an apple; she could at least munch on that while she attempted to figure out the day's menu.

But his hand held the box shut and the other gently grasped her hand and pulled her to the table. "Not today. Just you wait."

He reached for his gray bag, unnoticed near the door, and pulled out a wooden box. He set it on the table and lifted the lid with a flourish.

Ellisia caught her breath. Hotcakes! Towers of hotcakes, still steaming, with maple sauce dripping from the edges of each. Her stomach clenched, and she found herself reaching for one even as she met Caeleb's amused expression.

"Caeleb!" For the second time that morning, words failed her, and she shook her head.

"You're welcome." He produced the plates and deftly scooped a hotcake tower onto one, then slid it in front of her. "Breakfast for you. My compliments."

"*Cae*leb." She shook her head but dug into the stack. What amazing flavor. Almond, perhaps? Mae rarely had almonds in her stock.

"Glad you like it," he said. "I meant it to be a picnic, but Mae's not out yet, Jaeson's busy, and you're too hungry. But lunchtime. Picnic for sure. I'll help with the preparation. Promise."

"Right . . ." Ellisia murmured around bites. "'Help.'"

"Just you wait and see. Excuse me one moment . . ." A plate balanced in each hand, he stepped down the hall and knocked on Mae's door with his elbow. "Breakfast. Hotcakes! Cold cakes if you don't partake soon."

Ellisia sighed and shook her head. Caeleb. The brother she'd never had. The one who could turn out to be a spontaneous blessing or the most annoying nuisance at the flip of a page.

10

THE DAYS FLEW by, and under Uncle K's instruction, Ellisia gradually became increasingly proficient not only at grasping the philosophy of the effect of words on mind and matter but also working with words. While Uncle K experimented with a variety of sounds, Ellisia inflexibly focused solely on words. After all, the more time she spent on other sounds, the less proficient she'd be in words—and it was specifically words that fueled her dreams for learning, for understanding her own experiences, for influence, and perhaps even for the BookHall.

Both the sound visualization instrument and the sensory enhancement glove—for so Uncle K called the glove he was working on—became her special points of study. Uncle K remained hopeful that she'd one day be practiced enough to recognize simple sounds without assistive devices, and she grasped that affirmation deeply within and determinedly threw her heart and soul into practice.

And it wasn't only with Uncle K; everywhere, she practiced; everywhere wordology lodged foremost in her mind. When she spoke to her classmates, she visualized the vibration shapes of some of the simpler words in her head; when she studied alone for her classes, she muttered the words from her textbooks aloud, her hand pressed against her jaw to feel them as they emerged; when she talked with Caleb or Mae, she pictured her words emerging with power and transforming objects in ways she couldn't see. She cultivated the habit of aiming her voice directly towards the person or object she spoke of. She practiced speaking with conviction, cutting qualifying words and phrases out of her vocabulary. For words to truly work, she had to believe and act as if they did.

One evening, Uncle K waited for her, not in the midst of one of his projects, but sitting with Jolyn in one of the outer parlors.

"What's going on?" Ellisia halted at the doorway.

"Ellisia, a pleasant evening to you." Uncle K rose. "You've been with us for quite some time. You've shown much more promise and potential in your studies than even I would have dreamed."

"And?" Ellisia crossed her arms.

"When we met, we spoke of a trial partnership. I agreed to train you first with reciprocation at a later time. As I said, you've progressed faster than I calculated on. As we discussed, you are the spokesperson that we need to spread our advancement throughout Taerna, particularly to the students. I believe the time has now come to take the next step in our partnership."

"Go on." Ellisia stepped fully into the room and seated herself on one of the chairs.

"No, it's for Jolyn to go on. She will show you our situation here, and then return to this room and we'll chat. I want you to know what you are doing and have all the information you will need."

Ellisia's eyes flicked to Jolyn, seated quietly in another chair. At Ellisia's glance, it was as if a switch had turned on. Jolyn rose, flung her blonde locks behind her shoulders, and whirled purposely toward Ellisia.

"Come."

The next few hours passed in a blur. Ellisia glimpsed rooms and furnishings of the mansion-like abode through which Jolyn led her, chatting constantly about the purpose of each room and who lived where. Apparently at least a dozen people called this place home. She heard snatches of conversation on topics she didn't understand. She read bits of sentences on various papers that didn't make sense to her. But one thing stood out clearly: the moment when Jolyn showed her the vast dining table, set for the evening meal, ornamented in white and gold, with one place setting bearing a card with Ellisia's name resting atop a large, gold-covered book.

The Art of Using Words.

The title couldn't have been more perfect. Ellisia would have been happy to curl up in the corner and study for the rest of the evening, but Jolyn insisted on showing her the rest of the house and explaining various bits of information to Ellisia that she did not in the least understand the importance of.

At long last, the tour ended back in the dining room—this time filled with people coming and going: some carrying dishes, some talking with each other, some filling the ornately-carved dining chairs.

Jolyn led Ellisia to her place, then slipped into the next chair.

"We don't always have dinner so late," Jolyn murmured. "This is special on your behalf. Uncle K wanted you with us this time. You've impressed him, Ellisia."

Ellisia only nodded, her eyes raising for only an instant to meet Uncle K's as he filled the seat at the head of the table, directly to Ellisia's left.

Dinner, as Ellisia anticipated, proved to be a long, stately, elegant, and boring affair. She merely ate as much of the simplest foods that were set before her as she could. Conversation she ignored entirely, unless Jolyn directed a question or statement to her.

Instead, she studied the people. Jaefa and Jaeta filled chairs on the other side of Jolyn, and Ellisia was glad she was far enough down the table to avoid conversation with either of them, should they be disposed to make it.

Opposite her was a girl near her own age and a middle-aged woman whom Ellisia thought she'd seen at Academy. Beyond them, a woman in lab attire and another quiet-looking man sat next to Miss Loaw, whom Ellisia recognized as the bookseller from the marketplace. Next to an empty chair at the foot of the table, a middle-aged woman directed the meal in a precise manner.

Entertainment followed—yet another uninteresting affair to Ellisia, who didn't care anything about entertainment unless it related to the written word. Music, plays, shows, attractions—none of it had ever held any interest for her, despite Laelara's repeated invitations to join her at the ShowHall for something or another. But tonight Ellisia pretended to be amused—to laugh, to sigh, to smile at the appropriate points. When it devolved into table conversation, she grew impatient.

"Jolyn, I can't stay all night."

Jolyn contorted her face in an apparent effort to conceal her own tiredness and glanced at the timepiece above the mantle top.

"You are right. Uncle."

Back in Uncle K's parlor, Ellisia focused her wandering attention. This conversation could be meaningful to her future career.

"Did you enjoy the tour?"

"You have a pleasant house here."

"Indeed. I'm glad you approve of our Doekhan style. It is quite comfortable, if I praise it myself."

"What is it you'd like of me? What is the next step you wished to speak about?" Ellisia wasn't in the mood for further small chat. Nothing she'd seen in the house seemed to merit these hours of delay.

Uncle K twirled his thumb across his fingertips and gazed over her. "Straight to business. As you wish. You see, girl, in short, we need your ability. You have a way with words that none of us have. and words are a powerful force—a powerful motivator, a powerful tool. Words can do what other skills cannot. We, at present, are not in the best position to teach our research to the people and bring them our technology and knowledge. We need a little more influence among them. Certain factions within the city are doing nothing to help and much to hinder in our goals. It is from only these few factions that much of the violence and degradation, as well as the poverty, of this city stem from. Poverty and violence are not receptive to science, research, and improvements. If we can only sway the will and ear of the people in our direction and open their eyes to the hurtfulness of a few key factions, we will soon be able to restore complete prosperity to the city—to make it a city very much like our own capital in Central Doekh. You see, the majority of the people are quite willing to live peacefully, to hold a job, to raise their families—in short, to contribute their share to the well-being of the city. It is the ones who will not that must be persuaded otherwise."

"How do you plan to accomplish this persuasion?" Ellisia asked. "Surely not with force?"

The man's deep laugh echoed musically across the parlor. "Of course not, my girl. Would we need *you* for force? No, I could put an army of strong men towards the city if I were interested in taking that path. But no, we have a much better, much stronger, much more effective weapon in our hands. And it involves words, my girl. Words. Real words. Powerful words. Words of authority. Words of might. Words of persuasiveness. Words of reason. Convincing words. Cunning words. Clever words. And I know you have them all at your command."

"Waiving the implied flattery, I follow. Now just what do you wish for me to do with these words of mine?"

"In short—you have had ample time to observe our operations here. You've dined with us and met many of the group. What say you to formally partnering with our ASAA team?"

Ellisia digested his words for a full moment before

replying. "ASAA?"

"Ambassadors of Scientific Advancement and Application. Surely you've heard of our prestigious establishment in Central Doekh?"

"Ah. Yes." The name was familiar, though Ellisia knew little of it. "You're from ASAA?"

"I head up our Applied Physics team here in Syorien."

Ellisia nodded, pondering. "And you're here educating the citizens and students."

"In short, yes. I could philosophize on enlightenment, profit, and industrialization, of course, and share how our work in many parts of the four countries has wrought immense benefits in each of these areas in various cities; but this is not to the point. You've seen our work for yourself. You are competent to judge your own path, and the advantages or otherwise of crossing it with ours."

Ellisia remained silent for several moments. Hardly could she help feeling flattered by the offer of partnership, even though she remained well aware that many others could have filled the same position. An undefined longing tugged her heart—a realization of purpose, of fulfillment, of destiny—towards throwing her whole being into mastering wordology by all means possible. The dream was idealistic, lofty, perfection itself. It ushered in visions of power, of influence, of importance, of success, of truly high-level satisfaction.

And yet from somewhere deeper down, less strong and defined and yet equally craved, lay another desire—the hope awakened that first moment she'd stepped into the Palace BookHall. It was quiet among the books—quiet save for the many voices of knowledge and wisdom streaming from between the color-coordinated covers. Secure a position there, and she could disappear from the irritations of petty people and their choices forever.

"I would be willing to consider such a partnership," she replied at last. "I do have additional aspirations, however."

"As all students ought." Uncle K nodded.

"Let me guess, BookHall." Jolyn raised her head from the book she'd been reading during the conversation.

"Of course."

"Ah!" Uncle K's voice held a definite lilt. "In that case, I can be of assistance to you in more ways than one. I happen to know the BookHall employment manager who works at the palace."

"Truly?" Ellisia couldn't keep the fiery spark out of her eyes if she tried.

"Indeed. He studied under me for several months in my second year here. Ultimately he chose a different path, but we've remained friends. I am sure a word with him could land you almost any position you might desire."

"And you'd do that for me?"

"Surely; why not? That's what mutually beneficial working relationships are for. You can help me advance my own career aspirations, and I can help you advance yours. We both win. I'll do it for you, my girl. On the condition that you partner with us, of course."

"What would partnering with you involve?"

"For the present, continuing to study here under me as you have been. When special projects arise, you would accompany me to gatherings and speak words at my bidding. At times, a small group of us would travel to spread my research in various parts of the country, as needed. You'd be my aide—my assistant, right alongside Jolyn."

The corners of Ellisia's mouth tipped upwards, considering. Master wordology *and* work at the Book-Hall! Was it too good to be true?

"How would that balance with my BookHall work?"

"Of course, it would depend on the position," Uncle K answered. "But in general, such positions are flexible. We could work it out."

That sounded favorable. Ellisia let the grin spill onto her face. Another opportunity as good as this one may never open up. She recalled the conversation she'd had with the man at the BookHall. Gaining a position there for herself—as a woman—would be far more difficult than she wanted to admit. Her pride balked at accepting assistance from a comparative stranger, but she could sacrifice a bit of pride for her dreams. It was the least she could do.

She raised her head. "I will do it. At least, if I possibly can," she added, "on the condition that you will get me a position at the BookHall and teach me all you know about wordology."

"I will. No fear of that. And you will work under my instruction as I direct."

"If I can," Ellisia repeated firmly. "I make no promises regarding the extent of my skills, but I am willing to stretch them to whatever extent I can. And insofar as it does not interfere with my studies and my chores at home."

"Oh, come now, there are more important things than home chores or even studies," Jolyn argued. "You have a limited amount of time. You can't do everything well. Choose to use your time on the best possible experiences."

Ellisia sat back. "And how soon can you get me that BookHall position?"

"I can't say. Depends on how things go. Perhaps in a month or two, if all goes well, I can have that chat with my friend."

Her brow wrinkled. "And . . . why the delay?"

"Business, Ellisia, business. This will be a partnership. Businessmen don't hand over the entire payment before the goods or services have been received."

"Oh." Of course. She should have thought of that herself, but . . . she'd thought only of her own aspirations.

"To our Taernan student ally!" Uncle K tossed her a mint, then popped one in his own mouth. "And to enlightenment, profit, and industrialization."

Stars stared from overhead as Ellisia trudged home after the evening with Uncle K, her mind ricocheting between all she'd heard that night and the possibilities for the future. Under her arm she firmly grasped the gold-lettered book that had been at her place at the dinner table—a gift from the team, Uncle K had told her.

The Art of Using Words. If only she weren't already struggling to keep her eyes open, she'd love to sit up till the early morning hours and revel in the crisp words hidden within the pages. Her mind jumped back to her conversation with Caeleb. Why was he so set against her wordology books? Her lips pressed against each other as she marched up the path to Mae's. He just didn't understand. He didn't know what the book truly was, and he didn't know who she truly was.

But he'd asked her to stop reading the Wulf book—and he'd almost been in tears, if she was any judge of his inner state. Why did it mean so much to him? For a moment she paused, her hands brushing the door-latch. She *had* respected Caeleb. She'd valued his opinion and advice deeply. He'd turned out to be right more often than not. Was it possible that he knew something about this matter than she didn't know?

Silently she opened the door, stepped inside, and climbed the stairs to her room. She pulled out the textbook and leafed through it once more, her eyes stopping at various passages. Caeleb hadn't read it. In fact, he hadn't read many books. He'd read with her, certainly, but he seemed to have no particular interest in the written word more than in anything else. He'd taken joy in a little of everything, never settling down to one thing or devoting himself exclusively to any one passion.

How could she take his opinion as authority on this matter when he wasn't even knowledgeable about it? She herself knew much more about books and their content than Caeleb ever had. Yes, she had much to learn, and her past held a book or two that cut her heart and conscience to recall, but she'd learned from those experiences. She'd spent her entire life in books and all things related to them.

No, Caeleb simply did not know what he was talking about. He meant well, but she couldn't let him guide her in this matter. There was potential here. There was opportunity for her to fulfill her purpose in life—to do something to make her birth of worth to the world. She couldn't turn her back on this now. Whatever happened, she must go forward in the path shining before her. Someday even Caeleb would see and acknowledge who she'd become through her choice today.

11

"A NEW REPORT from headquarters." A neatly bound sheaf plunked onto the physics lab table, sending new vibrations to disturb the sound waves already lingering in the air.

Kraevyn shut the sound machine off and glanced at Don Rhaea before sliding his gaze down to the report. "Anything new?"

No progress in physics. That had been the conclusion of the reports for the past year. Only Professor Phlygia and her dedicated team, back home, continued his own line of wordology. He pushed the report away and spun back to his work, his brow twitching. Still no progress worth mentioning. What were they doing? The nerve enhancement glove at least ought to have been perfected a year ago, and here he was still tinkering with the mechanics. Certainly it worked in a crude way, but crude had never been good enough for ASAA, and crude wasn't good enough for Kraevyn either.

"You may find this of interest." Don Rhaea methodically flipped the top page over.

Kraevyn sighed and whirled back around. "Yes?" His mind still reworked the glove problem. The mechanics themselves just didn't provide enough sensitivity yet. It had to be smooth—to be perfect—something that could be applied more directly to the nerves.

Don Rhaea pulled up a chair and seated himself across from Kraevyn, his finger rhythmically tapping the page.

"The downgrade in receptivity to our operations in the middle sectors isn't new, and yet neither is it normal. The previous Syorien team has confirmed its emergence nearly a decade ago."

Kraevyn's eyes scanned the timeline. "A decade. Any downticks or relevant events in the time frame?"

"Not to speak of that I could find at first. But upon further research, there was one notable exception. A failed experiment, it was recorded. But with a bit of uncovering, I was able to find that it wasn't as much of a failure as the public records declare."

"Oh?"

"The farm experiment. Nine years ago, the kings granted farmland to a hundred revolutionaries in Syorien. Mixed results, they say, and officially it was written off. But I checked with the Director of Land. Eighty-seven of those farms are still operating under the original deed-holder from the experiment, four are running under a family member, and two others are running under a different person entirely. What's more, over forty or fifty are classified as mass productions."

Kraevyn nodded, saying nothing.

"It's subtle, but it's something. I theorize that the spreading availability of fresh local food works to unite the Taernans as a whole and the people of Syorien in particular. An undercurrent of power, of self-sufficiency, a traditional clinging to independence stemming, of course, all the way back from the 800s. Typical Taernan spirit."

"Of course." Kraevyn scanned the paper himself. Another parchment, lacking any sign of ASAA headquarters, fluttered atop it. "What's this?"

"A summary of my own findings when we pursued this trail." With one eyebrow raised slightly, he waited as Kraevyn's eyes flew across the lines.

Kraevyn felt his forehead scrunching as he perused the sheet down to the last word, then he shoved it back and lifted his face back to his colleague's. "So it wasn't simply a farm experiment."

"So it seems. A thinly disguised reintroduction of *Adon Olam* to the Taernan people. Turns out the farms weren't the kings' idea initially, though that's not the public story."

"Whose idea, then?"

"Indeed, that is the question. Who could turn the minds of these Taernan kings from their own pursuits to launch a campaign of this scale—a campaign that nearly worked—I might say, *did* work?"

"Well?" Kraevyn folded his arms under his well-worn cloak. Don Rhaea wouldn't be telling him the story now without some sort of conclusion already in mind.

"Some of my students located a band of farmers, and some of the farmers have mouths that outrun their prudence. Kaelan Ellith is the name. From a no-name town west of here, likely the journey of a day or two."

"A hothead?"

"Seems to be the type. Showed up, waltzed into the palace with his plan, twisted the kings around his finger, made a delightful little address to only the entire male populace of the city, handed out farms right and left, and disappeared at the end of the summer."

"Yet surely he had contacts here?"

"Caeleb Rohaea. You may have heard the name. Eldon Rohaea was one of the great scholars of the last century. Had a son who was a quieter figure but also prominent. Still around, but quieter now. The grandfather of this Caeleb."

"Ah." Kraevyn drew out the syllable. "And so he hopes to direct the Taernans into his wisdom instead of ours. I see how it is."

"Always foreigner prejudice to contend with in some of the sectors, of course. The Rohaea faction seems to encourage it. There's a reason I sent my students to speak with the farmers."

"Which has nothing to do with the allotment of your limited time, and certainly nothing to do with the training of the students themselves." Kraevyn quirked an eyebrow.

"Nothing whatsoever." Don Rhaea's face didn't shift in the slightest. "But to business. There's more—much more—but speaking of my valuable time, I don't have enough to spare to go over it all with you just now. If you like, scan my detailed report. The mainstays are there. You'll find the evidence to back my conclusion. But in short—this must stop. Now. Unrestricted independence, headstrong self-sufficiency, and superstitious fanaticism will never lend themselves to improvement, academic, economic, or socio-political."

"Of course. The Rohaea family?"

"I wasn't able to determine their current connection, if any." Don Rhaea stepped backwards towards the door. "My students will keep working on it. They are certainly a factor. And Kaelan—we must look into his case as well."

"You said he disappeared?"

"He did. But by all reports, he's likely back in that no-name town—yes, I will discover its name; don't look at me like that—and yes, he's another factor to consider. The farmers themselves have no clear leader or instigator in their midst, and I well imagine that if one appeared with vision and direction for improvement in a manner cohesive with their own, they would loyally follow."

"And that is where I come in." Kraevyn folded the

paper in his hand with a smile. "Or rather, my charge."

"Your charge. Yes." Don Rhaea's lips curved to match Kraevyn's own. "I'll instruct her during the day. You instruct her at night. She's a sponge."

"And I daresay the most valuable aid to our team we've seen since pitching here in the Palace District."

"Of that, time will judge."

"Time, and words."

12

LIFE IN SYORIEN progressed satisfactorily for Ellisia. She prepared meals at Mae's, quickly learning how to fix the midday and evening meals in the morning. She attended her regular lessons at Academy, using the lengthy stretches of unfilled time to read or peruse the BookHalls. She spent many evenings with Uncle K, mastering his instruments and discovering how to detect nuances in the ripples created by different sounds of various words.

One afternoon, with her Academy studies successfully behind her, Ellisia sailed down the front stairs, books in hand, eager to get to Uncle K's sound room. Her mind filled with plans for her research that evening, she stepped towards the next of the wide steps.

A black-haired girl with folded arms leaned against the wide pillar in the middle of the step. Ellisia, her mind elsewhere, automatically sidestepped to the opposite end, not even stopping to glare at the girl for the condescending down-her-nose stare.

The next moment she was stumbling backwards, her foot catching against the step behind her. She slid down and came to rest on the previous step, her eyes blinking uncomprehendingly up at a pair of dark eyes staring into hers.

They were not friendly eyes.

"You," the girl hissed. "How rude!"

Ellisia's countenance flashed. "I didn't do anything," she retorted, pushing herself up to a standing position. She didn't fancy facing this opposition sitting down. Her hip smarted.

"You walked right into me," the girl accused.

"*You* walked right into me!" Ellisia snapped. "I was walking down the steps minding my own business. You shouldn't jump out at people like that and then blame them for what was your own fault."

The girl shoved past Ellisia, then turned back, her long dark hair whipping behind her shoulders. "And you think you're so smart, closeting with the instructor. I will tell you this—no. No playing favorites. You're nothing special."

Ellisia rolled her eyes. "Just because I had personal business with Don Rhaea does *not* mean I'm trying to become a professor's pet."

But the girl tossed her head. "'Personal business' always means trouble."

"But what if that is my pleasure?" Ellisia challenged. She wasn't about to show intimidation before this brazen piece of impudence.

Pausing mid-step, the girl faced her once more. "You're new here. You haven't learned the system. You can learn the hard way if you wish."

Ellisia stood, her mouth open to reply, but the girl was gone. She shut it firmly and gazed after the bouncing dark hair. This would be war. That little piece of presumption had no right to dictate the system of the school or the code of conduct that Ellisia would follow. Was Don Rhaea aware of this bullying behavior? No doubt the girl had a following to back her up.

Her face burned as she bent to pick up the book she'd dropped when she fell. Its front pages bent sickeningly. She straightened them with an impatient gesture.

As she turned to continue down the steps, a small bit of paper on the ground near the next step caught her attention. It hadn't fallen out of her book, and it certainly hadn't been there before she had stumbled.

Rubbing her bruised hip, she swiped the paper with her other hand and dropped it into her book. She wanted to examine it, but she no longer felt secure on the Academy steps. Various students already exited around her.

Some other time would do. For now, she had to get back to Uncle K and the words.

"We would enjoy having a bit of chat with you, if you have no objection."

"No objections raised." Ellisia shut the lid over the sound visualization lens and turned back to Uncle K.

"Indeed." His tones were light. "About *Adon Olam*—have you seen Him?"

"No."

"Have you heard Him?"

Ellisia pondered before answering. "No . . . but my sister has."

"Is that why you are inclined to consider Him in a favorable light—because of your sister?"

Ellisia hesitated, her thoughts tumbling. "I don't know," she whispered.

"For discussion's sake, let's say that it is so. Did you first hear of Him from your sister?"

Ellisia thought back. Her parents had known *Adon Olam*—or so Carita said—but Ellisia had only been two years old when they died. She thought of the books she'd read, but that was only after she'd learned to read, and even then the books had initially been supplied by Carita. "I believe so," she answered at last.

"Do you pray to Him? Meet with those who say they know Him?"

She shrugged. "Sometimes."

"Has He ever answered a religious prayer of yours?"

Ellisia's brow furrowed as she concentrated. "I don't know. I can't think of a time . . ."

"Has He ever done anything for you?"

Had He? He'd done something in Carita's life years ago, but it had only seemed to make her less shy—and happier to do housework, care for other people's children, and accomplish other menial tasks. If that was all that *Adon Olam* had done . . .

She thought of the citizens of Frydael, mentally comparing her happy hometown with the stark contrast between the palace district and the lower districts of Syorien. Frydael was peaceful. Had *Adon Olam* done that?

"My town," she spoke hesitantly. "It seems more well-off than Syorien. Less poverty. Less crime. Safer. Happier. The people know *Adon Olam*."

He laughed. "That sounds like a wonderful town to grow up in, but reason, my girl. Safety and happiness have nothing to do with a Master. You've a sharp mind; let's do a little exercise here to develop it. Consider with me, and you answer for yourself: what if *you* were a slave, chained to the will and desires and whims of a master? At any moment he could do anything with you. Would you be happy? Would you be safe? Think carefully, then answer."

Ellisia shook her head. "I suppose not. Slavery has always sounded horrible."

"Indeed it is. And it's in the very word we use to speak of Him. *Adon.* Master. Is it not who He is?"

"That's not all He is, though . . ."

Uncle K lowered himself into one of the chairs. "Granted, for discussion's sake. If He indeed is real—you've already acknowledged you have not seen or heard Him—perhaps there is more to Him. After all, even a slave-master has other elements of his personality. He may be a father, a brother, a merchant, a scholar, many things.

Yet you call him *adon*. If you call Him *Adon,* that's His relationship to you. The other aspects of who He is aren't relevant to your life. Indeed?"

"That's a fair point," Ellisia acknowledged thoughtfully. It *did* seem strange that His people chose to speak of Him mainly as *Adon.*

"Therefore, if you're going to acknowledge Him, you're choosing to be a slave. No safety or happiness there."

"I see what you mean." Indeed, *Adon Olam* did seem to mostly ask of her—or expect of her—unpleasant things, things she didn't want to do. Comparing her relationship with Him to the relationship of a slave to his master didn't seem to be too farfetched.

"So, enough on the master. Think about the slave. Say the slave has a gift or a talent. Can he effectively use it when his master is dictating his every move?"

"I would say not." Ellisia had to agree, but she added, "Still, he can use it under the authority of the master."

"Of course. But not effectively or freely. The master—or rather the slavery—is a handicap on him. If the slave had a gift for painting, he might well be able to paint still if the master allowed it, but what then would happen?"

"The master would sell his paintings and receive the profit," Ellisia replied.

"And the master would also dictate what and when he painted. He wouldn't be free to enjoy his own talent."

"And if the master forced him to paint, the slave might not even enjoy it anymore."

Uncle K nodded. "So you see, as you learn to use your gift, don't let any slave-master slow you down. You need to be free—free to do what you want. Everything depends on it: your own safety, happiness, dreams, and goals."

Ellisia nodded, thoughtful as she packed up her bag to return to Mae's.

When she came downstairs in the morning, hotcakes waited at the stove and Caeleb chatted with Jaeson as they shoveled bites from plates to mouths. Mae sat at the other end of the table. Each of them held a fork with one hand and secured a baby in the other. The green bundle on Mae's lap appeared to be asleep, and the blue bundle on Caeleb's lap seemed restless. However, Caeleb apparently had the child well under control. Though Naethan made happy little baby noises, he looked content and even laughed at Caeleb a few times—if such a noise could be called a laugh, since it had little in common with the normally accepted sound considered as such—but Ellisia supposed it could pass as one since a large smile accompanied the cacophonic cackle.

The yellow bundle on Jaeson's lap, however, appeared to be doing her best to ensure that Caeleb and Jaeson could not have a proper conversation. She insisted on lifting her voice and emitting the loudest possible sound her tiny lungs could conjure up every time Jaeson turned his attention from her.

Ellisia comprehended the situation in one long glance. Then she sighed. She didn't want to talk to Caeleb—not after her last conversation with him. But she needed to eat. Already her stomach protested, and the next meal stretched hours away.

As quietly as she could, she found a plate and filled it with hotcakes from the stove, trying to sit down without attracting unnecessary attention. Surely it wouldn't be difficult to hide behind Elkaena's squalls.

But Caeleb's eyes fixed on her before she was seated. "Good morning, Ellisia." His voice sounded much too cheerful.

Unreasonably, her heart revolted against it. *Good morning.* How dare he pretend as though he didn't loathe her every choice and course of action. How dare he pretend he understood her, that he was on her level. Yes, it was a good morning, but not at all because of him. He wasn't helping. He hadn't helped. She didn't want to fight with him, and she couldn't push aside who she was and the choices she was making, so she'd just have to close up when she was around him. The less he knew of her heart just now, the better.

"Oh." Mae jerked her hand back from the bowl she had reached for.

The table around her fell silent. Only Elkaena and Naethan exchanged noises now. All three adults stared at the bowl of water in the center of the table, directly in front of Ellisia, and Elkaena chuckled and reached out towards Ellisia. Ellisia's gaze fell to the bowl.

Words.

The water in the bowl was rippling perceptibly. Instinctively Ellisia reached to touch the ripples, and her fingers confirmed what her eyes had translated. Words, appearing. Sound waves, rippling the water. Where had they come from? She hadn't spoken since she'd come down to the table. More ripples followed.

Forcefully, she closed her mind. Horror seized her, and a tremor shot through the ripples. Those were her thoughts. She couldn't interpret them all, but she recognized many of the patterns from her long hours in the lab: loathe, help, good morning, dare, understand, fight, heart.

Panicked, she tried her hardest to stop thinking. "Stop," she commanded in her mind, so intensely that it slipped out her lips. The word "stop" flittered in ripples over the bowl and continued across the table.

Elkaena, still reaching her chubby fists out towards Ellisia, giggled at the water bowl. She waved her arms, splashing one fist into the bowl, and one of the waves rippled across her face with a shower of droplets. She emitted a tiny sneeze, then giggled again.

In one motion, Ellisia swiped her hand across her face, and the vision of the sound waves disappeared. The water stilled, and the vibrations passed on.

Yet Ellisia lifted her eyes across the room and saw the

faintest disturbance in the dust-speckled light beams slanting through the window across the kitchen. The dust danced, but she saw the waves of her word pass through the sun-illuminated particles and continue to the opposite wall, seeming to Ellisia's horrified eyes to float and flutter and dance around the room in harmony with the dust.

There was nothing she could do. The others had already resumed eating and talking, laughing off the rippling water with a light jest. She picked up her fork, cutting and chewing the hotcakes as rapidly as she could, then disappeared out the door.

As she stepped down the path, the door clicked behind her and Caeleb's form appeared.

Not him. Not now.

She pinched off her thoughts just as she sensed sound waves around her beginning to ripple. How had the water rippled so strongly that the others had seen it too? She'd never seen sound waves that clearly before, and she hadn't even said anything.

Caeleb wouldn't know how to recognize the sounds as she did, but she definitely didn't want him to know what she was thinking. She tried her hardest to shut off her thoughts, but the more she thought about not thinking, the more she kept thinking. Instead, she tried to recraft her thoughts so that she wasn't using words in her mind. This was an intensely difficult task—especially since she'd been immersing herself in words since teaching herself to read at age three.

Walk, she told herself. Get away. But would her thoughts send ripples and vibrations spiraling all over Academy? She thought of fountains, basins, puddles, ponds, and her vivid imagination spun a frightening storm of vibrations and ripples outward from her across all visible water. Would the other students laugh at her? Would any of them be able to translate the sound waves as she had? Would her instructors read her innermost thoughts? Perhaps some of the Doekh teachers wore sensory-enhancing devices that Uncle K hadn't told her about. A heaviness draped her. She'd dived in over her head in wordology, and she now peered into a world she'd never known existed in the predictable reality of ordinary life.

Caeleb easily kept in step with her. Ellisia dared the tiniest sidelong peek. He didn't seem to be paying the least attention to the slight breeze wafting around her. Some of the pressure on her chest lifted. If only he would continue oblivious to anything unusual, she might be able to get through this. With a deep-drawn sigh, she ventured to glance around. Good! It *was* just a breeze.

"What's the matter, Ellisia?" Caeleb asked.

"Nothing." Her teeth clenched, and she didn't turn her head. The tempo of her footsteps increased. He kept pace with her.

Caeleb sighed. "Elli, you aren't yourself. What's happening?" Three steps. Ellisia remained silent. "Are you enjoying Academy?" Three more steps. "What have you been learning?"

Ellisia's frown deepened. She certainly wouldn't be telling him that. "Academy's fine," she said, "and I *am* myself. Reading. Studying. That's all I've ever done, right?"

At least she couldn't see her sound waves now. Control your mind, Ellisia, she told herself. Don't let externals take over. You can do this.

"Yes, but you've hardly said a word to me in the past many weeks, and Mae says you've barely spoken to her beyond what is absolutely necessary. That's not you."

She shrugged and looked both ways before stepping out into the street. Saera's form approached from the end of the road. Ellisia turned the other direction towards Academy, glad she wouldn't have to face Saera this morning too.

Silence spread. Why didn't Caeleb go home and leave her alone? Every moment, she imagined leaves rippling with the words she'd just spoken, pebbles below her feet vibrating, the skies themselves echoing her for the world to hear.

"Ellisia, how are you with *Adon Olam* these days?" The words jolted her out of the thoughts that were quickly wrapping themselves about her in a heavy cloak.

"*Adon Olam*?" She hadn't tasted that word on her tongue for a time, and it reminded her of her conversation with Uncle K.

"Are you walking in the Word of *Adon Olam*, Ellisia? Have you been speaking to Him? Have you been listening to Him?" The words rang soft and low, yet each one clearly penetrated Ellisia's ear.

"Stop it." Her tone was cross now. "You sound just like Carita. My life with *Adon Olam* is private. It's my own business. You have no right to barge into my life to try to induce guilt in me just because you fancy I'm talking less than I have in the past. Well, maybe I'm growing wiser. Maybe I don't need to talk every moment of the day. Maybe I'm too busy with more important things. Maybe my studies require my time and energy. And just maybe *Adon Olam* can handle me Himself. I don't need you."

Caeleb said nothing for several more strides. Then his words were lower still, yet their intense earnestness pricked Ellisia's conscience. "You are right, Ellisia. He can handle you. Forgive me. I'll be praying for you."

He stopped walking, and Ellisia reluctantly halted with him, though it irked her to be forced to do so. Caeleb held out his hand to her. "Let me know if you need anything or if I can help," he said. "God be with you, my friend."

She ignored his hand, but then at the last second touched it with her own out of politeness. She gave him a nod, then spun on her heel and marched toward the Academy steps. Always meddling.

At the center of the stairs, she turned, unable to resist a peek to see if he was still there. He was, but he no longer looked in her direction. From the safety of one of the tall pillars, she gazed at him. She'd admired him—once. She'd confided in him once. How could she? His gray-brown eyes overran with craftiness, of desire to control her life. Even from here she sensed in them a spark that she loathed. His short, broad build irritated her. She was almost taller than he. She tossed her head. Somehow that thought gave her a feeling of superiority. The very way he held his hands was revolting—as if he didn't care about their placement but simply allowed them to hang. His trimmed hair was such a dirty brown. Such a dirty brown. She had sometimes wished for brown hair, but now she was inexpressibly thankful that her hair shone bright red instead of such a common, everyday color.

She averted her eyes. Even the tones of his voice, though deep, had been so quiet—as if he didn't care to speak with authority or as if he were unsure of himself. And his prying into her personal matters! There was no end to it!

She stomped—inwardly anyway; she didn't care to portray that little mannerism outwardly—into the Academy, wishing it had been anyone but Caeleb to whom she was indebted for being here.

13

THE NEXT EVENING with Uncle K brought new questions from her lips. She didn't tell him the whole story, but she had to find out if he knew anything about why the others had been able to see the water ripple at her words—or was it at her mere thoughts?

"It's a special gift, girl," he said. "One that few have mastery of. You've picked it up quicker than anyone I've ever seen, and you've taken it farther than I would have thought possible. I myself do not have any abilities with words outside of the laboratory—although I hope that my sensory devices will change that—but I have studied from those who do. It's a mind game, as I said, as Wulf says repeatedly. Focus. Concentrate. Deliberately think about it. Your thoughts have power. You need to believe that your thoughts have power. If you truly believe in yourself, anything you want to do will be done. Eventually your will may start acting itself out through your thoughts—or through your words alone—it depends on how strong you are. Many people kill the impact of their words and thoughts through disbelief—or rather, too strong of belief in logic and reality as they perceive it with their outer senses and not in reality as it is independent of us."

"But how does this happen?" Ellisia asked, puzzled.

"Quite simple. Everything has a cause, does it not? If

something happens, something else made it happen. One example: you can possess power through your words through borrowing the ability from someone who can make it happen." He paused. "For instance, say you want to move my hand off of the table." He laid his arm across the table. "There are several ways you can do that."

"I want—your—arm—off—the—table." She spoke slowly and deliberately, concentrating on his arm.

Nothing happened. Ellisia didn't even sense a flicker of the sound waves that left her mouth. Uncle K laughed. "Your problem is a logical one, my girl," he said merrily. "Your own mind by wanting it cannot move my arm off of the table, correct? What *can* move it? Let's move away from wordology and philosophy for a moment and think about what can move it."

"You can," Ellisia stated.

"Correct. More specifically, the muscles in my arm can lift or push my hand off of the table. How else?"

"I—don't know . . ."

"Think, girl! Who could move it?"

"I could?"

"Correct! Or Jolyn could, or anyone else! Or something could fall on the table and push it off. Or you could upset the table and it would fall off. There are many ways to accomplish a single task. So you in your mind need to borrow that ability from me—or from yourself, or Jolyn, or the table, or whomever! Focus on thinking about something that could do it, and then snatch that power from them! Try it, try it now!"

Ellisia concentrated. She scrunched her eyes shut, imagining her arm pushing the man's hand off of the table. Over and over she repeated the scene in her head. When she thought she had it, she spoke quietly. "Move off the table."

For a moment, nothing happened. Then Uncle K's

hand moved slightly, but that was all.

"Excellent attempt, girl. It nearly worked. Look through the sound visualization lens and try again. Watch what happens. While you're at it, you might as well put on the glove too."

Ellisia obeyed. When she spoke, the vibrations swirled and blew as though with a breeze towards the man's hand, pushing against it, again wiggling it slightly.

Ellisia shoved back from the table. This wasn't anything different from what she'd been practicing with the recorded voices and the objects that the sound waves had moved. It was only the rearranging of atomic matter at some microscopic level she could only glimpse at through many instruments.

"Speak bolder this time. Maybe when you borrow, imagine it as a mighty push, not just a little nudge." Uncle K's voice said.

Ellisia closed her eyes and focused again. She imagined her arms thrusting out at the man's hand and shoving it off the table. She tried to "borrow" the power from her arms as she spoke, louder this time, opening her eyes at the lens of the sound visualization instrument. "Get off the table!"

This time the waves were even quicker to appear, but they were jerkier. They swirled more directly towards the table, and with a scraping of flesh against wood, the man's hand was in his lap.

"Well done!" Uncle K spoke, lifting his head from the second lens on the instrument. "You're quick to catch on. I didn't even see or feel it coming."

Ellisia stared. "You didn't see . . . ?"

"I saw nothing. I suppose you could see it all clearly, but not I. Not this time. Too fast, and I wouldn't have interpreted it regardless."

"Truly?" Perhaps her thoughts were safe after all, even

from advanced wordologists.

"Indeed. It's the nature of the gift." Uncle K leaned back. "Now try it again. Something else like that—simple and harmless, but evident. I won't tell you what it should be this time though—you come up with it."

Ellisia looked around the room. She knew exactly what she wanted to try first—with this man in her presence, this mysterious teacher, the uncle who always wore the black hood, the face behind that dark beard.

Ellisia closed her eyes and imagined. This time she thought of the man himself and his own arms performing the action. Her mind seemed to step into his body and steal his power, then step back. She squinted into the instrument, stretched out her gloved hand, and spoke—in a whisper because she didn't want him warned. "Remove your cloak."

The vibrations were crisp and flew straight to the goal. They twined themselves about the man's cloak strings and engulfed his hood. A few moments later, the cloak lay on the floor and Ellisia found herself gazing at the dark-haired stern-jawed figure with the gray eyes and set expression. He was tall and powerful, but he slouched.

Only a moment she gazed before he seized his cloak from the floor and threw it about his shoulders, an annoyed expression settling over his features. "What'd you do that for, girl?" he whined. "Something simple and harmless, I tell you. I'm teaching you, girl. Don't turn my own instruction against me."

"Seemed harmless enough to me, I should think," Ellisia murmured, blinking again through the instrument.

"Regardless," the man pulled the hood far over his forehead, "I think that's enough for one day."

He stood, sliding the chair back with a grating creak, and stomped towards the door.

"Enjoy yourself," he emphasized. "Go ahead and

practice on your own. Work on your skills. Read up on them. You'll learn. You'll hear from us later." He marched out, the door closing heavily behind him.

Left alone, Ellisia turned back toward the sound visualization instrument and flipped the lever for the recording of the voice Uncle K had used when he'd first introduced her to the instrument. She adjusted the controls, letting the words come at random as she peered through the glasses. The voice droned, drawing out each syllable with emphasis. The vibrations still flashed past, so quickly Ellisia had to pay close attention to distinguish them.

An.

Not a very notable word, but a word just the same. A crucial word. The building block of books.

The glove slipped over her fingers, and she reached out to sense the sound waves.

Eagle. Music. Thought. Swarmed.

She touched words at random, pushing them, mentally moving them into place. Fascinated, she slipped an ear protector helmet on her head, blocking the sound, forcing her to interpret the words by sight and feel.

Ten. The. Foretaste. Beckoned. Alliterate.

Her motions became more focused, more concrete. The sound recording stopped, and her own tongue took over, speaking words as they came to mind, hardly noting what they were until she saw and interpreted the vibrations before her.

Freedom. Light. Song. Ran. Taerna. Books. Learned. Word. Thought. Power. Fought. Victor. Spoken. Think. Gifted. Thirst. Living.

Words seemed to spin and rotate on the table in front of her. She was barely moving, hardly thinking. Each word, formed of those unique ripples of air, jumped next to another word. Sentences formed. She barely took in

the sense of them, only reveled in the action of creating. *Authority. Power. Commanded. Belief. Faith.*
The door opened. She barely noticed.
Jolyn stepped in.
Ellisia froze, a word still spinning in her throat.
Time seemed to stand still.
"What are you doing?"
The words caught her clearly, despite her blocked ears. Her eyes locked with Jolyn's.
"Studying." She kept her answer short, squeezing off the vibrations as they traveled through her fingers, though without the instrument, she couldn't feel them.
"I swear the lab was nearly shaking. I thought Uncle must have gotten lost in one of his projects again."
"No, just me."
Jolyn shook her head, backing out again. "Watch it or you'll be twice as lost as he's ever been."

14

IN ONE OF the private study areas at Academy, she flung her books to the table with little respect for how they landed. One toppled a moment on the edge, then clunked to the floor, pages sprawled, a tiny paper fluttering slowly after it.

Ellisia froze, following its flight with a mesmerized gaze. The paper! In the wake of everything that had happened since, she'd completely forgotten about the paper she'd found on the step. She caught it up just as it reached the ground.

Opening the book, she straightened a crinkled page corner with one hand while the fingers of her right hand gently smoothed out the wrinkles in the small paper.

At last it lay flat before her.

Jolaena,

That matters little. The discovery of which we previously spoke is confirmed. I make for F-1 as soon as practical, projected three weeks. Must seek out this E first, and quiet the continued influence over the madness he began once and for all. Then further. Posse will continue to uncover further information regarding R. You will cover, as we discussed previously. Household must not know yet in

case of repercussions. Meet in Rizdor Allaey in four days at last evening light for final details. Be ready to come to the house directly afterwards. Till then, continue business as usual, lay low.
DF - Destroy.

Ellisia froze, instinctively turning the book page over the bit of paper. This was serious business. This was no casual note or scrap. It was trouble. One of the political factions vying for power? Why "cover"? Why not spell out the names?

She forced her face to look normal, to be apparently studiously bent over the book. She *was* indeed studious—studiously puzzled over the note. Who—or what—were F-1, E, and R? "Must seek out this E." Her own name had instantly sprung to mind, but logic took over, quickly reassuring her that the person was obviously a male. "*. . . Put an end to the madness he began . . . I make for F-1.*" It had to be a place. Her mind raced over the names of various countries, but none fit. A city then . . . but R could be a place, a person, or something else entirely. "Further information"—it had to either be a person or some important object.

It was unsigned. There was no clue as to the writer's identity.

She stole a peek behind the pages at the note. Jolaena. She needed to find out who Jolaena was.

But perhaps the note was a prank—one of those harmless plays that unthinking citizens perpetrated for their own amusement. She closed the book firmly. The identity of Jolaena would determine that point. She felt as though she would be able to tell the purport of the note simply by gazing upon Jolaena.

She'd found the note on the steps, so it likely belonged to a student, or possibly a teacher. How could she set about this task? Academy was huge. She couldn't meet everyone. Besides, someone could have merely appointed the Academy steps as a meeting place—in which case Jolaena wouldn't be a student at all.

The dark-haired girl dropped it.

The thought flashed into her mind, and she replayed over and over the events of the encounter on the steps: how she had crossed to the other side, how the girl had appeared in front of her and bumped her, the words they'd exchanged, the abrupt departure. *Had* she dropped it? *Could* she have dropped it? Was her name Jolaena?

It had to be. A deep-seated conviction rooted itself in Ellisia's heart, though her brain recalled no clear memory of the girl being anywhere near the step where the note had been. But Ellisia hadn't paid attention—and there hadn't been anyone else ahead of them on the steps. It *could* have been the girl. She certainly seemed the type to be mixed up in something devious.

In the hall on the way to the Literature room, Ellisia scanned every face, tuned her ears to every conversation. Never did she hear the name "Jolaena" used, though she gathered a good bit of useless trivia on typical thoughtless student matters.

By the end of the day, she'd furtively remained close enough to the dark-haired girl to discover that her name was certainly not Jolaena. Once her studies ended, she slipped back to one of the private reading nooks to examine the note once more. Since the dark-haired girl wasn't Jolaena, she'd have to adjust her methods. There was no time to sift through every student at Academy to find the recipient of the note; the hints as to the note's purport seemed too suspicious to delay too long.

F-l. Frydael.

It couldn't be, but Ellisia's subconscious insisted. Why would someone in the Palace District head for her tiny no-name hometown?

A deep foreboding filled her heart. The E wasn't Ellisia, but . . .

"Ellith." She muttered the name. "Really?" But her mind insisted that no one else in Frydael had an E last name, and with a single initial, a last name was more likely than a first.

And Kaelan had started something in Syorien's Palace District that many might term "madness."

The foreboding in her chest sunk to an ache deep in her stomach. Urgency beat through her veins in harmony with her heart. Even if she were entirely wrong, she couldn't risk it.

The evening of the fourth day. When could that be? How long since the note had been penned? And how long since it had passed from Jolaena to the dark-haired girl? Why had this Jolaena passed it off? What part did the dark-haired girl have in this scheme? "Quiet the continued influence he had over this madness once and for all." It sounded ominous, vaguely threatening, and yet too casual at the same time. It could mean much or little. Ellisia's stomach knotted and re-knotted somewhere deep down as she reread the words.

Mentally she counted the days since her encounter with the girl on the steps, her brain stuttering as she hit three . . . four. Either the important meeting had already happened . . . or it was tonight.

It had to be tonight. It *had* to be. She couldn't have missed it. She dared not miss it.

But what farfetched chance was there that the writer of the note gave it to Jolaena at once that morning, and then somehow it went from Jolaena to the Academy steps on the very same day Ellisia had found it? She stuffed the note deep inside a cloak pocket and turned away. No doubt she'd missed her opportunity, like it or not. Why hadn't she remembered the paper before today?

But if there *was* a chance ... where was Rizdor Allaey?

Her steps quickened towards the Academy BookHall. Her finger scanned the shelves in search of information on the geography of Syorien. For several minutes, maps, guides, and detailed descriptions of the city flipped past her eager fingers. Most of the information related to the various entertainment halls and shows, but Ellisia ignored it and focused on the names of the various streets, roads, allaeys, and sideways that crowded the map. They were many and some proved difficult to decipher, but Ellisia eventually made out a tiny road marked "Rizdor."

Oh joy! It was near Academy! Furthermore, it was almost on her way home. She could probably find it quite easily.

The next question: what would she do when she got there? She couldn't just wander into the midst of a conversation. If it were truly as important as it sounded, she could be walking right into trouble. She wished she knew how to capture their words, but such a thought was beyond possibility. She'd make do with what she had.

Replacing the map book on the shelf, she shouldered her books, left the building, and directed herself straight towards Rizdor Allaey.

To the left and right, several blocks stretched, and left then right spun Ellisia. Where on the allaey would they meet? On the side closest to the main road, or furthest away? Either would be logical options.

She scanned the buildings. Gray angled corners shot up towards the sky, no color or pattern to relieve the monotony. Storage buildings, perhaps? Work buildings behind the gaudy show halls and entertainment centers?

She stepped into the allaey, feeling rather than seeing it narrow considerably. An unusual quiet pervaded the street—so strange after the noisy thoroughfares of the city she was used to passing through. No possibility of mingling in a crowd existed here, though she hadn't expected to.

Another thought tugged at her mind. Would she be safe here at dusk? There was no telling what her unknown targets might do to her if she thwarted their plans or even "unintentionally" overheard them. Maybe they would resent her simply for being in the area. Would they suspect her? Had Jolaena missed the note?

Ellisia meandered up the length of the street, hoping for a secure corner in which she could hide to observe a conversation. But none appeared. The best she could do, she decided, would be to squeeze between two of the buildings. Some of them were built directly against each other, but others had just enough space for a person to creep through.

No one was in sight. Impulsively she darted toward the nearest crack and sidled her way through to the end. As she suspected, there was no street on the other side. Large showy buildings rose around her in every direction, leaving only narrow spaces between them. She picked another tiny route and squeezed in. This one opened onto a wide street. A crack revealed passersby milling up and down on the brown cobblestones and periodically entering one of the showy buildings.

Ellisia pulled back. It wasn't the busiest street in the city by any means, but much busier than the one she'd left. How many townsfolk used these narrow corridors between the buildings to access these streets? It was the perfect route for anyone wishing to avoid observation. The path did seem a tad well-worn for such a locality. She bit her lip. If she had to use one of these hideaways this evening, she certainly didn't want to run into anyone back here.

She furtively explored several other passages, making careful mental note of which buildings had passages and which didn't. No matter which end of the allaey Jolaena and her contact met on, she could slip into place to observe them. She selected a spot near the middle of the allaey to begin from.

For a few moments more she deliberated. If they met at either end of the road, she wouldn't be able to get to them very quickly. They might not have much to discuss after all. She could miss them altogether.

She couldn't risk them seeing her unless it became necessary. That much was clear.

She'd have to take her chances.

Scanning the street once more, she turned towards her home. She'd have to prepare the evening meal and complete her chores quickly if she were to return by last light.

The foot traffic on Charlin Street hadn't lightened, though the sunlight streamed across the wide and well-lit cobblestones, leaving long crisp shadows. Ellisia paid no attention to the people who loitered or flowed in and out of the many Halls on the street. She attempted to blend in, to lose herself in the crowd, to appear as one of them.

When she reached the corridor she'd selected earlier, she hung back for a few moments until she was sure that she could slip in unobserved. Then she was gone, quickly sliding between the buildings until she reached Rizdor Allaey.

Once on the other side, she peered up and down the allaey, careful not to betray her location. No one was in sight. She slid back into the recesses of the building, sure that she would hear if anyone stepped onto the allaey anywhere near her.

She crouched, her hands supporting her face. The dust beneath her was uncomfortably dry, but at least it wasn't mud. The building walls loomed behind her, tall and grey. Her back pressed against the wall, and the soles of her feet slid to push against another in front of her. She wrapped her arms around herself, wishing she'd put on her cloak before leaving home. Spring evenings could be quite cool.

It seemed ages before she heard a furtive footstep. Immediately she straightened to attention, careful not to betray herself with any sound. Her senses strained against her body as every nerve morphed into alertness.

The steps weren't coming from the allaey. They came from the other side of the building. Evidently someone was approaching the allaey from the corridors, as she had.

She peered out. The allaey was still devoid of traffic. As Ellisia gazed, a door across the way opened and a dark figure stepped out. Ellisia squinted hard. The sun was very low now, and the dusk rendered the figure indiscernible.

In vain she strained her ears. The person, whoever he was, was being unnaturally silent. No footfalls reached her. No thud of a door being shut wended its way across the allaey.

A small sound from the other side of the building Ellisia hugged snapped her attention away from the figure, and she instinctively shrank back into her hiding place. Another form—that of a girl—emerged from the opposite end of the building. Darting glances up and down the allaey, the girl took a step or two away from the shelter of the building. Once again, she gazed up the allaey, then down—in Ellisia's direction.

Ellisia nearly gasped but caught herself in time. The

profile against the darkening sky! Ellisia fixed her eyes upon her even as she herself slowly shrank back into the shadows. The long blonde hair, the tall figure, the airy look—it was Jolyn all over. Her friend. What was she doing here?

Disbelief flooded her as Jolyn moved a few steps away. She wanted to cry out—to direct Jolyn's attention to herself, to ask her what she was doing—to confide in her. But there was the other figure.

The dark-cloaked person stepped slowly and silently down the allaey towards Jolyn. It, too, looked around, then at the sky. After several pauses, the figure finally met Jolyn—not far from where Ellisia still crouched.

Ellisia carefully glanced both directions. No one else was in sight. Based on the dark figure's cautious behavior, this had to be the planned meeting. But what was Jolyn doing?

The figure finally stopped next to her classmate, and the reality of what she was seeing broke upon Ellisia. It couldn't be! Jolyn: her first friend—her protection as a new girl, the one who'd introduced her to the BookHall. They'd shared experiences. They understood each other. Jolyn couldn't be involved in whatever scheme this was. It was impossible. It was crazy. It was unthinkable. Not Jolyn. Anyone else.

She was so shaky she could barely focus. She sank her head down into her hands. Jolyn. It couldn't be.

Soft voices drifted towards her. She was supposed to be listening. She pushed away the sensations of betrayal and horror that crowded at her mind and tried to focus on the figures in the street.

Her ears strained once more. She distinctly heard the whispered word "Jolaena," but had a difficult time deciphering the other words.

Then she caught another word that nearly froze her.

"Kaelan." Her mind tumbled, trying to piece together what she'd heard, desperate to know if it could possibly be any other word, frantic to be wrong.

Her head sank into her lap and she tried to think rapidly and logically. Kaelan was the "E" in the note, then, and Kaelan must be in trouble. That dark-cloaked man would be going after him. If she interrupted her studies for a trip home, she'd lose her place at Academy. Even if she did manage to warn Kaelan, she could not travel faster than the man himself. She wouldn't be able to continue her personal studies or her wordology at home. If she didn't get certified in Taernan Literature, she would have no chance of getting a position at the BookHall. All things considered, *she* couldn't be the one mixed up in this—not now.

But there were no law men in Syorien to whom she could appeal.

She'd have to send Caeleb to warn Kaelan. She had no choice. And she'd rather have Caeleb out of her way at the moment anyway.

She raised her head and struggled to hear more of what the two were saying, but the words failed to reach her ear. Frustrated, she inched closer to the opening, moving her head into the open air. What good was it for her to be here if she couldn't even hear them? She rose to her feet, still crouching, and inched forward, hoping the shadows would keep her invisible.

At the same instant, the man turned his head. Ellisia froze, her eyes locked with his. The next second she was on her feet, racing back to the safety of the corridor. In a moment he had caught her, pinning her arms behind her. She screamed, but the man's other hand pressed hard against her mouth. She tried to bite him but couldn't reach.

"What are you doing, girl?" He hissed directly in her

ear.

    She couldn't have answered if she'd have wanted to. He dragged her out to the open allaey.

    Her gaze traveled down both sides of the allaey once more. The fading light of the sun barely illuminated the street. Ellisia struggled to get a good look at the man who held her, but her back was to him. Still, she couldn't mistake that voice.

    Jolyn approached with an odd mixture of casualness and indifferent disgust. "Oh. It's Ellisia." Her nose turned up slightly, just visible as her profile stood out against the dark blue of the sky.

    "Whatever are you doing here?" Uncle K's voice still hissed, but his arms released her at last.

    She straightened and shrugged. "What are *you* doing here?"

    The man looked from one girl to the other. "My niece will be spending the evening with me. I work here on occasion and I was late tonight," he added, almost apologetically.

    "Indeed. I never knew this." Freed from his grasp, Ellisia examined him as she never had before.

    Yet the effort revealed little. As always, a dark cloak floated from shoulder to ankles, and tonight the hood obscured his head. His beard bristled over his chin, but in the dimness accentuated by the hood, she could not make out his expression. "May I ask why you have detained me?" Her heart beat rapidly. Uncle K was going to Frydael—to hurt Kaelan. There had to be an explanation—a mistake.

    He swept his cloak more closely around him. Ellisia shivered equally at the motion and the breeze.

    "May I ask why you are lurking in the shadows?" he returned.

    She lifted her eyes to where she imagined his must

be. "May I ask why you and your niece have selected this hour and this deserted allaey to whisper to each other when you live in the same house?"

He tipped his head. "May I ask what gives you the right to question our doings?"

She leveled her chin. If he wanted to play this game, she could play along. "May I ask why as a respectable gentleman you have no justification for your actions?"

He stretched out his arm. "May I ask why the reasons I have given are insufficient?"

"May I ask why you expect the lady to answer before answering yourself?"

"May I ask why you are not home where you belong at this very moment?"

She pressed her lips together. "May I not ask the same of you?"

"May I ask whether we two could more profitably use our time elsewhere and not in fruitless questionings?"

"May I ask why you began this train of questions by answering my question with a question?"

"May I ask when you will begin to answer me?"

His words were still polite, but a shade of hostility lurked in his manner. She parried with another question. "May I ask what right you have to demand an answer?"

"May I ask what right you have to deny one?"

"May I ask what you will do when I do not answer?"

"May I ask what you will do when I don't let you go home?" he challenged.

She paused. That above all things must not happen—not now. Like it or not, she needed to let Caeleb know that Kaelan was in danger. "May I ask when you will allow me to continue on my way home?"

"May I ask why you were on the streets at this late and dangerous hour?"

"May I ask if there is anything amiss in exploring the

various lanes and byways of the city?" She tilted her chin up innocently.

"May I ask if you care for your life and security?"

"May I ask if you—"

"This is nonsense!" Jolyn burst out at last, indignation spilling from each hissed word.

Uncle K turned to Jolyn. "My dear Jolaena, please calm yourself. Your friend and I were just having a delightful bit of a chat here. There is surely no need for such vehemence."

Ellisia regarded her friend critically. "You are not Jolaena."

"A little nickname that I've called her ever since she was a wee lass." Uncle K's head tipped in Jolyn's direction.

Jolyn's eyes fixed on Ellisia's face. "Didn't I warn you to mind your business and of the dangers of too many of the wrong questions? And here you've done nothing but ask questions for the last five minutes!" Jolyn's heel tapped the pavement to emphasize her statement.

"One must ask questions if one is to become wiser," Ellisia murmured.

"One must *not* ask questions if one wishes to be safe," Jolyn emphasized.

"Why, whatever could be unsafe about conversing with my teacher-partner and my school friend?" Ellisia opened her eyes wide, hoping she appeared innocent and child-like. Then she shook her head. "This is madness. Are we going to stand here in the allaey all night long, or do we have homes to get back to?"

"There you go with your questions again!" Jolyn exclaimed.

"Very well. I have a home to get to tonight, and you certainly have a home to get to tonight. I will see you early—too early—in Literature tomorrow."

"I'm afraid I won't be there. Family matters . . .

money and all . . . I've had to drop out of Literature for this term."

Ellisia didn't let her gaze flinch. "This is sudden."

"I know. I got the news when I got home today."

"Hence our irregular meeting here tonight," Uncle K broke in, "discussing her position, the matters, and how I may assist her and her family. So, no, my dear Jolaena, money isn't the obstacle here."

Ellisia flicked her eyes from one to the other. Both were lying. However, she had no means of either figuring out their true intentions here or proving her suspicions without endangering herself. "Jolyn, school dues are paid at the beginning of the term. Money shouldn't be an issue for weeks yet anyway, Uncle K's assistance or not."

"No, Uncle's right. It's not money—not for that," Jolyn murmured. "Family . . ."

Ellisia waited, but Jolyn didn't continue.

"Then you are in a fix, and my condolences to your family. All the more reason why I ought to be on my way and let you be on yours."

"Unlike us, you have not given satisfactory account of yourself yet, girl," Uncle K spoke up suddenly. "Is this what you do on your nights off? Roam the allaeys of Syorien?"

"First time." She sighed. "I was ambling up Charlin Street exploring on my way home. I saw a gap in the Halls and decided to see what was on the other side. Only you were right there—I didn't want to disturb you. Instinctual self-protection. It could have been anyone on this dark, deserted street." All true, she told herself inwardly.

"And that explains why you know this is an allaey." Jolyn's harsh voice wasn't trying to keep quiet anymore.

"It's obvious." Ellisia motioned to the narrow packed dirt track, as if anyone with eyes couldn't help but know the term for such a road.

"Enough, Jolaena." The man's voice was low.

"But she . . ." Jolyn leaned closer to him and the rest of her sentence was lost in the quiet whisperings that followed.

"We could just . . ." Uncle K's voice also softened too far for her to hear.

"But . . ."

Ellisia glanced from one to the other, engrossed in their whisperings, then slowly edged away. If they meant harm to Kaelan or anyone else she knew, she'd prefer not to remain alone with them in the Allaey for any longer than she had to. If she'd hoped to learn the meaning of the note from them here, that hope now lay dead and buried twenty feet below the cobblestones.

Step by furtive step she shifted.

But her flight could hardly be called three steps long before the man pulled away from Jolaena and glanced at Ellisia. She imagined that his face hardened, but in the darkness she could detect no change.

"You're right." He stepped towards Ellisia, his tones conversational. "Girl, we've discussed your aspirations toward the BookHall as well as in mastering wordology. You've made significant progress in the latter, and it's time we begin to look into the former, as well as into your side of our agreement."

Ellisia halted, torn yet listening. She wasn't certain she trusted this man anymore. But he *had* taught her more than she'd ever hoped to learn about words. And he *had* promised to get her a BookHall position, and she *had* promised to assist him. So far she was only in his debt. She'd listen, and if she still felt misgivings, she'd see what she could do about extracting herself from the partnership. "Say on."

"I know you have not yet perfected your mastery of the science. But at the rate you are going, you will soon surpass me in certain areas. You've mastered quite enough to serve your country, and we do have a task for you. At the same time, I'd like to perfect your knowledge of a few specific areas in a way I find difficult in the short hour we normally have together. In the meanwhile, you would do us a service by remaining at our humble abode."

"But what about my friends ... my home?"

"You can notify them that you will be paying a visit to your friends for a short time. They will hardly hold you back in pursuit of your dreams, or in your social life. No doubt they will scarcely notice your absence."

"I'm not so sure of that," Ellisia muttered. Weary Mae juggling her three babies, Jaeson in the fields, and Saera working as best she could during the day—would they miss her? They might miss her help, but surely they wouldn't very much miss her personally. Besides, a longing tugged her heart to master the areas Uncle K had mentioned, to see what else he had for her, to—oh! perhaps quite soon!—work among the rainbow rows of books. Surely the faint misgiving she harbored regarding their motives and operations was misplaced. Surely, even if they proved untrustworthy, she could watch her back and return to Mae's at any moment. It was only a temporary position.

"What about my Academy tuition?" she said aloud.

"What about it, my girl?"

"I—I was earning ..." she stammered, unwilling to reveal that she worked for her living, schooling, and board at the place that she called "home."

But Uncle K held his hand up as though he sensed and respected her hesitancy. "No matter, girl. We will take care of that, I can assure you. No worries there. As long as you remain with us, we will see that you have all you need to continue your studies. No outlay required on your part. I feel sure that you will well repay us with your services."

"I'll stay," she sighed, fatigue fogging her brain and pulling at the corners of her eyes. "Just let me collect my things at home, and I'll be over after Academy tomorrow."

"Make it sooner. I have business to attend to that I'd like your assistance with."

"Fine. I'll come tonight, but it might be quite late."

"Perfect." Uncle K sent her a nod. "I'll have someone at the door to show you to your room. Come, Jolaena. The evening lengthens."

Left alone, Ellisia stepped quickly towards home, her mind reviewing the evening. She'd intercepted the meeting arranged in the note. She'd discovered that uncle and niece had to be plotting something against Kaelan. By logical deduction, Uncle K would be traveling to Frydael within the next few weeks. Yet . . . how would he "end Kaelan's madness once and for all"? The patter of her heart kept time with her footsteps as she quickened her pace. She wasn't sure she wanted to know; she could only suspect and imagine.

15

THE DOOR BEHIND Caeleb clicked even more quietly than usual despite the rusty latch, yet Grandfather still glanced up from the pile of parchment he sorted at the table. Caeleb knew Grandfather had already read his face and a conversation was coming. He stifled thoughts of retreating to the stillness of his own chamber, strode across the room, pulled out the chair opposite, sat, and ran his fingers through his hair before massaging his forehead and cheeks. He drew a deep breath and downed a mouthful of water from his tumbler, then turned his attention upon Grandfather.

"Rough patches again?" Grandfather's voice was low.

"You have no idea." Caeleb shook his head. "Dissention. Grumblings and hard feelings over the tiniest things. It's wearying."

"I do know." Grandfather placed a hand over Caeleb's for a moment. "Human nature never changes, apart from the transformation of the Spirit of *Adon Olam*."

"I just feel so—I should be preventing some of this tension. I should be shepherding these people. They think I'm not the type, and I know they're right."

"Of course." Grandmother appeared behind her husband. "Of course you're not the type. But *Adon Olam* is, and who leads and feeds those dear souls through you?"

"I know." Caeleb sighed. "But I hate this—I hate the fights. I hate the sideways looks and murmured disagreements. The body of *Adon Olam* shouldn't be this way—shouldn't be divided. Shouldn't be at war with itself. With such division among our own, what strength and unity remains for warring against the enemy?"

"With much tribulation we enter the kingdom of *Adon Olam*," Grandfather reminded him.

"I know. But sometimes I wonder if these people even want to enter His kingdom at all. Seems as though they're seeking to build their own kingdom. Usually I can move past some of the petty dissenters—much of the time the issue doesn't even matter. But this time, it's the very Word of *Adon Olam* at stake."

"How so?" Grandfather asked.

Caeleb shook his head. "I don't want to rehash the details. Just that certain people want to justify certain choices or lifestyles or activities, and that desire inside them is so intense that it's the spectacles through which they view all of life . . . including the Word."

"Ah, the enemy himself as an angel of light, twisting *Adon Olam*'s words for his own purposes," mused Grandfather.

"It's difficult to deal with." Caeleb clenched his fists. "There's nothing I can do but pray."

"Which is, of course, enough." Grandmother lowered herself into a chair.

"Yes." Caeleb sighed, then stood. He needed to get on that without further delay.

"We'll keep praying for you, Caeleb." Grandfather held his eye a moment before turning back to his papers.

Grandmother gave a gentle nod as Caeleb climbed the solid wooden stairs. Usually he slept in the downstairs bedroom, but on evenings like this, he craved the seclusion of the upper level. It was to him a bit of holy ground, a sanctuary, a refuge.

Up in the quiet darkness of his old room, kneeling—no, prostrate—upon the worn green stripes in the rug, he tried to pray. He tried to bring before his *Adon* the difficulties of the gathering he oversaw. Yet he couldn't speak; he couldn't pray.

After several futile minutes, he lit a candle and reached for the Word.

> (As it is written, I have made thee a father of many nations,) before him whom he believed, even *Adon Olam*, who quickeneth the dead, and calleth those things which be not as though they were.

"Calls those things which are not as though they are ... calls those things which are not as though they are ..." The rhythmic cadence reechoed in his head. "Quickens the dead—makes them alive; believed ... father of many ... calls those things which are not as though they are ..."

Again and again Caeleb read the words before him; again and again they circled through his mind.

> It is not ye that speak, but the Spirit of your Father which speaketh in you.

> And hath given him authority to execute judgment also, because he is the Son of man.

> I live; yet not I, but Yeshua liveth in me: and the life which I now live in the flesh I live by the faith of the Son of *Adon Olam,* who loved me, and gave himself for me.

"Calls those things which are not as though they are . . ." he whispered again. By Yeshua's faith, that power was his.

His mind flicked back to the gathering—the bitter voices, the spite, the hypocritical holy arrogance ricocheting through him.

And just as quickly, it flicked away.

This wasn't all that was weighing on him just now. Ellisia.

Her words, voiced from a place of intellect, of reason, of ambition, of delight at a prize unseen but yet before her.

Her eyes, set eagerly on books, now glazing over in so many other situations, now nearly imperceptibly darkening when meeting his.

Her mind, a keen and eager sponge, always drinking in books and their content, yet worryingly unrestrained by her morals.

Her voice—her voice! Repeating words she'd heard, words that weren't hers, words of truth that yet left a subtle taste of poison to Caeleb's spiritual taste. That voice! So many times he'd heard it—lighthearted, encouraging, joking, bantering, laughing, debating, speaking wisdom. She must not lose that—lose who she was. To be sure, she was growing up, discovering who she was, forming her own opinions—but she had so little experience. She couldn't rely on herself quite as much as she thought she could.

And she herself couldn't see that. There was nothing he could say. He could only pray—pray that *Adon Olam* would guide her steps, pray that He would hold fast to her mind, pray that He would speak through her voice, pray that her choices would be His.

So pray he did. For protection, for wisdom, for power, for truth, for her, for the kingdom of *Adon Olam*—for himself.

It wasn't an hour later that he quietly yet firmly retraced his steps to the main room. His grandparents glanced up, smiles touching each of their faces at his changed demeanor.

"Looks like the enemy's lost." Grandfather nodded.

"*Adon Olam* told me to make disciples. I certainly don't feel like the right sort of chap for that, but He never said I had to be. I don't enjoy this job in the least, but He didn't promise I would. I go about everything wrong and make all sorts of mistakes, but He never asked for perfection. He just told me to do it. I'm going back to it. Now."

Grandmother glanced at the timepiece, but her smile didn't waver while she nodded. "Go, Caeleb. We'll keep battling it out for you here."

The wall lamp flickered, drawing up the last of its oil, as Caeleb listened to the words that flowed—sometimes hesitatingly, sometimes in a fountain—from the middle-aged man before him in a private office of the gathering hall. Caeleb had found him there, distraught and alone in the growing darkness, and for the past hour he'd simply listened, asking a question once or twice, but mainly listening—listening, and praying, from the depths of his heart. Compassion filled him, tingling from his forehead to his toes. If only *Adon Olam* would tonight reveal Himself as the Prince of Peace to this poor, struggling soul! If only his eyes could be opened now to the powerlessness of the enemy.

"There's no way in Taerna I can reconcile with

Lionel. He's past the point of fellowship for me. It breaks my heart, but I just can't tolerate this slander—this public injustice among the people of *Adon Olam*. There can be no overlooking such blatant hatred, such willful disregard of His work in my life. I just . . ." The man shook his head, language evidently failing him to express the vehemence of his feelings.

Caeleb swallowed. Again, Poe was only feeding the enemy and his lies. He was shutting the door in the face of the Spirit of *Adon Olam*. No, Lionel and Poe couldn't reconcile now, and Poe's insistence was making it a fact and a reality.

"Poe, I hear you. I understand where you stand, and I understand what Lionel is doing. I've been praying for both of you, and I will continue. I'm asking you now to pray—pray yourself—seek His face on your knees before you act. That's all. Pray. And search the Word yourself."

"Of course." The man rose, pivoting his hat from the hook to his head in one smooth motion. "I do hope you've advised Lionel the same. I cannot believe he's not believing the evident work of *Adon Olam*. But I apologize for my moping here when I ought to be out doing the work of *Adon Olam*. Without that scum, I hope."

His words died away with a knock at the door. "A pleasant night to you." Caeleb sighed. "I'll see to the door."

Wood scraped over the floor as Poe opened the back door and slipped into the dusk with a muttered "good night." Two other figures stepped inside the front door.

"Mr. Rohaea?"

"Yes. What can I do for you?" Caeleb rubbed a hand across his forehead, willing his eyes to appear open and alert. *Don't get weary in well doing, Caeleb.* He stifled a yawn and turned his attention towards the newcomers.

A man and a women stood before him. "Be seated, if

you please." Caeleb waved to the chairs, and in a rustle of dark cloaks, the pair sat. It was difficult to tell underneath the thick folds, but Caeleb thought he recognized the figures from one or another of the gatherings.

"A pleasant evening to you," the woman continued, brushing a long dark strand behind her ear as she claimed a chair with ease and professionalism. "My name is Maeve. We've been present at several of these gatherings. I understand that you oversee them generally in this area?"

"That is correct." Caeleb watched the pair, patiently waiting.

"We can't help but notice the unrest among your following here."

Caeleb nodded.

"As you may have noticed, we're foreigners. We're from Doekh. And, to be quite frank with you, we've felt shunned. Rejected. Unwelcome in your circles. In the Palace District, we receive warmth and acceptance—yet here in the Lower District, it's otherwise."

Again, Caeleb nodded.

"Can you explain this to me?"

Caeleb considered, then spoke. "Human nature tends to wrongly look down upon that which it perceives as different. The Word of *Adon Olam*, however, clearly makes no distinction between foreigner or native. We are all one in Yeshua."

The woman's critical gaze pierced him. "That is what you say. That is not what we observe. Does not the Word you preach also say to test every teacher by his fruit?"

The question lingered.

"Yes, it does," Caeleb agreed. "Yet sin is not a product of *Adon Olam* or His Word, but of the human heart, which is deceitful and desperately wicked."

"It's more than that." The man spoke for the first time, his dark hood rippling and settling over his black hair. "We've seen a rejection of progress, of improvement. We've seen resistance to scientific advancements and philosophical modernity—all stemming from this area. Farmers, middle-class citizens, religious fanatics. And we're here to ask why. What do you have against progress? Against bettering your country?"

"Nothing against progress or improvements, if they truly do improve." Caeleb answered in as few words as possible.

The man leaned forward. He hadn't yet introduced himself, Caeleb noticed. "Mr. Rohaea, I don't believe you understand the seriousness of this. You might think you are part of only a small group, that it won't affect the majority of the population or the success of the city as a whole. But I'm here to tell you that your efforts are more far-reaching than you could ever believe. I've seen what progress has done in Central Doekh; I've witnessed the profound differences in the quality of life there and here. And I must ask: what stands in the way?"

"True progress and advancement do not always look like it. Often it looks like regress: going back to the original ways of *Adon Olam*."

"And I'm quite worried that this is the issue here. Your people are reading ancient, outdated works and listening to the theories of hundreds of years ago. Is clinging to ancient ideas just for the sake of tradition healthy?"

"Of course not. But clinging to the Word of the One who created the world—the Master of eternity, who sees the past and the future just as the present—is true wisdom, though our limited perspective might not say so."

Maeve withdrew a volume from her bag. "We have some facts for you." She laid the book on the table before them, flipping to various charts and numbers as she spoke. "I'd like to point out the differences between Syorien and Central Doekh. You will see clearly written here the numbers of those who are in poverty, the number of those dependent on the kings as well as dependent entirely on imports, the number of crimes, the law enforcement standards, the reported levels of satisfaction. We have here the number of people who die young, as well as your chances of reaching the age you are now. We have educational numbers here, and, frankly, it's shocking. The upcoming generation will fare even worse than our current society."

For the next ten minutes, their language flowed, doling out figures and numbers and comparisons, backed with clear evidence in Maeve's book. Caeleb listened at first with a sinking heart—for no one could argue with these facts. He'd known all this for fifteen years or more—perhaps not the exact numbers, but he'd lived in this city his entire life. He'd experienced the very statistics his visitors laid out. He couldn't argue. He had nothing to say. Even as Maeve turned another page and began pointing out in detail how many children had died of starvation in Syorien already that year, Caeleb fixed his thoughts on *Adon Olam* in supplication, in prayer. He needed a heavenly perspective.

And then came the poison—the subtle hints, the looks, the gestures—sympathizing, helpful, concerned, eager to assist with whatever solution he would provide—yet slipping bits of lies straight from the invisible spiritual kingdom.

The book closed. Both visitors looked expectantly to him for his answer—no doubt awaiting his inevitable reluctant acceptance of their facts, and, before long, their methods.

His mind wanted to agree with them. They *were* right. The way of *Adon Olam* was slow, and so many continued to suffer within it. He couldn't help everyone at once. Wouldn't—oh, could it not—be better to join a larger force to lift the oppressing physical forces off the nation so that their attention could then turn to spiritual matters? He could be the messenger of *Adon Olam,* meeting physical needs and then introducing spiritual solutions. His audience would be that much wider . . .

But no. He could not join with the forces of darkness to bring the message of the light. *Woe unto them that put evil for good and good for evil . . . Agree with thine adversary quickly.* And then give him the *full* truth.

"*Adon Olam!*" He spoke aloud. "Reveal to me Your purpose, Your hand. Embolden me. Keep me strong in the calling You've given, even though I may not like it. I do not lay claim to any part of the forces of the enemy, and he has no place in my life. I am Yours. You live in me. I don't speak of myself. You speak in me. I say that You have finished Your work in these people, and I call upon You to reveal it. Make it seen in this physical realm. Silence the lies of the enemy . . ."

He trailed off. This wasn't exactly what *Adon Olam* was leading him to say right now. What should he say? Nothing to his visitors, that much he felt sure of. They sat still and puzzled.

The man opened his mouth. "You're an influence. You've got the power. Don't let it be hindered by your perceived obligations. The true moral duty is for the good of all the people. There's more to that than your small corner here. Wouldn't you like to use your position to actually impact people's lives? So you could see a difference, instead of this bad fruit you've been experiencing?"

"*Yes,*" whispered Caeleb's heart, but a stronger voice within him urged, "No."

Caeleb drew a deep breath, torn. Yet he knew now what *Adon Olam* wanted him to say, and he said it, even though it was the last thing he felt like doing just now.

"Thank You, *Adon Olam,* for Your victory and

power. Thank You that the battle is won. Thank You that You've put me in this position. Thank You that I'm nothing of myself and I can't make the right choices. Thank You that in You I'm a man of Your strength. Thank You that Your truth is revealed. Thank You that Your kingdom has come. Thank You that I'm in it. Thank You, thank You, thank You!"

As the words fell, he lost awareness of his companions. He spoke with his King; in the King's presence, all others were only witnesses.

When he finally moved, his two visitors' eyes were shifting repeatedly, slanting between each other and him as if they didn't quite know what to make of him.

The tiniest smile welled up within Caeleb's mouth, but his lip barely twitched. *Adon Olam* had this. The condition of the country, the hearts of these people—his own heart.

As one, the visitors stood. "We are going to leave you now," Maeve said as they stepped backwards.

Caeleb resisted the urge to nod. Nothing must take his focus off *Adon Olam*. The man glanced at Caeleb once, twice, three times, four times before following his colleague out the door. It shut. Caeleb breathed again.

Spinning to put his back to the door, he stared at the wall, exhaling, inhaling. The man would have begun all over had he seen the tiniest crack in Caeleb's prayers.

And yet the presence that lingered in the room wasn't that depressing aura that radiated from the man's dark cloak and hood. Something indefinable, something glorious, something triumphant—something that reminded him of the whiff of spring lilacs on Grandmother's old farm. Something peaceful: the kind of peace that brought to mind wiping off his sword and sheathing it. Infinite satisfaction. Messy satisfaction. Life. Victory.

16

AT THE TURNOFF to Caeleb's house, Ellisia drew up, catching her breath. Now was decision time. Should she warn Caeleb that Kaelan might be in danger? Or should she go home, hoping to get word to Kaelan later?

Rapidly she weighed her options. The uncle would be traveling and Jolyn would be covering for him back home. He'd said he had business for Ellisia—that business might involve traveling with him or covering for him with Jolyn—or possibly it would be entirely unrelated. Covering for him while he was gone *did* seem like a logical option, especially considering what he'd said about her abilities soon surpassing his own.

He'd likely keep her busy. She couldn't count on warning Kaelan herself unless she entirely deserted the team.

Carefully she weighed the alternatives. She could drop everything and race to Frydael to warn Kaelan. Or she could keep quiet and continue her responsibilities here, increasing her opportunities for the future.

The BookHall. Mastering words. Achieving the pinnacle of education. All these teetered on one side of her mind, towering over all else with the lofty brightness of her ambitions.

And on the other, her family. Kaelan. Her sister

Carita. Her own baby niece. Their *safety* could be at stake. The gravity of the unknown weighed upon her chest with a desperate internal clutching at something, anything, that might ensure their wellbeing. *Nothing* must happen to them—no matter what.

Yet she couldn't lose the BookHall opportunity. It would never come again—there was no doubt on that point. Her heart turned to lead at the mere thought of throwing away what lay before her. Desperation seeped through her. The choice was impossible.

No, she would *not* succumb to negative words or thoughts. She *would* get through this. She would find a way. Taking a deep breath, she thought carefully.

Traveling to Frydael on her own was out of the question. It would use up all her savings for the next Academy term. She'd lose her place in the class. Mae would probably replace her. And worst of all, even if she could manage to get there and back, her partnership with the Applied Physics team would be forever gone, and with it her chances for advancement.

Furthermore, what could she say to Kaelan and Carita? "I overheard your name whispered in a Syorien allaey"? Ridiculous. She still had the note, but it proved little—and what could Kaelan do on her information? Probably nothing except to distrust any black-cloaked stranger who might show up in town. What if Uncle K found out? Would she merely jeopardize her own safety along with Kaelan's?

No, all things considered, traveling to Frydael couldn't be managed just now.

That left Caeleb, and Ellisia turned her steps towards his home. She'd talk to him now before collecting her belongings at Mae's, notwithstanding her resolve to be wary around him.

She found him in the backyard, locking a shed door

behind him. His hands occupied, he lifted an elbow in greeting upon hearing her footsteps. She stopped behind him, waiting as he fiddled with the lock and finally turned towards her.

"Elli. What is it? How's life?"

"Great. Learning more than I'd ever have dreamed. Studies are going well."

"What is it you've been learning?" His voice was gentle.

She shrugged. "We have been studying various literature as well as literary philosophy. It's fascinating. One professor of mine, born in Doekh, has some interesting theories on the philosophical side that I've been researching. He wants me to focus more on that line."

"Indeed." Caeleb's smile flashed as he pocketed the keys in his hand. "What is it exactly he wants you to study?"

She turned suddenly, scanning the dark horizon, its buildings jutting up like the teeth of a saw against the starry background. "Caeleb. This isn't about me. We have a bigger issue here than my studies and what I'm learning." She bit her lip, wondering how to drop the subject on him, but glad that she had a valid reason to avoid his prying.

He just stared at her.

She dropped her voice, stepping towards him against her will. "Kaelan is in trouble, Caeleb. Big trouble. And I can't do anything about it. It'll have to be you."

"But—*what*?"

"Kaelan's in trouble. A man's headed for Frydael, maybe at this moment, maybe next week, I don't know. I don't know what he means to do, but he's going to shut Kaelan down. You know that means trouble."

"Elli, how do you know this?"

"Doesn't matter. The important thing is that I do

know it."

Caeleb stepped forward. "Listen. If I'm going to help you with whatever mess this might be, I need to know the details. What man? Who is he? How did you find out?"

Ellisia hesitated. She didn't want to give out more information than necessary, but she needed to do what she had to for Kaelan's sake. "I—actually don't know his name. He has dark hair, grey eyes, and a determined look about him. He's tall. Professional. Black cloak, hood, and boots, most of the time."

"And he's leaving . . . ?"

"I don't know when. 'As soon as practical,' and that was at least two weeks ago he said that. I don't think he's left yet—maybe not for a few days."

"You saw him?"

Ellisia nodded.

"Where?"

"On one of the streets between here and Academy."

"He's going to Frydael? What for? Does he have a plan? Does he know Kaelan?"

"All I know is that he has some skill in wordology. That's how I found out. He's planning to go to Frydael as soon as is practical, because he wants to put an end 'once and for all' to the 'madness' Kaelan began. And then 'further.' Someone's covering for him here, and he met with this person tonight to give the person the final details. Seriously, I think that's all I know."

Caeleb took another step. "Did you hear him say all of that?"

"Yes—no—some of it. Some of it was—written."

"Ellisia, this is serious. Does anyone else know about this?"

She shook her head, stepping backwards towards the road, hoping he wouldn't ask any further questions. She wasn't in the mood for answering. She needed him for this, but she wasn't about to go any further than she had to.

"Ellisia!"

She didn't turn around.

"Ellisia." His voice was gentle now. "Ellisia, I'd like to help you. I—I don't know what this is about. I'm worried for my friend—your brother-in-law, but I need to know as much as I can about the situation."

"I told you what I know." Her voice was muffled yet determined.

He waited.

After several long minutes of silence, Caeleb finally stepped to her side. "Then, thank you. It's handled. It's out of your hands. You may study with an easy mind. Think no more of it." His footsteps receded down the path towards the house. At the house door, he turned for a moment. "Good night, Ellisia."

She whirled around, her foot stepping towards him with her mouth opening to protest. She hadn't meant for that to happen! She'd only meant to get him concerned about Kaelan—enough to warn him—not lose Caeleb's ear or her control over the situation.

But Caeleb was gone. And she wasn't about to go running after him no matter what he had done. She'd delivered her message; it was his responsibility now.

She marched to Mae's, collected her clothing and books quietly in her room, and penned a note explaining and apologizing for her absence. Study with an easy mind. She would do that, at any rate.

Still, helplessness washed over her, mingled with undefined guilt. She wasn't doing much of anything to help her family—and in the hour of perhaps their greatest need. Why had Caeleb reacted so strongly? Ellisia swallowed, adding her textbook to her bag. If anything happened to Kaelan, the guilt would hound her, she knew. She'd told herself she wouldn't care as long as they and her ambitions were both safe, but she was afraid that wasn't quite true. And now Caeleb would be the hero, Caeleb would save them somehow, Caeleb would receive the credit and admiration for his quickness and shrewdness. No one would ever know she had anything to do with it.

And . . . she was associating freely with the one who plotted this terrible unknown against her kin.

But she'd made her choice, and she wasn't about to back down. Perhaps she could even use her knowledge here to foil Uncle K's scheme from within—whatever it might be. Determinedly scanning the room, she shouldered her bag and tiptoed down the stairs, pausing to leave the note on the table. At the doorway she sighed, set down her bag, and silently readied everything for the morning meal—that at least she owed Mae for leaving with no notice.

More and more the dreadful feeling nagged at her that she was sacrificing her family on the altar of her education.

Yet no—she'd weighed the situation; she could do nothing. It wasn't her fault; she didn't have the money. And the assistance she could provide to her family in the future with a completed education would far surpass anything she could do for them even now, even if she had the funds. It would be worth it in the end, when her family and her career both emerged unscathed.

An early morning followed an outrageously late

night, and Ellisia scarcely noticed the elegant surroundings of the room they'd given her at Uncle K's home. She carried a blurred impression of teal and cream and clean lines as she stopped outside his sitting room to gather her thoughts before entering. He'd requested her presence first thing this morning.

Drawing a breath in an attempt to clear the fogginess in her head, she rapped, waiting for his voice before entering.

"We have need of your services for an important task, girl." Uncle K faced her, setting down his papers to give her his complete attention. "A group from a dissenting faction meets this morning, and it is the prime opportunity for you to exercise your skills for bettering the populace."

"What would you have me do?" Ellisia asked. She cared little for his factions and causes and revolutions. She would play her part and have nothing more to do with it. She'd focus on the skills, the words, and the BookHall.

"Simply this." Uncle K scooped up a brown sheet of paper and fingered it. "Accompany us to the meeting and direct your thoughts and words towards a certain person we shall point out to you. Keep your thoughts focused strongly against the core of what said person believes. Use your techniques: mutter if you must, but unobtrusively. Make sure to keep logic at the forefront of your mind. Do not send him any form of well-wishes, not even mentally. Keep your mind open but hostile in a general yet overt way. We will do the rest."

"Very well. I can do that." Simple enough. "How long will this meeting be?"

"We don't know for sure. Perhaps a couple of hours, perhaps less, perhaps more. We will leave directly. Are you prepared for departure?"

"I can be in a very few moments," she replied. "I was

just wondering about Academy."

"Once the meeting is over, you are free to attend your classes. Meet in the front entry as soon as you can."

Morning sunlight lent houses and people alike a white-toned glow and cast long shadows behind Ellisia and Uncle K as they walked. The cobblestones in this part of the city joined together much more smoothly than those in the part of the city where Mae lived.

Ellisia's steps dragged more and more. Why was she so inexplicably tired these days? She hadn't been doing much more than usual—just studies and housework. She blinked and hurried to keep up with Uncle K. This wasn't a good day to get lost in the city alone.

By the time they arrived, everything blurred before Ellisia's vision. She moved as though in a daze. She heard herself speak, felt herself sit, and sensed that Uncle K sat closely beside her, but she did not take it in. Impressions of a dim crowd, warm lamp, and rough bench penetrated her consciousness.

She shook herself. She had to be ready to concentrate. Uncle K caught her eyes and directed her attention to a man near the front of the room. Ellisia sat up, willed away her sleepiness, and focused on the man.

The rest was relatively easy. She only had to keep her thoughts centered on that person. She willed opposition for him into her mind and directed it at him. At Uncle K's prodding, spoken words started flowing—barely in a whisper, not even loud enough for him to hear.

She hardly noticed when the man she was focused on moved around the room or spoke. She was vaguely aware of a low murmur of words—not loud, but strong and penetrating. The room seemed dark—and stuffy—but she ignored it. Her one focus was getting her task done, for then that BookHall position would be that much closer to her reality.

When Uncle K nudged her arm, she trailed him out of the building onto the streets, her steps following his until she recognized the Academy turn-off. It would be a long day of studying.

That day proved but a foretaste of the ensuing week. During the mornings, she attended Academy or read at the mansion; in the evening, Uncle K always requested her presence at some meeting, Hall, or event in town. She would go with him or Jolyn and direct words towards anyone they pointed out. Through these ordeals, her only interest was the experience of word influence that she gained.

Gradually, she began to notice that her words had a much more powerful effect than she had realized. Often as she spoke something, she would slowly detect similar signs in the mind, attitudes, or even actions of the person she focused on. What troubled her a little was that often when the person began speaking or acting on her words, he didn't repeat them just as she had said them; they were different somehow. Something seemed added or removed, yet she could not identify any particular change. They *were* her words—only they weren't.

One day, Uncle K gave Ellisia instructions to pack her belongings and be ready for a journey of a week or two in the morning. He had already spoken with the Academy on her behalf, and not only did the normal Academy-wide three-day holiday fall that week, but her instructors were perfectly amenable to Uncle K's request.

In the complacent manner quickly becoming habitual to her in her dealings with these people, she agreed. Uncle K gave her almost all she desired. He provided her with as many books as she cared to read; he oversaw her wordology experiments; he would get her a BookHall position. Under the circumstances, even Academy seemed slightly less important. After all, hours counted, and at

Academy, accounting and history, science and herbology, and more required yet dull studies occupied nearly as many hours as literature. Why spend her time there when she could spend all her time on books and words?

The afternoon rolled in foggy, and Ellisia's mind felt the same as she readied her pack for the journey. They'd be riding, Uncle K had said—he, Ellisia, Jolyn, and Maeve, the molecular scientist. Ellisia tried her best not to pack too much, but it was always so difficult to leave any of her well-beloved books behind. Why were books so weighty, anyway? Perhaps someday she could invent a lightweight book.

Dinner was in progress by the time she'd readied her simple bag and walked over to Mae's to give a brief explanation. Mae hadn't said much, but Jaeson had looked sober. Ellisia resolutely blocked his face from her memory, refusing to allow either guilt or duty to invade her heart. She couldn't help it if her teacher-employer was sending her elsewhere, could she? She'd ultimately come here for the studies, not to shoulder the responsibility of Jaeson's family struggles. It might be her room and board for the moment, yet she couldn't let even that stand in the way of her life's course. After all, if all turned out as it ought, Uncle K might well be her path forward regarding room and board.

Belatedly she thought again of Caeleb. She owed her opportunity to him; surely she owed him a personal notice of her absence. She slipped out the door and into the fog, wending her way to the home owned by Caeleb's grandparents.

After several moments' delay, the door opened to reveal Caeleb's father.

"Is—is Caeleb home?" Ellisia stammered. Words fled her command. She hadn't thought about how she would respond if someone else were to answer the door—but then, she'd never knocked on this door, either. Caeleb had always accompanied her here.

Caeleb's father shook his head. "He has not been here for some days. He didn't say when he'd be back. Would you care to leave a message for him?"

Her head shook in turn. "No, no message." Somehow she shrank from communicating her plans to this near-stranger, father or no. "I just wondered—I hoped to see him if he was home, but if he's not, that's quite all right."

"Very well," Caeleb's father replied. "I hope your day is blessed by *Adon Olam*." He bowed slightly, and she bowed in return.

"And—yours." Already her mind had flown far past Caeleb's front door or the man behind it.

Her footsteps turned for home, her thoughts a jumble. Caeleb was gone. Had he gone to Frydael? He must be at some unusual business, at any rate. Why hadn't he told her? "Worry about it no more," he'd said—or something along those lines. He'd make sure of it, too. Well, that was that. Hopefully she could wash her hands of the whole Kaelan business. Caeleb and Kaelan would be able to make plans for whatever might come, and she wouldn't have to worry her head over the matter.

She had no time to spend on it, anyway.

Adon Olam. His father's parting words echoed in her ear. It had been so long since she'd heard anyone use the familiar phrase. Nearly everyone in Frydael did, but here, very few even acknowledged *Adon Olam.*

Was her day blessed by *Adon Olam*?

But why would *Adon Olam* want to bless her day? What was she doing that He would see fit to bless? And why would He—the Master of the Universe, the One Whose Kingdom Extends Beyond the Horizon—even care to bless her day? That wasn't what a master would do. Masters would only wish blessings upon their servants insofar as it would benefit themselves—and surely she could be of no use to *Adon Olam*. The very word *bless* itself meant to kneel—to bow down, to prostrate one's self. Ellisia repeated the engrained and memorized definition in her head as her footsteps rhythmically crunched pebbles. Kneel. That was something a slave would do for a master, not something a master would ever do for a slave!

Ellisia sputtered, smothering a sudden laugh. The idea of *Adon Olam* kneeling to confer benefits upon her—blessing her day! It was preposterous! It was unheard of. It was a silly idea. Truly those who believed such a thing could hardly be termed other than "rather backwards" in their thinking.

But Carita believed it. She truly believed it. And so did Kaelan—and Ellrick—and many others Ellisia had known in Frydael. What logical reason could such well-meaning, intelligent, kind people have for adhering to such a line of thought? *Adon Olam*, at best, had to be a Being to control the people—to prevent them from wrong conduct. And Taerna certainly boasted more than its share of wrong conduct at present. The world could do with a bit more of *Adon Olam* in it. But not as much as some people claimed. As Uncle K had said, what good was a gift—or by extension an ability, a skill, a possession, a thought—if the person was barred from using it?

The balance, Ellisia decided as she avoided the crumbling cobblestones, had to be somewhere between the two. Too much *Adon Olam* limited. But too little *Adon Olam* encouraged lawlessness and crime. Just the right amount of Him would therefore be perfect. It wouldn't limit the exercising of truly good abilities, gifts, and skills, but it would put a check on bad ones. *Adon Olam* must be a rather benevolent Master—standing back from the good people in Taerna to let them use their abilities and perform their dreams while reining in the bad ones.

So thinking, Ellisia opened the door to Mae's home and trudged upstairs. As she lifted her packed bag from the floor to the table in her room, she realized that tonight the house stood strangely silent. No babies screamed. No one whimpered, gurgled, or yelled happily. No creaks shivered her attic walls to betray someone persistently walking a wakeful infant in an attempt to keep siblings asleep. One last evening in her room—she might as well take the opportunity, now that she was here, instead of hurrying back to the uncle's.

Instead of turning to her books, Ellisia practiced her word skills. Alone in her room, how limited her abilities seemed. She soon stole back out of the door and headed down to the sunset-lit streets where the fog had dissipated. There she amused herself by playing with the strength of the passersby—subtly stealing their volition to perform harmless tasks such as touching a certain fence post, peeling bark off of a tree, picking up a piece of trash from the road, or plucking one of the few flowers that grew in the ditches.

It was all very satisfying to Ellisia. To see before her own eyes the power of words proved incredible to her. Her imagination soared, dreaming of what she could do once she gained further knowledge and strength. Sometimes she tested out larger tasks, trying the power of her words. Over the past several days, she'd focused on honing her ability. Learning to choose her words with precision, to select just the right moment to slip her will into someone else's, she soon had the satisfaction of seeing her words enact whatever she spoke almost as soon as she had spoken it.

Her ambitions spiraled. Uncle K or not, she'd use her abilities to gain that position in the BookHall. Perhaps she could even use it to get through her studies more quickly.

While she wasn't entirely sure how speaking could accomplish non-physical tasks, no doubt it was only a matter of further learning. At some point, perhaps she could use her ability to protect her family.

All she really wanted was to work with words—and if that was now possible, it was the best thing that had ever happened to her.

17

THE GRAY-SPECKLED TAIL of Jolyn's mount disappeared beyond a ridge against the cloud-streaked horizon, and Ellisia's horse followed an instant after. Kraevyn slowed, keeping pace with Maeve. The woman had scarcely uttered a sound since they'd departed Syorien, and her face was set, her eyes fixed on some distant point.

Fine. So she wasn't even looking at him. What was her issue now?

"Is this about the girl?" Kraevyn shifted in the saddle.

Now Maeve certainly looked at him—but only for one long moment before turning her eyes back to the ridge ahead. "What?"

"What's irritating you?"

"Nothing."

Kraevyn nudged his steed as hers began to edge ahead. "You're deep in thought."

"Yes."

"And?"

"Working out the possibilities if things don't go as smoothly on this little journey as you seem to expect."

"Maeve, you know I've gone over this for months now. I've prepared for every possible risk. *You've* prepared a backup to my backup plans. Words work; we've tested this; we know how to manage the science. It isn't new anymore."

"Who are you trying to convince, yourself?" Her voice lent a knifed edge to the words. "*I* know the science. You know your inventions. And you *say* you know this stranger we're carting along."

"I know quite enough of her, at any rate. You certainly could have improved the opportunity the last few months to cultivate her acquaintance, should you have cared to do so—or should you have distrusted my judgment so highly." He strove to keep his tones level, though he had no intention of arguing with her for the entire journey. He hadn't earned the position of overseer of Syorien's Applied Physics Team by fruitless disagreements.

"I had no idea you'd take her this far so quickly. She has months to our many years—our entire lifetime."

"And there is just where you are mistaken. She also has a lifetime of relevant experience and skill. To be sure, she is young yet, and her experience is at an entirely different level from our own. But to watch her! To hear her! Honestly, I wouldn't have been ready for this trip for months more at least had I not discovered her. She has some grasp upon words that even I cannot yet attain. Words move for me; they leap for her."

"Erg." Maeve grunted, facing stubbornly forward.

"I can experience words through my instruments; I begin to wonder if she even needs instruments. She has a keen eye and the most sensitive ear I've encountered or heard of in the four countries. And her mind's open to work with it. She's a jewel. A girl in the right place at the right time."

"For you."

"Of course. I'm a man in the right place at the right time." Kraevyn laughed, not caring what pardonable pride he might allow on display.

"No one's that perfect," Maeve argued still. "Where

is the thorn in this rose of yours? Where's the weakness of this jewel? And when will the rod of power you wield prove to be a serpent that turns and bites your hand?"

Another laugh, so long and loud this time that Jolyn, ahead, turned around to stare at him a moment. "Never, I hope and trust, my Maeve. I'm not merely plucking an unknown serpent for my task. No, I've trained her myself. I've given her the tools and knowledge to access and use the poison. She could use words to my disadvantage, but I'm still the teacher and she only the pupil. I am well equipped to match her should that unlikely circumstance occur. But why should it? She's been the most amenable little thing. She aspires to the BookHall, and she loves words for their own sake. She'll do anything for either, and I can offer her both. No, what weakness she may have is not in this direction. Of that I am confident."

"If you are right, I am glad enough to secure her assistance on this journey. She's the mouthpiece we need to retain our own positions while simultaneously ingratiating our cause in the favor of the Taernans."

"Undoubtedly. You don't know the influence and strength we have by taking the girls, both girls. Especially her. A word from her, and the whole city—well, there's no telling what all the city might do once her message penetrates."

Kraevyn's words died away, and in a few moments his horse overtook the lagging steps of the girls' mounts. It was time to think of a noonday stop. The destination still lay several days ahead at this rate.

18

THE JOURNEY WAS monotonous. In Ellisia's mind the only proper word was "jolting." Her saddle was certainly not the most relaxing seat she'd ever had, and before two hours had passed, she wished herself back at Academy in her own comfortable chair.

Other than the general discomfort, however, she had little to complain about. The ride might be dull enough, but the discovery that she could read while riding distracted her. Directing the horse was unnecessary, and, though potholes and slopes rendered the pages difficult to decipher, she could read with tolerable ease—although proper studying remained out of question.

As the shadows lengthened in the afternoon of—was it the third day, or the fourth now?—Ellisia jerked to attention when Uncle K spurred his horse to ride ahead of the girls. Ellisia blinked—once, twice. Surely the town before her was Frydael! It couldn't be! But she could not doubt the evidence of her senses regarding the town she'd been born and raised in. Her eyes locked on building after building, one following the other with that slight shock of one who expects to see wholly unfamiliar territory and instead finds the mind placing every detail with such easy precision that everything requires a second look and a third, familiar and unfamiliar clashing so sharply that even one's own front door seems suspect for a moment. The

Mercantile ... the mostly unused Halls ... the meeting place ... house after house belonging to neighbors and friends. There was no mistaking it; this was Frydael.

But surely even that wasn't terribly surprising. She'd known that Uncle K would travel to Frydael at one point or another. She'd expected him to have done so already. The nagging at her heart began. Why had he brought *her* along? And Jolyn?

Jolyn. Jolyn was supposed to be "covering" for Uncle K back home while Uncle K traveled to Frydael. Why was Jolyn here now? Could she dare to hope that this wasn't the journey they'd spoken of in the note?

But how could she hope? Why else would he travel to such an out-of-the-way town?

Terror gripped her chest. What was she expected to do? Something with words, she had no doubt. But what? Suddenly this no longer seemed like simply a harmless alliance. That which was a matter of indifference to her in a foreign city loomed dark and foreboding in her own town. What if Uncle K pitted her skills against Kaelan? She couldn't turn against her own brother-in-law.

Her eyes darted here and there. She was close to home now—a curse in her present circumstances, but it still could also prove a blessing. If trouble struck, she could ask Carita for help or advice. Kaelan would protect her personally if it came to that. Would Uncle K allow her free time—long enough to visit home without scrutiny? And what would the homefolks say to her visiting so unexpectedly now? She couldn't explain everything to them, not now.

Just so long as she didn't have to visit home in a way she didn't want to ...

As they rounded the square and entered Market Street, Ellisia stiffened on her horse. A familiar figure stood in the road before her, her hand resting against a corner of a building. A basket swung from the other hand, and her face lifted curiously towards the party of travelers.

It was Laelara. Ellisia knew it even before her eyes reached Laelara's face. She could almost feel Laelara's feelings, think her thoughts. It wasn't often that a party of travelers on horseback clattered through town; Ellisia would be observing the group, too, if she were in Laelara's place.

Ellisia slumped in the saddle. O to avoid recognition! What would their family think of seeing her here now? Had Caeleb arrived? Powerlessness surged through her. She needed information.

She averted her eyes and tried to pull her cloak over her face. But Laelara's eyes were already on her, and she knew her bright red curls hadn't escaped recognition.

For one step, Laelara started forward, as though she would speak to Ellisia. Then she seemed to see Ellisia's companions. She fell back to lean against the side of the building and merely scowled in Ellisia's general direction as she passed. Ellisia tried to avoid meeting those piercing brown eyes, but she couldn't help but sneak a tiny glance at Laelara as she passed. By that set of her eyebrows, Laelara was not thrilled to see her. But then, the two of them had never been particularly close friends. They were always at odds with one another.

Then the horses had turned onto Beacon Road and were stopping in front of the inn.

The idea of staying in an inn in her own hometown!

But she smothered her thoughts and slid off the horse, wincing as she did so. She hoped to the West Taernan Hills that she wouldn't have to climb back on this steed in a hurry.

Stiffly she followed the others into the inn, not caring who saw her in her present condition. Oh, for a hot bath to wash away the aches from her legs! But such luxuries had never reached the simple Frydael inn.

She trailed behind the others as Uncle K ordered their rooms. The innkeeper wouldn't glimpse her tell-tale curls if she kept her cloak well pulled up until she'd safely disappeared in her second-floor room.

Mercifully, Uncle K reserved separate rooms for each person. Once behind her closed door—which she tried twice to make sure it was locked from the inside and not from the outside—she immediately went to bed. She needed to sort this situation out, and she could best do that with a full reserve of energy.

Morning would come too soon.

She arose even before the birds on the two lone trees outside her window began their chirping. A sensation of knowing lodged within her heart, enmeshing itself deeper each moment into the furrows of her consciousness, yielding unanticipated peace. Proactivity. Here there could be no playing along or pretending she didn't know or care what game it was. She'd have to anticipate, to place her tokens well, to provide for every contingency. Uncle K might possess the plan, but she held one of his figurative keys. She held the power to run the game her way, and she'd try her best without letting on to him. That much was certain.

The sun hadn't crossed the horizon when she quietly stole down the stairs. With her cloak wrapped snugly around her face, she wandered out to the road.

Unlike the streets of Syorien, every path in Frydael had long-since traced its duplicate on her mental map. She knew exactly where she was going, and she knew exactly how to best get there without being detected—though at this hour, detection concerned her but little.

Once away from the town and striding past the country homes, she loosened her cloak a bit. Considering how far these houses stood from the road, few would see or recognize her. The spring air hadn't warmed yet, but it wasn't quite cool enough to need the extra warmth a tightly-fastened cloak provided.

And then she was at her own front door—the door of the home she'd lived in all her life. With only a few rooms rebuilt since the fire, much of the house remained unchanged. Upon Carita's marriage to Kaelan a few years ago, Kaelan had joined Carita in the sisters' own home, and Ellisia's life had continued almost unchanged until—that visit from Caeleb.

She halted on the tiny porch, hesitating. Sometimes in those years since the marriage, she'd felt out of place—as though Carita needed solitude with Kaelan. At those times, Ellisia had retreated even more heavily than usual into her books and studies, trying her best not to intrude on Carita's home life. She'd wished she could live elsewhere, but she was too young to set out on her own, and Carita wouldn't have heard of it even if age wasn't a factor.

Ellisia smiled. Caeleb's offer had certainly solved those difficulties for her rapidly. Her hand drooped, trembling over the scratched and dented door frame. The offer had, however, created a host of new difficulties that she'd never thought she'd have to deal with.

She knocked. How strange to knock on the door of her own home, but Carita wasn't expecting her. Ellisia didn't want to upset her or scare her. The corner of her mouth quirked. As if Carita were easily scared.

The door flung open and Carita herself stood on the doorstep, her little daughter resting on her hip. "Ellisia!" The next moment both sisters and the baby were nearly smothered in an enthusiastic embrace.

Ellisia tensed and her gaze flicked back to the door frame. Carita, crushing her in hugs?

"Is Kaelan home?" Ellisia asked the moment she broke away from the embrace. No time must be wasted on formalities. At any moment, Uncle K or one of the others might miss her.

"Yes, he hasn't gone anywhere yet today." Carita's eye

twitched as puzzlement passed over her features.

"Is Caeleb here?"

"Not that I'm aware of." Carita's voice lifted slightly on the final syllable.

Ellisia hesitated. Now what? She'd fully expected Caeleb to have arrived days ago. "He hasn't visited recently? Kaelan hasn't heard from him?"

"I don't think so. Is there trouble? Why are you back here in Frydael now? We didn't expect . . ."

"I have a job—we came here on business. I didn't know either that this would be our destination." Ellisia glanced over her shoulder to the empty street behind her.

Carita stepped aside, allowing Ellisia to enter. "I can't stay long—not this time. I'll be missed," Ellisia murmured. "But I had to tell you. Kaelan's in danger."

"Danger? How?" Only the twitch of Carita's lips betrayed her inner fear, for the tones remained perfectly level.

"I—I'm not sure how much I can explain . . ." Ellisia's words forsook her. "I'm a bit confused myself. But there's a man who wishes to shut him down, and I believe he has the power to do so if he wishes."

"From the kings?"

"No . . . it's complicated." Ellisia sighed. "I can't explain it now. Some time I will. It's more subtle than that. More scientific. I don't think it's his life in danger as much as his work—his message. And yet . . ." She couldn't help but remember afresh the choke of fear she'd felt as she read the note. Shut him down. Silence him. For good this time. "Warn him," she whispered. "I must go—I can't stay now—I'll return later if I can."

Carita's eyes locked with hers for a long moment. Ellisia shifted uncomfortably, wondering how much of her mind Carita could read. At last, Carita spoke. "This is your home, Ellisia. You're always welcome here as long as you can stay."

Ellisia nodded, her gaze fixed on the baby, whose tiny

fingers played with the embroidery on Carita's shoulder seam. If only she could stay longer just to hold her niece. "I shall try. For now, I'm at the inn, but don't seek me out. I'll come when I can. Just . . . warn Kaelan. Beware deceit." She swallowed, backing towards the door. One more glance, then she was jogging back down the road towards Frydael.

She ran until she reached the outskirts of the town, then she slowed to a brisk walk more in keeping with her station. She pulled her cloak tightly around herself again. Truly, she had wanted to speak with Carita—to ask her advice, to tell her about herself and her own position, to inquire what she ought to do. But there was no time—and Kaelan's safety was more immediately important.

Once she'd reinstated herself in her room at the inn, barely five minutes elapsed before a knock interrupted her.

"Who is there?"

"Time to go!" Uncle K's voice called.

After his footsteps retreated, she opened the door and crossed the hall to the open area at the end where a bench lined a wall and a window looked out over the town. Ellisia slid onto the bench, leaned against the wall, and let her gaze drift over the shops and homes across the street. A speck of purple lay in the ditch across the street—a stray spring blossom? A forgotten apple rested in the walkway, dusty and forlorn. The grey paint on the sign across the way was so worn and faded that Ellisia could scarcely make out the letters.

A door slammed. Jolyn approached. Moments later, both Maeve and Uncle K joined them. "Come. We have much to do."

Down the steps they trudged, the older ones chatting in low tones. Ellisia trailed behind, feeling quite out of place. She caught words every now and then. ". . .trouble in town here. More than we knew. That fellow isn't behind it all either. It's rampant all over the neighborhood.

The matter of those three boys . . ." His words trailed off.

Ellisia stepped forward after him even more quickly, trying to remain directly behind him so as to overhear his conversation. How could the man speak so quietly?

"It'll take a while. We'll have to be alert. And take our time. It will take longer than we previously thought. But at least we are here . . ."

The meeting-house. Ellisia had forgotten. Strange flashbacks filled her senses as she followed the others inside—everything was so familiar, yet so wrong. How often had she unthinkingly entered a meeting-place similar to this one in Syorien over the last several weeks? How often had she sat mindlessly where Uncle K dictated, directing her thoughts and words in whatever direction he instructed towards whatever person he pointed out, herself heedless as to the target or any consequences? And how often had she entered this very meeting-house with Carita—ever since her own childhood? How often had she sat with her attention fixed on a neighbor or friend who spoke of *Adon Olam* or read from His Book? How often had she and Dresie played behind the chairs once the meeting had finished? She knew where the walls joined unevenly; she could glide directly to the Y-shaped crack in the plaster that was just large enough to hold a tiny note; she knew which chairs to avoid due to the unevenness of the floor below. Forty-seven beams on the ceiling, four hundred and seventy-six nails in the front wall; and one pink stain three-quarters of the way up the left side of the floor where Mrs. Totaen had once spilled acai juice.

All her senses heightened as she slid along the wall next to Jolyn. She couldn't do this—not here. She'd never be able to focus her thoughts long enough. What did Uncle K want of her?

Protect Kaelan. Her brother-in-law. Carita's husband. Elanor's father.

She seized onto the single idea, concentrating hard.

Whatever the uncle wanted, she'd keep her own personal mission in the front of her mind. Under the circumstances, she was better here than elsewhere.

"Listen. Observe. Learn." The single whispered instruction from the uncle reached Ellisia's ears, breaking into her thoughts. She met his eyes and nodded once before quickly averting her gaze. Certainly she'd listen, observe, and learn. No problem there.

People filed in. Ellisia pulled her cloak further over her head. *No one* must recognize her or speak to her now. She knew several of her neighbors would speak to the newcomers—they always did. If only she could escape recognition, just this once . . .

She tucked every curl inside her cloak, for once not caring how warm she was. She kept her eyes down and her cloak over as much of her face as she dared. Thankfully, Uncle K and Maeve handled speaking with everyone who stopped to greet them, and by the time the meeting began, no one paid any attention to her.

Readings, prayers, songs, stories from the community: familiar it certainly was, yet somehow time, distance, and experience had introduced a strangeness—a distantness, an undefinable feeling of not quite belonging. Home was the same as ever, but Ellisia was not. She'd changed, she'd expanded, she'd grown, and she didn't quite fit here anymore. What if the people here knew about the power of words the way she did? What if people here understood the entirely unknown world of science and philosophy and their impact on the mind?

No. They wouldn't understand. They'd reject it as "science falsely so called." They'd warn her of the dangers of mingling too much with the philosophies of the world. They might even denounce her pursuits as dabbling in the world of witchcraft. And they, in their simple lifestyle coupled with their simple devotion to *Adon Olam, would* be perfectly content with their simple mindset—if only those such as Uncle K weren't in the picture. They wouldn't have a prayer against him. Or rather, prayer was all they'd have against him.

19

"I SUPPOSE YOU'VE been wondering what your task here involves, my girl." Uncle K seated himself on one of the straight-backed wooden chairs in the small meeting-room adjoining the bedrooms of the inn.

Ellisia nodded. "No doubt quite important, to bring us all the way out here."

"Indeed. Of utmost importance. It is also of utmost secrecy, and before I divulge the details, I must have your promise that they will not pass your lips in any respect without my express permission."

"I understand that." Ellisia swallowed. "However, as I am your mouthpiece, would it not be better for me to remain ignorant of the details? I cannot absolutely promise what may or may not pass my lips in the midst of any heated persuasion."

A beat followed, then another, then a third. Ellisia counted them carefully. She couldn't promise, but telling him why was out of the question. He had to agree with her reasoning.

"There is something to that," he admitted. "I will withhold full details, then, but surely you must know what we are doing. I've already impressed on you the need for total secrecy. If our mission here fails, our work in Syorien will be undermined, and I can't promise what will happen to my lab or your ambitions if I'm forced back to my home country."

"Understood."

The thud of horse hooves drifted through the open window and stopped below. Uncle K's words trailed off as he crossed the room to peer outside. "Ryna?" he breathed. "You're supposed to be holding it all together for me . . ." The whisper died away.

Ellisia leaned towards the window. A tall girl with long black hair sat astride her gray mount—a girl Ellisia recognized both from the Academy steps and from Uncle K's dinner table back in Syorien. Perhaps Jolyn had passed to her the task of keeping Syorien's research running, but that didn't explain why Jolyn was needed here—nor why this girl was here now. Pursing her lips, Ellisia glanced from Ryna to Uncle K. The lift of his eyebrow, the slight crease above, the set of his lip—he wasn't expecting her, that was plain. She leaned back, awaiting developments.

The door opened. Ryna entered, disheveled clothing and hair betokening a speedy ride.

"There's trouble."

"You rode after us so quickly?"

"I've been riding most of the night. It's urgent." For the first time, Ryna's eyes fell on Ellisia and immediately darkened.

Uncle K inclined his head in Ellisia's direction. "We will talk later."

Ellisia nodded and wordlessly exited. Trouble. What could that mean for her?

Back in her room, books beckoned. It seemed only moments before a summons to the meeting room arrived, but a quick glance at the timepiece revealed that it had been a half an hour.

"I have just received urgent news from home. I must return immediately." Uncle K's gaze encompassed all three girls and Maeve.

Ellisia stole a peek at Jolyn, and Jolyn glanced back. Evidently she had no more idea of this than Ellisia had.

"Our business here is important, but I have no time to attend to it now. I will return as soon as I can. It is best for the present that you, Ellisia and Ryna, remain here at the inn. I have arranged it. I must travel rapidly and will return so soon that it is not worthwhile for you to make the long journey back home and then here again. Jolaena and Maeve, I will need you to accompany me. If any developments occur that prevent my immediate return or necessitate you joining me, Jolyn will carry the message."

"What about Academy?" Ellisia's voice was more of a squeak than she meant it to be.

"Never fear; I shall arrange for that. You will not lose your place; that I assure you."

Satisfied, Ellisia nodded. She didn't want to gallop all the way back to Syorien anyway just now. It would take her a week just to recover from the first trip.

"Any other questions? I must leave directly." He paced across the room and back again.

Ellisia and Ryna both shook their heads, and Ellisia glanced towards Ryna just in time to exchange a curious look with her. For the first time, a spark of understanding flashed between them. Both were left out of something—both were being set aside.

Ryna folded her arms and stared at Uncle K. Ellisia pulled her eyes from the girl and glanced at Jolyn. She seemed as calm, cool, collected, and disinterested as always.

Ellisia huffed and pushed herself to her feet. "We will see you later, then. And we will wish that your journey and business goes as it ought." That was a safe goodbye, at least. "As it ought" might not be what he thought it meant. Or what she thought, either, for that matter, but what did she care? He was leaving. She was free—for the present.

Visiting Carita wouldn't be a problem now. All she had to do now was to wait for Uncle K to leave and she could do what she liked.

She was vaguely aware when the others departed, but hours passed before she wearily tore her gaze from the pages of her book. Hunger assailed her. She'd forgotten to ask how they expected her to take meals in their absence.

Downstairs in the dining room, she accosted the innkeeper. "Excuse me. Do you know the meal arrangements for the group staying upstairs?"

The innkeeper looked over his wire-rimmed spectacles at the girl. She shrunk back, wary of such observation. He would recognize her, given the chance. "If you pay for the board-and-meals package, meals can be taken here. Otherwise, you may purchase them separately."

"I'm with the group that came in the other night—Maeve ... Jolyn ..." Ellisia modulated her voice to hide her natural tones.

"Maeve ..." He flipped records. "Kraevyn?"

Uncle K ... that must be his name. *Kraevyn.* She repeated it twice over. Not the sort of name she'd expected of him. "Yes," she muttered.

"Oh, you have the full package." The innkeeper lifted a hand-spun cup to sip a steaming beverage. "Eat. Enjoy. Let me know if you need anything."

"I will."

She retreated to the farthest corner and sank into a chair. Moments later, a grinning boy brought her a plate of food and an earthen hand-spun mug full of something spicy and sweet she'd never tasted before.

She quirked the corner of her mouth as he retreated. Never in her seventeen years of living in Frydael had she taken a meal at the inn. Yet, under these circumstances, why not? Uncle K—Kraevyn—had paid; she might as well eat.

Kraevyn. In all this time, why had he never told her

his name? Something foreign intermingled with the accented syllables. A Doekhan name, assuredly.

After the meal, she slipped out onto the streets. How she would love to stroll through town, taking in all the old sights and perhaps speaking with some of the townsfolk, but she didn't dare. Her position here remained too precarious for her to be able to announce herself openly.

Instead, she traced her path back home. Home! She'd never dreamed that she'd be returning home under these circumstances. She wasn't just an Academy student on holiday now; she was caught up in the midst of—of what? Something strange, something mysterious, the implications of which she didn't even know herself. Her family was in danger. And she herself possessed skills that she'd never known about while living her quiet childhood here.

Yes, she was home, but home was not the same. Or rather, it was *too* much the same. As she passed through town, faces were visible through windows. Passersby called out greetings to one another. The rough wooden walks spurted dust clouds as they did every spring. The window of the Mercantile displayed the usual array of merchandise for the season: washboards, garden trowels, aprons, new shoes, plow blades, and the like. Yes, everything was precisely the same as ever—only she had changed.

Knocking on the door wasn't so unusual this time. Carita opened it even more rapidly than she had that morning. Evident relief shone on her face upon seeing Ellisia. "Is all well?" she asked.

"Well," Ellisia replied. "Evidently the trouble I spoke of has been postponed. I think. Anyway, I'm here now, and I can stay. For a time, at least."

"Come in." Carita stepped out of the way and motioned Ellisia into the main room.

Ellisia entered and collapsed into a chair. "Apologies. My legs haven't recovered from horseback yet."

"I can imagine not." Carita smiled as she rearranged a blanket on a chair and sat down with Ellisia. "What is going on? How is Academy? Are you learning a lot?"

"More than you know." Ellisia drew in a long breath, stretching out her legs and massaging her hands down her calves. "Academy's fine. Everything's fine. I mean . . . except . . ."

"Ellisia, what is it?"

"I just happened to come across a—" Ellisia looked around carefully before lowering her voice, "—a note. Threatening harm to Kaelan. I imagine perhaps for his work in Syorien years ago, and maybe his present work. And they were here—but they've gone back now. For the present."

"Praise *Adon Olam*. We prayed that He would send them away from us." Carita's words were simple, but her eyes closed in infinite trust, joy, and hope. Ellisia knew what she meant. When Carita prayed, *Adon Olam* worked.

Yet Ellisia sat back, not sure she was in the mood for *Adon Olam* prayer talk at the moment. "They promised to give me a position at the Palace BookHall." A wave of longing swept up from her heart—she missed the long rows of books, the scent of paper and ink, the quiet hours hidden away alone among the rows. Did homesickness exist for places other than home?

"Who?" Carita's eyes flew open.

"A man . . . a teacher . . ." Her heart raced and heat warmed her cheeks. What would Carita think? How could Ellisia explain it to Carita's satisfaction and understanding? She certainly didn't want a similar reaction to the one that she imagined Caeleb would give her.

"How does this man have access to the Palace Book-Hall?" Carita asked.

"I'm not sure exactly, but I know he knows the right people and has the right influence. He was quite confident in his promise, though—I'm certain he meant it."

"What did he ask for in return?" Carita asked quietly.

Her heartbeat seemed loud in her chest. Seven surges

suffused her ears in crimson as she hesitated. "Just a bit of my services," she said at last.

"What kind of services?"

Again Ellisia was silent.

"You do not have to tell me if you'd rather not," Carita said at last. "But I *am* interested in what's going on in your life, if you choose to tell me."

Ellisia sat silently. She wanted to confide in Carita, but she didn't want Carita to think ill of her. After a moment she began describing the situation in a subdued tone.

"I found a note—Jolyn—I tried to overhear a conversation—it didn't work—they are friendly—I think—and he promised a place at the BookHall if only I'd help him. Persuade people—words—they're using them—or I'm using them, and they are . . . oh, I don't know what it's all about! I only know that if I cooperate, they'll get me that position."

"And why do you want that position?" Carita's voice was even.

"Why? It's books! Living with books, working with books, reading them, knowing them—it's all there. And I wouldn't have to—" She halted abruptly, not wanting to admit her dislike of helping Mae and the babies. "They would pay me," she finished lamely.

Carita rocked back and forth slightly in her chair, still emitting an aura of perfect relaxation.

Three times the rocker tilted backwards. "What kinds of things are you learning in Syorien?"

She shrugged. "Books. Words. Mind." How could she explain this?

"Words and the mind," Carita repeated. "Words. Such power, words are."

"Yes?"

"When your mind and your words are under the power of *Adon Olam*," Carita stated slowly, "you have more authority than you can imagine."

Ellisia bit her lip. She nodded slowly. "The mind holds

power."

"As it is in subjection to *Adon Olam*, yes," Carita agreed simply.

How could she respond? She needed to tread lightly in this conversation.

"Don't you think it has authority in itself—willpower, or something of that sort?"

"The Son of *Adon Olam* said, '*All* authority is given to me in heaven and earth; you go into all the world and make disciples of all peoples.' If it is all His, how can it be ours?"

Ellisia didn't respond.

"Only as we are in Him," Carita answered her own question softly.

"But the mind ... He gave us our mind," Ellisia protested.

"'Be not conformed to this world, but be transformed by the renewing of your mind,'" Carita quoted.

"Yes—and renewing our mind is a process, and we can learn to do that more effectively and precisely."

"True—by letting Him do that in us."

"It *is* our mind, though. We have control over our thoughts and decisions." Ellisia pressed her fists together. Why was it so difficult to express herself today?

"'Let this mind be in you, which was also in Christ Jesus.'" Carita rose in response to a whimper from upstairs. "Just a moment."

While Carita was gone, Ellisia concentrated, trying to recall what she had been taught. She focused, using her mental willpower. Could she pick up the book that lay on the shelf without moving her hands first?

She could. In a moment it was in her hands, and the quiet words she'd spoken—a bit self-consciously in the empty room—left their aftertaste in the air. A grin overtook her lips. She'd come so far in the last weeks. She could make words work for her. She'd have to think of the perfect way to use them on Carita and convince her that there was something wonderful in all this.

In a few moments, Carita emerged, carrying a smiling baby on her arm. The baby made happy coos in Ellisia's direction and waved a tiny fist at her.

Ellisia grinned.

"I am pleased to hear that you are learning about the mind, Ellisia," Carita said. "I pray that through it, *Adon Olam* will teach you His ways and give you His mind. For we have the mind of the Son of *Adon Olam*."

Ellisia let a slight bit of a pout appear on her face. "We have our own minds," she maintained, but not loudly. She didn't want to argue the question with Carita. "Otherwise why would everyone have such different minds? You and I are sisters, and we don't even agree. And some people hardly have any intelligence at all. We can't all have the mind of His Son or we all wouldn't think so differently."

A smile appeared at the corners of Carita's mouth. "It is a mystery. Nevertheless, what His Book says is true."

Ellisia shrugged. "Maybe. But we do have our own practical lives to worry about."

Carita's voice was almost a murmur as she sank back into the rocking chair and bounced the baby on her lap. "'Take no thought for your life.'"

"That's ridiculous!" Ellisia could no longer contain her indignation. On top of everything else, Carita couldn't even speak in her own words today. "That's not literal. If we didn't take thought for our life, we would go hungry. We'd freeze. We'd die. We'd be a mess. We have to take thought. It's common sense. It's daily life."

Carita made no answer, which infuriated Ellisia even more. However, she determined to control the course of this conversation. Her emotions wouldn't get the better of her mind. Not this time. Not in front of Carita.

A thought struck her. If her words were so powerful, then why couldn't she make them have any power over Carita? Why did everything she said seem to fall to the ground with no impact on her sister? Perhaps she wasn't concentrating carefully enough.

Focusing deliberately, she spoke slowly and as calmly as she could manage. "Carita, believe that the mind is important."

Carita's eyes snagged on Ellisia's in shock. For a moment a hint of fear glowed, but immediately it was veiled by the same calm confidence that was her wont.

"I can control my mind," Ellisia continued. "I can control you."

She desperately wanted to make Carita physically do something, but she didn't dare with the baby on her sister's lap. Even though she had a fairly good grasp of her own abilities, she didn't trust them yet to do exactly what she wished every time.

Concentrating hard, she let words tumble out of her mouth. At first, she was shocked. She didn't even understand the words, but she could instinctively feel that they matched her thoughts.

Ah! This would work! Now she could speak her thoughts and the other person wouldn't be able to know what she was saying or what was happening! Boldly she continued, bringing forward in her mind all her strongest arguments for the power of words and her methods. She started explaining what Uncle K had done, surprising even herself with her interpretation of his words. She kept her eyes locked on Carita.

Carita's gaze hadn't wavered. Ellisia felt Carita staring deeply into her eyes, but she fought off the urge to consciously look, as it would only distract her.

Suddenly Carita tore her eyes away. "*Adon Olam!*" she cried.

Ellisia started at the suddenness and volume of the cry, and her words ground to a halt.

"I am in the name of Your Son Yeshua! The evil one has no place here! Remove the power of the enemy that seeks to destroy and corrupt all that it touches. Bring down his schemes. Deliver us from evil! Enemy! This home belongs to *Adon Olam*, and you have no place here. It isn't yours. Get out!"

She ceased speaking, and Ellisia sank back down into the chair that she had risen from when she first began concentrating. Her focus lay broken. She could hardly breathe, let alone think. Why was she shaking? She'd heard Carita pray many times before.

From somewhere, the baby whimpered, and Carita rose, shushing her. Ellisia sank her head down and buried it in her hands. She hoped Carita would not speak to her. Her stomach twisted as her face flushed in embarrassment—not about herself or her own efforts, but because of Carita's behavior. Since when did a woman shriek out like that in the middle of a polite conversation? It sounded insane, but Ellisia knew her sister was far from insane. If only she could have reached her mind . . . it had been going so well for a moment. So well. And then this.

The bouncing beside her ceased and Ellisia could feel Carita taking a step closer to her. A soft hand caressed her shoulder—kind and gentle—but the words were serious. "Ellisia. You are my joy and delight. Please don't meddle in things that are too high for you."

A rebellious feeling stirred in Ellisia's heart. "Nothing is too high for me. I'm going upward."

"Oh, do beware, Ellisia. Those are the very words that the wicked one said before he was cast out from before the presence of *Adon Olam.*" She paused. "Ellisia, I need to warn you. I love you. I'm your sister. I've lived with you all of your life until now. I've tried to take care of you, but now you're growing up and you can make your own choices. I've tried to teach you the ways of *Adon Olam*, but perhaps I haven't always done the best job of it." She sighed, and the hand pulled away from Ellisia's shoulder. Ellisia lifted her head a bit to see the hand stroking the dark hair of the child in her arms. "*Adon Olam,* be with me." Ellisia barely caught the whisper.

Carita continued. "You speak of the power of the

mind." Her eyes searched Ellisia's face.

Ellisia threw her head back and leaned against the chair, her eyes boldly meeting Carita's gaze.

"There are many types of power in the world, but only two sources. Light—and darkness. Right—and wrong. Truth—and falsehood. 'If a man is not against Me, he is on My side.' 'My kingdom is not of this world. If My kingdom were of this world, then would My servants fight . . . but now is My kingdom not from hence.' 'The kingdom of this world has become the kingdom of our *Adon* and of His Son.' Ellisia, you need to understand that there are two kingdoms—a kingdom of *Adon Olam* and a kingdom of this world. Both desire your soul, your heart—your life."

Ellisia sighed. Her eyes strayed to the long planks of the wooden floor. "I know. I've heard this before."

"This power of the mind—we have no power of our own. Power comes from this spiritual kingdom—a realm that is more real around us than we can imagine, but one that we cannot physically sense. There are things going on around us, often even in this very room, that we have no idea of. The more connected we are with *Adon Olam*— the more we learn to listen to Him—the more we are able to sense His kingdom and what He is doing."

Ellisia twisted her fingers together. "What does this have to do with the mind?" she grunted, though she wasn't sure that she wanted to know. Of course things happened that she couldn't see—witnessing the physics of sound waves through the sound visualization instrument for many weeks had shown her that. But Carita knew nothing of science.

"Just this. The enemy wants your mind. Both kingdoms desire to communicate with people and will use whatever means they are allowed. *Adon Olam* uses what we are willing to give Him, and the enemy snatches and steals anything he can get. Your words are a form of communication for this. If you allow your mind and words to be used by the kingdom of darkness, then you are fighting for the enemy and against *Adon Olam*—and you know that this is serious."

"Seriously." Ellisia's words were only a mutter.

They said nothing for several moments. The baby squirmed and Carita stroked her daughter's head.

At last, Ellisia rose to her feet. "Is it time to eat?"

"We can make it be," Carita replied, still in a subdued voice.

The meal was quiet, as was the rest of the day. Ellisia remained with Carita, despite the misgivings of her heart.

Ellisia split the next several days between home and the inn, daydreaming, studying, practicing, and reading, usually secluded in her room. During meals, Ellisia asked Carita about home life, and Carita filled her in on the details of Elanor's growth, the happenings at the homestead, and the needs she'd filled for the neighbors.

As Ellisia listened day after day, restlessness tore at her heart. Part of her longed for the peaceful home life—so unlike her life in Syorien. Even her life as part of Mae's household seemed chaotic—a rush of trying to figure out what meals to make, blundering over cooking, screaming babies, a weary mother, messes continually, escaping upstairs to study and to be away from everyone else. She thought about Academy—always on a strict schedule—listening to the instructor in one room for an hour, then studying her books for an hour, writing this or reading that or working on a project with certain people. She pondered the rush at noon when everyone pushed to be the first to get their hands on the free meal that the kings provided for Academy students. She thought of the endless chattering in the hallways and the competitions for a certain book, game, or show. She remembered the many confrontations she'd observed between students on the steps, in the halls—anywhere and everywhere in the Academy.

Ambition and adventure did have their price, that was

certain.

But it was a price she'd willingly pay.

The door scratched open. Kaelan's familiar presence seemed to fill the room. Yet Ellisia's heart jumped at the foreignness of his pale cheeks and anguished eyes.

Carita flew to his side before he could cross the room. "Kaelan?"

Ellisia couldn't speak.

Kaelan passed his hand over his forehead, then his hair, before letting it rest on his wife's shoulder. His eyes lingered a moment on her, then bore into Ellisia. His tone was uncharacteristically spiritless.

"Caeleb has been abducted."

20

"WHAT?" ELLISIA DIDN'T recognize her own voice. Shapes and shadows tore at her vision. This was her fault. Somehow or another, she was responsible. Her last conversation with him—the way she'd shut him out—had she been mistaken all along? Was it Caeleb that Kraevyn had targeted, not Kaelan at all? *Seek out this E...* no, it couldn't be Caeleb. And yet...

Uncover further information regarding R.

Rohaea. If E was Kaelan Ellith, R was definitely Caeleb Rohaea. It made sense now ... why had she been so blinded before? She'd thought only of her own family, never once dreaming that Caeleb could be involved. And now ...

She barely heard the worried murmurs between Kaelan and Carita. Concern etched grooves into Kaelan's countenance, deeper than Ellisia had ever known.

"Ellisia." His urgent voice cut through her fog. "Ellisia, tell me. Why are you here? What do you know?"

She shook her head. "What I told Carita—that's about all I know. I don't know. I'm confused myself."

"But why are you here? What brought you here now?"

"They said they had a job for me here."

"Who?"

"The man who's teaching me physics."

"And what's the job?"

"I don't know. He didn't tell me. He had to leave for something. He said he'd be back."

"Highly suspicious," muttered Kaelan, but Carita's small hand found his arm and he cleared his throat. "Do you know anything about Caeleb? When did you last see him?"

Ellisia explained in as few words as she could, leaving Kaelan clearly unsatisfied.

"So you have reason to believe that this incident is connected with a threat to me."

Ellisia lifted a shoulder, not making eye contact.

"Carita, send word to Father and my siblings. I'll notify the others. Prayer meeting here, as soon as can be arranged. Ellisia, you may join us in prayer if you wish."

"I—I should probably be going . . ." A nameless fear swept through her heart. If Caeleb had been kidnapped by Uncle K, who could say what may happen next? Surely Ellisia shouldn't be found in Kaelan's house once he returned. Perhaps she could still talk reason into the uncle—or at least mitigate the effects of his plans. He still relied on *her* skills, at any rate.

Both the others were staring at her. Heat swept across her face, and she seized up her bag. "I—I hope it goes well for you. I—will be seeing you—later."

"We love you, Ellisia. Go with *Adon Olam*."

The door thudded shut as Carita's lingering voice gave way to the squalls of a baby. She *had* to go. Now.

The uncle had returned. She'd barely closed the door to her room at the inn when a familiar step sounded outside in the hall. Ellisia tensed automatically, her mind racing.

The summons came. Ellisia wordlessly joined Ryna in the meeting room, her heart beating as though pumping extra blood would protect her in the coming encounter.

The door opened. When the black cloak didn't

immediately cast a shadow over her, she glanced up—and what breath she had left her chest in a whoosh. It wasn't the uncle.

It was Caeleb.

Caeleb!

Those eyes . . . she couldn't look away, though she felt that a dagger pierced her heart. Heaviness dragged at her.

The black cloak fluttered behind him, vaguely betokening Uncle K, but Ellisia felt her whole soul sinking, sinking. Nothing good could come of this.

Yet there was nothing she could say, nothing she could do—nothing? Nothing now. All words fled.

Kraevyn stepped into the room, his manner professional and easy as usual. "Business in Syorien was settled to satisfaction even more quickly than I'd anticipated. All very well, as now our real business can begin."

The smile stretching his countenance bloomed broader than Ellisia had ever before seen, and somehow, with the silent and subdued Caeleb beside him, it no longer seemed benevolent. He'd taught her; she'd thought she knew his mannerisms—but this one inexplicably sent a tremor through her already-tense heart.

"To the Meeting Hall. Directly after dinner. We begin there. I've spoken with the overseers. I'm to have a speaking slot tonight. Ellisia, you are to have another. I will coach you on the message and mannerisms to convey, leaving it to your abilities to devise the exact words."

Ellisia swallowed, hardly daring to sneak a glance at Caeleb. Torn between wanting to speak to Caeleb alone and speak to the uncle alone, she merely nodded. Questions burned in her mind. What would Caeleb say? What had happened? Why was he so silent? Why had the uncle failed to mention him at all? What would Kraevyn do with him?

The intense gaze startled her from her troubled reveries. He was reading her. Too well.

"I'll speak with you after the meeting," he said.

21

"Have you ever wondered why some towns improve to the point of large cities so rapidly? Or why some country farm communities grow to success while others remain close to poverty? Have you ever wondered what occurred to place tiny towns such as Rivera and Joynway on the map while many villages of similar size fade into obscurity?"

Ellisia ducked her head low and yet lower as Uncle Kraevyn's voice filled Frydael's meeting room. Benches in front of her bore her neighbors, her friends, and acquaintances from town she didn't know but had seen all her life. Dressed in Syorien-style, a veil hiding her hair and as much of her face as she dared, Ellisia wasn't afraid of being recognized now—not if she kept to herself along with Ryna—but her heart thumped at the thought of addressing these people. Once all their eyes rested upon her, *someone* would know her, surely.

"...some of you might be content to be small farmers, unknown and uncared for by the rest of the world. Some of you might seek seclusion and obscurity. Yet I know some of you long for more. Some of you question your place in this world, your ultimate reason for existence. We all struggle with quiet moments wondering where our legacy lies, whether anyone beyond our own children and grandchildren will ever remember we existed. It's human nature to desire to make a mark on society, to make a difference, to do something worth noticing, to be someone worth remembering.

"And that's the question I put before you today. What is it? Examine your own lives. Think about your circumstances. Remember your own grandparents, your parents. How did they live, and how are you living? Will it make a difference? Is there anything to your life other than waking up, working yourself into a backache simply to feed your family, sleeping when you can, and repeating the cycle the next day?

"And then ask yourself—does it have to be this way?" Kraevyn paused, his eyes lingering for a moment and then another on face after face. "Some of you have never been more than a day's journey from this little town, and yet I, who have seen the best and the worst of the four countries, stand before you telling you that so many people don't live this way. It doesn't have to be a struggle simply to put food in your mouth. There can be time for leisure pursuits, for family togetherness outside of the fields, for the journey to academic knowledge.

"That's the good news." His voice was low now and earnest, spilling each word so lightly and yet deliberately, yielding the taste of hope but not its fullness yet. "Good news—if you examine yourselves and find that you are discontent with any element of your life, it can be changed. You might think you don't have the time or the resources, but I'm here to tell you it doesn't matter. It can be done. And that's the message I want to leave you with today." He stepped to the side, waiting for the scattered applause that met him only after a significant delay, then he smiled.

"One final question I wish to propose for your meditation. *What is holding you back*?" He let the question linger in the stillness. "When we return following a short recess, my colleague will address this question." His eyes landed on Ellisia now for the briefest of moments, and her heart thumped.

She'd be expected not only to speak, but to lecture her neighbors on a topic she'd never thought she'd address.

Half an hour later, she stood in the front, her fingers damp. The short curls at her temples clung to her face, and a nervous hand swiped them back under the concealing veil. She couldn't do this. Not here. Not now. Her whole body tingled, sharp pricks assailing her skin now here, now there. Uncle K's instructions burned in her mind. She'd have to try. Yet she couldn't . . .

Her mouth opened. Her words would work. That one thought paralyzed her heart. Whatever she spoke would be done in the lives of her friends, and the words she was under orders to speak ought to never pass her lips—not here.

"The question I will address is this: what is holding you back?" She heard her voice as if it were far away, the unnatural tones in which she spoke rendering her own words alien to her ears. All the better for disguising her identity. "I won't make you guess. I won't expound on the nature of the question for a half an hour. I'll tell you, though I do encourage you to seek out your personal answer for yourselves."

She swallowed, willing the slight tremor that betrayed itself through her tones to still. Here it came. So far Kraevyn could have put the words in her mouth himself. And yet . . .

"It's you."

Hearing the quiet words out loud startled even her.

Kraevyn's countenance was lit with attentiveness. She wouldn't be slipping anything past him.

"You are what holds you back from the life you were meant to live. You are what controls your thoughts, your actions, your attitudes. The more you seek to live for yourself and your own pleasure, the more discontented you become."

Ouch. Her mind fixed on her BookHall ambitions, guilt stabbing her. Did she even believe the words she was saying?

"You know the answer. You know it better than I. In this town, you seek *Adon Olam* more than many towns do. Already you've seen His blessing. Yet when you turn from Him—when you doubt Him—you aren't walking in His covenant, and His blessing is withdrawn."

What had she just said? The words flowed unbidden now, though the trembling hadn't ceased. Kraevyn stared at her, a frown creasing his entire face. As her eyes caught his, he mouthed, "Stop."

She glanced away. He'd told her she was to speak, so she'd speak.

"The only truth is in His Word. Seek it with your whole heart, and beware deceit. The enemy seeks to turn your ears away from *Adon Olam* . . ."

"Stop!" Kraevyn's word rang aloud this time.

Ellisia started, the single syllable freezing her mental processes. Only then did she realize that the pressure in her mind she'd been ignoring must have come from him. He'd been mentally willing her to stop for the past several sentences.

Her mind fixated on all that must be behind that word, and suddenly all memory of what she'd been about to say fled. Somehow Kraevyn was beside her, his smooth words plowing over whatever she had been about to say.

"My colleague was attempting to demonstrate that which you've heard all your lives, but it seems she got a bit carried away. She can be prone to that; it's a condition.

Yet I will cut to the point to give you the answer we bring. Personally, I have studied these things in the best Academies in three countries. I've spoken with professors and teachers who have entire lives of research and experience behind them. I've seen what effects different philosophies have in cities and countries. And it grieves my heart to see the differences. Some have so much, others so little, and so many who have much care nothing about the others. That's why I've devoted my life to bringing the knowledge and success of the few to all the rest. Students have studied under me, and I'm proud to see their success now. And it's not just me ... our team is seeing results across the four countries..."

Ellisia found herself inching to the back of the room. Kraevyn had entirely taken over; his words filled the room. No one was looking at her anymore. Did anyone even remember her words?

"In short, what I've experienced is that it all comes down to your ideology. What you think is who you are. And to move your life in a positive direction, you need to take charge..."

Unobtrusively Ellisia slipped out the back door. She didn't want to hear more of Kraevyn's put-on drivel at the moment. One thing was abundantly clear right now: it wasn't the flesh-and-blood Kraevyn she'd have to worry about. Something behind him was speaking—something even beyond the philosophy and wordology and science and mind. She'd studied enough of the science to recognize that.

What was she doing trying to fight unseen power with practical science and words?

Her heart weighed heavily within her as she dragged herself around the back of the Meeting House. She didn't dare leave, but how could she stay? She needed to school her mind to speak with him afterwards, for of course he'd have something to say about her behavior this evening.

Perhaps she could indeed pass it off as a physical or mental abnormality. Despite all her misgivings, she still did want his influence for the BookHall position. At this point, even her Academy status might hinge on him—not to mention her continued access to his lab instruments.

"*Adon Olam?*" She whispered the name quite unlike she had proclaimed it aloud only moments ago, hesitantly now. It felt as though she ought to speak to Him, since she'd spoken *of* Him, but she wasn't even sure she truly believed all of what she said. What's more, where was Caeleb, and what part would Uncle K assign him in these schemes? She *had* to help him as well as protect Kaelan. Heaviness weighed upon her.

"You gave me wordology. You gave me sensitivity. You gave me love of books. You gave me my dreams. You brought me here. I don't know what's happening, and I don't know what I'm doing." The words emerged, challenging, bold, almost accusing. She stepped between the slim birches behind the building, breathing a bit freer once hidden behind them.

"If You can help, please do. Tell me what to do and say. I do want to do what You want, but I want what I want. So I'm going to ask You—please keep my family and friends safe first. Please grant me a BookHall position, and help me know what to do about Kraevyn and all the rest. And if You can help me to develop my wordology—please do. But first, I ask You to straighten out this situation here."

Get me back to Syorien, her mind added, but her heart didn't quite want to acknowledge that wish as a prayer. As awkward as it was for her here, she didn't wish to leave without assurance of Kaelan's safety.

Once her cheeks had cooled and her mind was partially calmed by the evening breeze, she slipped back into the building, reclaiming her seat.

The restless air murmured around her in keeping with the shifting of the people and the mutters of voices. Evidently some change had occurred in her absence. Different tones took shape and rose above the others before another overtook prominence.

"You can't tell us our lives don't matter," a deep voice somewhere on the other side of the room grumbled.

"Yes! Some of us like our ways."

"Wouldn't keep 'em if we didn't think we'd got the right ones," another put in.

"You're a foreigner, isn't that right?" a female tone piped up.

"Don't want any foreigner telling us what to do. We're Frydaelers. We . . ."

"But don't you think . . ."

"Uff, listen to the chap. I for one . . ."

". . .right. All this propaganda is driving us to complacency. Maybe if . . ."

"But if we'd just listen . . .!"

"He's not preaching *Adon Olam*. I at least won't . . ."

"But he's right! What has *Adon Olam* ever done for us besides keep us from the . . ."

Ellisia inhaled deeply, her eyes falling shut as torrents of words crashed against her mind, pulsing in her brain and threatening the formation of a headache.

"You see!" Kraevyn's deep tone penetrated the chaos. "You're divided. Disagreement thrives; where disunity abounds, you have no chance of success and progress. Those of you who are interested and wish to know more, meet me at the Inn tomorrow morning."

The thumping of Ellisia's heart rivaled that in her brain. "Don't do it! Don't do it!" her mind screamed in the direction of the people, but her mouth and hands felt equally powerless. She fell in line as Kraevyn dismissed the seething crowd, winding her way back to the Inn. For the moment, she was glad only to get away.

Yet her relief was short-lived once she found herself alone with Kraevyn. His dark eyebrows knit together threateningly, and her heart quaked.

"What was all that about tonight, girl?" He threw the door shut, his cloak whirling. "I was counting on you. We could have made real progress. Wrapped things up maybe even tomorrow and gotten back to Syorien. Now—what a mess! What were you thinking?"

"I don't know—I have a headache," she whispered. "Something came over me . . ."

"See that it doesn't happen again. What, is this of no importance to you? I set before you a job; I expect you to complete it according to directions. I realize you've been faithful to your tasks before this, but this was the most crucial as of yet, and you bungled it entirely."

Ellisia drew in a breath, holding it for a full moment before exhaling and meeting the uncle's eyes. "And what of all the other tasks I've completed successfully?" she challenged. "What of the BookHall position? Isn't it about time I saw some progress in that direction? How many meetings have I sat through, directing my thoughts at your command? How many days have I waited idle here while you were back in Syorien? Don't you think some compensation is warranted?"

Kraevyn threw back his head, the hood falling into the back of the cloak as his laughter rattled the candlesticks. "Good one, girl! If we're keeping accounts, what of the days of training I've invested in you already?"

"I should think the weeks of meetings in Syorien would have covered that by this time." Ellisia met his eye.

"Girl, girl. For all your smarts, you don't understand yet? Look at what we've seen tonight. The division, the restlessness, the longing. I would wager that the Inn's meeting room will be full tomorrow morning. Look at how oppressed these people are. They are practically begging for leadership and liberation. Can't you see how important it is that we stop the dissention, the rebellion, the stubborn persistence in ways so ancient that most societies have left them behind long ago? This is the core of our opposition, and if we can gain the ears of this town, you'll soon see prosperity spread across Taerna, just as it has in Doekh."

"That's all very well. But I'm only seeking academic advancement, and you've promised me the BookHall."

Again his laugh rang out, grating on Ellisia's ears. "Girl, you're mad indeed! What's come over you tonight? Any position is minor in the face of what we're doing here. I'm busy. I have a job to do, and I begin to fear you're wasting my time."

"You need my abilities." Confidence laced her tone.

"Ha! Yes, I would do better with them. But never fear, I shall accomplish my purposes with or without you. I'd greatly prefer *with,* both for my sake and yours, but if it's without, so be it. You failed me tonight, and yet I didn't fail."

"But it was in exchange for a position. And you dare to laugh in my face at this?"

"Girl, girl. You're beginning to be something of a pest. Go away and put that ridiculous little idea out of your head, and fill it instead with that new Wulf I've put on your table. 'Twould be a much better use of your time and mine."

"Do you mean to say that you won't get me that position?"

"Tut, I said no such thing. But you certainly don't understand. I know of far loftier positions you can't even dream of—full of power, influence, fame, money, comfort, pleasure, leisure, freedom—and that's where I'm placing you. Measly BookHall, indeed!" A chuckle let loose.

Ellisia seethed yet stood her ground. "You made a promise. If you break it, you will regret it."

"Oh little girl. You forget you're here in this no-name town on my money, and your Academy standing hinges on my goodwill. If you're leaving the team, you leave it all."

She only stared at him, her hands mentally forming fists, though outwardly she didn't move.

"One more thing. We have another meeting tomorrow afternoon. That will be the most important one. Do *not* mess this one up." He emphasized each word. "You won't be speaking. You'll be directing your thoughts at the speaker, as usual, only concentration is key. Knowledge is supreme—that's the theme we wish to impress on him. Seeking knowledge and not backwards ways. You understand?"

Ellisia nodded. Of course she understood—perhaps much better than Kraevyn hoped.

"I'm depending on you to persuade him," he said. "If you accomplish this, I can send back your name to my superiors as a candidate for promotion. You'd have access to so much more knowledge and learning. And, between you and I, I believe you'd gain a promotion or two immediately with this little task."

Her chest heaved, then she spun on her heel and left the room, each measured step clacking ominously in the hall. Back in her own room, the fire leaped from her, her heart giving itself up to rage. To think that he'd laughed in her face at her mention of his half of the bargain! To think that he imagined she'd cater to every whim simply because of her position. Why had she ever trusted him? Why hadn't she been more wary—or extricated herself from the bargain sooner while she still could easily?

Well! He didn't know she was in her hometown,

surrounded by friends and family who would give everything to shield her were she to leave his service ... but would those friends see her as a traitor? Would they think it was simply another ploy to gain their ear for him?

She sighed. Carita would stand by her, but she hated the thought of giving up now.

Yet the crisis at hand was too evident to let slip by. The name of *Adon Olam* was being attacked, chipped away from her neighbor's minds and hearts by logic and deceit.

And she had to stand by and watch it all, their demise on her hands.

Or did she?

He'd said he'd move forward with or without her, but she still had her training.

Clearly now the choice appeared before her eyes. She could speak for Kraevyn and whatever spiritual kingdom he strove to bring to the people.

Or she could speak for *Adon Olam* and His spiritual kingdom.

There could be no compromise. She knew that now. The decision was hers, and choosing ambition meant forever renouncing the name of *Adon Olam.*

And as much as she'd strayed from and doubted Him lately, she couldn't forsake Him. In her heart, she knew Him as truth. She'd seen Him and His power in Carita's life. She'd read His Word, and it resonated with her spirit. Despite all the questions and doubts, when it came down to it, she couldn't deny the One who was the support of her entire existence.

And with that realization, her ambitions crumbled in the ground at her feet even as her body crumpled up in her bed, shaken with weeping as she'd never known.

22

CALM SETTLED ITSELF firmly in her heart even as she awoke. The grief of losing the BookHall, losing her studies, and losing her standing stung bitterly, its sharp ache unmitigated by sleep, yet somehow peace gripped her in the midst of it. She'd renounced herself entirely to choose *Adon Olam*, and somehow, sacrifice for Him wasn't as dark and awful as it had appeared.

She wouldn't have to play both sides any longer, at any rate. No more two-facedness. She could fight for her family openly, free from any fear of consequences from Kraevyn. Every dream was relinquished, and her head and heart soared lighter than they had in weeks. Freedom. Truly Kraevyn knew nothing of such real freedom when he spoke of masters and slaves and pleasure. Who would have guessed that choosing to crush her cherished life-hopes could be so—freeing?

But the question remained, troubling her heart as she prepared for the day. What ought she to do now? What was Kraevyn planning for the meeting with her neighbors that morning? What would he have for her? And what ought her response to be—what did *Adon Olam* want from her that day?

Surely Ellrick could give her his wisdom. The elderly gentleman been a firm and faithful family friend for so long. To be sure, hadn't he helped Carita and Kaelan so many times when they seemed to be in the midst of soul struggles? Carita was such a pillar of *Adon Olam*'s kingdom herself, and yet she'd always spoken of Ellrick almost as someone from another realm, another dimension, another sphere of living . . .

And there her bookish imagination had run off with her again. She'd go to Ellrick. He'd tell her what to do. And she'd listen, no matter what. Even if it involved going against everything she'd dreamed of.

Ensconced in one of the many wool-stuffed chairs in Ellrick's front room—Ellisia had always marveled that one small room could possess so many soft chairs—she told Ellrick the whole story. He listened, quietly, just as she remembered he always had to Carita, nodding now and then, his chin tilted slightly and leaning on the thumb buried in the white beard, his forehead sympathetic yet strong, perhaps more deeply creased than in her childhood, perhaps not.

". . .and so I have come to you to receive the wisdom of *Adon Olam* that He has granted you over your lifetime. I can't use my words for *Adon Olam*—not to bring His kingdom to the people as I know He wants me to. I don't understand it. I can feel most of the other words; I can see, I can sense what they do, and yet somehow my mind is powerless to form the words that would bring the kingdom to the people. And I'm here now at this crisis. I'm ready to do whatever it takes. I must—I must learn. And I'm here asking you to teach me."

Her voice died away, and only the bobwhite beyond the open window broke the silence for several minutes. Ellrick's head dipped once, twice, as he stared at the vacant wall beyond Ellisia's shoulder. Then a slight frown creased the broad forehead, and his eyes escaped.

"Give—give me a moment." His voice sounded

strangely husky, something Ellisia couldn't recall hearing from him before. Before she could reply, he rose and disappeared into the back room.

Ellisia focused on breathing. In and out. In and out. What was the matter with Ellrick? Where was his wisdom and eloquence?

Yet it was scarcely three minutes later that Ellrick returned, a small parchment-bound volume of the Word enclosed in his hands. He sat down again, his eyes studying Ellisia soberly. What *was* the matter?

After an uncomfortable moment on Ellisia's part, Ellrick spoke at last.

"No, Ellisia." The words were kind yet deliberate, welcoming no argument. "I cannot help you with this. Not as you ask."

"But . . ." She knew the word was futile, but she couldn't help it. "Why ever not? I *know* you have the wisdom I need here. Look at your life."

Ellrick's eyes escaped again and grew soft for a brief moment, as if remembering his past. "It is not what *Adon Olam* has called me to at this time. He has given me a word, and I must not depart from it—not even for you."

"You can't share some of your wisdom with me?" Ellisia demanded.

"Not in that way." Gentleness threaded through his tone, and Ellisia caught a hint of yearning, of compassion, of something far deeper that she couldn't quite translate. He slid the Book in his hand towards her. "But in another, I can point you towards everything you need. The fullness of wisdom is contained in this Book. The more you read this Book down on your knees, the more your mind will conform to the mind of the Son of *Adon Olam*."

"I know that." Ellisia seized the volume a bit impatiently. "Of course I know that. But I came for practical help. And you can't give it?"

"Ellisia, listen. Your practical help is here." He tapped his finger on the brown cover. "I can't tell you anything you can't find in here."

"But it doesn't say anything about my particular situation."

Ellrick shook his head. "That is where you are mistaken. *Everything* in this Book speaks to your particular situation. The Spirit of *Adon Olam* grants you the understanding, interpretation, and application. Do not ask me to fill the Spirit's role. Get down on your knees and beg Him for it yourself. He loves to answer."

"You don't think I *have* asked Him for wisdom?" Ellisia was losing patience. "Believe me. If there's anything I could do, I've tried it. I've prayed. I've asked. I've searched this Book already. In the multitude of counsellors there is safety, it says, and so I'm here."

"There's not something more you need to do. It's someone you be, Someone you receive to live, pray, love, understand, and speak through you. And you know I'm not that Someone."

"But—I don't understand why you can't at least be a signpost to guide me along on my journey. You've done it for others. Why not me? What's wrong with me?"

"Ellisia . . ." Ellrick's smile radiated compassion. "It's not you. You are a marvelous and powerful creation of *Adon Olam*. As His life lives in you and as you bathe yourself in the beauty of His presence . . . I dare not tell you the impact He can have through you for the coming of His kingdom. Bring it before Him. *He* is your guide."

"Didn't He ordain ministers and servants to assist others on the way?"

"He did. But such is not my call."

"You teach others, though."

Ellrick shook his head. "Not to preach, not to speak, not to proclaim. To pray."

"But Kaelan preaches . . ."

"Praise be to *Adon Olam*." Ellrick breathed the words reverently.

"You mentored him."

"To pray," Ellrick repeated quietly.

Ellisia fell silent, mulling. At last, she heaved a deep breath. "So there's nothing more you can do for me? Nothing you can say? Nothing at all?"

"I will continue to pray for you." Now the spoken sentence was cheerful, excited even. "Take that volume with you. Read it on your knees. And may the humility and victory of *Adon Olam* go with you."

"I have the Book already," Ellisia muttered.

"Of course. But you've never read this copy." Ellrick's eyes were twinkling now. "Keep seeking Him, and He will be found."

Ellisia swept up the Book and turned towards the door. "Good day."

"A very good day, and to you also."

Was that laughter in his tone? Huff!

Voices radiated from the meeting room at the inn when Ellisia drew up on the step outside. As she debated her next course, the door before her opened and neighbors spilled out.

Ellisia yanked her hood over as much of her face as she could, stepping aside to allow them to pass. Animation throbbed in the voices, and each man, woman, and young person carried a thin orange-covered book.

"—can't wait to see a little bit of that city prosperity in my family—" Ellisia heard one man say to another as they stepped aside to allow her to enter.

Upstairs, Ryna lounged on a window seat in the hall, eyes fixed on the stairway.

"What did—what did Uncle K tell them?" Ellisia asked.

"You should have been there."

"Yes, but ..."

"He gave them a Wulf guidebook and told them to read it. Then they have to each get someone else to read it."

Ellisia nodded, passing on into her room.

"You'd better read it yourself," Ryna called after her. "Uncle was pretty clear about the importance of this one."

The door shut, and Ellisia's eyes fastened on the identical thin orange volume on her table. That must be the book Kraevyn had referred to last night ... she hadn't even noticed it in the turmoil of the evening. So he'd been in her room. She filed that fact away for future reference.

She stepped to the table, deliberately placing the volume Ellrick had given her directly next to the new Wulf. The parchment bindings were nearly identical in size, the brown-covered volume just a shade off from the orange one.

Two books. So opposite. The symbolism felt weighty to her, as if it were a signal of the momentous nature of her position and the decision she faced.

She cracked the cover on Wulf, scanning its contents detachedly. The usual. The basics. All laid out in a clear, simple fashion unlike the style of the more complex Wulf books she'd already studied.

More reverently, she opened Ellrick's Book. Like the other, she knew what this contained—yet each word seemed fresh to her, written for her.

> And I saw in the right hand of him that sat on the throne a book written within and on the backside, sealed with seven seals. And I saw a strong angel proclaiming with a loud voice, Who is worthy to open the book, and to loose the seals thereof?
> And no man in heaven, nor in earth, neither under the earth, was able to open the book, neither to look thereon. And I wept much, because no man was found worthy to open and to read the book, neither to look thereon.

A book. Ellisia would want to read that book too if she'd been there. Seven seals, and no one able to read it!

> And one of the elders saith unto me, Weep not: behold, the Lion of the tribe of Juda, the Root of David, hath prevailed to open the book, and to loose the seven seals thereof.

The Lion. The image stuck in Ellisia's mind as she read the brief story that followed:

> And I beheld, and, lo, in the midst of the throne and of the four beasts, and in the midst of the elders, stood a Lamb as it had been slain, having seven horns and seven eyes, which are the seven Spirits of *Adon Olam* sent forth into all the earth. And he came and took the book out of the right hand of him that sat upon the throne. And when he had taken the book, the four beasts and four and twenty elders fell down before the Lamb, having every one of them harps, and golden vials full of odours, which are the prayers of saints. And they sung a new song, saying, Thou

art worthy to take the book, and to open the seals thereof: for thou wast slain, and hast redeemed us to *Adon Olam* by thy blood out of every kindred, and tongue, and people, and nation; And hast made us unto our *Adon Olam* kings and priests: and we shall reign on the earth.

And I beheld, and I heard the voice of many angels round about the throne and the beasts and the elders: and the number of them was ten thousand times ten thousand, and thousands of thousands; Saying with a loud voice, Worthy is the Lamb that was slain to receive power, and riches, and wisdom, and strength, and honour, and glory, and blessing.

And every creature which is in heaven, and on the earth, and under the earth, and such as are in the sea, and all that are in them, heard I saying, Blessing, and honour, and glory, and power, be unto him that sitteth upon the throne, and unto the Lamb for ever and ever.

And the four beasts said, Amen. And the four and twenty elders fell down and worshipped him that liveth for ever and ever.

The impact and solemnity of the little story lingered in Ellisia's mind, though she did not understand it. The Lion—which showed itself as a Lamb—was the key figure in this story, the one who loosed the all-important book, the one receiving the blessing and praise of all other creatures in the account, the one who redeemed all people and caused them to reign.

Her eyes wandered back to the Lion section. This time, she noticed a faint underline of the word and a light note penciled in the margin.

PP Pt II Sec VI

Was that why Ellrick had insisted on her taking this copy of the Book?

Pages flipped. Barely visible in a pale gray ink, tiny notes studded the edges of the text. As the last page fell away to the left, another thin book slipped out of its pocket in the back cover.

Pilgrim's Progress. Ellisia should have known. She paged to Part II, Section VI, scanning the section quickly for anything that might mention a lion.

> ...Christiana said, Methinks I see something yonder upon the road before us, a thing of such a shape such as I have not seen.
> Then said Joseph, Mother, what is it?
> An ugly thing, Child, an ugly thing, said she.
> But Mother, what is it like? said he.
> 'Tis like I cannot tell what, said she. And now it was but a little way off. Then said she, It is nigh.
> Well, well, said Mr Great-heart, Let them that are most afraid keep close to me.
> So the Fiend came on, and the Conductor met it; but when it was just come to him, it vanished to all their sights. Then remembered they what had been said some time ago, Resist the Devil, and he will fly from you.
> They went therefore on, as being a little refreshed; but they had not gone far, before Mercy looking behind her, saw, as she thought, something most like a Lion, and it came a great padding pace after; and it had a hollow Voice of Roaring, and at every Roar that it gave it made all the Valley echo, and their hearts to ake, save the heart of him that was their Guide. So it came up, and Mr Great-heart went behind, and put the Pilgrims all before him. The Lion also came on

apace, and Mr Great-heart addressed himself to give him Battle. But when he saw that it was determined that resistance should be made, he also drew back and came no further.

Ellisia closed the book, her imagination fired in a way far deeper than she'd experienced for many months. What an inspiring illustration of victory in Yeshua the Son of *Adon Olam*! Two lions—a victorious one and a defeated one. The defeated one, of course, could only roar. It was not real—it was a trick of the imagination, an illusion spun by the enemy. Without doubt, the enemy was, as Carita had often proclaimed, a "liar and the father of lies." In her life as she followed *Adon Olam*, the enemy had no power to cause any harm; he remained a defeated foe.

Yet somehow, if she were to yield to him and treat him as if he were indeed some great one, she herself granted him the power to cause her to stumble. Of himself, he had no such power.

Ellisia grinned. She'd call the enemy's bluff, and he'd have no choice but to recognize his own powerlessness.

She'd forgotten about the orange-covered book. As her eyes landed on it, her grin intensified. Wulf knew nothing of the sort of mind power she was pondering. Taking words, taking truth, and helping people believe rightly in relation to the two spiritual kingdoms—that was the right use of her skills. So thinking, she set Ellrick's Book firmly on top of Wulf's.

In that sense, it wasn't as much a fight for victory as the claiming of victory—resting in the flaming sunlight of the victory possessed by Yeshua. Why would she exert all her human energy wrestling with a roaring vaporous lion when she possessed the fullness of the strength and victory of resting in the Lion of the Tribe of Juda?

23

ELLISIA SOUNDLESSLY PULLED her cloak's hood as far over her face as possible. Beside her, Kraevyn yanked open the Meeting Hall door, his own ever-present cloak fluttering about his ankles. He'd insisted she wear one that afternoon, though the heat of her nervousness combined with the glaring spring sunlight threatened to cause the entire thing to cling to her arms and neck.

Inside, she slipped to the back corner, partly secluded by high-backed chairs in front of her. As Kraevyn slid next to her, her mind sharpened even as her body relaxed into the seat.

Prickles shivered down her spine. At the inn, she'd lost track of the days—yet this *had* to be meeting-day. Carita and the baby sat in their usual place. Laelara, Kelton, Kethin, Liliora, and their father filed in directly behind Carita. Face after face Ellisia recognized—not just neighbors and acquaintances but friends and fellow-believers in *Adon Olam*. Ellrick, Thaecia Jaelrven and her brood of young ones, Dresie and Dixaen with their family, Mrs. Totaen, Mr. Trentyn: her closest friends, all present.

Ellisia's heart sank. Kaelan would be preaching today. There was no way she would be directing any hostile or anti-faith thoughts towards him.

Yet even as she watched him walk down the long

aisle to the front, her heart settled in her. She wouldn't have used skills against any preacher; the name didn't matter. She only had to stare at Kaelan hard enough to convince Kraevyn she was doing her job—and whatever else happened would not be up to her.

Turmoil warred with the contents of her stomach, despite her best efforts to relax. Questions swirled—could she keep up appearances? Would anyone else recognize her? Would they forever consider her a traitor? Would Kaelan be harmed?—and yet she steeled herself. The Lion of the Tribe of Juda was here. She could take on the vaporous lion.

She even couldn't help but bite back a smile as Kaelan read from the Book:

> Humble yourselves therefore under the mighty hand of *Adon Olam*, that he may exalt you in due time: Casting all your care upon him; for he careth for you. Be sober, be vigilant; because your adversary the devil, as a roaring lion, walketh about, seeking whom he may devour: Whom resist stedfast in the faith, knowing that the same afflictions are accomplished in your brethren that are in the world. But *Adon Olam* of all grace, who hath called us unto his eternal glory by Yeshua Mashiach after that ye have suffered a while, make you perfect, stablish, strengthen, settle you. To him be glory and dominion for ever and ever. Amen.

Ellisia pressed her hand against the bag at her side where she'd stashed Ellrick's Book. As Kraevyn stepped out for a moment, she slipped it out and let it fall open.

Balak the king of Moab hath brought me from

Aram, out of the mountains of the east, saying, Come, curse me Jacob, and come, defy Israel. How shall I curse, whom *Adon Olam* hath not cursed? or how shall I defy, whom *Adon Olam* hath not defied?

Firm footsteps sent the Book hurrying back to her bag, but a smile overtook the corners of her lips. It was as if *Adon Olam* had known she'd be in that exact same situation at this exact moment and caused the Book to open just for her. And she'd thought people were exaggerating when they said the Book just happened to fall open to what they needed.

Her eyes fastened back on Kaelan with intense concentration. She wasn't going to defy what *Adon Olam* had not defied.

Beside her, she felt Kraevyn's steady gaze. She didn't turn her head, only kept her own eyes fixed on Kaelan. What ought she to think towards him? Not what Kraevyn had asked, but—

The words he'd just read tumbled to mind, and she pointed them in his direction.

Cast all your care upon Him, Kaelan. He cares for you. He is protecting you. He is watching over you. Humble yourself under His mighty hand. Be vigilant. The enemy will not devour you. Resist him.

As Kaelan spoke *Adon Olam*'s word, it was easy for Ellisia to turn those exact phrases back upon him through her thoughts. She marveled at the ease with which the words came.

Suddenly, a barrier rose in her heart. The thought-words ceased, and she could barely comprehend what Kaelan said. A tiny glance revealed Kraevyn still staring at her, concentrating now. His lips twitched slightly, and Ellisia understood. *She* was his target.

Every tongue that rises in judgement against you, you shall condemn.

New words appeared in her heart, and she embraced them, her spirit recognizing them as from *Adon Olam.*

I condemn the lies, she thought. *By the power of* Adon Olam *in me, the lies have no power.*

But she felt herself wavering. Kraevyn had asked so little of her, and he had offered her so much in return: learning, academics beyond what she could access even in Syorien, perhaps still the BookHall position once this died down. He was only trying to help the poor citizens of Frydael . . . he was only trying to spread the knowledge that he'd been blessed with . . .

Her mind warred, and in the struggle she could focus her thoughts neither for nor against Kaelan. Kraevyn's gaze beside her shifted to Kaelan, and now his lips moved in earnest. What was he speaking to Kaelan?

Knowledge is king. Of course. *NO. Adon Olam is King,* her heart cried, but she could manage no more. Vainly she saw Kraevyn's words reach their mark.

But the crease deepened on Kraevyn's brow even as Ellisia's chest grew tighter and tighter. She quickly focused back on Kaelan, though her heart and mind felt entirely blank.

"I've never seen this," Kraevyn hissed. "Totally unfazed. Keep up the thought direction. Whisper if you must—don't be afraid. I'm switching to interception."

Ellisia swallowed, her eyes never leaving Kaelan's face. Waves of heat rushed over her, stifling her beneath the cloak. As she focused, she heard Kaelan's words, yet now their meaning seemed slightly shifted. She could sense the undercurrent of conflicting messages now being subtly broadcasted across the room. Ears would pick it up, but the brain wouldn't consciously register it. She tried to clamp her ears shut beneath her hood, but in the heat, she couldn't manage it.

Daring to glance away from Kaelan, she focused on the back of Carita's head for a moment. Her head was bowed slightly over the baby on her lap—praying, Ellisia knew, as she almost always did while Kaelan preached.

A wave of peace slipped over Ellisia at the sight. To get to Kaelan, the enemy would have to contend with her praying sister.

Yet just as quickly, the wave slipped away again. Kaelan's words flowed, just as usual, like something from another dimension, another reality, a place where only *Adon Olam* filled all. But an air of restlessness pervaded the atmosphere—a single message was being spoken, but mixed messages were being heard.

Kraevyn sensed it too. A muttered Doekhan word preceded a quick flutter of the black cloak, and he was gone.

Breathe freely or tense further? Ellisia wasn't sure which response would be more appropriate. Kaelan hadn't paused, and Ellisia debated sneaking out as well, but somehow she couldn't leave—not yet. A distant rumble of thunder grumbled. This heat was oppressive.

"The Son of *Adon Olam* gave these words plainly to His followers—to you and to me: 'If ye abide in me, and my words abide in you, ye shall ask what ye will, and it shall be done unto you.' Abide in me: that's relationship. My words abide in you: that's treasuring His Word day and night in our minds. Ask what you will: that's prayer. And it shall be done. That's victory."

Kaelan paused.

The back door burst open.

Heads spun.

Ellisia, heart in her throat, reluctantly pulled her eyes towards the source of the commotion, already knowing who she'd see.

But nothing, within or without, prepared her for the sight of Maeve, her purple sleeves hanging loose from her bronzed arms, black hair straight and shimmery, her dress billowing in the pre-storm breeze that filtered in around her.

Maeve took one step forward, and Kraevyn's dark figure slipped in behind her, reseating himself.

All eyes fastened upon Maeve. Tension knotted Ellisia's shoulders and chest. Kraevyn was still muttering, some small instrument in his hand. Words fell from his lips. "You can trust us. We're here to help you. Don't interfere; stay in the background; you'll be safe; it's danger to interfere. Be safe. We're on your side, your team . . ." Only Ellisia registered the murmurs, but she knew he was somehow broadcasting them throughout the room to the subconscious senses of her friends.

"Kaelan Ellith." Maeve's commanding voice rang out. "In the name of knowledge and progress, we ask you to cease perpetrating outdated propaganda. Immediate compliance secures you advanced education to your village at no cost using the latest books and research from the very best philosophers in the four countries."

Kaelan deliberately closed his Book, locking eyes with Maeve. "And non-compliance?"

Maeve stepped to the side, and Ellisia gasped. Into the room stepped Ryna, Caeleb at her side. Only his face and head were visible under the billowing red cloak. Barely detectable between his cloak and Ryna's, a rope hung between them.

"Non-compliance requires us to request you to turn yourself over to us immediately at the penalty of harm to your friend." Maeve's decree rang out, firm.

Ryna shifted. Now, with Caeleb in the center, Maeve, Kraevyn, and Ryna filled the back wall, effectively barring the door. Ellisia was sure they expected her to either join them or use psychology in her own mind to influence the people—but instead she shrank down further in her corner. Surely everyone was too focused on the figures in the back to notice that she too appeared to be a stranger in a dark cloak.

Kaelan stepped towards them, the shock he must be feeling only faintly hinted on his face, his eyes fixed on Caeleb. *"Adon Olam."* Ellisia read his lips rather than heard him. Carita wasn't even visible anymore—she must have slipped to her knees. Laelara and Kelton both had arms tightly around Liliora—her eyes big as she stared at the intruders.

Lightning flashed through windows and time seemed to stand still before Kaelan finally spoke. "What is the meaning of this? Who are you?"

This time Kraevyn spoke up, his voice reverberating with confidence. "We are researchers and professors from the Palace Academy who work under authorities to educate and improve the station of citizens across the country. We have proof that you are disrupting this progress and encouraging regress among the populace, especially the lower classes. Again, we ask you to immediately desist."

Kaelan's eyes fled in Carita's direction momentarily.

Ellisia's clammy hands pushed her cloak aside. *No.* This was impossible. Kaelan must not go with them. Her bag slipped off her shoulder into her lap, Ellrick's Book bumping her knee. Her fingers grasped it, tightening until each knuckle stood out pale.

How shall I defy whom He hath not defied?

Another sentence from the same story pierced her memory.

Must I not take heed to speak that which Adon *hath put in my mouth?*

Ellisia squeezed her eyes closed. Thunder growled, closer now, and stiff breezes sent their ominous breath through branches outside. Around her, voices whimpered. People shifted. Even the very air of the room felt like everyone had forgotten to breathe—not that breathing in this stuffy weather was pleasant anyway.

This was hopeless. What could she do?

She still had her skills.

Sitting up, she stared at Kraevyn, willing him to back down, willing him to forget about Kaelan, persuading him to think favorably towards the Book.

All her strength she directed towards thinking those thoughts. With every ounce of effort that was in her, she strained her mind, her words, her skills. Her lips moved; words fell. This had to work. It *had* to.

Kraevyn's eyes shifted from Kaelan to Ellisia. One moment. That was all. But she crumbled. Her mind melted, lost focus, couldn't fasten on anything. Everything became a blur, and she slipped down out of her seat.

"Well? Will you trade yourself for this so-called friend? Or will you allow him to suffer—ah, who knows what he may suffer? Because we *will* keep him, and we will be retraining his mind."

"Free him." Kaelan's tone held steady.

"Not until you comply. Will you cease your speaking of these matters and continue in your station as a farmer alone?"

Must I not take heed to speak that which Adon *hath put in my mouth?* He would never comply. Ellisia buried her head in her hands.

"No." The single syllable lingered, soft yet still steady.

"Then will you give yourself up to us?"

"If I must, I must." Footsteps shook the center of the room, but Ellisia couldn't look up.

"No, Kaelan! Don't do it! You have family that needs you . . . don't think of me. *Adon Olam* . . ." Caeleb's words were muffled suddenly.

"Caeleb, I can't . . ."

"Leave . . . Go . . . Don't mind me . . ." Caeleb's voice rang out again, fragmented.

"Silence!" Kraevyn said.

Ellisia's head snapped up. Faces blurred before her vision. Kaelan was walking—walking from the front directly to Kraevyn. *No!* He must not!

Step. Step. Step.

She again dropped her head. All she wanted was to be a quiet room somewhere with her books and no responsibilities—no demands on her time, no threats to her family and friends.

And yet she was here.

Nothing would ever be the same again.

Step. Step.

I promise.

The unexpected words burned sharply into her mind. What?

Two promises, Ellisia. For you. From Me.

Now she was listening.

If you extract the precious from the worthless, you shall be My spokesman. I promise.

Turn away. Sacrifice. Sit apart. Spend her time, her mind, her mental capabilities on what is truly precious . . . the commission was nearly impossible. But—to be His spokesman.

Ask of Me: I'll give you the heathen and the uttermost parts of the earth. I promise.

The heathen. The uttermost parts of the earth. That was a lot of possession—but why should she wonder? *Adon Olam* already gave her Himself as her possession: the whole earth was nothing to that. "I receive it," she whispered. "And I ask. Give it to me."

And she raised her face to the enemy.

Step. Step.

And her mind fought.

You're my possession. You have no power. Adon Olam *has the power.*

She hesitated, struggling for words, grasping for truth. Nothing came to mind. "*Adon Olam,* help."

She stood, hardly caring who noticed her. Confidence washed through her, and she threw back her head, feeling more like a warrior than ever before as she threw herself into the battle—on the right side this time. "It is written . . ." she muttered the words aloud.

But again, her mind blanked. *No.* She had to have something—she'd showed up for the battle. Her quiver couldn't prove empty now. For the first time, Carita's ceaseless prayers and poring over the Book made sense. One oughtn't to enter battle half-equipped. "*Adon Olam* so loved the world that He gave His only begotten Son . . ." The familiar words slipped from her lips. It was all she could remember, and as the depths of the truth of the verse wrapped themselves through the mesh of her inner heart, identity with all creation joined itself to her being, her very fibers at one with the warriors of *Adon Olam* from the beginning of time, when His words had flung the entire universe into existence in an instant, when the poisoned words of the Serpent Creature had instigated rebellion, when the true war began. That was the war—the ancient war. *Hath* Adon Olam *said . . .* ?

"*Adon Olam has* said." She let the phrase slip through the restless room. "He's said. He's done. He will do. Do, *Adon Olam!*"

Words—confident words, bold words, tense words—flew back and forth between Kaelan and Kraevyn—one from the middle of the room, in the very midst of his people, the other from the back door, flanked by his cohorts. Kraevyn's expression soured the spit on Ellisia's tongue. Such intensity she'd never seen from him. Ellisia buried her face in her hands again. It was hopeless. Not even she could think of the words to say—not with all her skills and training. She'd never trained for this side of the battle. It just wasn't in her.

Now Kaelan had reached Kraevyn, bravery evident in every set crease of his forehead and cheeks, in the open hand evidently kept relaxed only by resolute effort, in the real concern in the corner of his eye as he glanced one final time in Carita's direction.

"Come." Kraevyn beckoned. "We will settle this elsewhere." Business-like as ever he was, even now.

"Release Caeleb."

"Elsewhere. Not here."

"Release him. Or I refuse to come."

"Not much choice if we compel you. Cooperate, or we'll make certain he suffers for your choices."

"The enemy is bound!" The feminine shriek came somewhere from the front of the room. "The Spirit is loosed. He is here. Greater is He that is in me than you who are in the world. Be gone in the name of Yeshua!"

"Greater is He that is in us than he that is in the world . . . greater is He that is in us than he that is in the world . . ." Ellisia's mind took up the phrase, not even bothering to wonder at Carita's unusual public outburst. More serious matters lay at hand. Ellisia spoke aloud now, almost shouting over the confusion in her head. Kraevyn was launching something psychological at her, and Ryna's dark glare hadn't let up for the past five minutes.

"Ryna! Pay attention. Give me the cord," Ellisia heard Kraevyn's voice from somewhere seemingly far away. "No—Kaelan first. I swear, you are the most disorganized, inefficient—"

"You have no authority here!" Ellisia proclaimed.

"Girl!" Kraevyn's full attention was on her now. "What has gotten into you? Calm down, sit down. Let us handle this. Stop—now!"

"Never! Greater is He—"

The cord dangled loosely now, and Caeleb's eyebrow, still mostly concealed by the cloak, raised in Kaelan's direction. Wordlessly Kaelan's lips set, and Ellisia sensed his entire body trembling. If only he could speak with Carita . . . the next moment, both Kaelan and Caeleb had slipped out the door.

"—than he that is in the world!" Ellisia finished, her eyes shifting back to Kraevyn, still shouting at her.

Then he turned to Ryna. "Wait—where's the Bookman? Behind you—secure him." He bumbled into Ellisia and an elder woman in a dark shawl, then spun upon Maeve. "Take Kaelan; let's get out of here."

"You had him, not me," she returned.

"What? No, he was with you. WHAT?" The thunder of his voice rivaled the thunder outside. "You let them both escape?" He whirled on the congregation. "The crowning rule of knowledge and science will yet have its place in Taerna. Prepare yourselves to see the day."

The next moment, he was gone, and only driving rain clattered upon the roof. Congregants collapsed back on the benches, children raised their heads again, women sighed and relaxed their hold on their small ones. Ellisia drew in a breath, her knees crumbling beneath her as she slumped back to the bench.

A moment she rested, catching her breath, then she yanked off the cloak. Not a moment too soon. Her eyes closed in the ecstasy of a faint breeze reaching her skin. Then she slowly sidestepped through the crowds until she reached her sister's side.

"Ellisia—you were here?" Carita breathed, one hand reaching out to clasp Ellisia's shoulder. "You saw?"

"Yes. Yes, I was here." A heavy sigh escaped.

"You think—Kaelan—I didn't quite see . . ."

"He escaped. No fear of that."

"Even from the speedy pursuit?"

Ellisia nodded. "These people know nothing of this town. Kaelan knows the hideaways and backstreets as well as anyone. And in this weather? No, they won't catch them. But—" She bolted upright as a thought struck her. "We need to get everyone home. I don't know what might happen next, but it's best if you all disperse now."

Carita glanced at her baby, then at the murmuring congregation. "No, we need our oneness now, more than ever," she whispered, her arm tightening around little Elanor. "And there's no one. . ."

Reluctantly yet firmly, Carita rose and approached the front of the room. "Brothers and sisters, neighbors, friends—let us give thanks." The quiet voice rose in the room, somehow commanding attention despite its lack of volume. "O give thanks unto *Adon,* for He is good; for His *hesed* endures forever."

"O give thanks to the *Adon* of adons, for his *hesed* endures forever." Another voice took up the praise.

Ellisia sank back to the bench, finally allowing her body to fully relax as the worship rose around her. She wanted to soak in it, to be truly a part of it—but she was the traitor. She'd worked against them. She could have prevented this altogether. She'd been one of them, and yet she wasn't.

No. Something within warned her that wasn't true. That wasn't the way of *Adon Olam.* As her hands massaged her temples, the night at Kraevyn's returned to mind—the night she'd claimed she had a headache and later a severe one had struck. She'd caused it to be so by her words. Words had power. Thoughts had power. *Every tongue that rises in judgment against you, you shall condemn.* That's what *Adon Olam* had said, and if that didn't mean her, it didn't mean anybody.

A resolve formed in her mind, right there in the meeting house. From that day forward, she'd never let anyone say anything negative or contrary to the Book without countering it with truth.

24

THE STORM WORKED itself through its own fury and merely rumbled and mumbled grumpily as the long hours of the afternoon stretched on. Ellisia, in her dim room back in Frydael inn, her head in her hands, had ample time to cogitate—something she hadn't let herself do for quite some time.

She had plenty to ponder—especially her own seeming failures that very day. *Why,* Adon Olam? She'd been there, ready for the battle, ready to speak the words that would dramatically tumble the kingdom of the enemy, and nothing had happened.

Kaelan and Caeleb had both managed to escape, but that wasn't on her.

Never would she forget that feeling of helplessness of looking the enemy in the face and realizing she had no weapons.

Ellrick's Book lay open on the bed before her, but as of yet, she hadn't mustered up the strength to try for a single word. The answer rested somewhere there, she knew, but she wasn't in the mood for answers. She'd rather mope. She knew her self-pity wasn't helping anything—least of all herself—but she couldn't seem to help herself. There was something penance-like in wallowing in her own self-despair.

Even though her heart rebelled, she pulled the Book towards herself and listlessly cast her eyes on the page. Nothing. Just as she expected.

But she made herself flip a section of pages over, again scanning the page. Still nothing. *Come on,* Adon Olam.

But then it caught her eye out of nowhere.

If you abide in me, and my words abide in you, ye shall ask what ye will, and it shall be done unto you.

Ellisia stared the opposite wall down. Kaelan's voice, reading those very words right before the Doekh group invaded, played repeatedly in her head. If she extracted the precious from the worthless... condition led to promise... she'd be His spokesman.

She could only speak words powerfully for His kingdom when she'd been abiding in Him and keeping His words as precious within her mind.

And that was one thing she certainly hadn't been doing these last months.

Again her head bowed until her forehead touched the blanket. She had some straightening out to do with *Adon Olam,* immediately. The next battle wouldn't find her quiver so empty.

This *is the battle,* His Spirit whispered in her heart. *Now.*

The sun had begun to play shy wolf with the gently receding clouds by the time a rap preceded Ryna's dark head at the door. "Make sure you pack your bag this afternoon. We're leaving for Syorien in the morning."

Back to Syorien. Turmoil rattled Ellisia's soul. What ought she to do now? She'd determined not to continue using her wordology skills for anyone defying *Adon Olam* and His ways, but her agreement with Kraevyn still stood. Strange that he had said nothing to her since the meeting.

Once introduced, the thought pounded in her head.

This wasn't like him. As her instructor, her traitorous behavior would be at the forefront of his mind. Surely he'd have requested her presence—or said *something* to her. Perhaps the escape of Caeleb and Kaelan had been urgent enough to direct his attention elsewhere for the moment. But she was not looking forward to seeing Kraevyn again.

Again her head bowed to the bed, and she remained immovable for several long moments. At last, she rose and slipped on the shoes she'd kicked off.

Mud squirted beneath them as the familiar streets fell away beneath her feet. Raindrops glistened on grass blades, robins merrily pecked away at the moistened path, and patches of sunlight fell about her here and there. The trail to Carita's front door hadn't changed a bit, however.

Neither had the atmosphere inside, despite the experiences of the afternoon. The conversation passed in a blur, Ellisia's mind and heart a whirlwind of thoughts and feelings, each striving for the upper hand. If only she had more time in Frydael . . . but now was not that time.

She'd return. She had commitments to Mae, to the Academy, and to Kraevyn—though she now couldn't wait to formally terminate the latter. Her months in Syorien had opened her eyes to so much she'd never dreamed existed, but now she'd return. She'd care for Mae's house, she'd finish her literature line—everything would be back to normal. No ambitions for her; they'd already propelled her far enough in the wrong direction.

What was it that the little book in the back of Ellrick's Book had said? "When the lion saw resistance should be made, he drew back, and came no further." Something like that, anyway. Hopefully that would prove true in her case. The enemy would see her resistance and leave her alone. But in her case, the enemy seemed very real—very much flesh and blood, very threatening.

When she said as much to Carita, her sister's lips curved gently upwards even as a spark lit her eye. "Indeed, that is the very tactic of the enemy of our souls. He walks about as a roaring lion, seeking whom he may devour, and yes, he wants to devour you. But we know him. We know who he is in reality. He's a defeated foe. And when we call him out as a defeated foe by the blood of Yeshua, all power over us vanishes instantly."

"A soap-bubble in lion form," Ellisia commented. "But the Lion of the Tribe of Juda isn't really a Lion either. The writer looked for a lion and saw only a lamb."

"And that is the mystery—a Lion who is a Lamb, not conquering his dominion through power, fear, or force, but by being led silently to slaughter, covering over the sins of the world with His dying blood, and then defeating death itself by the power of His endless resurrection life."

"So . . . the battle of the two lions is the Battle of the Soap Bubble and the Lamb?" Absurdity forced a laugh from Ellisia.

"Yes, only far more deadly. Don't forget, the enemy is the master deceiver who works in illusions, but without the shield of faith, illusion becomes reality. If we believe the appearance, its deadly effect upon our lives is real."

"Oh! That makes sense!" Ellisia sat up suddenly. Words worked that way, too; when she refused to believe their power over her, they had none. "So . . . the battle is in the mind, and the shield of faith is actually the offensive weapon. That's absurd."

"There's a reason the Book says, 'Bring them down, O *Adon* our shield.'"

"Oh . . .because shields don't generally bring anyone down? But the shield of faith destroys the illusions . . ." Ellisia's mind busily sorted this bit of information.

"But no, the shield as an offensive weapon only works along with the sword," Carita added.

"Yes . . . like I couldn't have faith when none of the Word was in my mind."

"In your heart, part of your life," Carita corrected gently. "Receive with humility the engrafted word, which is able to save your soul. Faith only comes by hearing, and hearing by the Word."

Ellisia sat silently for several minutes, her head again in her hands. This was all well and good, but how did it truly relate to her daily life—her Academy studies, even the Wulf philosophy? It was so similar and yet so different.

It was late. She couldn't figure it all out in one night. She had a long journey ahead of her to puzzle it out.

Back in Syorien, Ellisia slid surprisingly smoothly back into her studies and her life at Mae's. *Surprisingly* because Kraevyn said almost nothing to her, and Mae required only the simple explanation that she'd been home because of a family emergency. As far as everything around Ellisia was concerned, it was almost as if she'd never left.

Yet a tense undercurrent flowed through her during her classes. She'd avoided Jolyn and Ryna in the halls, even completing her studying in her own room at Mae's instead of lingering in her beloved BookHall alcove.

She'd still heard nothing from Kraevyn.

All at once, the news changed. Meetings were being called. News bulletins changed their tone and blatantly used a baffling combination of humor, logic, and entertainment to spread their message that knowledge and science reigned, not pleasure, and certainly not *Adon Olam*. Street criers' content—usually dripping with encouragement to indulge in personal pleasures—now was laced with the subtle theme of the all-powerful, all-benevolent knowledge. The Show Halls showcased dark-haired professors, all cunningly weaving the message into the normal trivia contests, the story performances—everything. All continued as normal, but to Ellisia's senses, heightened by nature and honed by much practice, the message seemed different. The tone had been damaging before, but now it was outright deadly.

One day as the end of the long spring approached, she returned as usual to Mae's home to complete her afternoon routine and start supper. Jaeson stood in the middle of the kitchen, his arms crossed, Elkaena clinging to his foot while her brothers shook blocks of wood on a blanket in the corner, occasionally tasting one. Nearby, Mae drew her needle in and out of a tiny shirt with sudden, jerky motions.

"What?" Ellisia froze, glancing from one to the other.

"It's begun—the silent invasion of Taerna." Jaeson shifted to avoid knocking over his persistent daughter.

"Jaeson." Mae's word was clipped.

"What?"

"No dramatics necessary."

"Mae, you know how I feel about this."

"Yes, I know, and we pray you are wrong."

"What's happened?" Ellisia put in.

"Audio implants for homes have happened. Courtesy of the all-powerful Doekh, of course."

"Those have been widespread in the Palace District for some time now."

"Yes, but only because the kings wanted them there. Helped the shows and entertainments and such, and I understand that. But now they're giving them—no cost—to private homes. They say it's for our benefit, of course: we won't miss any announcements or broadcasts from the palace; all the news will be directly in our homes; we can overhear shows right from home. Most of the city is wild for the idea."

"And you're not." Ellisia's mind spun. Kraevyn had showed her the basic science of the devices used in Central Doekh. She'd known about their use in the ShowHalls and the Palace, but . . . "They've offered *you* one? Here in the Lower District?"

"That's what bothers me. You'd think they'd move down gradually from the Palace District, but no. They're starting with the Lower Districts and moving up. Makes me wonder why—no one starts with us."

"Maybe they feel sorry for us?" Mae asked.

"Not a chance." Jaeson scooped up Elkaena and crossed the room to sit with his wife.

Ellisia moved towards the stove to begin supper. "You refused?"

"For now. But I'm afraid I won't have a choice for long. Someone's coming to set them up in every house as a courtesy—because of *course everyone* wants them, obviously."

"And you don't want it because . . .?" Ellisia pulled out plates, spreading them out on the table.

"Because I don't want the kings, or any foreigners, for that matter, up in my personal business. I don't want them in my home, able to say who knows what."

"Maybe the gatherings could be sent to each home through these devices," Ellisia suggested.

"I'm sure they could. But these aren't controlled by followers of *Adon Olam.* Neither the kings nor the professors would want the gatherings spread like that."

Ellisia nodded. Words again—this time in the homes. Where would it lead? Certainly the Doekh group could use something along these lines to spread their research and knowledge to all Syorien—it would be the quickest and most effective method to reach directly into the homes and lives of the people, especially the lower districts that were the farthest removed from the influence of the palace.

She silently boiled the sweet potatoes over the stove as Mae jerkily sewed and Jaeson watched the triplets. This science had so much potential for good—for improvement of the people, for education of the poorer ones as well as the richer. It held the potential to be all that Kraevyn had declared in his idealistic speeches to her.

But Ellisia had seen where his ambitions were taking him. Without *Adon Olam*, his power of words must stem from the wrong source. The roaring lion. The serpent-creature. The enemy of souls, who ultimately wished no true prosperity or good upon the Taernans. In those hands, this new device could be nothing but evil. The announcements, the shows, the education—it would all drive Taernans further from *Adon Olam*. It had to.

No, there could be no going back to normal life for her. A war was on, and every fiber of her inner being vibrated with the personal call to battle. She'd be equipped this time.

And so, once supper was finished and the dishes tidily tucked back onto the shelves, she disappeared up to her room as usual.

But not to read, at least not the books she was used to.

An hour or two with Ellrick's Book was time most precious to her just now, despite what her mind craved.

25

SHE ATTENDED ACADEMY as usual during the day, yet her soul felt more unsettled than she'd ever noticed before. When had studying ever impacted her spiritual well-being?

Yet somehow she sensed, vaguely and dimly through the newness of the experience, that something within her had changed. For the first time, her pursuit of *Adon Olam* and His Word was something highly personal. For the first time, she recognized all that lay at stake. And for the first time, she noticed how all she immersed her mind in tugged in opposition to the life of *Adon Olam* in her.

If she studied world literature for the majority of the day's hours, how could a few hours at night in Ellrick's Book counterbalance that intake?

Characteristically, her decision to withdraw from all but the required classes rapidly followed. No longer were free hours spent in the BookHall or reading in her corner. Ellrick's Book found its way to her hand more and more often—while eating her midday meal, while waiting for the next class, even while walking to and from Academy on occasion. This was war, and she couldn't be found compromising with the enemy.

Yet the struggle within her continued. The Book of *Adon Olam* didn't fill the mental and intellectual voids.

She found herself craving something more interesting, more challenging, more fascinating. She found her mind wandering more than she would ever care to admit.

Yet she persevered.

One afternoon when she simply couldn't sit still with the Book any longer (an anomaly with her), she paced the halls of Academy, unwittingly wandering farther than she'd ever been, her mind fixed on the passage she'd just encountered, captivated by that enticing word *victory*. Over and over she whispered it to herself:

"For this is the love of *Adon Olam*, that we keep his commandments: and his commandments are not grievous. For whatsoever is born of *Adon Olam* overcometh the world: and this is the victory that overcometh the world, even our faith."

Into her reveries weaseled strains of music. She glanced from the painted red door on one side to the long row of narrow transparent doors on the other. This must be the music hall. Curious, she ambled past the first door, casually glancing at it as she passed. A bushy-headed young man slouched, a flute to his lips, yet the sealed room shut out his tune.

Ellisia continued. A raven-haired girl with intellectual eyes stood in the next, plucking the strings of a futuristic-looking harp or lute of some sort. Boys and girls of all descriptions, playing instruments just as varied, lined the hall, interspersed with vacant practice rooms.

The last door lay ajar ever so slightly, and Ellisia approached with increasing curiosity. It must be from here that the faint notes she'd first heard had originated, though the tune had since fallen silent.

Even as she stepped towards the door, a clear voice—simplistic in style, surprisingly innocent in tones and quality, youthful even—lilted in an acapella melody. Ellisia halted, reluctant to startle or disturb the singer, who might not know the door cracked open enough to project the notes.

> *Messengers came to Jehoshaphat's throne.*
> *"King, there is trouble as we've never known.*
> *Armies are coming—a great mighty host.*
> *We have no power of which we can boast."*
> *The king in fear, yet trusting, began to seek his Lord.*
> *He cried for all His wisdom and might to be outpoured.*
> *He held a fast in Judah and led them in this cry:*
> *"In You we trust; be near,* Adon—*are You not God on high?*

Adon. This was a story from the Word then, one Ellisia hadn't heard for many years, but one she well remembered. That meant that someone who knew *Adon Olam* was here at Academy—and singing about Him openly.

> *"You are* Olam *of all heaven and earth.*
> *You are* Adon *who has given us birth.*
> *And You have promised our savior to be.*
> *In our affliction, we're waiting on Thee.*
> Adon, *will You not judge them? We have no might at all.*
> *We have no strength or wisdom, but Your strength is not small,*
> *Nor has Your hand been shortened; 'tis strength eternally.*
> *We know not what to do,* Adon—*but our eyes are on Thee."*

The clear notes fascinated her, and the trusting words

meshed with the melody in such a powerful way. Ellisia inched to the wall, listening.

> *While they were waiting, He answered their cry.*
> *"Be not afraid nor dismayed; I am nigh.*
> *Mine is the battle, so you need not fight.*
> *Go forth tomorrow beholding My might."*
> *The people bowed and worshipped while trusting what they'd heard.*
> *They rose up very early to carry out His word.*
> *They marched forth to the battle where victory was sure.*
> *With voices raised they sang His praise:*
> *"Praise Him; His love endures."*

Victory. There it was again. "This is the victory that overcometh the world, even our faith." Now Ellisia *had* to hear the rest of this song. If only the other musicians would stay in their rooms until she was gone.

> Adon *heard their worship and moved in His might.*
> *Israel's enemies started to fight,*
> *Not with His people, but among their own.*
> *In sight of all men, His power was shown.*
> *No enemies remained there when Israel reached that place.*
> *They gathered up the spoil. It took them three days' space.*
> *Proclaiming thankful gladness,* Adon Olam *they blessed.*
> *With joy the men returned again—and* Adon *gave them rest.*

The light, feeling tones shifted to a softer dynamic,

yet each word wended clearly to the silent listener as a heartfelt prayer.

> Adon, *when a trial You send unto me,*
> *Teach me to trust You, whatever it be.*
> *Teach me to silently wait for Your best,*
> *Letting You work as I patiently rest.*
> *I am but foolish weakness, but You are still my might.*
> *I will not use my own strength, but let You for me fight.*
> *I'll seek You first and early till peace You have restored.*
> *So I will trust* Adon Olam—*my strength is in my Lord.*

The final note sustained three beats, then fell away. Ellisia couldn't move, her mind far away, her back still hugging the wall. The picture the girl had sung was so far removed from anything Ellisia had ever seen, heard, or read in her life—well, perhaps anything but Carita. "Silently wait . . . letting You work . . ." Yes, Carita had lived that. But had Carita ever had to battle anything but her own timidity and the expectations of her neighbors for everyday chores? As usual, Ellisia couldn't begin to compare her own life with her sister's.

But perhaps *Adon Olam* was the same. If He came through for a king in a serious battle, perhaps He would come through for her.

The click of the door sliding open startled her, and she raised her eyes to find herself face to face with the singer. Blue eyes, open in surprise, an angled chin, and straw-tinted hair caught back from her face in some loose manner, stray wisps escaping about her ears and her forehead—shorter than average, she looked much more mature and womanly than her voice had suggested. A black high-neck vest partly covered a simple deep brown dress that suited her and somehow hung with noticeable grace over her form.

Ellisia balked between scarlet embarrassment and friendly ease.

"I'm Anthea—Anni," the singer volunteered, a trifle timidly.

"Ellisia. Pleasure to meet you."

"Vocal music line."

"World literature."

"Second year."

"First year."

"From Syorien's West District."

"Lower District."

Information exchanged, the silence lingered far too long. At last, Ellisia cleared her throat. "Where did you learn of *Adon Olam*?" She kept her voice as soft and non-threatening as she could.

"My parents." Anni didn't even hesitate.

"And you really believe Him—and you came to Academy?"

"Yes."

Ellisia nodded. "I too." A pause followed. "I know a quiet corner of the BookHall. Want to talk?"

"I have an hour before my next voice lesson." Anni nodded, her cheeks dimpling. "Lead on."

Ellisia spun around and wound back down the hall, but as she passed the rooms, yet another door opened in front of her and a curly-headed girl flashed a giant smile. "Where are you off to, Anni-Anni?"

"I just met Ellisia from world literature, and she's about to show me a BookHall corner she knows. Ellisia, this is Aethelwyn. Wyn, Ellisia."

"A definite pleasure to meet you, Lise-lise. You're in

lit, then? Not music? Of course, certainly not, or I'd met you long before this."

"Yes, I'm in world literature. But—Lise-lise?" Ellisia's tongue nearly tripped over the unfamiliar name.

Anni laughed. "I've never known Wyn to fail to shorten and double a name in that way, not in the three years I've known her."

"Oh. Okay, then— *Wyn-wyn.*" Ellisia winked.

"Believe me, I get called that more often than not these days."

"Even by yourself," Anni put in. "Would you like to join us? We have an hour."

"But—" Ellisia cast a glance between Anni and Wyn. She'd wanted to ask more about *Adon Olam,* to find out from Anni what she'd known of Him while at Academy and how she'd kept her focus among the high academic standards here . . . so much to ask, but not in front of a stranger whose attitude towards *Adon Olam* was yet unknown.

"We will probably talk about *Adon Olam,*" Anni interrupted. "So you can choose to come or not. No offense either way."

"Oh, I'll come," Wyn stated immediately. "Just got to bring out my—" She disappeared back into her practice room, then returned a moment later, a cello tucked under her arm with apparent ease and the bow clasped between her fingers.

Once she'd deposited it behind yet another door, she fell in behind Ellisia and Wyn. "Lead on."

"So . . . you know *Adon Olam,* too?" Ellisia let the question drop as she again began her trek back to the BookHall.

"*Know* is a relative word." Wyn shrugged. "I know who He is. I've heard most of what anyone has to say."

"And what do you think?"

"I'm open. I think most of the people I know who believe or claim Him are sincere, and I think He really does make a difference to them and in their lives. But me? I don't know. I've never seen much of a need to make up my mind one way or the other what I think. I guess I think He's out there. But I know a lot of people who don't even think that, and they seem fine. So, believe what you want, say what you like. I'm happy to listen to anything. That's why I'm here at Academy."

Ellisia entered the BookHall in silence. At her usual corner, she motioned the others in. Once all three were seated, she turned to Wyn. "Do you believe *Adon Olam* is the maker of all things?"

"Why, yes, I suppose so. Things came from somewhere."

"So you think He made you specifically?"

"Well, He made people, then, so by extension, yes, I would say He made me."

"Do you think He had a reason for making you?"

"Eh. I don't know. He might have. Or He might just have made people and I happened to be one of them. No special purpose."

"Before I formed you in the womb, I knew you, and before you were born, I sanctified you—set you apart." Anni chimed in softly with a quote from the Book.

"Hmm..." Wyn pushed her black curls behind her shoulders and tilted her nose upwards. "Another one to think about, eh."

"Specifically the one thing I was thinking of was this." Ellisia drew in a breath. "There are two kingdoms at work here. There's the kingdom of *Adon Olam* that His Book tells about, and there's the kingdom of the enemy. Neither one can be seen, but they are real around us. We do see them at work. We see their effects. And we're all subjects of one kingdom or the other. In Syorien today I see pleasure reigning, working chaos within families, promising happiness but somehow never quite delivering. I see people devoting their lives to pursuit of this pleasure, and I see the older generation with hopeless eyes and disillusioned hearts. Then again, I see people devoting themselves to knowledge and learning—that's the big temptation for me. Proclaiming that the ultimate aim in life is intellect, or knowing the most, or using that knowledge for power. Yet look at the older professors—the ones living in the Palace Retirement Home. What a sad condition to aspire to."

"I see what you mean," Wyn put in. "But what then should we aim at? Satisfaction in what we do? In the little things, perhaps. Making others' lives a little easier and better."

"If *Adon Olam* is our maker, perhaps we ought to ask Him that question." Ellisia's hand slid towards Ellrick's Book. "But right now, even here in the Academy, the enemy's working. Turning people towards self-fulfillment and pleasure, which will equal disillusionment. I wouldn't be surprised if you start to see a shift in what's taught here. And it's up to us who know to stand against it for truth—for life." *For victory.*

"But how?" Anni spoke up. "I've seen that—I've felt it—the subtle shift, even in the year and a half I've been here. I knew the tone of this place wasn't what I believed, but I didn't know it was this godless. It's getting harder for an individual to even claim *Adon Olam* publicly here."

"If you abide in me, and my words abide in you, you shall ask whatever you will, and it shall be done." Ellisia quoted the passage that had been continually on her mind recently. "When the enemy comes in like a flood, the Spirit of *Adon Olam* will lift up a standard against him."

"Oh! I know!" Anni put in suddenly. "I was just

reading it last week, wondering about it. 'And they overcame him by the blood of the Lamb, and by the word of their testimony, and they loved not their lives unto the death.'"

"'Therefore rejoice, ye heavens, and them that dwell in them,'" Ellisia chimed in.

"Because *we* live in the heavens." Anni's face was alight now. "The word of their testimony—walking with Him alone, and willing to stand against the enemy in whatever ways need be."

"Exactly. And the word—words are powerful. That's one thing I've learned here. Mostly in a worldly way so far, but I know that the same is true in the kingdom of *Adon Olam*. I just have to learn how to use them right."

"I'm sure He'll teach you. It's in the little things—the choosing to claim Him when it's easier to stay quiet. Or to pray when you want to relax. Or sit apart with His Word when you'd rather be talking to your friends. Speaking of which . . ." Anni glanced at the clock in the alcove across from them. ". . .oh, I still have time."

"But I don't. I've got to get to my room." Wyn stood. "But seriously, this is fascinating. I'd love to talk more another day. I'll be thinking on what you said, Anni-Anni, and you too, Lise-lise." With a wave, she bounced off, her curls dancing after her and her blue dress swirling.

"That's Wyn." Anni's smile bloomed as she looked after her friend. "She'll be back. She seemed more interested than usual today with such topics."

"How do you maintain your life in *Adon Olam* here?" Ellisia's fingers traced the lining of the Book in the bag that hung beside her. "When you spend the whole day thinking about other things—studies and all?"

A smile played around Anni's cheeks and scrunched her eyes. "I told you already. Did you forget?"

"What? When?"

The smile widened, and the clear voice rang low yet distinct.

I am but foolish weakness, but You are still my might.
I will not use my own strength, but let You for me fight.
I'll seek You first and early till peace You have restored.
So I will trust Adon Olam—*my strength is in my Lord.*

"Oh. You did."

There wasn't much else to be said. Ellisia's eyes followed the lines in the flooring, contemplating. It wasn't anything new, but somehow that one little verse seemed to say everything.

"Anni," she said at last, lifting her eyes to her new friend. "When a crisis comes—as I'm afraid it may quite soon—may I count on you to be by my side?"

"If your side is *Adon Olam*'s, yes, of course." The blue eyes locked with the dark ones, and in that instant, a friendship birthed, begotten deeply within by the solidarity of a mutually-shared passion for something far beyond either of themselves, a common goal, a shared yearning to be part of something eternal—difficult and self-sacrificing though it may be.

"Do you know, are there others—here at Academy? Honestly, yours is the first positive mention of *Adon Olam* I've heard within these walls."

"There are more than you would think." Anni crossed her boots and leaned back. "I know of some. Many are reticent and won't be vocal, but I think it would be of mutual benefit for you to meet them. You seem to have this way of speaking that's just—compelling." Again her face lifted as her beaming countenance beheld Ellisia.

"Or *Adon Olam* does," mumbled Ellisia. "But yes, I'd like to meet them."

"Come. I'll introduce you to a few immediately, and the rest as they come. I have a few moments yet."

For the rest of the hour, Ellisia met name after name as Anni performed the introductions. Male and female, older and younger, a variety of study lines, a variety of experience and beliefs of *Adon Olam*—Ellisia never ceased to be astonished at the sheer vastness of the differences in those she was meeting. Back in Frydael, it seemed that everyone who claimed *Adon Olam* appeared to be more or less similar in beliefs and ideas. To all, she spoke words of encouragement, of exhortation, of a thankful heart. Some of the students knew of still others to whom they introduced her.

By the end of the next day, she'd met so many students she doubted she'd be able to locate and speak again with each one in the Academy halls.

"Perhaps we could meet in my home. Some would definitely come, and then you could speak with them all uninterrupted," Anni suggested towards the end of the week.

Ellisia eagerly consented, the date and time were set, and Anni proceeded upon the business of informing her friends of the event. Ellisia, meanwhile, retreated further into Ellrick's Book. She was only beginning to realize that she barely knew the Book herself; how could she ever influence others in the direction of the kingdom of *Adon Olam*?

Yet even as she studied in the seclusion of her own private room, thoughts and ideas kept forming, and eventually she reached for a blank book and began keeping notes. By the time the day to meet with the others at Anni's home arrived, many pages of thoughts and passages had spilled from the Book to her mind to her heart to the page.

When Anni caught her jotting down yet another thought and Ellisia reluctantly agreed to her request to see the little book, Anni's face lit up. "Ellisia! You need to copy this. Give it to the students. There's truth here. Everyone needs to read this. What you say about the nature of thanksgiving, truth, and power and victory ... this is a needed message!"

"But Anni, I can't. This is just for me. This is what *Adon Olam* has given me. I'm still learning this."

"It's not just for you. It's for everyone. This is the powerful truth of the kingdom we're working for. This is something you've been given for others—I know it. Why, I've been speaking with these people for two years now—this is where they are at. They'll understand this. From you especially, an intellectual student. I can't put words together like this for anything."

"Yes, you can," Ellisia protested. "You don't have to speak. Your songs can do it all."

"No one here wants to hear my songs—not anything helpful."

"Someone will."

"I've wondered why I was here at all—why I've made so many friends. I don't seem to be doing them any good. But now I think I know. It's because of you, Ellisia. I'll arrange to have this copied if you'll agree. I'll even give it to the students myself."

"Go ahead, then." A sigh twinged Ellisia's heart at the thought of her personal words being widely distributed. She pulled the book back towards herself, scanning the pages.

At least it wasn't as bad as she'd thought. *She'd* written this? She'd never done much writing, nor wanted to. She'd been too busy reading books to bother with creating her own. Somehow she'd never had much talent for written words—always so much more troublesome than spoken words. But this ... perhaps *Adon Olam* had directed her pen, for this certainly didn't sound like anything she'd say.

"Copy it. I'll help distribute it. Copies for every student, if we can."

Twenty neat copies of Ellisia's work lay tidily on the kitchen table when she walked into Anni's home that afternoon after Academy.

"Ellisia! Pleased to meet you!" A woman even shorter than Anni but with eyes just as blue and her silver hair in the same style slipped in from the next room. "I'm Elen, Anthea's mother. Welcome to our home. I was so pleased to hear that Anni met you and invited you here. I look forward to getting to know you more."

Ellisia exchanged greetings with Elen and Anni, met the writing student that had made the twenty copies, and was soon engaged in pleasant conversation. One by one and two by two, other students joined them, and Ellisia found the conversation moving towards a concept that had been occurring and reoccurring in her Book reading recently.

"When I was praying passages yesterday, I came across this one." A young man with spectacles and dark hair combed precisely to the side pointed at the open Book in his hand. "'Thou that inhabitest the praises of Israel.' Do you think *Adon Olam* literally lives in the praises of His people? When we praise Him, that's where He puts Himself?"

"That would make sense," Ellisia replied. "That's

what it says." Her mind flew back to her experiments with words in Kraevyn's lab. The Spirit—the breath—it all fit together.

"It's like the story in the song I'm learning," Anni added. "It's only when *Adon Olam*'s people marched out singing and praising that their enemies began fighting each other."

"Or when the disciples in prison prayed and sang, and *Adon Olam* sent an earthquake to free them." Elen set down a tray of pastries.

Ellisia plucked one off the plate and bit into it thoughtfully. "He made a point of telling us 'In everything give thanks, for this is the will of *Adon Olam* in Yeshua concerning you.'" She glanced around the room, at the black, brown, and blonde heads seated around the perimeter—as usual, she was the only redhead. Among the girls, curls bounced, straight locks swished, and braids bobbed as various ones nodded or tilted heads in agreement or thought.

"I think there's something in the story of that song of yours, Anni. That's unprecedented victory. It is the attitude—the attitude that matters," Ellisia continued. "If we don't have a mindset of thankfulness towards *Adon Olam*, we'll never be able to give thanks when the difficult moment arrives."

"There's something to be thankful about in everything," Anni agreed.

"Even if we're not thankful *for* the thing itself," the same young man spoke up.

Ellisia chewed her pastry, savoring the flavors of cinnamon and spice. The conversation continued around her, but she felt herself oddly withdrawn. For the rest of the evening, she observed and listened, strangely humbled in the presence of so many students who also sought *Adon Olam*.

Before the evening ended, Wyn approached her. "Lise-lise, happy to see you again. Pardon the bluntness, but I wanted to know—have you ever seen *Adon Olam* do something for you? I mean, asked Him something specific and had it happen. Something real."

Ellisia's mind flew back over her childhood and youth, awash with the memories. "Yes."

"Okay." Wyn nodded. "Then I'm in."

"In what?"

"In the *Adon Olam* camp. Kingdom. Whatever you called it. I'm in."

"You're in?"

"Yes. Now, tell me, what do I do? Read the Book?"

"You're in? Just like that?"

"It can't hurt, right? You seem more real than other groups I've seen. I think that about the two kingdoms sums up life better than most people who try to explain life. Anyway, I'm going to try it, and if *Adon Olam* doesn't show up anywhere in my life, I can always change my mind later."

"If you seek Him, you will find Him . . ." Ellisia faltered. What was one supposed to say in such a situation? She wished Carita or Kaelan were here to speak to Wyn. She'd never spoken with someone who'd just declared their intention to seek *Adon Olam*. "Read the Book. Yes. That's a good place to start."

"But what else?"

"The Book will tell you."

"You don't understand though." Wyn backed against the wall, her eyes searching Ellisia's. "I did believe *Adon Olam* once. As a child. *Adon Olam* told me His will was for me to be a nurse. Now, I can't stand anything about nursing. Not the people, not the system, not the processes themselves. Nothing. So I begged Him twice a day to let me be a cellist instead. For years. One day He told me I'd be a cellist. Now, I know it was His will for me to be a nurse. But now I know it's His will for me to study cello. And when I left *Adon Olam*, that was part of the deal. If He's really *Adon Olam,* why would He change His mind? How could I change His mind?" Her dark eyes earnestly searched Ellisia's.

Ellisia drew in a deep breath. Not only was this side of Wyn entirely opposite of her normal lighthearted bubbliness, this theological question was far too deep for her. *Adon Olam!* her heart cried. She didn't have the words. Not one. How *could Adon Olam* change His mind? Had He? How could she be sure?

Speak, my daughter. My Spirit will give you the words.

Ellisia froze. How could she speak when she didn't even know the first word? But she opened her mouth.

A word came.

"Jacob."

What? Seriously, Adon Olam*?*

"Hezekiah. Jonah. Saul."

Come on. Now I sound like a fool. But Wyn still stared at her as though she held the ultimate answer on life and the kingdom, not as though she were spouting male names like a maniac.

Ellisia retreated a step. "Okay. I have to look at the Book. One moment."

Wyn nodded, and Ellisia pulled out Ellrick's Book. *Saul.* Somewhere near the middle. She opened the Book.

Highlighted in a faint ink, words stood out on the page she opened. It wasn't Saul, but it caught her eye.

"But my people would not hearken to my voice; and Israel would none of me. So I gave them up unto their own hearts' lust: and they walked in their own counsels."

Softly she read the words aloud, then paged to the story of each of the men that she'd named. One by one she spoke the passages:

"And *Adon Olam* said unto Samuel, Hearken unto the voice of the people in all that they say unto thee: for they have not rejected thee, but they have rejected me, that I should not reign over them."

"And Jonah . . . said, Yet forty days, and Nineveh shall be overthrown. So the people of Nineveh believed *Adon Olam* . . . and *Adon Olam* repented of the evil, that he had said that he would do unto them; and he did it not."

Ellisia's voice trailed off, and she paged to Isaiah. Wyn leaned closer, reading the words herself aloud:

"In those days was Hezekiah sick unto death. And Isaiah the prophet the son of Amoz came unto him, and said unto him, Thus saith *Adon Olam* . . ."

Ellisia's voice joined in: "Set thine house in order: for thou shalt die, and not live. Then Hezekiah turned his face toward the wall, and prayed unto *Adon Olam* . . . Then came the word of *Adon Olam* to Isaiah, saying, Go, and say to Hezekiah, Thus saith *Adon Olam* . . . I have heard thy prayer, I have seen thy tears: behold, I will add unto thy days fifteen years."

"So *Adon Olam* did it for him! This Hezekiah-kiah man changed His mind too!" Wyn gazed awestruck at the page. "But how can it be? And *why*?"

Silently Ellisia paged to the beginning of the Book, praying *Adon Olam* would show her the passage He desired, for she had no idea where she was going.

"As a prince hast thou power with *Adon Olam* and with men, and hast prevailed."

Wyn glanced up quickly. "Oh! That's a passage. I thought you were just answering my question."

"*Adon Olam* was answering your question," Ellisia said. "And that's the answer. There's power in the tongue. He gives us our desires as we persist in them. He's given us power with Himself and with man—and we prevail."

Soberly she closed the Book, much subdued. *I could ruin someone's life with my words if I have that much power. Do I even want to mess with this?*

But she didn't have a choice. The power was *Adon Olam*'s, and if He'd given it to her and worked it through her, she could only receive it from His hand.

"Thank you," Wyn declared. "Thank you. I'm standing by that—for now. If He wants to do something, I'm ready. I want to see Him."

26

LENGTHY EASTERN SUNBEAMS danced across the grass and touched the heads of the wildflowers with sparkling gold as Ellisia swayed across the path from Mae's house to the road. A dove cooed, birds twittered, a sandhill crane honked in the distance, and overhead, an early falcon soared. Miniature frogs crisscrossed dewdrops on bright green grass; a rabbit in the field twitched its ears. Ellisia felt the sunbeams pierce her very soul, springing delight and joy to every fiber of her being. Disregarding her seventeen years, she twirled until the shimmering seafoam green skirt puffed out around her and tiny stones fled from under her sandals.

Hoisting her white bookbag back to her shoulder, she pranced towards the road. It might be a school day, but it was no ordinary school day. It was Spring Festival—for *Adon Olam* lovers, Resurrection Festival. Back in Frydael, the celebration generally passed quietly without much fanfare—an extra-fancy meal, a moment of remembrance, time outdoors if the weather cooperated—but here in Syorien! Every house boasted wildflowers, banners and streamers flew over the streets, citizens paraded the walks in their best spring attire.

Speeches had been prepared for Academy—

speeches of joy, growth, and celebration—and Ellisia's spirits soared. Even the most pleasure-seeking or academic-loving people of Syorien could come together to focus on joy and unity, if even just for a day or two.

Early as it was, the Academy steps and grounds already swarmed with people—students in party gowns in all shades of yellow, lavender, blue, green, pink, and white, or in smart-looking suits and polished boots; teachers and professors similarly attired; personages from the Palace; family members and general populace, all in their most festive attire and aspect. Long tables spread across the grounds, loaded with pastries, pancakes, porridge, and a wide assortment of fruits in a dazzling rainbow of colors.

Ellisia mingled with the crowd, quite at her ease, stopping to speak with one and another of her acquaintances from the past few weeks, thanks to Anni's introductions. Wyn's bubbling figure, draped in gorgeous yet simplistic lavender chiffon, her black curls bouncing freely as always yet ornamented with a single white lily, slipped to her side. "A Pleasant Spring, Lise-lise! Isn't it a gorgeous day? And aren't these lemon pastries scrumptious?"

"I haven't tried one yet, Wyn-wyn. But I'll take your word for it." Ellisia's smile flashed to her. "It's almost time for the speeches to begin, though, so I ought to grab one when I refill my canteen."

"Oh, you know you ought! Can't come to the Spring Festival and not have a lemon pastry. By the by, *Adon Olam* still owes me one. I haven't seen Him anywhere doing anything since that night at Anni's. I'm still reading that Book I got, but it's on Him. I told Him I'm giving Him till the end of the spring term, and then if

He hasn't showed up yet, I get to reevaluate."

Ellisia shrugged, not quite willing to agree with Wyn's flippant way of speaking, yet at the same time adoring the passion for *Adon Olam* concealed beneath the casual words. Somehow, deep within Wyn's heart, lay a genuine love for *Adon Olam* mingled with the very natural doubts of human nature. One couldn't help but admire her very Wyn-ness. But Wyn still spoke.

"You know, I was reading just this morning, and did you know that Yeshua says, 'I am the resurrection and the life'? Never knew that. I thought He *did* the resurrection, and He *has* life, but He *is*? Strange way of speaking that one had. You know what else He said? 'I am the good shepherd,' and far as I can tell, He never had any actual bleating sheep. And a few days ago, 'I am the bread. Eat me.' Never heard anyone talk like that!"

"He listened to His Father," Ellisia remarked.

"Well, perhaps if we listened a whole lot better, we'd talk a whole lot stranger." Wyn glided to the table to nip up another lemon pastry.

Wyn chatted on as the girls enjoyed the pastries. Ellisia listened, sometimes interjecting a remark or two, until the appearance of a gentleman on the Academy steps signaled a slow silence to creep across the gathered crowds.

Ellisia listened with interest to the standard welcomes, announcements, tributes to the kings and other organizers, and other miscellaneous minutiae. Balancing her canteen in one hand, she leaned against an oak, careful not to scrape her satiny dress against the bark.

One by one, various speakers took the steps. Pontifications on diverse topics followed: the history of Syorien, the history of the festival, the typical late spring weather trends, the latest technological advancements, the schedule of upcoming shows and trivia contests, readings from books, updates on the latest developments at the Academy, and customized messages thought to interest the general public. The sun rays lengthened across the square, and Ellisia gradually sank to a sitting position as the speeches continued.

Then a figure mounted the steps that jolted her upright.

Kraevyn.

The sight of him sent a chill down her spine. She had seen neither him nor Jolyn for many days, and she'd hoped that he'd been sent elsewhere for the rest of the term.

Not a chance. He was here—speaking at the Spring Festival. Terror jolted through her, and she inconspicuously lowered herself again, praying no one would spot her. Where were the others? He was not here alone. Automatically her eyes searched the crowd for any sign of Jolyn, of Maeve, of Ryna, of any of his associates. But no. If they were present, they were well disguised.

"Citizens of Syorien, students, royalty—a pleasant Spring's Eve to you. I come before you today to speak of this fine Academy, of your students, of your advancement, of your future."

He carried on, his voice projecting clearly through the masses with its customary weight and authority. The confidence—the persuasiveness—was he using one of his devices to assist his delivery? Were his associates manning one of the instruments from some secluded location in the crowd to manipulate the minds of the people? Ellisia swallowed, glancing around nervously.

"Wyn," she whispered.

"What is it, Lise-lise?"

"Hush! You remember what I said about the two

kingdoms, about battling for the right kingdom?"

"Of course."

"This might be the time. That man speaking? I know him. He works for the enemy. No one would know it, but I've seen it and know who he is."

"Oh-ho! So it's war-time then? Hope you're all prayed up, Lise-lise. We're about to blow the enemy's boots off. I'm 'xpecting *Adon Olam* to show up today or never, then, because I'm here, and He is too, and it's time."

Ellisia wanted to laugh at the fierceness contained in the whisper, but dread gripped her heart too strongly. "Okay. Just wanted to alert you. Yes. Pray. And be alert."

"Sure thing, Lise-lise. Wyn-wyn's here." The petite dark figure clasped her hands tightly together, her eyes shutting at once and her lips moving in silent prayer. Then her eyes popped open. "Nope. Got that one wrong again. *Adon Olam*'s here. No worries." The eyes shut.

Ellisia couldn't help a smile. Praise *Adon Olam* for Aethelwyn.

But Kraevyn still spoke—lauding the academies of surrounding nations and promising to open their secrets to Amadel Academy today.

"Has tradition told you things must go a certain way? Have old religions spoken that specific studies must be taught? Have authorities mandated rules for their own pleasure? It's not for your profit. If you are a free society, if you are a forward-moving people, if you are indeed advancing citizens of a great nation—let's show it right here in the Academy! Let us institute a reform, that your Academy may prove the greatest in the four countries. You have the wisdom of the four countries at hand. Among you even now are the most highly studied professors of all four countries. At a word from you—the citizens—we are at your command. Install us in your Academy, and you will see knowledge rain down like hail on the hottest summer day. You will see prosperity and wealth return to your city. Your students will prosper—they will rise and rebuild your city one step at a time with the brightest of tomorrow, the best of today, and the greatest of yesterday. Together, you can make your city of Syorien a beacon on a hilltop, a light to which the eyes of all nations are drawn. What say you, friends of Syorien? Are you with me? Shall we install the new professors? Shall we overhaul the teachings to the advancement of the nations around you? Shall we begin right now building with the best of the best?"

He raised his arms, and, with one voice, the crowd surged to its feet. "Yes! Yes!"

Students and adults alike took up the cry and the cheer. "Down with the old. Up with the best!"

Ellisia shrank back against her oak, breathless with the suddenness of it all. They were moving now—marching, forming, following Kraevyn, though Ellisia could not tell where they were going or what they were doing. Spellbound, she could only watch. Kraevyn directed them now. Somewhere in the crowd, voices rose louder—instigating, suggesting, pressing the crowd on. A long row of teachers, all in dark capes, formed on the steps behind Kraevyn. Ellisia gulped. Kraevyn must have received reinforcements from Doekh. None of the teachers looked remotely Taernan.

Marching, marching, marching . . . what were they doing? Suddenly stacks of books appeared, thrown into the center of the square from seemingly nowhere. Copies of the Word. Books that quoted the Word. At once a thin spurt of smoke rose from the pile, then a tiny flame shot from one book, then another. She had to stop this madness! Was the whole city under the influence of Kraevyn's persuasive lies?

Do something! She had the words, the skills, the matching persuasiveness. *Speak up!* Her entire being shook with terror. She couldn't let herself think what might happen if Kraevyn caught her. "Pray, Wyn," she hissed, and then she was running, dodging the crowd, speeding towards the steps, her heart keeping pace with her slapping sandals, heedless of the seafoam green satin.

One by one she raced up the steps. They seemed to come too slowly. She was at the top. There was an alcove—she could get there; she would be out of the people's reach there ... up she heaved. "People of Taerna!" she shrieked. "Listen! *Adon Olam* reigns. He is master of your life. Listen to Him. Let us have no more of this madness. These lies."

It was no use. She could hear her voice going on, but she knew it wasn't penetrating. No one could even hear her over the madness. Desperately, frantically she carried on. Perhaps her words could still have power even if no one heard them.

Her tongue stuck in her throat, and she couldn't even think of what to say. She fell to her knees, whispering now. "*Adon Olam*! Save us! Help us! Help me. Save the school! Save Your Word! Rebuke the lies!" Tears ran down her face, losing themselves in her hair. Her hands shook as she brushed back both the tears and the hair, peering down over the crowd. Somewhere—ah, there was the oak!—Wyn still prayed. Wyn still waited to see *Adon Olam*. "*Adon Olam*! Show up! We need you!" Ellisia was begging now. "Please!" She hurled the words out. "Lies, stop! Kraevyn, halt! People, stop! This madness ends now."

The people still marched, a mob now, crazily doing the bidding of Kraevyn and anyone else moving under the current. Ellisia drew a deep breath. She had to try one more time. "*Adon Olam!*" *Give thanks.* "Thank—thank You—that You are here—that You are the victor—that . . ." She couldn't think of anything else to thank Him for. She faltered, unable to stop the shaking either of her hands or her heart.

It wasn't enough. She could feel it within her being. She wasn't strong enough. She couldn't do it. She couldn't stand against the combined forces of flesh and spirit. The full power of the enemy crashed against her soul, and she crumbled. Her eyes fell shut. She couldn't win. Not now, not ever.

It was over.

And with that realization, she laughed.

The enemy is a spirit. What am I doing trying to fight him in the flesh?

Of course. She couldn't fight the enemy. With all her skills and training, she didn't have the authority, power, or intellect to match him. He deceived the entire world long before she ever showed up. When called to match an eternal being, she didn't have a shot.

I can't do it. The realization sank in, and finally she understood. *That's victory.*

And in the midst of the chaos, the smoke, the shouts—a smile rose on her face.

"Wyn!" she shouted. "Wyn!"

Faster than Ellisia would have imagined, Wyn covered the ground between them and stood directly under her. "Help. Tell the others. Tell Anni. Speak. Praise. Sing."

Wyn blinked twice.

"I'm not strong enough. It's a spiritual battle. Something unseen is fighting here. We need more voices—more people to stand against the enemy. As many as we can! Tell them. Speak, praise, give thanks—sing! Remember Anni's song! Overcome by the Word!"

A light sparked in Wyn's dark eyes. "Lise-lise?"

"Yes?" Ellisia caught her breath.

Wyn's eyebrow quirked. "Got to remember. We're the attacker. We don't walk into this saying, 'Here comes the darkness.'"

Ellisia blinked, uncomprehending.

"The darkness backs up and says, 'Here comes the light!'" And Wyn spun, bounding down the wide steps two at a time. "Anni!"

Ellisia spotted Anni briefly in the mass, but then the girl disappeared. Ellisia clasped her hands tightly. "*Adon Olam,*" she whispered. "I choose to use my words *now* for Your kingdom. Enemy: here comes the light."

Singing. Praising. Speaking. What should she sing? The shouts around her echoed in her head, drowning out the still, small voice that spoke in her heart. She had to squeeze her eyes tightly shut, cram her fists in her ears, and take a few deep breaths.

Now is come salvation . . .

Without stopping to think, she sang it aloud.

Now is come salvation,
Salvation and strength,
And the kingdom of Adon Olam,
The kingdom of Adon Olam,
And the power of His Son,
The power of His Son.

Her voice quavered and could hardly hold the notes, but from somewhere down below a clear, familiar voice took up the melody.

Now is come salvation,
Salvation and strength,
And the kingdom of Adon Olam,
The kingdom of Adon Olam,
And the power of His Son.
The power of His Son.

From all across the grounds, voices joined in the tune—faint and difficult to hear over the commotion of the crowd, but still there—more than Ellisia would ever have guessed. Men and women, boys and girls, students she knew and students she'd never met—more and more voices took up the words, singing louder and louder still.

With increased courage, Ellisia licked her lips and

continued:

> For the accuser of our brethren is cast down,
> Which accused them before Adon Olam day and night.
>
> And they overcame Him by the blood of the Lamb,
> And by the word of their testimony,
> And they loved not their lives unto the death.

The blood of the Lamb. Ellisia's mind flashed back to the Lion of the Tribe of Juda. She visualized Him standing against the roaring lion, disguised as a blood-covered Lamb.

"I claim the blood by the word spoken!" she shouted. In that moment, everything rushed back to her: the BookHall, her wordology studies, the Literature line, even her beloved books, her family, her purpose. "No. I relinquish it all. My whole life. *Adon Olam,* I am Yours."

"I will praise Him with my whole heart . . ." she sang. "Thanks be to *Adon Olam* for this place, these happenings, Himself."

Once more she sang.

> Now is come salvation,
> Salvation and strength,
> And the kingdom of Adon Olam,
> The kingdom of Adon Olam,
> And the power of His Son.
> The power of His Son.

This time as the words throbbed they swelled in volume. Ellisia felt the power of the Spirit within her, rising and battling on her behalf. She heard the might of *Adon Olam* in the voices. Her eyes locked on Kraevyn's—just one moment—but her voice never faltered. His eyes held defeat.

"Thank You, *Adon Olam,* that it's not my victory. It's Yours. And it's ours."

Her voice was only one in the multitude—one tiny voice proclaiming the truth, in faith that *Adon Olam* would show up and show Himself strong on their behalf.

Only one tiny voice—but it was enough.

27

As the song again swelled across the grounds, a breeze whipped Ellisia's hair. She pulled it behind her, scanning the sunny skies. Out of the clear day, charcoal-toned clouds rolled in.

Now is come salvation . . .

It rang confidently now. Ellisia straightened. She'd just be there watching *Adon Olam* show up. That's all. Prayers swirled through her.

The torrents of rain hit in full force, dousing the bonfire along with the crowd's spirits. As quickly as the rain arrived, it passed, the wind still whipping strongly from the south before softening to a gentle breeze.

Now the only sound heard was the song—the song rising, stilling the unruly crowd as a lullaby might soothe an upset child.

The kingdom of Adon Olam . . .

Ellisia smiled, secure in the peace of *Adon Olam,* whatever might happen next.

The power of His Son.

The song ended, and from all around voices arose, no longer singing, but speaking, praising. Male and female, young and old, voices blended and cadenced in words of truth, of power, of life. Ellisia found herself repeating with a confidence far beyond herself the familiar words:

"In the beginning was the Word, and the Word was with *Adon Olam*, and the Word was *Adon Olam*. The same was in the beginning with *Adon Olam*. All things were made by Him, and without Him was not anything made that was made. In Him was life, and that life was the light of men."

From somewhere near the bonfire, Caeleb's familiar figure rose. A grin nearly split Ellisia's face in two—it had been *so* long since she'd seen him, and now here! Now! Then he was on the steps, exhorting, encouraging, speaking truth, sharing, grinning as only Caeleb could. The people listened; at his encouragement, they salvaged the books they'd just thoughtlessly tossed to the flames; they cleared the steps of the foreign teachers. Somewhere in the middle of everything Ellisia heard shouting and threats, and she pieced together that Kraevyn and his team were banished back to Doekh.

From her perch, she could see the dark cloaks streaming away—and she breathed a sigh that was thanksgiving. "*Adon Olam*," she whispered, her breath shaky. "You did it. You showed up." Tears flowed again now, and her hands shook—not from fear or desperation this time, but from the humility of the experience. He'd done it. She'd watched, and how gratefully humbled she was to witness His power show up in such a potent way.

And more than that—He'd shown up in her. Where she'd been filled with confident pride, she now possessed His Spirit. Somewhere in her brokenness, He'd shown His mighty power. And somewhere in her shaky voice, He'd revealed His ultimate victory.

28

BABIES CRIED AND dinner burned at Mae's as though no spectacular display of spiritual power had been exhibited on the Academy steps two days before.

Ellisia could almost believe it hadn't happened, despite the soiled gown with the soot smell still clinging to it that hung in her attic room. Yet something within her had shifted, altered permanently. She was the same, yet not the same.

The Spring Festival, shut down prematurely, would linger in memory as an anomaly. What remained from the madness of the crowd had been damaged by the rain, and by the time order had been restored, there was little to do but clean up the mess and return home.

Home. Ellisia's thoughts wended towards Frydael. If only she could be there, seeing family again, living among those who'd known and loved her forever. How they would laugh and cry over her story, mourning at what she'd nearly entangled herself in and rejoicing over what *Adon Olam* had done in her. She stifled a sigh. It would be a long while before she could manage another trip home, now that she again lived on and paid her Academy expenses from what she could earn at Mae's.

When Academy resumed, all carried on as normal. Don Rhaea was gone, replaced with a soft-spoken gentleman Ellisia didn't remember seeing before. Yet Ellisia found that his teachings possessed a purpose and depth that Don Rhaea's had sorely lacked. Once class finished, she lingered, pondering the beauty of reality encased within written words by ancients long past, contemplating the connections between the kingdom of *Adon Olam* and bare shadows of those truths revealed in printed literature. Purpose, mistakes, falls, sin, redemption, holiness, renewal, resurrection, accomplishment, meaning, mission, love, joy, peace: concepts simple and complex merged and stood forth on the printed pages, shining dark or light varying with how they were portrayed. For the first time, the pieces fit together—and Ellisia couldn't wait to discover more.

With that thought, she reached for her book bag—and felt a tap on her shoulder.

"Ryna?"

The dark-haired girl stood behind her, her eyes cast down.

"I—I thought you'd gone back to Doekh?"

"No. I'm here. I stayed. The others . . . the rest of the team went back."

"But—why?" Suspicion rose within Ellisia, but she tamped it down. *Whatsoever things are true . . . think on these things.* She whispered the words to herself.

Ryna twisted her hands together. "Because . . . I didn't cooperate with them. I didn't do my part, and when I wished to remain, they gladly allowed it. Even my mother—"

"Mother?"

"The physics professor here—the *old* professor. I never thought she'd leave me. I never dreamed she was more dedicated to her work than to—oh, but I should have known. I see it now . . ."

"I—I'm sorry." Ellisia drew her book bag to her chest,

uncertain what to say.

"I want to tell you what happened that day—at the Festival. I don't know why. But I feel we've wronged you personally—I've wronged you, and I'm sorry. This is my due."

"Shall we go elsewhere?" Ellisia glanced around.

"No. I'll sit here." Ryna suited action to her words. "That day—I was supposed to target you. I was supposed to make sure you didn't mess anything up. I suppose you never saw me—I watched you the entire morning."

"You—were watching me?" Ellisia recalled her conversations with Wyn, with other believing students.

"Yes, why do you think you were left alone in the midst of all that happened?"

Ellisia shrugged. "I suppose I just thought Kraevyn lost sight of me."

Ryna loosed a short chuckle. "Never. Not for a moment. I was watching you long before that day."

"No wonder . . . I never saw Jolyn or Kraevyn. Not that day nor any before it. But I wasn't looking for you."

"Which is why I was the one chosen to do it. But yes, you were my target, psychologically speaking, that day."

Realization broke over Ellisia. "And you refused."

"Certainly I refused. I had to tackle Jolyn when she came as my replacement last minute. How she spotted you up in the alcove in the midst of *her* tasks is more than I know. I suppose her eyes were on me."

"Oh." No wonder Kraevyn hadn't even glanced in her direction. No wonder she'd felt hidden in the crowd. "Thank you. But . . . why? Why wouldn't you carry out your orders?"

"Because of you."

"Me?"

"I've watched you even longer than that, Ellisia. I've watched you almost since you first arrived at Academy. I saw your love of learning, your eagerness for books, your skill with words. I hated you then. I was envious, especially when my team began taking notice of you. I knew you'd easily surpass me and be given honors I've been working my whole life to achieve. But then . . . I saw you turn your back on all of it. Trust me, I *know* how deep-rooted your love of books is—and that BookHall, and studying wordology. I watched you. And then I watched you leave it all for what you believe. I knew you were crushing your dreams—everything *you've* worked towards all your life. And—I know how that feels. I couldn't work against you, couldn't crush you even further. You were out of my way already, but even if you hadn't been . . . well, I changed my mind. I don't hate you. I wish you well." Ryna held out her hand, and silently Ellisia clasped it.

"Oh," Ellisia murmured softly. "Oh. I didn't know." That hatred—it had been mutual. Irritation had always bubbled inside at the sight of Ryna—those haughty eyes, that uplifted stare, the mannerisms that had screamed "I'm better than you." But now . . . Ellisia lifted her eyes afresh to Ryna's face. Her eyes were softened in love, her stare was warm and gentle, the lines on her face had softened to something akin to friendship and loyalty. Could they yet be friends?

"It's the power of *Adon Olam* at work in both of us," Ellisia said at last. "I'm not who I was. You're not who you were. Let's move past that. But what are your plans?"

"I'm still in the house rented by ASAA. I can't stay there long, but I'll try to find other arrangements. I intend to remain in Syorien and finish my line at Academy and then apply as a teacher. And—I met a man yesterday who heads up distributing copies of the Book. I'll be meeting with his group as soon as I can."

"You mean—to seek *Adon Olam*?"

"I believe that's the phrase. That's the one area in

which I always felt severely undereducated in Doekh. The one study where you Taernans are ahead of us."

"I'm afraid not by much." Ellisia let out a disappointed breath, but she immediately straightened. "No—that is, I mean I pray that the knowledge of *Adon Olam* will soon cover the four countries. It shall be so."

"Perhaps it shall." Ryna's lips quirked. "Now, I need to pop over to physics, but, Ellisia, I'll see you again, true?"

"True!" Ellisia couldn't have wiped the grin off her face if she'd wanted to as Ryna disappeared out the door. They'd both come so far since the day they bumped into each other on the Academy steps.

Gathering her bookbag, she stepped into the hall, rapidly covering the distance to her usual corner in the Academy BookHall.

But a figure reclined on the purple couch Ellisia usually claimed, her eyes engrossed with a familiar-looking Book.

"Wyn?"

"A pleasure to see you too, Lise-lise! I thought I'd run into you here as soon as you possibly had a moment. Wasn't that grand, that *Adon Olam*-ness three days ago here? I wouldn't have believed it if I hadn't been there! I'm sure glad I was there; wouldn't have missed it for anything. Bang! Sing. *Adon Olam.* Bam! What a sight!"

Ellisia couldn't help but laugh. "So He answered you, and before spring was over, too."

"Sure did! Whee-oh! Makes me want to curl up under the big star quilt and hide my face to think of it. I told Him to show up, and that's what He did. Little ol' Wyn-wyn, what *were* you thinking there? Making deals with the Master, were we? Well, never again. We know who He is now. We know His power. We've seen Him. And we're never going back." She shook the Book she held for emphasis.

Ellisia grinned. "Guess you've made up your mind, then, I see."

"Yes, I have."

"And the cello?"

"Oh, we're sticking with the cello. I know He wants it, and I like it, and there's not much more to be said. But I have ideas . . ." Now her countenance softened to wistfulness, thoughtfulness, her eyes narrowing and focusing with the hopes and fears of a thousand possible futures. Then she shook herself, and her eyes met Ellisia's. "On that *note*—ha!—I have something to show you. Just something we worked up this morning. Come on!"

Swinging herself up, Wyn strode towards the music hall, passing the many practice rooms until reaching a familiar one on the very end. Ellisia followed silently.

"Anni!" Wyn banged on the door. "Let's show Ellisia what we were working on!"

"Come in." Anni smiled, holding the door for Ellisia.

"One moment." Wyn disappeared, then reappeared the next moment, lugging in her cello.

Flattening herself into the corner, Ellisia squeezed up next to Anni in the tiny room that barely accommodated the three of them with the cello.

"Not the best performance room here, but it will do. Now." Wyn pursed her lips, positioned the fingers of her left hand, and set the bow on the strings. A familiar four-four melody filled the room, and Wyn glanced at Ellisia with a grin.

At the right moment, Anni's clear voice soared and reverberated off the ceiling.

Messengers came to Jehoshaphat's throne.
"King, there is trouble as we've never known . . ."

Ellisia's lips quivered into a tiny smile even as she

swallowed a lump that had risen in her throat. Dear Anni. Dear Wyn. *Thank You,* Adon Olam. Silently, thanksgiving rose and fell within her in time to the song, and by the time the cello lilted the bridge before the final verse, Ellisia's own lips opened to softly sing along:

> Adon, *when a trial You send unto me,*
> *Teach me to trust You, whatever it be.*
> *Teach me to silently wait for Your best,*
> *Letting You work as I patiently rest.*
> *I am but foolish weakness, but You are still my might.*
> *I will not use my own strength, but let You for me fight.*
> *I'll seek You first and early till peace You have restored.*
> *So I will trust* Adon Olam—*my strength is in my Lord.*

The last cello note soared and faded. The three friends shared a smile—a smile of understanding, of purpose, of mutual encouragement to press on.

Purpose. What was *Adon Olam*'s purpose for her here?

This question niggled at her brain during the weeks that followed and worried her to open sighs one morning as she scrubbed the porridge pot. It was one thing to expose the minds of students to the truth, to lead them in following life, and stand beside them claiming victory—but what about here? She never had become quite comfortable in conversation with Mae, try as she might, and Mae always seemed busy. Jaeson was even worse, and the babies far too young.

A knock sounded at the door, and Ellisia turned her head just far enough to see Saera slip inside.

Saera.

Did Saera know *Adon Olam*? What was her home life like?

Ellisia suddenly quieted, her scrubbing as silent as possible. How did she know nothing about Saera? In all those days of working side by side, listening to her streams of chatter, how had she failed to learn anything that mattered?

"Good morning, Ellisia."

"Good morning, Saera." Ellisia pulled the pan from the water, turned, and really looked at the girl before her.

She was growing taller—on the very brink of womanhood. That curly brown hair was pulled back from her face, just as always, leaving the broad forehead. Those eyes—they hadn't changed. She even wore the same blue dress she'd had on the first time Ellisia had met her. As Ellisia watched, Saera seized the broom.

As Ellisia silently washed the last few dishes, her heart suspended in a prayer to *Adon Olam* for the girl behind her that she didn't even know.

With an unusual smile, she dried her hands on the kitchen towel. "Saera, have you heard of *Adon Olam*?"

"Yes." The answer was as immediate and cheerful as usual, but Ellisia raised an eyebrow when Saera didn't seem inclined to say anything else.

"Do you—does your family know Him?"

"Some of them."

"Do you believe Him?"

A hesitation this time. "Some."

Ellisia twisted the dish towel into a tight wad, then

smoothed it again. How was she to get on in conversation like this?

"You know Him?" Saera asked, almost whispering, almost fearful.

Ellisia nodded, biting her lip.

They worked the rest of the morning in unusual silence, hardly looking at each other or crossing each other's paths. Passages ran through Ellisia's head, something about it not being *Adon Olam*'s will for any of these little ones to perish. Perhaps this was why *Adon Olam* had put her here.

Just before Saera was about to leave for the day, Ellisia brought her own copy of the Book downstairs. "Here, Saera. This is for you."

"Thank you." The earlier fear seemed gone, but Saera still didn't volunteer further information.

"*Adon Olam* bless your reading of it." What else could she say? "Be filled with the knowing of Him."

For just a moment, a smile of pure delight beamed across Saera's face. Then she nodded and was gone.

Week after week, Ellisia spoke truth over Saera, both privately and aloud when she could. Gradually Saera began asking questions—tiny ones at first, just barely touching on stories or concepts she'd read in the Book—but with increased understanding came increased boldness. One day, Saera entered Mae's home earlier than usual, a strange look in her eye.

"May we go upstairs to your room?" she asked at once, not even stopping for a good morning.

"Why, certainly. Do you need something?"

"I'll tell you upstairs."

An eyebrow raised, Ellisia led the way to her room. Saera shut the door quietly yet firmly behind them, then leaned on it.

"I want to know more."

"Yes?"

"About *Adon Olam*."

"Certainly. What brought this on?"

Saera shrugged. "Nothing. I just always wanted to."

Ellisia felt her brow wrinkle. "I don't understand. Why didn't you say so before? And why do we have to be up here?"

"Because—you don't just talk openly about it," Saera declared, emphasizing the words with a determined nod. "It's the way to get into trouble."

"Oh! Someone at home told you that?"

Saera shrugged, clearly unwilling to say more than she had to.

"Well, anyway, it's all right here. Jaeson and Mae know *Adon Olam,* as you probably know by now, and I do too, and there's no one else here."

"They could be anywhere." Saera's voice remained low. "People are always listening. That's what Papa said."

"Oh! But Jaeson and Mae don't have the new devices, and besides, the group behind those has been sent out of Syorien."

"But sometimes they've put them in without anyone knowing. And I would think that they'd be controlling the devices from their place in Doekh. That's what I'd do, anyway."

Ellisia bit her lip. "It is true," she said at last. "We don't know who might be listening, or when something we might say might get us in trouble. But we know *Adon Olam,* and He's said He is our shield. He says in the time of trouble, He will hide us." Ellisia sat on her bed, her hand reaching for Ellrick's Book, grateful that she'd taken the time to read those very words just that morning.

"But how can I be sure?" Saera glanced around. "Anything could happen! Things *do* happen, all the time." Evident worry creased her eyes.

"Then stop believing the lies. Say they aren't true. *Adon Olam*'s Word is true, even when all else says otherwise. That's faith. So, I speak it. *Adon Olam* is our shield. He will hide you, Saera, in time of trouble."

Slowly Saera nodded. "He will hide me in time of trouble. He will. He is my shield." She repeated the words as if to herself, then heaved a sigh, as if all her cares had rolled off her shoulders. "I have so many questions. I've read the Book you gave me—"

"All of it?" Ellisia's eyes widened.

"Why, yes. It's a small Book. And I have plenty of time after I leave here."

Ellisia shook her head. Here was a girl hungry for *Adon Olam*. Ellisia couldn't even say *she'd* ever read the Book completely, and she'd been reading it all her life, more or less.

For the next hour, Ellisia tried her best to answer Saera's eager questions, but more and more she found herself wholly inadequate. Adon Olam, *give her understanding,* her heart repeated continually. *Receive understanding. Become a powerful warrior in the kingdom of* Adon Olam.

Over the ensuing months, as Ellisia diligently worked through her Academy line, she saw it come to pass. In just a few short months, Saera transformed from shy and quiet regarding spiritual matters to a vibrant, confident young girl radiating the kingdom of *Adon Olam* and bubbling over with her enthusiasm for His Word. Already she'd committed large portions to memory, and she couldn't wait to memorize the entire Book one day. Instead of simply helping with the housework, she became a second mother to the triplets, and Daenia, Naethan, and Elkaena each received ample doses of spiritual songs and passages recited from the Word from Saera every time one of them needed to wake up, rock, or go to sleep.

Gradually, Ellisia began to follow the example of the younger girl. Even though she'd viewed such people as overly zealous, she found herself slowly becoming that which she'd once despised. The urgency of the kingdom of *Adon Olam* and the spiritual battle fought within each soul weighed higher than her own perception of such things as "fanatic" or "over the top." At each crib, Ellisia daily spoke a specific truth directly from the Word to and over each baby—and eventually, her mind began to repeat the habit any time she encountered a student, friend, or stranger at home, at Academy, or on the street.

The habit also carried over to her studies. Instead of reading with abandon as had been her wont, she set the Word of *Adon Olam* as a filter over her mind, carefully weighing every book and chapter against the mind of *Adon Olam*. In this way, when she encountered shreds of untruth, no matter how small or harmless, she was able to immediately condemn them, speak the truth, and prevent them from lodging permanently in the untouched depths of her heart or mind.

Yet even secure in the knowledge that this was the right kingdom and she was abiding as its citizen, moments and entire days of struggle, doubts, and tears overtook her. She longed for the BookHall; she struggled against the constant envy that assailed her whenever she spotted one of its caretakers; she wrestled with bitterness against Kraevyn for promising what he did not fulfill; she yearned in longing and loneliness for a career that could never now be hers. For seven long months, she even banned herself from the Palace BookHall doors to avoid facing her tumultuous emotions, using the time to instead dive deeply into *Adon Olam*'s Word, reading the Book from cover to cover for the first time in her life, wrestling in quiet moments alone with meaning, purpose, and fulfillment, and surrendering once and again her life dreams.

Yet even here, victory prevailed. Regardless of the feelings of her flesh in weaker moments, by the time she triumphantly walked across the Academy steps with her brand-new world literature certification in hand to the joyful sound of Anni, Wyn, and Ryna cheering from the grounds and the triplet toddlers roaring behind them, she truly did believe she was now satisfied in *Adon Olam*. She wasn't the same person who had crossed the Academy steps three years before. She knew her King. Whatever the future might hold for her, she'd face it with Him—and His Word.

29

OAK AND FRESH-CUT hay. The wind rustling the birch leaves. Truly nothing in Syorien could quite compare to Frydael right on the crux of midsummer. In Ellisia's twenty years, she'd never appreciated the scents of her country home quite so much. There was nothing like being away for three years to cause her to value what she didn't even know she'd missed.

The house door creaked open, and Caeleb's broad form moved to stand behind her.

"Morning, Ellisia."

"Good morning, Caeleb."

"Happy to be home, I see."

"More than happy. It's glorious here."

"It's been a short three years."

"That it has. Both short and long. I missed home, but I know I'll miss Academy too. And the children—so talkative and active they were! Hardly a moment's peace for Mae, though I don't know that I've ever seen her have much more than a moment's peace since I've known her."

"Patient Mae. Glorious here just to have a bit of quiet, eh?"

"Oh. I suppose. But I do miss them already. They'll be grown up before I get to see them again, I suppose!

Funny how I've seen them practically every day since their babyhood, and now . . ."

"I'll keep you updated." Caeleb's voice sounded just a bit husky, and Ellisia started to turn to face him, but despite his tones, he was grinning. "But you're glad to be home. Even without the BookHall."

"Stop it." This was the Caeleb she was more used to. "What do you know of books, Mr. Laboring Man? When are *you* going to get an Academy certification, young sir?"

"Young sir, indeed, to a man full ten years your senior. Watch your respectfulness, old lady, or you won't get the news I bear to you especially today."

"News? For me? Then I'll wait, for I know you can't keep it long from me."

"Oh, indeed I can. But in this case, I'm almost as anxious to tell you as you will be to hear when you know what it is. Actually . . . let me show you. Come with me?"

"Where are we going?"

"Just into Frydael."

Ellisia wordlessly followed Caeleb down the road and into the town. Turning off the main road, she strolled by his side until he halted at a small building tucked away between a shoe shop and a quilt shop. "The pastry shop?"

"Wait and see." Caeleb fitted a key into the door and twisted it. Ellisia scanned him doubtfully.

The door creaked open. Empty shelves lined the back wall, but shelves along the side wall held—

"Books?"

"This is what I wanted to show you. This is the news. It's a BookHall."

"Oh?" Her half-distracted gaze snapped directly to him.

"Ellisia"—his voice was serious—"I've been praying about this longer than you've been at Academy, and I'm convinced that now is the time to tell you. Everything is in place. It's up to you now." He cleared his throat, shifting on the path where they stood. "The pastry shop here closed a year ago. The owner is headed out in the direction of Joynway. Thanks to the group efforts of many, the deed of ownership is here." He produced a document, laid it on the short counter, and motioned her to see. "Like I said, I've been praying about this, and—well, this place is for you. If you'll accept it."

"For—a BookHall? Here? In Frydael?" A wave of unexpected emotion washed over Ellisia from stomach to head. "Me?" *Adon Olam.* It couldn't be. She'd given up her dreams long ago, but . . .

The struggles of that very morning, earlier that week, the journey home—everything raced back to her. A new transition. She was back home. She'd found her purpose in Syorien, at Academy, at Mae's—but what about home? What would she return to? And she'd argued with *Adon Olam,* with herself . . . and all this time . . . in all His silence . . . He'd been planning *this.* For her.

It was too much. Ellisia's lip trembled as her head bowed. *Thank You,* Adon Olam. Oh, how unworthy she was of this gift—but so she was of all blessings, all gifts, all good.

The next moment, she had flung her arms around Caeleb, catching him completely off guard. "Oh!" he exclaimed, but after only an instant's hesitation, his arms closed about her—gentle, steadfast, kind, upright.

"Thank you, Caeleb. *Thank you.*" She was almost as unworthy of any gifts from Caeleb as from *Adon Olam,* but the humility that enabled her to receive whatever *Adon Olam* sent her from His loving hand enabled her to do the same for Caeleb—dear old Caeleb. He'd done so much for her, and she'd only repaid him with childish spite that first summer at Academy.

"It's from our *Adon,* Elli. Him and many others. I'm

just blessed to be the messenger."

"And the books!" She pulled herself away from him, swirling to the shelves, ecstasy thrilling through her. "Where in Taerna did you get all these books? Oh, they are fine!"

Caeleb grinned, crossing his arms as he watched her. "That's my little secret, but I have plenty of sources you'll never know of."

"So many copies of the Word! And I've never seen many of these."

"They ought to be the best to start any BookHall with. I've been assured of that by a trusted source, and I wanted to make sure your BookHall started with only the best. Kingdom-speaking, of course." He winked.

"Of course! Oh, I don't know what to say! What do I do first? Sign the papers, I suppose." She whirled back towards the counter, her purple skirt following an instant later.

"Sign the papers, arrange your books, make your catalogue and system, advertise the place, share your love of words, and keep speaking truth." Caeleb handed her a pen. "You'll want more books, of course. This is only a start, but I hope it is enough to begin with. We're on your side, Ellisia, and I'm thrilled to be able to put you in the way of a position you'll love as you keep on going right where He's put you for His kingdom."

She scanned the documents, then sighed, laying down the pen, the paper unsigned. He studied her, his brown eyes sober. "You've grown *so* much in three years, Ellisia. Even more than I've seen since you were eight. Before, I knew a book-loving, opinionated, friendly, chatty little girl. Now I see in that same girl a devoted, steadfast, strong, and determined woman—a woman who knows weakness is power and faith is victory."

Ellisia swallowed, then looked up brightly. "Now,

now, you *are* sounding like an old man. My, Caeleb..." She glanced around the room, her eyes lingering on the shelves, the books, more unopened boxes in a corner, the counters, the bare walls... the empty space by the window where she could place a study table or perhaps some reading chairs. Mentally she decorated the walls, the shelves, the counter.

Moving towards the full side shelf, she slipped one of the copies of the Word off, placing it reverently open on one side of the counter. "There. First start to the BookHall."

Stepping to the doorway, she looked up and down the street. Shops, homes, places of business, places of entertainment—Frydael might not be Syorien, but it too was filled with people. Real people. People who needed the power of *Adon Olam* spoken into their lives.

From somewhere out of sight, a man's harsh tones yelled at someone. Down the street, a boy sneaked an acai fruit away from another and made off, the other giving chase. A woman struggled under the burden of a heavy load and two active children.

Ellisia looked, and she saw it all. Yet she saw more: in the shouts, she heard the lies of power and control. In the thefts, she saw the enemies of greed and lust. In the struggles of the woman, she heard the whispers of fear and discouragement.

And in that one moment, her whole world stretched again. Everything recalled the thin volume slipped into the back of Ellrick's Book: the roaring lion that sought to devour, but only had power when people granted him power.

That enemy was bound in her life—but not everywhere. He had no power in her because of the faith of *Adon Olam* within her—but all around her, men, women, and children granted that roaring lion power over them.

All around, his roars translated to whispers, murmurs, fear, greed, lies, control, and hate.

And for just that one moment, she glimpsed a vision of her purpose. Spoken faith through the Word granted victory—not for her alone, but for all. She was that messenger, the meditator, the ambassador.

She saw it now—words spoken by her voice, yet coming from one far greater than she—words flying throughout these very streets, gentling the shouting man, bringing kindness to the boys' hearts, whispering courage and hope to the weary woman. Real words—*His* words—could and would become reality. She had only to speak them at His bidding.

And this very BookHall would be the hub by which she, one prayer at a time, would speak *Adon Olam*'s power into Frydael—and the world.

She turned back to Caeleb, a smile creasing her cheeks.

"Victory BookHall," she said, and signed the deed.

DEAR READER,

While *Promise's Prayer* was originally intended to be a standalone, God had different plans. A year after writing *Promise's Prayer*, I sat down to pen a second unrelated novel with nothing more than the theme of the power of spoken words in the spiritual realm. After two days of false starts and dead ends, an idea emerged: what if I combined the theme with the characters and setting of *Promise's Prayer*? Book-lover Ellisia proved to be the perfect main character for this theme, and *Victory's Voice* was born.

Yet the writing process wasn't smooth sailing. The first draft ended up as an unfinished mess, and it wasn't until several years later and a complete rewrite that my excitement for this story emerged. Praise God for His work in shaping this book into something for His glory. Every time I reread *Victory's Voice,* I'm excited, humbled, and amazed at how God delights in taking a broken vessel and pouring His fullness and life through it—for others.

My prayer for *Victory's Voice* is that it inspires, motivates, and challenges you to battle in the spiritual realm through the power of the Word of God known, internalized, prayed, and proclaimed. My hope is that the world may see and shake with the echoes of God's Word spoken by God's people for generations to come—and that His kingdom would reign and be known on this earth.

Readers, thank you so much for participating in the journey of this story! For behind-the-scenes book goodies, character interviews, storyboards, updates on future books, and more, I invite you to visit restinglife.com.

If you enjoyed this novel, would you consider leaving me a review on Amazon or Goodreads? Reviews are a vital to help other readers discover a book. Even one sentence is valuable.

Truth from Taerna is a six-book series born from a

heart to communicate the truths of God's kingdom—the spiritual realm hidden from our physical senses—in an engaging story format. Each book focuses on an aspect of spiritual truth that today's church often downplays. My desire is to demonstrate how the powerful, life-changing truths of God's kingdom could play out in a fictional setting. My goal is that God will use this series to reveal His kingdom to you as the reader.

My prayer is that by spending time seeing and knowing God within these pages, you may know and experience Him more intimately in your daily life.

Resting in Christ,

Erika Mathews

WITH MANY THANKS TO

- Jesus Christ: for revealing Himself to me
- Joshua Mathews and Danny and Heidi Wenzel: for encouraging me and being my biggest fans
- IMI: for the atmosphere in which I learned the power of spoken words
- Megan McCullough: for the gorgeous cover
- Angela Watts: for editing assistance
- Lani Koons, Tara Savanna: for beta reading feedback
- My wonderful launch team, Abigail Harris, Chelsea Burden, Jenavieve Rose, Katja Labonté, Kylie Hunt, Ryana Lynn, and Tara Savanna: for awesome support!
- All my writing friends at The Chatter Box, Prayerful Pens, Restful Readers, and King's Daughters Writing Camp: for brainstorming, encouragement, and love

Continue the journey with Laelara's story!

SURRENDER'S STRENGTH

TRUTH FROM TAERNA BOOK THREE
ERIKA MATHEWS

*Her only ambition is keeping her old familiar identity.
But she isn't given that choice.*

Ever since her mother's death, all Laelara wants is to keep doing what she's good at: managing the household. She definitely isn't interested in higher education. When she's sent to the city to further her schooling, Laelara finds herself caught up in a case of mistaken identity that seems like the perfect opportunity to avoid the despised Academy. Amid the whirlwind of new friends, new jobs, and the glitzy social life of the Palace District—particularly the trivia contests—her double life becomes more and more precarious. For the first time in her twenty years, everything spirals out of her careful control: her family's security, her job, her friendships, and her very identity. With her lifelong purpose and identity stripped away, to what will Laelara surrender, and where will she find the strength to persevere?

RESTINGLIFE.COM

RESTING LIFE
EDITING

**YOUR CONTENT:
PROFESSIONALLY
PRESENTED**

Flawless content

Comprehensive analysis

Excellence and integrity

**YOUR MESSAGE:
CLEARLY
COMMUNICATED**

Thorough

Professional

Affordable

ERIKA MATHEWS,
FREELANCE
EDITOR

WWW.RESTINGLIFE.COM

BOOKS BY ERIKA MATHEWS
www.restinglife.com

Truth from Taerna
Promise's Prayer
Victory's Voice
Surrender's Strength
Sustainer's Smile
Memory's Mind
Romance's Rest

Short Stories
Gather 'Round the Fables
Happiness Below

Inspirational Poetry
Overrun By Your Love

Christian Living
Resting Life: Jesus' Rest for the Busy or Burdened Believer

ABOUT THE AUTHOR

Erika Mathews writes Christian living books, both fiction and non-fiction, that demonstrate the power of the kingdom of God through ordinary people, transforming daily life into His resting life. She's a homeschool graduate with a Bachelor's in Communications, a Master's in Biblical Ministries, and a passion for sharing Jesus Christ and His truth. Outside of writing, she spends time with her husband Josh, mothers her little ones, reads, edits, enjoys the great Minnesota outdoors, plays piano and violin, makes heroic ventures into minimalism, clean eating, and gardening, and uses the Oxford comma. You can connect with Erika at restinglife.com.

Website:	restinglife.com
Blog:	writtenrest.wordpress.com
Instagram:	instagram.com/ErikaMathewsAuthor
Facebook:	facebook.com/ErikaMathewsAuthor
Amazon:	amazon.com/-/e/B06XK4TFQL
Goodreads:	goodreads.com/resterwen
Pinterest:	pinterest.com/resterwen

Sign up for Erika's newsletter and receive a free digital copy of her short story
Happiness Below!

Restinglife.com/signup

Made in the USA
Columbia, SC
09 May 2023